I0838162

SOUL WARS

AN ADVENTURE INTO THE SUPERNATURAL

CHRIS KLINE

WORKBOOK PRESS LLC
187 E Warm Springs Rd,
Suite B285, Las Vegas, NV 89119, USA

Website: https://workbookpress.com/
Hotline: 1-888-818-4856
Email: admin@workbookpress.com

Ordering Information:
Quantity sales. Special discounts are available on quantity purchases by corporations, associations, and others.
For details, contact the publisher at the address above.

Library of Congress Control Number:
ISBN-13:   978-1-956876-12-3 (Paperback Version)
               978-1-956876-13-0 (Digital Version)

REV. DATE: 11/08/2021

P.S.: Quotations taken from NAS Version of the Bible

This story was written and birthed from the spirit and imagination of the author, and therefore, is open to conjecture. My prayer is that the readers will see and understand why people do what they do and why they become what they are. Instead of ignoring and disliking them, we might consider loving them and doing some spiritual praying on their behalf.

No one is good and the darkness that lurks in us all has outside assistance to keep it festering. There is only one way to overcome...

The characters and situations will hold the reader's attention because they are so believable and common. The workings of all concerned in the spirit realm have been depicted in a variety of manner to encompass many schools of thought. This book will teach, encourage, rebuke, and challenge any reader with an open heart.

PREFACE

High above the city, among the twinkling lights, glittered a different kind of light. There were billions of them, and they came in various shapes and sizes, peering in sets of two. Glimmering here and there were the eyes of all the witnesses who helped regulate earth's functions and the people who live here. On one side of the expanse were gathered the steadfast, immovable, dazzling Army of the Lord God of Heaven. They stand guard, patiently waiting for their cues to go and minister to those who will inherit salvation. Each radiant being must look for a sign indicating that they have permission to intervene. Looking down from the Celestial City, all seems dark and foreboding. A light, a glimmer of light no matter how small, is what theses beings search for. The lights causing the most joy for these angels is those glowing from the hearts of the redeemed. The slightest flicker of light shows an angel is needed. Immediately the angels respond.

On the opposite side of the cosmos is another group of beings. These malicious, evil creatures are bent on the destruction of any human they can influence with their poisonous ideas. These demons search for cues too. They search the earth for any indication of darkness, of and sin. They seek out the hearts of those having no light and even some who do-- hearts from which many an evil thing can emanate. Thoughts of lust, theft, murder, adultery, coveting, deceit, envy, slander, pride and all other human folly. These creatures thrive on the darkness and grow more impatient as they search for any kind of darkness and of sin, hoping to find a heart that is surrounded by a crust of darkness, a sure indication that the soul is in readiness for the demon to come and agitate the circumstances. These demons look for the darkness while the angels search for the light.

The Lord of Glory is building His Kingdom, a Holy Nation. In it there will be no darkness once it is established. A new race is being set apart on earth, a people who are called the Light Bearers. These people who were chosen so they would declare the praises of Him who called them out of darkness.

But over the cities reside the rulers and principalities in the heavenlies whose Master designated their ranks and strategies. To keep men's hearts in darkness, each area has three princes ruling it: the spirits of Death and Hell, Antichrist, and Jezebel. Each has its own army, whose ranks include powers, spiritual forces of wickedness and evil spirits of this darkness. Their only objective is to stamp out the light of God and His purposes wherever they can.

The celestial angels are positioned to destroy these plans, but they can only be effective when given the directive that comes through prayer. Dark spiritual poisons or righteous insights are released depending on what emanates from the particular heart in question. Those with light glow into the spiritual realm; the others secrete blackness that will increase as the demonic hosts attach themselves.

The battle is on. Will those whom God has called fulfill their destiny? Who decides?

Example of Soul Wars

"I saw the Lord sitting on His throne, and all the hosts of Heaven standing by and the Lord said

"Who will entice King Ahab to go up and fall at Ramoth-Gilead?" And one said this and another said that.

Then a spirit came forward and said "I will entice him" The Lord said how?" And he said "I will go and be a lying spirit in the mouths of all his prophets" Then He said"" You are to entice him and also prevail. Go and do so."

(1 Kings 22:19-22)

Sam
Esther
Evans Family
George
Mary
Walter
Soul
Wars
Larry
Janet
Rose
Marvin
Silverstone Family
Olson's Family
Walter
Josh

SOUL WARS
TABLE OF CONTENTS

Chapter One
Young and Innocent

During the season of autumn in 1958 in the town of Cambridge, Iowa, the future looked bright for its residents. All had hopes of a fairly good and prosperous life, expecting to live to a ripe old age. The town was like most others in the Midwest with its share of problems and trials, and almost everyone enjoyed the "average" American lifestyle (or was living the "American Dream.") In one neighborhood on the south side of town lived four families whose comfortable American lifestyle would be drastically changed due to outside powers. The Olson's daughter Debbie, the Silverstone's and daughter Eva, George and Mary Smith with a son Walt, and Samuel and Esther Evans with their sons Sam Jr. and Josh. Their community and their lives were the battleground of human failure and unseen forces. There was a battle of invisible kingdoms and some fell victim to the darkness while others gained wisdom and strength and emerged victorious. Each family was unique in itself, although they were alike in many ways. But there was one main difference: which powers they allowed to affect their destiny. What sin line owned them?

Whatever had brought Sam and Esther together and had kept them together was a binding secret for they were as different as night and day. Their son Josh was smart and athletic, two assets that had drawn the girls to him as a young boy; but over the years he had become reclusive, demanding, selfish and downright cruel. His younger brother Sam Jr. was taking on the same behaviors.

Esther was petite, barely reaching Sam's broad shoulders, with a gentleness and sweetness about her despite all that Sam had inflicted upon her. In fact, she was someone who could be praised for her long suffering and patience through difficult times (if only others had known what life was like in their marriage).

The only similarities between them were their auburn hair and green eyes, an inheritance from their Irish ancestors. This made them look more like brother and sister than husband and wife. As a youth she was more optimistic with a stronger faith, but now she had grown somewhat cold and withdrawn. Yet underneath the pain and disappointment were a flickering hope that at least she would have a wonderful afterlife.

In reality her life was falling apart. Sam came in the back door shaking rain from his boots. The look on his face showed anger and Esther, determined not to give him reason to abuse her again, sat quietly. Sam strutted by, opened the icebox and grabbed an old bottle of cooking wine. He took several long gulps, then bellowed, "Those creeps at the Power Company did it again. They've doubled our power bill!" Throwing the empty bottle into the garbage bin, he disappeared down the basement stairs, returning shortly with a bottle of scotch.

Esther spoke quietly, "Be careful drinking that on top of wine, dear. You know you're not much of a drinker."

Pouring a large glass, he snapped, "Don't start that again!" just as Sam Jr. ran out the back door, letting it slam behind him.

Joshua, still full of innocence, came slowly around the corner. He was used to hearing his father snap; but seeing the grief etched on his mother's face, his young heart ached for her. Esther reached out for him, but he stood there not caring to reciprocate this motherly gesture of affection.

"Joshua, come sit here." Esther gently brushed back his blonde hair, noticing how much he looked like his father. The auburn tints were obvious only in certain lights. Though Joshua's hair had youthful golden highlights, his green eyes reflected the same anguish his father was carrying inside. Esther wasn't quite sure what to say to him because he had already hardened his heart towards his father and much of the world around him.

In his innocence, Joshua began, "Mom, in Sunday School they taught us to pray to Jesus when we have a problem."

"They're right, sweetheart. That's a good idea," Esther said, painfully aware of how few times she ever asked God for help. "Why don't we go upstairs now, and let's pray for Dad.

Esther reached for his hand, and they climbed the stairs. Esther noticed the peeling paint on the walls and the traces of Josh's dirty fingerprints covering the banister. Glancing at her husband's work shirt that was tossed carelessly over the railing, she noticed lipstick on the sleeve that wasn't her shade. Pushing it aside, she was determined she wouldn't allow it to distract her from the task at hand; she would deal with that later. As Esther and her son sat on the bed together, little did they realize what was happening in the unseen world, the Heavens were actually opening up to hear their cries.

Being a bit uncomfortable with this first-time attempt of a prayer together, Esther was relieved when Joshua began, "Dear God, can you please help Dad not to be so mean?" Esther was warmed by her son's simple, honest prayer. She folded her hands and closed her eyes. "God, I've prayed to you before and even though I can't say I've really known when you've answered my prayers or when coincidences have occurred, I do believe you're up there somewhere and you hear me. Please show yourself to me by answering this prayer. Help Samuel, my husband, amount to something and help me to put up with his ways. He's not an easy man to live with. And Lord, please help him to love us and maybe even to love you to get some of you in his life too. Do whatever it takes."

God was willing ... but was Samuel?

Like lightening, their prayers flew up to the heavens and before the King of Glory. He was more than willing to do this new work in Samuel's life but was Samuel willing?

Later that night at dinner, Joshua, Sam Jr., and Esther sat staring at the empty place at the table. It was unusual for Sam to miss a meal because he loved food so much. "He loves food more than me" had crossed Esther's mind more than once.

She had gone to great lengths to prepare his favorite meal--home cooked meatloaf--but once again she and her sons ate alone.

What had been happening to their marriage? A sense of dejection crept into Esther. "Where have I failed?" she sighed. "I try my very best to please him, but it's never enough."

Joshua didn't care that his father wasn't at the table, for even when he was there, Sam only degraded him, spewing comments, like, "I'll be glad when you're older and can-do things for yourself." Joshua longed to be affirmed by his dad. Sam Jr. didn't know how to do that, nor did he care.

Labor Day had passed, which meant school was in full swing; and now the cherished free time Esther had with Josh was gone. Despite the tension in the house, she had tried to be a good mother. Having Joshua there and caring for him brought her a certain amount of comfort and purpose, yet her purpose as a mom was fading along with her marriage. Sam Jr. was now in preschool. Josh was starting first grade.

✱ ✱ ✱

With a big hug, she gave him also a quick kiss on the forehead and tiptoed out the door. As Joshua lay there, an emptiness swept over him. Dad wasn't home and Mom was preoccupied. "Couldn't she have stayed with me just one minute?" he asked himself. "Grownups never seem to have time for kids. Josh wondered how much time she gave Sam Jr. since he was younger.

He nestled there in the dark, listening to the drizzling rain on the roof while sinister thoughts swirled through his mind ... "They didn't want you in the first place ... You're just a problem to them." Feeling insecure and unwanted, Josh tossed and turned, harassed by the tormenting thoughts until exhaustion silenced the cries in his heart and his weary body fell asleep.

Esther pulled back the sheets on her bed with shoulders drooping as she glanced over at the empty side where Sam should be. "I wonder where he is this time." Memories flowed of how happy they had been the first couple years together, but slowly they had drifted apart. He'd been on the football team and she was a high school cheerleader. Though they met in storybook fashion, by necessity they both dropped out of college to start a family—bad timing. Sam's dream to play pro football was crushed. The routine of married life had invaded their love, and each was forced to find other fulfillment – or ways to release their frustrations.

"He's a loser and he blames you." The poisonous suggestion darted through her mind. As she crawled under the covers and reached for the lamp, the door suddenly swung open and in stumbled Sam. He was dripping wet and his curly red hair was sweaty and matted. Her eyes were drawn to his sleeve.

There it was again. The telltale smudge of pink lipstick, and she hurriedly averted her head to hide the tears which quickly welled up in her eyes. What neither saw was the ebony demon standing directly behind Sam, determined to destroy him and his family. Its task was to use every means possible to hinder salvation from this home.

Esther sat up. "Where's the car. I didn't hear you drive up."

Avoiding her eyes, Sam mumbled, "Um, I wrecked it."

"You what?" Esther exclaimed.

"I wrecked it."

"Sam," Esther growled, "You're with another woman *and* you wreck our car?! What are you doing? What's happened to you?" Torn between wanting to beat him with her fists or break down sobbing, she lamented, "You are not the man I married."

Sam took a deep breath, then expelled some of the frustration that had built up. He stood staring coldly at Esther, realizing he didn't love her anymore. Darkness radiated from within his heart as his thoughts despised her.

The fiend signaled his comrade waiting by the window. It took its cue and released verbal judgments that wafted into Sam's mind. "She's ruined your life . . . you're trapped."

Sam accepted those thoughts, dwelling on the satisfaction injected into his already callous and vicious heart. The intruding venom intensified the sin possessing his malignant soul.

The dark entity shuffled over, coming as close as possible to mesh its evil with Sam's misplaced emotions. An overwhelming feeling of hopelessness saturated his spirit. His own pain etched deep within, screamed, "You're a failure, and you'll never amount to anything." Dropping to the floor and burying his face in his hands, Sam exploded into sobs which wracked his body from deep inside. He could no longer keep his petrified emotions locked inside, they now erupted to the surface, detonating the self-made bomb within. Esther sat silently, watching his display, keeping a tight rein on any compassion she might have felt towards Sam in his dilemma. The sight of lipstick was still too vivid to pretend everything was okay.

Esther, you're just like your father, you expect too much of me. I'm not going to pretend anymore. I'm going to be who I want to be, not who you want me to be."

Though Sam was adamant in justifying his actions he still felt the shame and worthlessness inflicted upon him for years by his father. Many times, Sam heard from his father that he was unwanted. The Ghouls snickered. They knew that to keep hammering at his self-worth would keep Sam running to women to feel attractive, and he would use booze to cover the guilt.

Chapter Two
Inheritance Has Good Timing

The next day at Sam's car dealership, a distinguished looking black man came into the showroom. Sam and his colleague chuckled. "What's the bet he's here to buy with hot cash?"

Sam took off his glasses and strode towards him. "What do you want? We don't finance cars for your kind."

Taken off guard, but used to such inappropriate remarks, the man smiled, extending his right hand in courtesy curtailing several of his emotions due to Sam's attitude.

"I have the money," the man replied politely. "Let me introduce myself. My name is George Smith. I'm from Macon, Georgia, and I can pay for a car without financing it."

His commonsense told him "don't bother", but Sam consented to show him around, engaging him in small talk.

"So where do you live now?" he asked, thinking more of his commission than George's answer.

"We just moved in on Sherman Way."

"You're kidding! That's where I live ... you mean you're my neighbor?" George didn't reply, instead he opened the door of an orange pick-up. Glancing at Sam, he asked, "May I?"

"Sure, why not?"

"Excuse me," George said, "But would you mind leaving me alone for a few minutes? I'd like to discuss this with the Lord to see if this is the truck, he wants me to have."

"What?" Sam asked, unsure he had heard correctly.

"Could you please leave me alone a moment so I can pray and ask God if I should buy this particular truck?"

Sam quietly walked back to his office, shaking his head in amazement. Then, he called out, "Listen to this, guys! He's got the money to pay for the truck, but he's got to ask God's permission to buy it. I've heard everything now!"

As the men sat there entertaining their own thoughts and prejudices, George approached them. "Well, the Lord says yes," he beamed. Keenly aware of what they were most likely thinking he continued, "Gentlemen, let me put your minds at rest. I didn't steal this money. I inherited a coin set that's been in my family for a couple of generations and it turned out to be quite valuable. We just came from a visit in New York where an entrepreneur was desperate for it and paid handsomely. Does that answer your question?"

"I'm just so thankful we waited on the Lord for the right time to sell those coins because the buyer he led us to was willing to pay so much more than the coins were actually worth."

"Sounds like someone upstairs is smiling on you," one of Sam's co-workers shot back playfully.

That's right," George proudly replied with a big smile, "And now He's getting me a mighty fine truck. All cash. No money down. And no payments.

After George Smith had signed the documents and paid for the truck, he left giving praise to God while the men sat there in silence, oblivious to what they had just witnessed. George was operating in realm of an invisible kingdom, the kingdom of God. He followed kingdom principles and experienced the benefits.

Sam returned to his desk, pondering, "Why can't I be that lucky?" Luck had nothing to do with it!

A few weeks later, as the nippy breezes of autumn began to blow, Sam had a visitor at work. It was Larry Olson, one of his neighbors on Sherman Way who owned the tire company across the street. Larry was a very handsome man with dark, wavy hair and piercing dark eyes. His wife, Rose, was a fashionable woman who enjoyed spending his money on fancy clothes and jewelry. Unfortunately, that didn't leave much money or time for her daughter, Debbie.

"Hey, Sam, you'd better sell some more cars so I can sell some more tires. My wife's bleeding me dry."

Sam, sympathetic to Larry's situation, motioned him into his office. Reaching into his desk drawer, he pulled out a half-empty bottle of scotch and tipped it towards the shot glass. "Can I fill you up?"

"Oh, no. I'm all right, but you go ahead."

Drinking alone was something Sam was getting used to, but sadly he had begun dipping into the petty cash to finance his habit. At first it bothered him, but soon his continual wrongdoing desensitized his conscience. Besides, he rationalized that the money could always be replaced later.

Reluctant to waste his time watching Sam slowly get drunk, Larry explained he better get back to work; but before he opened the door, Sam motioned him to sit down. Pouring his drink, Sam began, "You got to hear this one, Larry! I had this nigger guy come in the other week . . . in fact, he's just moved in on our block. You know the red brick house on the corner with the hedge in front--been for sale for a while."

"Yes, I saw it had sold. A colored guy moved in there?"

"Yeah. Anyway," Sam continued, "he came in and bought a pick-up for cash. But get this! First, he asked the man upstairs if it was all right by Him to buy it! Have you ever heard anything so ridiculous?"

Larry looked solemn. "So, you don't believe in God?"

Sam swallowed a large swig of the liquid, then shot back, "Well, I guess He's out there somewhere."

Slowly and stealthily in the spirit realm, a new demonic host descended, looking for the ever-increasing signs of darkness that consummated Sam's heart.

Swallowing another large gulp, Sam revealed the blindness of his soul by declaring, "No, actually, I don't believe He's out there. And if He is, then He must be asleep, and he sure isn't done nothing good for me."

Sam's declaration of unbelief triggered an immediate and unusual response. A rancor, bitter power was discharged, bridging a connection between Sam and the demon who stood nearby. Swelling up like a proud peacock, the spirit relished the strength those words gave him. Unbelief within Sam had a new home. Its spirit meshed with Sam.

When Larry got back to his office, little did he realize there was a major conference going on up in the corner of the building. Suspended in a weightless dimension were several twisted, devious creatures, discussing their strategies of how to dismantle Larry's faith in God and totally ruin his life.

Larry closed the door and strutted over to his huge oak desk, glancing at the empty order tray as he sat down. The spirits emerged through the far wall and hovered, observing him and encroaching his space.

The demons conspired. "We all know our master, Lucifer, the god of this world, who blinds the minds of the unbelieving, but since this Larry has a measure of putrid faith, and we need to get him off into some kind of deep deception. He needs to believe in something else, anything, except of course the truth."

They all snickered. Confusion, eager for an assignment, spoke up. "I know I could be of help. I could get him to read several books that confuse him and lead him to believe that no one can really know the truth."

There was silence. Then the spirit of Pride and his ever-present sidekick, Deception, spoke in unison, "No. Confusion only postpones a belief. We can't take the chance that someone's prayers could break through that confusion and lead him to truth." The demons drooled, thinking of their prey. "Just leave him to us; we know what to do and how to entice him away."

Chapter Three
Huge Black Mist

At home later that evening, Larry's wife, Rose, was her usual prima donna self. She had once been the apple of his eye and the dream girl of most of the boys at college. She was still very beautiful with her dark hair always in perfect place, but her pale blue eyes, which once sparked a vitality, now appeared lifeless.

She was obsessed with the way she looked, and her constant spending and self-adoration were beginning to disgust Larry.

They were all seated at the mahogany-inlaid dining table which, as usual, was adorned as though waiting for a magazine shoot to take place. "Nothing but the best" was Rose's motto.

Across from Rose sat their 6-year-old, Debbie, who, like Joshua Evans, had just started school. Both parents had forgotten just how traumatic that could be and didn't bother to inquire.

Dinner had been served, but Rose sat there painting her nails instead of eating. She was convinced her model-like figure needed extra help, so she almost starved herself. This was at great cost to her personality because since she was usually hungry, and she was often snippy.

Larry put down his fork. "Do you mind if I ask what you did today?"

Smirking, Rose replied, "I went shopping." Larry grunted, "Somehow I expected that!"

Debbie sat there waiting for someone to ask her how she was doing at school and if she liked 1st grade. Aware that they weren't taking any notice of her, she peeked under the table and spotted Chipper, her beloved poodle, the only one who really knew what school had been like for her. She slyly tossed him some meat. Each afternoon she had come home to an empty house, which only added to her tears and anguish. It seemed she had become the new 'whipping post' at school. Wearing glasses had made her the brunt of many a cruel joke. Between her parents and the kids at school, Rejection was beginning to gain access. All it needed was a little more ammunition.

Amidst all Debbie's trials that day, she had still remembered her mom's birthday. Reaching under the table, she grasped the present she had hidden, a bouquet of hand-picked wild wildflowers. As she pulled them out yelling "Surprise!" she knocked her glass of milk over, spilling it onto her peas and over the table where it dripped to the floor. Debbie cringed as her face went from a look of joy to one of horror.

"That's just great!" snapped Rose, grabbing the flowers and using them to stop the flow of liquid traveling across the table. "You've ruined my beautiful dinner, but you're going to eat yours even if it is soaked in milk!"

Larry addressed Rose angrily. "How dare you talk to her that way and look what you've done with her present."

Tossing the flowers into a nearby trash can, Rose slammed her hand on the table. Her countenance changed, and her eyes seemed almost inhuman. "Look, I didn't want to be pregnant. You know she was an accident."

Debbie gasped as the words racing around her head. "Accident."

Rose turned to her abruptly. "Go to your room and stay there." She glared down at Chipper, adding, "And take that stupid dog with you."

With lethal darts aimed, ready to fire and eyes filled with malice, the spirit of Rejection flapped its wings, stretched its grotesque claws and followed Debbie up the stairs. Chipper seemed to sense something in the air and didn't adhere. Instead, he crawled under the breakfront, timorous to the evil pervading the house.

As Deborah slowly climbed the stairs, tears stung her innocent brown eyes. How she ached in her heart, a harsh pain that would haunt her for years. While she lay on her bed, Rejection fired the first one. "You weren't supposed to be born. You're an accident!" Expelling a noxious breath, another was released. "No one wants you!"

Hardening her heart and holding back the tears, she answered aloud, "My Dad wants me."

Rejection replied, "No, he doesn't. He's going to leave all of you." That's a lot for her to accept without some damage.

Just then the yelling from below filled her room. She heard the screams back and forth from the dining area. Often her parents fought, but it was usually over money. The demon flung another thought at her. "They're fighting over you this time. You don't belong here."

Debbie looked around for Chipper, but realizing he'd deserted her too, she began to weep. Cautiously, she went to the landing, debating whether or not to go down and get him. Rejection followed, hissing the word of God. "A crushed spirit who can bear?" Proverbs 18:14

Her insecurity and anguish were multiplied as her mom shrieked, "I don't want to be a mother. I'm tired of all this and I'm bored with you and this house. I want to go someplace warm and fun."

Larry rose, along with his blood pressure at her outburst. "Go! Go ahead and leave, see if I care." Enraged, he strode over to her purse and opened it. "But you better say goodbye to these!" he snarled, holding up her credit cards before stuffing them in his pocket.

Overcome with panic, Rose jumped up, grabbed her purse and slapped him across the face. Darkness embraced Larry's heart as hate gripped his emotions. Immediately, a brute force named Anger began to revolve around his head, lancing its unobserved spirit into his mind. Larry's embittered heart relished that familiar sensation of madness. An almost supernatural strength displayed as his blood pressure exploded and he shoved Rose to the floor. In a trance-like state, Larry abruptly stormed out the door, slamming it in complete depravity, unaware that Chipper had followed him. All were alarmed as the dog let out a horrible yelp and fell lifeless to the floor.

Debbie came running down the stairs in time to see Larry meekly open the door and step over the dog. Scooping him up in her arms, she cuddled him to her chest. The demons in the room hovered ominously; waiting expectantly for the humans to react. Debbie was in shock.

"Well, good riddance!" snapped Rose, sauntering out of the room, clutching her purse to her heart. "You and your father can clean up this mess." Debbie looked up and glared as her mother disappeared out of sight. She sat there silently, her emotions mixed, unsure of what she actually felt, then focusing on the strongest reaction, she allowed the bitterness into her heart. The chosen sin surfaced the darkness already inherited from mankind; and, as the impurity was given permission to reside unchecked, her opaque heart gave the cue to the spirit realm. In a well-deserved but dangerous fit, Debbie snarled, "I hate you. I hate you both and hope you die."

The demons roared with sadistic laughter as her words penetrated the air in expression now waiting for fulfillment.

* * *

The Lord looked down from Heaven, His angels by his side. "Is there anyone who will stand in the gap?" (Ezekiel 22:30) A tear fell from His eye.

The atmosphere at the Smith family dinner table was the opposite. George and Mary were always eager to hear how their son, Walter, was getting along in school. They knew it wasn't easy being colored and especially at a new school. They were sure he would have some rough days, but they also knew the Lord wanted them in Cambridge. Even George's lawn service business was starting to thrive, and he had hired some more men. Sadly, though the family was ignorant of the fact that some wretched creatures had also been assigned to their house to do within their power any intent to hinder Walt's becoming born again. Fortunately, there were some blessings on this family, but the savage ghouls wanted to see a curse replace it.

Being raised Christian themselves, both George and Mary knew the importance of affirming their son, but also giving credit to the Lord for his achievements. The coin inheritance had enabled them to get a head start in middle-class America, yet each knew work for God's Kingdom must take first place.

Leaving behind the oppression and bleakness of the south and all that encompassed for other black families, George and Mary were eternally grateful yet leery of the struggles that lay ahead.

"So, Walter," his dad began, "how do you like your new school?" "Well, the kids aren't really friendly. They were teasing a girl named Debbie about wearing glasses. They called her four eyes and took turns trying to pull her hair."

"And what did you do about it?" his dad asked.

Walter paused, then looked earnestly at his father. "I tried to make friends with her, but the kids told her not to talk to me because I'm a nigger. At 7, Walt was just starting his road of racism. George paused, then looked at his wife to help him explain something Walt would have to contend with. Prejudice, it was an ugly fact of life. The demon that dispensed Hate and fueled prejudice on willing vessels was eager to descend on Walter as his father explained about slavery and how only recently Negroes had obtained their freedom.

"Don't worry, Walter," his father reassured him. "God will raise someone up to help us."

Walter's face beamed. "You mean like Moses?"

"Well, yes. A deliverer to make sure we are really free."

Sipping his chocolate milk through a crazy straw, Walt then set his glass down carefully, obviously deep in thought. "Why don't you do it Dad."

"No, son. The Lord already has someone in mind, and when he comes forward, I'll step in and do my part as the Lord leads. It must be done peacefully and in His way."

Anger was becoming agitated. This sort of talk made it nauseous. It began to descend when it was stopped short. Mary's angel, Odessa, glistening by her side, swooped on it and tossed it through the spirit realm.

Odessa smiled down at Mary. She was glowing, a sign that her spirit was in communion with God. "Oh, Lord," she prayed, "protect Walter from falling into the hate pattern between the whites and colored people. Give him a white friend so he can learn we are all the same."

Perfectly, deep in the heart of Walter, the Holy Spirit placed a tiny parcel. The purpose of it would lead him into his calling. Over the years, the Lord would bless Walt's life by giving him a vision and a destiny. It would be his choice whether or not to accept God's plan. Just as his father, George, had heard what he was supposed to do, young Walter would have to listen for his orders too. God would speak to him through the Bible and other ways until he stepped into his mantle or chose to ignore it.

"Walter," his dad said, then cleared his throat. "You will often hear that man was created equal, but that's not the real issue. The Bible says we were created in God's image, and all of his children are predestined to be conformed into the image of Jesus Christ. (Romans 8:25)

"God is Spirit, He is invisible, and He is immortal. You, son, are the same. What actually makes you who you are is your spirit. It too is invisible and immortal. Your true image is only seen in the invisible realm. God gave you a soul and that's what makes you an individual. With your soul comes the responsibility of choosing right from wrong. Just as God is immortal, because your spirit is immortal, you will never cease to exist either. All men are to be brought into fellowship with God and fulfill the purpose for which they were created. The word is redeemed.

Now I want you to remember that when you're older, God will show you

His purpose for your life, the job he has picked out just for you to do. Until then, don't fight with those kids no matter what they say. And pray for that little girl, that she won't be hardened by their name calling and that she too will come to know Jesus.

Walter had his commission.

Chapter Four
Prejudice Shows Its Ugly Face

Down a few blocks in one of the fanciest homes a huge black mist hung over the roof, expelling a toxic vapor. Circling purposefully was the principality called Death. It was enormous, ranting and raving as it released noxious fumes which caused the black mist to thicken while penetrating the roof. In the guest bedroom, Marvin and Janet Silverstone were keeping a vigil over her mother as she slowly passed away. Even with all their money and Marvin's occupational influence, there was nothing they could do to save her life.

It seemed no one was concerned where this woman was actually going to be going any minute soon. All just had assumed she'd go to Heaven. The spirit hosts were all enshrouding her, anxious to greet this lady into their dark domain. She lay wheezing from the years of cigarettes, barely able to catch her breath. Her once beautiful face, now frail and wrinkled, was ravaged by disease. She was a nice person who'd never hurt a soul, but the hosts knew her heart. It was void of the Spirit of God.

Suddenly, a look of terror came over her mother's face, and Janet quickly reached across to hold her hand, attempting to reassure her. She gave a last shudder, and then Marvin, sensing the life had gone, put his hand over her glazed eyes and gently closed the lids for the last time.

Marvin reached for Janet to hold her in his arms. Her eyes filled with tears as she embraced him and said, "She was such a good lady. I'm sure she is with God now."

Marvin, a distinguished lawyer who always needed the facts, could only give a pat answer. "Whatever you say, dear." He went downstairs to ring the undertakers.

While he was away, Janet took Eva's hand then realized Eva's blue eyes were the image of the woman's who had just closed hers for the last time. Both features had been in the family for generations. So had the spirits.

Eva's innocence and serenity were most precious, but the powers of darkness would soon begin their ugliness on her. The Godly principals and protection expected to be passed on from one generation to the next were not present in this family; therefore, neither was the Spirit of Christ.

At the funeral Eva and her mother, Janet, softy kissed the cold forehead of the woman in the plush coffin. As the shell of the old woman lay there, a secret was about to be buried with her--she was cursed. Challenged into a dare as a young woman, she had let someone hypnotize her at a party. While in a trance state, she had crossed over a supernatural barrier which had opened her up to a spirit of Witchcraft. Now that force had an "in" to be part of her family's heritage--a foolish action her entire family would unwittingly pay for. Once the sin had come forth, a fear set in, almost paranoia. In order to overcome this, she began filling her house with every kind of good luck charm. Horseshoes, four leaf clovers, rabbits' feet, and all different saintly medallions that were meant to give protection. Seeking more assurance, she then graduated to idols, statues from around the world--Buddha, Vishnu, Ashtoreth, a goddess from the Middle East, Idols from the South Pacific and for extra support, one of the Virgin Mary kept by her bedside.

Eventually, she became possessed with collecting ceramic gods; and as time went by, they became her secret little friends she communed with. What seemed innocent enough to her actually carried with it a severe penalty and consequence. God legally judges those who look to idols to received guidance, comfort or protection.

The moment Janet kissed her mother, the departing familiar spirit began contemplating ways to instigate a curse on Janet as well. The verse in Lamentations would soon ring true. "Our fathers sinned, and we have born their iniquity." Lamentations 5:7

As Eva stood there, transfixed, trying to envision what death must be like, an unannounced visitor entered the room. The humans didn't see it, but the ghouls all bowed low. Jezebel, the ruling demon of sorcery, had come to unleash its air of supremacy. It haughtily eyed the new victims, then reached over to Janet, proudly placing his intention upon her. It was a significant mark that was an indication to all the heavenly hosts as to what generational sin was now being transferred to manipulate her.

As the service continued, the few who were there listened to the sermon, pondering to themselves the actual existence of God or heaven. "The Lord is my Shepherd," the priest solemnly declared. "And I shall dwell in the house of the Lord forever."

In the spirit realm, the creatures were mocking the minister. They knew full well the grandmother had never known Jesus and had slipped into eternity without ever receiving the Spirit of God within her.

As the weeks passed, depression seemed to press in on Janet from every side. She also became bitter at God for letting her mother suffer so much during her last days. There had been so many things Janet wanted to tell her mom, but now she couldn't. With all the painkillers her mother had been taking, she was almost zombie-like; and in her rare moments of lucidness, there never seemed to be the opportunity to say what was on her heart.

One day while flipping through the newspaper, she came across an advertisement for séances held by a medium. "Has someone died that you haven't finished talking to?"

"Just what I need!" thought Janet, and so she read on. That month a lady would be visiting who called up relatives from the dead-on request for a small fee, of course.

Janet sat there with the article in her hand while the powerful demon of Witchcraft stood by her. Its slimy tentacles were covered with tiny pinions which secreted a defiling fungus. Janet toyed with the idea of talking to her dead mother as the venomous visitor encircled her forehead in the invisible dimension.

"Can I actually talk to my mother?" Janet asked out loud. It sounded fascinating.

As she cemented the excitement of it in her heart, ever so slowly, the dark luster began its deadly construction. She too had now crossed that dangerous line into the sphere of demonic oppression. "Well, it certainly would give me something to talk about at the country club!" Janet laughed. Witchcraft injected some of its living decay into her desires, strengthening its grip and pollution. "Yes, I'll do it!" Janet decided.

The demon congratulated itself and hastened away to prepare the medium with a decadent plan. Leaving behind a vapor, and snickering as it went, (God forbids this), now she'll keep the curse on her family.

The dusty Bible over on the corner bookshelf held the answers had she chosen truth instead. Even in Moses' day those who went to mediums and called forth spirits were cut off from God. It was all there for her to read. (Isaiah 8:9)

Her first encounter at the séance left Janet with an insatiable desire to know more about the occult. As they sat there in the darkened room, an apparition resembling her mother had materialized in front of her, hovered three feet off the floor, nodded and then vanished. If she wanted to talk to her again, she'd have to come back; but at thirty dollars a session, Janet decided she'd try it herself at home.

First thing the next morning Janet was off to the library to read up on spiritism and decided she too could contact the other side. The darkness in her heart deepened; and because of her mother's idol worship, witchcraft could now include two other beings to accelerate the deception. All three would have access as the curse obstructed any blessing or protection from "Above". The demons of Spiritism and Necromancy, and Witchcraft determinedly had their mission field.

There was only one way to reverse the ultimate outcome of the presence of these unyielding creatures, so the Holy Spirit began looking for someone to prevent the inevitable. Would He find a person willing and wanting His good pleasure?

Janet returned one last time to the medium to ask permission to bring her mother's spirit to her old bedroom. Her request was granted with a little encouragement from Necromancy. Janet knew Marvin would scoff at the idea of ghosts, especially his mother-in-law being one, so she kept her secret rendezvous to herself for the first few months. In the end, in her excitement and pride, she told Marvin, who candidly commented, "Anything you say, dear."

Each week, she would put aside a time to beckon her mother's spirit, and every time Necromancy was only too willing to oblige. The resemblance was uncanny and only reinforced the deception Janet was in. The spirit was kind and gentle, even the mannerisms and gestures were the same.

As time went by, her involvement opened her soul up for all kinds of demonic entry. Her heart took on the depth and shade of ebony, until only a flicker of truth remained.

Early in the spring, after one of these visits, Janet went straight to her room. The session had brought about a hypnotic sensation that had Janet's body crying for sleep.

The spirit went to make its usual second appearance, but this one was always in Eva's bedroom. Since Janet had begun dabbling in this, Eva who was six had been visited each night after her parents went to bed. She was too afraid to tell anyone; certain she'd be called a liar by her unfeeling mother. Her dreams had changed drastically from the offset of the demonic manifestations with Janet. In the dream, Eva would slowly sink in quicksand while her mother stood by with a switch to strap her if she tried to get out. Usually, she awoke with silent screams and soaked in perspiration.

But this time was different, for when she awoke the spirit was hovering above her. It was large and charcoal black. It was almost 7 feet tall built like a man covered with scales that waved about systematically. Its face was a mass of prickly hair and in the center was one eye that looked like fire. It didn't blink, it didn't incite, it only stared. Vindictively, it vibrated, setting off a deplorable odor. Eva was so frightened she lost all muscle control and wet the bed.

One of the heinous hands reached out and covered her mouth. She tried screaming, but no sound came out. Petrified, she lay there as a picture of her dead grandmother flashed through her mind. "I'm going to die!" she cried to herself. A deathly fear gripped her emotions, and her soul responded by accepting this trauma. As a result, her heart's illumination became nimbus, for fear blackened out faith. Loosening its hold, the felon then backed off, gave a hideous laugh, and disappeared beyond the wall. The fiend was gone, but its arsenic remained.

Linked with Eva's flesh was now the spirit of Fear. This dominating villain would remain to impregnate her, keeping her bound and unconscious to God's love. The presence haunted every part of her being, and it was hours before she fell asleep. Too scared to leave her bed, the anguished little child slept in the urine surrounding her.

The morning sunshine was flooding her room when she was abruptly wrench out of bed by her mother, furious that she had wet the bed. Janet commanded her to bend over as she took off the silver belt encircling her waist. Whimpering softly, Eva obeyed, her tiny frail body trembling with terror at the thought of being whipped and the humiliation accompanying it.

First Janet pulled off the musty, sodden nightgown, yelling, "How could you sleep in this thing all night?"

"Mommy, I'm sorry," Eva sobbed, panic-stricken by the anger reflected on her mother's face.

"I was afraid to get out of bed." With that the sting of the belt thrashed across her slender thighs. Then another, then another. Welts swelled instantly across her fragile frame. She wanted to scream but knew that would only bring more lashes. She bit her lip, then her tongue because of the pain, until blood appeared at the corner of her mouth.

Suddenly, the realization of what was happening registered in Janet's befuddled brain. "Oh my God," she cried. "What am I doing?" She threw the belt across the room as though it had turned into a shining, writhing snake.

"Oh, Eva, honey. I'm so sorry. I don't know what came over me." She clasped the trembling little girl tightly against her chest and both began crying. "Honey, I promise I'll never beat you like that again. I just got so angry."

The vixen of violence stood in the corner, taunting the tiny child. Eva wanted to believe her mother, but her emotions were dictating something else. Already in the recess of her heart, Hate and Anger had deposited their color, intertwining with the darkness that begot them. Their presence would dictate the choices Eva would make in her life.

Only the Prince of Peace could set her free. When would His opportunity come?

It was a beautiful spring morning, and the trees showed off their bright green foliage. The scent of flowers drifted everywhere, and it felt good to be alive. George Smith was dropping Walter off at his elementary school, when some boys ran by shouting "Nigger!". Walt looked at his father, the hurt obvious in his eyes.

"Their prejudice towards you is something they have learned. By cutting you down, it makes them feel better. Prejudice is not limited to the color of one's skin, either.

As you grow up, you'll see it in all aspects of life. Just remember, they have problems that we don't even know about. People have hurt them and that's why they like hurting others."

"I'm not the only one they tease," Walt said. "There's this girl from Japan and they call her "Miss Eggroll."

"What's her name?"

"Yasha."

"Well, you pray for her too, since you know what it's like to be called names."

George reached over, hugged his son goodbye, and as he watched him scamper across the street, a prayer rose in his heart that the Lord would give Walt a loyal friend. The moment his request was birthed, his heart radiated a light, the sign to his angel, Gallant, that a summons had gone forth.

Gallant, hastening to the throne room of God, stood in adoration and worship as he gazed in his Master's face. The Lord of Glory surveyed his host of angelic beings and called out for their unity in standing for the ways of righteousness. He knew without their intervention, His people would be defenseless in standing against their unseen enemies, foes that were always ready to discharge their malice upon the children of God.

The Lord issued forth the order for Regal to carry out the duties required of him to answer George's prayer. Immediately, Regal was by Walt's side, eager to do as the Lord bid. A delicate gossamer wing brushed against Walt's face and a smile lit his eyes as the Holy Spirit brought to his remembrance his father's words, "God has a job for you to do."

✳ ✳ ✳

Just as George pulled away from the curb, Sam Evans pulled in to drop off his son, Joshua. "Now pay attention. I expect you to get the best marks in class, all right? Don't fail me in this, son," Sam bellowed.

Chapter Five
The Spirits Are Busy

Joshua was out of the car before his father had finished speaking, and he didn't even bother looking back. Since he had started school that was all he ever heard. "Do the best; I don't want a loser for a son." It kept ringing in Joshua's mind.

As Sam began driving down the road, he noticed George's new pickup pulling off to the side ahead of him, so he pulled over too. "Hey, George! Is there something wrong with your new truck?" he called out the window, signaling he'd park in front.

He studied George's face as he walked towards him and noticed how different his features were from white people. Hate was waiting on the side, ready. Suddenly, Sam felt a rush of scorn towards George and was about to make a snide comment when George grinned, causing his whole face to light up. Immediately, something in Sam relaxed and the thought came, "He isn't so different after all."

The demon sneered in disgust.

"Great little pickup you sold me, but there seems to be something wrong with the back hubcap."

"Can you drive it okay?"

"Yeah, but it's making a very loud clicking noise as though something is loose."

"Well, follow me over to Olson's tire repair, and we'll soon see what the problem is."

As George was following Sam, he pondered over what God might be setting up for him, hopefully, a way to meet some of the town's folks so he could share his faith with them. I better ask you Lord for forgiveness for my temper this morning, he whispered. Gallant, His angel stood by, ready. "Father," George prayed, "help me make friends with them so I can lead them to you. Whatever this tire problem is, I commit it to you as your will for me today. I know that you'll help me get the things done I need to do."

As soon as they arrived, Sam reached under his car seat and pulled out a small flask filled with Scotch. Glancing to see if anyone was watching, he took a long swig. George saw him from the rear-view mirror just as Larry too spied Sam from the hallway entrance. Seeing the guilty look on Sam's face, George sent up prayer. "Lord, soften his heart towards you and also the man we are about to see."

Like turning channels of water, the Holy Spirit moved on Larry's heart. Reacting to Sam's sneaky cocktail, he thought, "I'm sure there is more to life. I hope I don't end up sneaking sips of Scotch to get through the day."

George strolled over to Sam, acting as though he hadn't seen him take the drink. He realized it could be a further hindrance if Sam felt embarrassed towards him so early in their relationship. They both walked up to Larry.

"This is George, the guy I told you about who asked God's permission to buy that truck."

Larry extended his hand. "Well, I always wanted to meet someone who had an "in" with the "Big Boss.""

Grinning, George shook his hand. "Well, you can have it, too."

"I doubt it. Anyway, what's going on with your truck? It sounded a bit strange when you pulled in."

"The sound seems to be coming from the back hubcap. Do you have time to check it out for me?"

"Yeah, sure. The only thing is I'm pretty busy at this hour of the day, but if you could leave it here, I'll get to it later."

George leaned against the hood. "My wife is waiting for me to take her to the dentist, and it's my turn to pick up our son at school."

From the Third Heaven, the Holy Spirit descended on Sam, stirring his heart and moving him to compassion.

"Well, I sold you the truck, so I'll take care of this, including retrieving your son at school. I saw you drop him off, so I'll get him when I get my son.

Across town, George's wife, Mary, had a sudden urge to pray for her husband. She had expected him home by now and wanted to cover him in prayer for whatever might be causing his delay.

In the spirit realm near Larry's tire shop there was much activity going on. The principality Antichrist, a ruling spirit, had arrived. Its sole purpose was to instruct its underlings on how to stop humans from knowing Jesus. Its flaring nostrils emitted a chalky white mist as its face changed from a rancid yellow to silky black. Its eyes stared full of hatred as it gnashed its teeth while communicating.

"What are you out here waiting for?" Antichrist quipped emanated a foul stench as each syllable ejected into the atmosphere. "You're supposed to be aggravating the circumstances in there and give them reason to dislike George. Why haven't you propelled any thoughts into their minds?"

Pride spoke up. "We can't do anything because Gallant, his guardian angel, is there, plus George's wife bound us in Jesus's name."

Antichrist's impatience exploded. "Which one of you did she bind?"

"She wasn't specific," offered Deception, trembling. "She bound all the works of the enemy, so temporarily there is nothing any of us can do."

"Well, once George leaves, attack them then. They'll be unprotected when he's gone since they willingly walk according to the course of the world. The binding doesn't last long once the vessel with God's presence leaves. And make sure they don't take George seriously." Disdainfully,

Antichrist surveyed his army. Then, turning to Deception, he glared using his piercing innumerable eyes and snorted, "I thought you had a plan to deceive Larry. When are you going to implement it?"

"We have," Pride burst in. "We've arranged a meeting between him and Sonny Weston from the Freeson's Lodge."

Antichrist smiled, his mouth resembling a scar from some cruel instrument of torture. "Good! That will keep him away from the truth. They compromise so much he'll never be able to decide what's right or wrong. Nail him good!" With a flash, he sped off to further spread his seeds of destruction.

The phone rang in Larry's office, and he called to Sam, "It's your wife."

Once on the phone, Esther snapped at him, "What are you doing? You told me I could have the car today."

"Where are you," Sam asked.

"I'm waiting in your office across the street. There's a sale at the market, and I have to get there soon."

Sam glanced at George. "I'll be right over, but you better be ready for a change of plans."

Leaving his car with Larry, George joined Sam in his car, and they drove across the street to find Esther looking very perturbed. "What have you been doing? I thought you might've wrecked the car again!"

"Just simmer down," Sam said, giving her a quick peck on the cheek for show. Esther was startled by the smell of Scotch, and it added to the growing coldness she felt towards him.

Noticing the look on her face, Sam abruptly changed the subject. "This is the man I told you about who asked God's permission to buy the truck. He needs a ride home, so maybe you can learn his secret on the way!"

Sam walked off, smirking to himself, leaving the two staring in awe. On the one hand Esther, wondering how to react to someone on such close terms with God, and George because God had opened the door for him to share his beliefs so quickly after praying.

On the drive home, Esther was in a quandary as to how to talk to him. She wanted to know how God had spoken to him when He gave the OK to buy the truck, and why did he have to ask God in the first place. Sitting silently, she recalled her mother telling her, "Never discuss religion, especially with strangers."

Abruptly, from the high places came a demon who sat next to Esther on the front seat. Of course, no one saw it except Gallant who stood immobile as no order had been given.

Pride stretched out its black gauzy wings and fired a thought into her mind. "Don't ask him about God. You'll only look stupid."

Esther looked over as God's Spirit within her revived a verse she had read as a child in Sunday school. "If you seek Him, you shall find Him." (Jer 29:13)

She took a deep breath. "Ah, George?"

Pride wrapped its wings around her forehead ever so gently, squeezing and engraving a word, "STOP."

"Oh, never mind," she replied, rubbing her temples.

The Holy Spirit spoke to George in his spirit. "She's searching for the truth. You take the initiative and I'll do the rest."

George turned off the radio. "Esther, I suppose you think it's strange I asked God for permission to buy this truck."

Relieved and grateful he had started the conversation; Esther began to answer him.

Pride shot out of the car to look for another ominous cohort. "You, Deception. Get over here now. This lady is about to hear the Gospel."

George, fully aware how the spirits work, prayed under his breath, "Lord, call on Mary. I need her prayers to strengthen me."

* * *

At home, Mary waited by the door, ready for George to take her to the dentist. A tiny demon, Anger, hovered near by trying to incite her to retaliate at him for being late.

The Lord spoke to her heart. "Pray. George is witnessing and needs your support."

Back in the car, Deception joined Pride, and both repeatedly shot their poisonous darts into Esther's mind. She tried to concentrate. "I often talk to God; I wonder …Well… No, I'm sure He hears me."

Deception chuckled as Pride released another dart. "In fact," she continued, "my parents were Christians, and so I must be one too."

George thought to himself, "I've sure heard that one before." Guided by the Holy Spirit's leading, he replied, "Esther, just because your parents were not Christians doesn't mean you are one also. The Bible says if anyone doesn't have the Spirit of Christ in them, they don't belong to God" (Romans 8:9)

As Esther hurriedly began defending herself, Pride and Deception were pulled unceremoniously through the roof. Holding them by their misshapen wings was Gallant, George's angel. In a resounding voice, the brilliant being commanded, "You must stop now. His wife has prayed, and I'm here to enforce it."

The two ghouls disappeared, and Gallant smiled. Looking toward Heaven, he offerred praise to the King of Kings.

Mary finished praying and looked up to see an unfamiliar car pulling into her driveway. "The lady driver," she thought. "She must be who I was interceding for. Thank you, Father, for bringing someone to me who I can pray into your Kingdom."

The Holy Spirit whispered into her spirit, "I have placed a mantle on her to witness and pray. Lift her to me in daily prayer, calling upon my heavenly host to bring protection from Satan, for her ruling and reigning with me will touch many lives."

George paused and turned to Esther. "I don't know quite how to say this, but your husband volunteered you to take my wife to the dentist and then pick up our son from Cambridge Elementary School.

Esther's gaze fell on Mary, and she felt an immediate liking for her. That was odd because she'd never had anything to do with a colored lady before. "Sure, I'll do whatever I can."

An ogre flew past, shouting, "People will talk if they see you with her!"

Gallant raised his powerful arm; and with one smooth backhand, knocked the little demon of Pride across town!

Chapter Six
Recruiting from the Spirit World

The small, red brick building was typical of any other elementary school. It had its playground, classrooms and share of spiteful teachers. Every school seemed to contain at least one rotten apple who would do enough damage to turn the kids off school forever. Mrs. Bladen appeared to be the one chosen for Cambridge. Her parents had beaten and neglected her as a child; and consequently, she had grown into a bitter woman taking her frustration out on her pupils.

She was one of the demons' favorite vessels, for with her dark heart, they could do all sorts of things to the kids through her. Despite the young ages of the children, the creatures wanted to get them to hate authority, especially targeting those who had Christian parents. The younger they could influence them, the easier it would be to sway them as they grew up.

That afternoon, coming in from recess, Walter was following Eva when he noticed a red mark on her skirt. He caught up with her and softly tapped her on the shoulder. "Eva, you must have sat in red paint."

Eva looked puzzled. "No, I didn't."

"Yes, you did. Look at your skirt."

As they looked, they both realized it wasn't paint. It was blood stain. Concerned and curious, Walt asked, "How did that happen?"

Eva flushed with embarrassment, knowing it was from her belt wounds, darted off into the classroom. Some boys noticing her hurried departure, called out,

"Hey, nigger boy! You're not allowed to play with white girls. Stay away, or you'll give her cooties." They all roared with laughter until they heard the smack of Mrs. Bladen's ruler on the desk. A hush fell over the room, and they sat quietly with their gazes glued to the floor.

"Walter Smith, stand up!" Mrs. Bladen bellowed. Walter gingerly rose to his feet, anguished in his spirit because he wasn't used to being spoken to so harshly. "Come up here and put your hand out right now!" she demanded. "Eva, did he bother you?"

The little girl, too afraid to speak, sat fearfully in her seat. Without warning, Mrs. Bladen brought the ruler down hard across Walt's knuckles. It made a loud cracking noise. No one moved as she raised her hand again, and Walt tried to hold back the tears.

"No!" Eva blurted out. "He didn't bother me." Seeing what he was going through, and reminded of her own undeserved thrashing, she added, "He only asked me a question."

Mrs. Bladen brought the ruler crashing down again. "It's none of your business to ask white girls questions. Now go to your seat and remember that next time."

An undersized demon of Anger buzzed around the room. Bitterness abruptly appeared, taking note of the situation, and demanding, "What are you doing up there? Go and aggravate Walt while he is still in pain."

"I can't," Anger replied. "His mother put the blood coverings on him this morning before he came to school."

"His mother! What are we going to do about that saint?"

Anger snarled, "You say you have been watching her. Well, where is she now?"

"She's with Esther!"

Both ghouls looked at each other, then without another word, disappeared, materializing at the dentist's office.

Mary and Esther sat patiently waiting for Mary's turn and trying to get acquainted. Pride stood in the corner watching them disdainfully. The two new demons didn't need to ask why no harassment was going on. Next to Mary stood Odessa, her guardian angel, dressed in full armor of light, a sign to show he was responding to prayer. In his brilliance, he towered over the demons, the power he commanded came from God Almighty. He raised his arm, fully aware that the slightest movement shot off tiny beams of light. A demon could be severely wounded if one of those shafts hit it. All stood completely still, waiting. In a thunderous voice Odessa decreed, "You have no authority to be here. Mary has committed this time to the Lord. Leave at once!"

Pride, Bitterness and Anger vanished, leaving behind a stifling quietness.

Mary reached over to take Esther's hand. As the two touched, a fresh aroma filled the room. It was sweet like potpourri of rose petals and baby powder. Esther commented, "What a lovely fragrance? Is that your perfume?"

"No." Mary smiled. "It's the presence of the Lord."

"You mean He's here? Right now? I feel so dirty!"

That's conviction. The Holy Spirit is showing you yourself in comparison to a Holy God. You can't be good enough or clean enough to know Him. They only way is to ask Christ's Spirit to come and unite Him with you. Because Jesus died and rose again, you too become a new person and the old you is passed away."

"But God already answers my prayers," Esther replied proudly. "I've always talked to Him" Then she remembered, silently prompted by the Holy Spirit, what George had said. "Unless you have the Spirit of Christ, you do not belong to Him."(Romans 8:9)

"Esther," Mary said, squeezing her hand gently, "King David spoke about how men with their bellies full and lots of blessings would assume they were at peace with God."

"What do you mean?"

"It can seem your prayers have been answered when in fact God didn't answer them at all. God will do things in your life that show His goodness so you will repent and come to Him, but not all circumstances in your life have been instigated by God."

"What do you mean, repent and come to Him? Repent from what?"

"From thinking you know God when you haven't accepted Jesus Christ as your Lord. That's like saying you know the president just because you heard someone talk about him. You don't really know anyone until you have spent time with them."

Just then the door opened and a nurse appeared. "Mary, it's your turn."

She got up to follow her and turned back. "Oh, Esther, you'll pick up Walt at school, won't you? You can't miss him. He's the only Negro child there. Oh, and thanks for bringing me here and waiting with me too."

"It was my pleasure. I'm glad I met you and don't worry about Walt. In fact, I'll take the boys for some ice cream on the way home."

Mary reached the door of the waiting room and looked back at Esther's retreating form. Aware of a serenity following Esther which hadn't been there before, she lifted a silent prayer of thanks for the work God was already doing in her life.

Nova, a shimmering angel, walked abreast of Esther, his presence infusing a circle of protection around the seeds that had been planted in her heart.

Later that afternoon on the drive home with George, the Lord reminded Mary of the different things she had been told, adding a lost scripture from years before. "If you seek Him, you shall find Him." (Jer 29:13)

Out on the school curb, stood Walt, Joshua and Debbie. All were waiting for their parents, but with varying degrees of expectancy.

Walter, of course, was expecting his father, so he wandered over to the steps to sit and wait. Usually if his dad wasn't there when he came out, then it meant he was tied up and would get there as soon as he could. He prayed a little prayer. "Lord, please take care of Daddy." Just then he noticed a somber look on Debbie's face and wondered what had upset her. After his experience in class, he was afraid to ask her, but Mrs. Bladen was gone and his father's statement danced in his thoughts. "Those kids have problems we don't even know about."

"Hey, Debbie, are you all, right?"

Sitting dejectedly on the stairs near him, she began crying softly.

"What's the matter?" he slid a little closer to her, wanting to comfort her in his childish way.

"I miss my dog. He was all I had to look forward to when I got home, and now he's dead."

"How did he die?"

"My Daddy got angry and slammed the door and Chipper was squashed in it." At those words, she started sobbing brokenly. Then her eyes glazed over in remembrance of the incident as they went from a look of hurt and pain to cold and calculating. Anger began gaining access to her. How much of a foothold it got depended on her? She could nurse the wound and add bitterness and resentment or she could reach out for the love of God.

Unfortunately, she chose resentment because no one had told her how to receive God's comfort.

As they were talking, Esther pulled up and Joshua ran up and got in the car. "Honey, is there a little Negro boy here?"

"Oh, the nigger!" he said, pointing his finger. "He's over there."

"Joshua!" his mother rebuked him. "I don't ever want you to say that again."

"What? Nigger?"

"Yes."

"But that's what everybody calls him."

"Maybe so, but I don't want you calling him that. Besides, you don't like it when kids call you names, do you? I met his mother today, and she is a lovely lady. I won't allow you to discredit her son that way."

He hung his head, ashamed. "Okay, Mom, I'm sorry. Hey, Walt," he called. "Come over here."

"Walter, your dad couldn't come so he asked me to pick you up. Hop in, and we'll stop for some ice cream on the way home."

Jumping in the car, Walt's unerring heart leapt with excitement while under his breath, he thanked the Lord for this rare treat. He had had a bad day, too many knocks for a 6-year-old to cope with.

He glanced back just in time to see Debbie's mom yank her hair. In his innocence, he thought to himself, "There certainly are a lot of kids to pray for. I'm happy to have something this important to do."

Chapter Seven
Invasion of Rock & Roll

The noisy air compressors wheezed in the garage. A smell of rubber filtered through the halls, Larry sat back in his chair, looked out to his warehouse and began reminiscing.

He remembered how Rose's father, Kent, had given him the money for this business as a wedding gift. Kent saw the future being in cars, therefore, there would also be a future for tires. Larry had wanted to be a doctor, but his lack of self-control had found him trapped in marriage and a mortgage. His father-in-law deemed a local business more practical and was especially persuasive.

Rose had been his high school sweetheart, and he recollected how beautiful she had been as homecoming queen. Their date that night had ended in the creation of another human being, their daughter, Debbie, a child Rose had always resented. Being pregnant at 18 had cut her off from the things she had dreamed of doing. Losing her reputation put her in exile from her family and their fortune, so with plenty of guilt and a corral of unseen hosts, Rose took her resentment out on Debbie.

Larry had always wanted to be somebody, to mingle with the rich and influential. He longed to belong to organized clubs and to amount to something. But now he was stuck in a garage that reeked like burned tacos and had to live with a woman with no desire to be a loving wife. The two, like many other couples, just tolerated each other and did their best not to intrude on the other. But for Larry, the pressure was mounting as the monthly bills kept climbing. Even after receiving his credit cards for her personal spending, Rose still managed to squander the food money on things for herself. As Larry looked around, his spirit sank in hopelessness.

Pride and Deception sat opposite him on the couch, ready for their mission to begin. Pride asked, "When does Sonny get here?"

Deception twitched. "He's here now. Get ready to activate." Both demons turned to watch Sonny, their favorite initiator, walk into the building. He was one of their best recruiters and knew how to make men feel noticed and special while unwittingly leading them down a path of spiritual deception.

Larry got up and walked towards the flamboyantly dressed man who had just entered the garage. "Larry Olson?" "Yes. How can I help you?"

"I'm Sonny Weston of the Freeson's Lodge. One of our brothers told me I should come and talk to you about joining our exclusive men's club."

Larry's ego responded and darkness emanated. Pride, taking his cue, placing its hand on Larry's shoulder and shot arrows of flattery and self-adoration into his emotions.

"Well, I'm flattered you should ask. What's it all about?" he questioned, standing a little taller.

"A demon penetrated its lethal pinions into Larry, dripping an invisible mist of its nature into his heart which meshed quickly with the darkness already there.

"Yes, I deserve to be on some committees, doing something people will take notice of," he thought to himself. "In fact, I'd be an asset to any fraternity I joined. I'm surprised nobody asked me before this."

"Our club is simply a group of guys who get together once a month. We discuss things that are happening in the community and look for ways to improve on things beneficially. Afterwards, we have a couple of drinks to unwind from work and the pressure of family life and play cards or something. We're like a family away from home." Sonny added," Our next meeting is tomorrow night. Why don't you come as my special guest?"

"Sounds great!" Larry responded. "I'll wait for you here and follow you over. What time?"

"I'll see you here at 6:00."

Pride and Deception grinned wickedly at each other. "Good! Once he's joined their ranks, we've got him further in our grip and we'll have an easier job of keeping him from the truth. Once he's a member, he wouldn't dare disagree with their beliefs."

That evening at the Smith's the aroma wafting from the dining room was whetting George's and Walt's appetites. Mary gave thanks to God for the food, then turned to Walter. "Did you have a good day at school, honey?"

Walt reached for his milk, a lump forming in his throat. He tried unsuccessfully to dissolve it with the liquid. He was unusually somber, and his parents knew something was wrong.

"One of the girls in my class had blood on her skirt. I think she had been strapped. When I asked her about it, she became scared and ran away. Then some boys yelled at me to leave her alone, and my teacher heard them and called me up front and hit me with a ruler."

George and Mary exchanged worried glances. The demon of Hate flittered about anxiously but wouldn't settle due to the presence of Gallant and Odessa. The family clasped hands, and George began praying. "Father, we pray that you would come and heal the hurt in our son's heart from what happened today. Don't allow any hate or bitterness to spring forth from this."

As they prayed, their hearts glowed, and beams of light flickered all about them. The angels shone even more brightly. After all, they were united in this to bring honor to their King.

During the prayer, Hate couldn't project, so it huddled in the corner to avoid contact with the shafts of light ricocheting around the room.

The Smith's resumed eating, and George asked his wife about her time with Esther at the dentist's office.

"You know, dear, her husband, Sam, is a bit of a mocker; but he certainly is babbling around town how you talk to God!"

They both laughed, and Mary put down her fork. The Lord has a great purpose for that Esther. He told me one day she would touch many lives for Him."

"Well," declared George, "we must certainly intercede for her salvation then."

Walt spoke up. "Can I pray for her son, Joshua?"

"Of course, you can, but what are you going to pray about, son?"

"That he will be my friend, and I can teach him about Jesus," Walt replied with determination.

Mary was touched. Her heart filled with love for this young ambassador for God. "That will be good for you." She looked at her son and remembered the day she dedicated him to the Lord as a baby. She knew, though, he would have to make that decision himself as an adult.

Walt added, "Hey, Mom! What's for dessert?"

Did he really understand the importance of praying for his friends?

At the Silverstone's it was cocktail hour. Marvin and Janet sat silently in the ornate living room until Eva came in singing.

Marvin looked over, pride radiating from his eyes. She was his precious jewel, and he motioned for her to come and sit on his lap. With soft, curly blonde hair, pale blue eyes and her perfectly formed features, she was a little doll. He lifted her up, and she let out a strange whimper. "What's the matter, sweetheart?" he asked, lifting the hem of her skirt. He was shocked by what he saw there. Black and blue bruises crossed her thighs.

"What happened?" He glared at his wife and snapped, "Did you do this, Janet?"

Janet downed her drink defiantly, then shrugged her shoulders. "I don't know what came over me. Maybe during meditation, I can find the answer." She got up and walked out, oblivious to the expression engraved on her husband's face.

He growled after her, "Don't you ever do something like this again. I want you to stop this hocus-pocus too. You've been getting weirder and weirder since you started this nonsense. I don't understand what's gotten into you." The demons did.

Eva sat on her father' lap relishing the closeness of being with him. Wrapping her arms around his neck, she felt safe in the haven of his love. She clung tightly and whispered in his ear, "Daddy, this monster came into my room. It wouldn't let me scream, and I was so scared."

"Oh, honey," Marvin chuckled, straightening the bow in her hair. "You were just having a bad dream." He was unaware that the tormenting vixen was sitting on his lap with her, leering in his face. Being totally grossed out by any indication of love when Marvin kissed his daughter, the ghoul fled to wait upstairs for Eva to come to bed.

In the darkened den, surrounded by a hundred of Marvin's law books, Janet sat Indian style on the floor. She was about to do her nightly spiritual routine.

"Oh, Mother, I beseech you to come from the valley beyond, past the port holes of time and death itself. I ask you, God, to let my mother come from the grave that I might speak with her."

By the big bay window, beginning to materialize as a faded misty specter and then becoming clearer and clearer, the spirit approached, disguised as her mother.

"What do you want?" it bellowed, floating to the side of the room.

"Mother, what's the matter?"

"Look, you wench, I have better things to do than to come and visit you all the time. Why don't you just leave the dead in their grave?"

Janet was stunned.

"And, furthermore, wench, you were a nuisance even when I was alive. Don't call me anymore!" With that, the apparition vanished.

Janet sat still, confusion racing in her mind. What had happened to cause this rejection from her mother? Usually, the spirit had been soothing, even loving. Janet felt betrayed. "Maybe I'll give her some time and call her up later. I wonder what she does with her time in Heaven."

Sorcery sent out a call into the darkness. "I need two more assistants to bring her down."

In a flash, Anger and Depression appeared, eager for a conquest. In unison, they inquired, "Is anyone praying for her?"

"No," came the reply.

Evil glee echoed through the atmosphere.

Angels pronounced, "Praise be the Lord who sets up circumstances to prevent them perishing forever."

* * *

The next day, the children were very excited about their outing to the local swimming pool. Eagerly, they gathered at the bus, each exchanging stories of the last time they had swam. There was only one pool in town, so many had never swum before at all. Because Walter was black, he'd never been allowed to swim in the pool, but he was excited to go, nonetheless. As they tumbled into the bus, Walt watched Eva slowly and stiffly climbed the steps. He knew by the way she walked, she must be in pain, and realized her swimsuit would reveal the belt marks. Walt sent up a prayer for her and added one for himself. "God, please bring a friend for me soon."

Once at the pool, the children were cautioned to stay near the shallow end. Walt, since he couldn't go in anyway, wandered down to the deep end. He looked down at the water and the design on the bottom of the pool. The sign said 15'. He was disappointed he couldn't feel the sensation of water all around him, but the thought of swimming in 15' of water seemed a bit scary anyway, so he was content to be an observer.

All the commotion and noise were at the other end of the pool, and Walt felt isolated as the laughter reverberated about him. He looked down at his black arms and glanced around at all the white children. "I'm no different from them. Why do they say I am?"

Self-rejection, a most subtle demon, waited nearby. Walt tried staying calm but was deeply hurt and a minimum trace of darkness was forming on the edge of his heart.

His thoughts were interrupted by a sharp crack. It sounded like a whip at the rodeo, and he turned directly to where the sound had come from. There under the diving board a few drops of blood floated on the water, and Joshua's body was swiftly sinking to the bottom.

The Lord spoke. "Rescue him."

Panicked, Walt kicked off his shoes and jumped in. The cold water surprised him, but he didn't have to relish the sensation. "How do I get to the bottom of the pool?" He took a deep breath and dove under, paddling furiously as he tried to go deeper. Thinking to himself, "God help me!" he reached out and grabbed Joshua by the hair, then his arm, and finally after what seemed an eternity, he pulled Joshua pulled him to the surface. It was as though someone had given him supernatural strength. It had been too easy for a child who couldn't even swim. Walt was out of energy but used this hidden strength to drag Joshua over to the side.

At Walt's cries for help, a lifeguard raced out of the locker room, pulled Joshua out of the water and ran with him to the bench. He began mouth-to-mouth resuscitation while Walt hung onto the side to catch his breath.

Insensitive to Joshua's dilemma, Mrs. Bladen came down and demanded that Walt get out of the pool. As soon as he had obeyed, she slapped him in the face. "Don't you ever let me see you in the pool again? I told you Negroes aren't allowed to swim with white people."

The pain and insult brought flames of anger to Walt's emotions, and abruptly he turned and ran down the side of the bench to escape this new enemy, Mrs. Bladen.

The tiles were slippery, and he lost his balance, falling headfirst into the bench in front of the other kids. They all shouted with laughter, and the darkness deepened as Walt held onto the anguish, engraving a scar in his soul.

The darkness signaled Anger who took its cue and released sin into his mind. Sadly, Walter received it, responding maliciously, "I hate you; I hate all of you!" He ran out the door, Anger clinging to his back. This force would compel and manipulate him for years to come, and eventually one he loved.

Was there anyone who could rescue him? Yes, His name is Jesus.

The next day, after much coaxing from his parents, Walt returned to school. He was quite surprised by the attention he received upon his arrival. The truth had come out. Walter himself had saved Joshua's life. He was now a hero, and God had answered his prayers. Joshua and Walter would become the best of friends. But what would he do with the anger in his heart?

Chapter Eight
<u>Civil Rights</u>

The beatnik movement had been replaced by the British invasion of the Beatles, and parents had a new fad to deal with.

Boys wanted to look like the Beatles and girls wanted to marry them. The clean-cut look was out, while scruffy, mod, long hair was in. Although the songs seemed innocent at first, they soon changed as demonic hosts help to glamorize sex, drugs and rock and roll. A new era had begun, and all it represented, split households apart in every neighborhood. Their appearance changed the course of hairstyles and bankrupted many a small-time barber.

Joshua, now ten, had a two-year-old brother, whom Esther had named Sam Jr., she was hoping the young one might endear Sam more than he had been to Josh. Although she enjoyed the tot, her husband didn't. Instead, he repeated his own father's sin, unwittingly accusing and condemning.

The Holy Spirit had continued working in Esther's life, drawing her to Jesus. The battle had been uphill, but God had freedom to rest on her in answer to the Smith's prayers.

The angels knew the calling on Esther, but did the ghouls see her potential in Christ? They were determined to sabotage any destiny God had for her.

One autumn day, the family was gathered in the living room admiring Sam's newest toy, a television set. The telephone rang, and he rushed to answer it. He listened for a moment, and then without bothering to cover the mouthpiece, he turned to Esther and sneered, "Its Mary, that negro friend of yours. And, no, you can't go to church with her, so don't even think about it!"

Accustomed to his rudeness, Esther ignored his abuse; and as she walked over to the phone, she smiled at the persistence of this lady to try and help her know God better. For Esther, it was like taking one step forward and two steps back. The Holy Spirit would show her the need for repentance and acceptance of Christ, and then a deceptive demon would convince her she knew God and was on her way to Heaven. "After all," she rationalized, "I was baptized when I was little, and I never miss a Sunday in church."

She was a member of the Bethesdian denomination, and of course, every Bethesdian was a Christian! Just that morning when the car wouldn't start, she had asked God to fix it and He did. What she didn't know was that a ghoul had been sitting on the hood and set up the whole episode to convince her God had favored her and answered her prayer.

As Esther took the phone from Sam, chills ran up and down her spine. The eyes glaring at here weren't his. They had an alien look about them as if someone else was in him looking out. She shrugged it off, assuming it was an effect from the booze he'd just consumed. Esther commented, "I'm sorry you had to hear that, Mary."

"I'm used to it," she responded with a sigh. "With all Martin Luther King's doing for civil rights, I've heard much worse than Sam's remarks. I'm sure being Jewish, Jesus was called a few names. In fact, certainly the disciples were badgered by insulting names, so I'm in good company."

They chatted briefly about the service that evening which Esther obviously wouldn't be able to attend. As she hung up, Esther said to herself, "That woman knows God in a way I didn't think was possible. I must talk with her again about it. She intrigues me."

That Monday, in the center of town many people converged on City Hall to hear an evangelist from New York. People said wherever he preached, people were changed when he left.

Mary slipped into the back row and bowed her head. "Father, I have tried to be a good witness for you. If there is something more I can do, please show me tonight. Speak to me through this man. And, Lord, please forgive Sam for his hatred towards me. I know it's not really me he dislikes, but rather my color. I pray for the work Dr. King is doing and bless him in that mission you raised him up for. With your help maybe this horrible barrier between whites and coloreds will be demolished."

After a few songs, a quietness came over the room. Onto the stage walked a silver-haired man in his mid-fifties, carrying the biggest Bible Mary had ever seen.

"Let us stand," he began, "and join hands in prayer." With great authority, he spoke, commanding Satan and his cohorts be bound. "In Jesus' name we command all works and schemes of Satan to cease, and for all demonic hosts to leave this building at once. Antichrist, Jezebel, Death and Hell, with all your assistants, go now! Jesus said He gave us all authority over the power of the enemy and the spirits are subject to us. The weapons we fight with are not the weapons of the world. Instead, they have divine power to demolish strongholds. Holy Spirit, we call on you to come and anoint the message for those who have ears to hear."

Mary sat down, reflecting on what she'd just heard. "He named the powers!" she thought He was specific. What a new concept in prayer. She sat, enthralled by the idea.

A new dimension was being added to her understanding of something Jesus had said. "I will send you my Comforter, and He will be with you forever." (Jn 14:16)

The preacher lay his glasses aside and took a sip of water. "Now, honestly, folks, how many of you love the Lord? Raise your hand." Mary didn't hesitate in openly declaring her devotion towards the Lord.

"How many of you feel there is more to walking with Jesus and you want it? You lack power. You're not walking in the victory you desire in all areas of your life. The people around you aren't coming to Jesus. Acts 1:5 says, "You shall receive power when the Holy Ghost comes upon you and you shall be my witnesses." How many of you want to witness for Christ?"

Mary's hand shot up along with many others all over the auditorium.

"Well, come down to the front and we're going to ask Jesus to empower you with His Holy Spirit. Some of you have the Holy Spirit in you because you belong to God, but now He's going to baptize you with fire from Heaven. You will see a change and give glory to God. If there is something you need to repent of, now is the time, for God gives His Holy Spirit to those who obey Him and desire to live for Him."

As the people got out of their seats and began walking forward, a voice whispered to Mary. "This is only for white folks. You don't think God would favor you with them to get His Spirit, do you?" She pushed the thought away, recognizing where it had come from. "Don't go down there!" she heard again. Fearlessly, Odessa clasped the tiny demon in a vise-like grip and hurled it through the air right out of the building. Odessa shook his magnificent head. "Some demons are so rebellious! I'll deal with that one later."

The Holy Spirit spoke to Mary's heart. "How much more would the Father give the Holy Spirit to them who ask?" Joy filled her heart, and she walked down the aisle knowing what she was doing was an important step in her Christian walk but unaware of the full purpose this would bring. She joined the thirty others who stood at the front, ready to partake of this great gift from God. Hundreds had come to hear the message, but only this handful were willing to seek the fullness of God's Holy Spirit.

The preacher asked for silence. "Now, I know some of you have been told there is no such thing as baptism in the Holy Spirit. In fact, you've probably been told you have all of God you can get. Well, I'm here to tell you that those who tell you that it can't happen, say it only because they never had it happen to them. But those of us who have had this baptism know something wonderful happened that changed us. So, look to Jesus, the author and the finisher of your faith. If He has more to give you, then don't let any man or preacher talk you out of His blessing. Don't allow someone else's wall to become a barrier for you to reach your fullest potential in God."

People began getting up all over the room. Another fifty or so people shuffled forward. Standing in silence, a soft breeze blew across the congregation, carrying with it that certain aroma of baby powder and roses.

The preacher took a deep breath and smiled. "Now some of you while I pray may feel a joy you never knew before well up inside you. You'll feel such happiness you might think you'll burst. You may laugh or you may cry. Some of you may begin speaking in a language you don't know. Simply allow it to flow from you. The Bible says, "forbid not the speaking in tongues" (1 Cor 14:39)

Suddenly, it was like the auditorium erupted into a celebration as the people in front began laughing and crying as a new awareness of God's presence and love enveloped them. Some had fallen on the floor and looked so peaceful and serene, almost like they had left this world. Others lay with beautiful smiles on their faces as if in direct communion with God Himself. A look of completeness was on each of their faces. Voices began calling out, "I'm healed. Oh, Jesus! Thank you, Jesus!"

Mary stood; her arms raised as though reaching up as a child to her Daddy. "Oh, God, I want to give you more and ..." Before she finished, the power of God came on her. It seemed like she actually floated backwards to the ground and lay there shining, while an incredible joy filled her. She bubbled over with excitement and then began speaking in another tongue. It kept coming and she couldn't stop it. In fact, she didn't want to stop it, it was so exhilarating. Her body tingled all over as she expressed this heavenly gift. She was ecstatic and laughed as the new language flowed out from her mouth. She felt the love of God shed abroad in her heart.

One of the town's beauty parlor directors, Mrs. Kraus, stood beside Mary's prostrate form. She had migrated to America as a child and upon hearing Mary's new language, lifted her arms to praise God. Mary was speaking "Praise God" in her native tongue, German.

Fifteen minutes later, when it seemed the power of God was deposited in each spirit willing to receive, people began slowly going back to their seats, and the choir sang softly, "Just as I Am."

Mrs. Kraus helped Mary to her feet and noticed the warm glow about her. "Excuse me, but I must tell you. The language you were speaking was German!"

Mary beamed. "Praise the Lord. Oh, that was wonderful!"

Mrs. Kraus cautioned, "Just be careful who you share this with because many will try to ridicule what happened and also attempt to talk you out of it. Use your new tongue every day and then it will add power to your prayer."

The lights came on and people began filing out. As Mary looked around for a familiar face, she noticed a group of ladies near the door staring at her. Just then one of them began walking towards her. "I wanted to tell you how positively radiant you look. It's just as though the Lord was shining right through you."

Odessa, Mary's angel, released his hand from above the woman and smiled. Sometimes it takes an angel to prompt us to say what needs to be said.

As Mary climbed into her car, she sat for a moment. Tears welled up in her eyes and she thanked God for all the blessings he had bestowed on her, her beautiful family, friends and financial security. She was especially grateful for the work Dr. King was doing to integrate peacefully her people into all phases of society. Now God had baptized her in his Holy Spirit and empowered her in a new way. Her thoughts were interrupted by a loving command from the Lord. "Don't give up, for in due time you shall reap if you faint not." (Galatians 6:9) As she turned the ignition, another verse came to her. "Pray for the city, for in it you shall have welfare too." (Jeremiah 29:7)

Chapter Nine
Spirits Manifest

Janet and Marvin were growing further and further apart. He was spending more and more time away from home and she was rapidly spilling into a psychotic depression. For no reason at all, she would fly into rages which often resulted in her locking Eva in the closet "to teach her a lesson". It had been four years since the apparition she believe to be her mother's spirit had rebuked her and since that time, never materialized again, no matter how hard Janet tried. The result was a bitter and dejected woman.

Her daughter was now ten and like most girls her age, enjoyed playing house and dressing up Barbie dolls. One afternoon, some unseen visitors were observing Eva and Debbie playing quietly in Eva's room. Debbie was only two years older and already bossy. They were looking for any vantage point where they could affect the girls.

"No!" Eva declared vehemently. "You can't have a new dress; the one you have is fine." She walked determinedly over to her drawer, opened it and flung the doll inside. "This will teach you a lesson!"

Influenced by Eva's actions, Debbie began pulling her doll's hair. "I'm sorry you were born. It's your fault I'm a bored mother. I want to move to Florida, and you're in the way."

With that, she flung her doll across the room. Both girls laughed and decided to go outside and play. Darkness had been given plenty of access into each girl's personality. Both had been rejected in different ways, but Eva had a worse problem. Fear gripped her spirit and the demons kept coming at night to keep that darkness growing.

Relationships at the Silverstone's were declining even further. That chilly afternoon, Marvin stopped by the drive-in to get a vanilla shake. While waiting for his order to be taken, he was drawn to a tall, shapely blonde who roller skated between cars with the greatest of ease.

He sat, infatuated as she glided by, carrying the tray of food without the slightest stumble in her maneuvers. As he watched, he noticed an uncanny resemblance to his daughter. I bet that is what Eva will look like in a few years' time. I'm going to have to fight off the boys, he chuckled to himself.

Perched jauntily on the roof of his car was a principality and two demons in submission to this higher authority. Jezebel, who had been a strongman in several generations of Marvin's family, along with Lust and Deception. They were discussing their strategies to bring their evil into Marvin's life.

Deep in thought, he was brought sharply back to reality as the girl skated up to his window. "Hey, big guy, what can I get you?" she asked with a wide smile.

Marvin was captivated by her crystal-blue eyes. They spoke to him. "I'm yours if you want me."

She leaned her elbow on the roof of the car, unaware it was strategically placed between the two demonic creatures. Elated at her proximity, they quickly ran their ugly claws up and down her forearm. Her body tingled as she looked into the handsome stranger's face. She assumed he was the cause of her rush.

"Well, gorgeous, what can I get you?"

"I'm not sure. My appetite changed while I was sitting here. Never mind, I'll get something at home."

He followed her with his eyes as she skated to the next car, staring at her long smooth legs. He could almost imagine what was hidden under her short, pleated skirt. As his mind conceived the thought, enticing him with his own fleshly desires, he felt sensual and while relishing the sensation, a black mist encircled his heart. Lust, ever alert for an opening, saw the sin and began waving its tentacles about like an octopus protecting itself. The demon released its power through the car roof into Marvin's mind. His thoughts turned from the girl in his sight to his daughter Eva. What would she look like now undressed at ten years old? He toyed with the perversion too long, and Lust invaded him, making his body a new target.

Once home, Marvin headed straight for the vodka to conceal his erotic feelings. He sat in his favorite chair, thinking again about the waitress. He took a long drink just as the hall door slammed and Eva sidled around the corner. She stood in the doorway a moment with the hall light shining on her from behind. Marvin could just make out a faint outline through her nightgown. "Hello, baby. Come and sit on Daddy's lap and tell me what you've been up to."

Lust began pricking Marvin's heart with its purpose. The darkness resident there consummated it and as Eva climbed onto his lap, Marvin's body responded to the enticing arousal.

"Daddy, will you come watch me in the school play tomorrow?"

"Oh course, honey," he said quickly. "Now go get ready for bed." He gave her a quick kiss and then removed her hurriedly from his lap.

She scampered off , and he sat in deep though, a worried frown across his brow. "What am I doing? She's, my daughter. Where are these feelings coming from?"

Lust retreated. Now that the seeds had been sown, it would have another opportunity.

Eva slowly climbed the stairs, reluctant to go to bed. Fear embellished her as she contemplated being in the dark and tormented by that monster again. Lately she had been hearing voices telling her to go kill herself. "If you don't you will have a horrible death by us."

She didn't know which was worse, being locked in the closet by her mother, or hearing those terrifying voices. Whenever she tried getting some sympathy from her parents, she was simply told, "All kids have nightmares, it's part of growing up!"

Janet came into the living room. "Are you going to her school play tomorrow night?"

"Yes, I told her I'd be there. I'll have to meet you at the school after work."

Watching Marvin, Janet thought, "Once he'd been so in love with me, he would have surely come home to get me so I didn't show up alone. All he cares about now is himself and his career."

He was the county's District Attorney and had his sights set on becoming mayor someday. He desperately wanted the prestige and the power that went with the position. God had similar plans, but for a different reason. God's desire was to instill righteousness in the laws to keep man from detouring too far into lawlessness, thus inciting God's curse on the land.

"I'm going upstairs to watch the news," Marvin announced.

A sarcastic retort was quickly forthcoming. "So, what else is new? That's all you do at home."

Marvin shrugged it off and mounted the stairs. As he got closer to the top, he heard Eva splashing merrily in the bathtub. Hearing her laughter brought a smile to his face. She was his little ray of sunshine. In his soul the emotions were mixed. The temptation to look in on her was great. He obeyed the impulse and opened the door slowly.

Pleased to have an audience share her bubble wonderland, Eva stood up to show him a handful of bubbles she could blow away. The remaining white foam slowly cascaded down her tiny innocent body. "Hi, Daddy. Look what I can do," she giggled, sending the foam puffs to flight.

Lust tightened its position and a perverted spirit landed on his shoulder. This demon was determined to twist Marvin's pure love for Eva and make it something sinful and wicked. As he eyed his daughter, the alarm bells went off in his conscience.

Just then Janet grabbed his shoulder. Guilt flooded him as she demanded he go answer the phone. Relieved, Marvin backed out the doorway and proceeded to the receiver lying on the table. In the background, he heard his wife bellow, "Sit down, you show off. No one wants to see your naked body."

As Marvin tried falling asleep, his thoughts accused him of this pervading draw toward Eva. Why was his child causing this reaction? He didn't understand it and certainly didn't like it. During the night, his dreams were invaded by human desires for the waitress and the guilt of seeing Eva in the tub. Deception propelled data into his mind that was so realistic that Marvin awoke so convinced the waitress could be his for the asking, and so purposed himself to go collect his prize before she got away.

During the day his business was often interrupted by the face of the blonde. Each time he felt a glow, a draw as it were, towards her. When the day came to a close, he was so hyped up to see her that as he headed for the drive-in and he completely forgot about the school play.

While he sat in the parking lot sipping his coffee and deceiving himself into a love affair with the girl, his own little girl was having a crisis of her own. Rejection was driving its ugly wedge into her spirit because not only had her father not come, but neither had her mom. Eva was crushed and another brick was added to her heart. "I mustn't depend on anyone, only myself," she declared. The creatures were willing to help cement that thought.

Across town at the Smith dinner table, Mary was filled with joy as she shared her experience from the seminar.

"It was amazing!" She smiled. "People were laughing, crying, some were healed, and I spoke in German for almost 10 minutes!" Mary went on to explain about Mrs. Kraus and suggested they have her to dinner soon. George was happy for his wife, but Walter wasn't too sure.

Just last week in Sunday school, Walter had raised his hand to ask a question. "Yes?" the teacher acknowledged, "what is it?"

"What is speaking in tongues?"

The teacher looked perturbed. "Where did you hear about that, young man? Let me tell you that speaking in tongues is the work of the devil. I don't ever want to hear that subject brought up here again. Is that clear?"

"Yes, ma'am."

Walter sat silently for a moment, pondering in his inquiring mind.

For the first time in his life, Walter doubted his mother, which meant other things she'd told him about God weren't fact either. He was confused. "Maybe everything about God and Jesus aren't true," he thought.

The fiends were nearby, and a seed of doubt had just been planted. Walter was reminded of a children's program he'd seen early on a Saturday morning. The host was talking about all sorts of things with two girls who were identical twins. The man had said that the girls had evolved like that, there was no first couple named Adam and Eve. People had just evolved and scientists could prove it. Then he added there was no God, the world had come from a cosmic explosion.

At the same time, Walter had heard that praying wasn't going to be allowed in school anymore. That was one of his favorite times because he could say the Lord's prayer all the way through. He would miss that opportunity.

Walter wondered, "Did God go away? Maybe we were too bad."

People and society were succumbing to the subtle influence of the powers of the air. Antichrist and Unbelief were masterminding a delusion to unleash their presence in a multitude of media. The demonic powers were ready to chisel away at the precious foundation Walter's parents had laid. Second period class on Monday would add to Walter's confusion. Mr. Bodsworth had disillusioned many a young person in his days at Cambridge. The ghouls went to stir him into action.

Sure enough, Monday morning in his class, the subject of God was hot on his lips. He had Sunday's paper in his hand and read from the front page to the class, "Prayer Banned from Public School." Antichrist leaned on his shoulder, shooting invisible plasma-like poison into his heart, already blackened by sin.

Bodsworth reminded himself of his hellish days at Catholic Boys School. The hours of repetitious prayer and countless times running the beads on the rosary through his restless fingers. "For what?" he thought. "From dust to d u s t. There's nothing else."

The class sat expectantly, waiting for his reaction. Good riddance! We didn't need another ritual anyway. Now stand and face the flag. Someday you may not be able to do either".

" . . . With liberty and justice for all." The class quietly slid into their desks.

Eva raised her hand. "Why aren't we allowed to pray anymore?"

To make his point, Bodsworth slammed down his book. "Because it's all rubbish, that's why! There is no God. Tell me, can you see Him? No! There was no Garden of Eden and I'll even prove to you there was no Adam and Eve."

He read from his science book with convincing authority, which made the class accept what he said about the theory of evolution.

Walter thought to himself, "It must be true. That's what the man said on TV too."

CHAPTER TEN
LOVE STARTS TOO EARLY

The New Year brought with it mixed emotions all through America. It had been over a year since the tragic assassination of President Kennedy and the Vietnam War was no closer to ending. Human spirits were low, and the usually strong United States was being split in half over the issue of this useless conflict. Malcom X was stirring up the Black communities against the white rich and riots were all over the states. (Sound familiar) This type of thing only made it worse on relationships between black and white families.

Across the world in certain major cities, a new principality was being birthed. It had always been around, but was taking on a new dimension, a new purpose. It was called the spirit of rock and roll. Its impact would be slow and seemingly harmless at first, but it would increase very rapidly within a decade. The influence it would make would change the course and purpose of songs forever. Music which was created to worship God would now accelerate the degradation and depravity of most nations. A new wave of hosts was in the heavenlies, preparing strategies that would raise hell and divide families for the next twenty-five years.

Hem lines became shorter while boy's hair grew longer. Pants got tighter and the clothing prints loud and obnoxious. Fashion screamed, "Look at me! I'm somebody!" The lyrics on records were no longer about simple things like puppies in the window for sale or "purple people eaters". In a couple of years, they had passed from "I wanna hold your hand" (Beatles) to "Let's Spend the Night Together." (Rolling Stones)

Music deteriorated the morals of an entire generation who would eventually pass it on to their children. It advocated rebellion, drugs, immortality, homosexuality, and the worship of evil. Those who succumbed to its demonic influence would, little by little, be deadened spiritually. Eventually they would have little desire of obtaining contact with God.

Although the three kids had been baptized, their parents knew they would have to make the decision themselves to be a Christian when a bit older. Now, several years later Walt was able to understand the responsibility and the need to be born again. Unfortunately, circumstances over the years had stolen the seeds that had been planted. Darkness had appeared in his heart on more than one occasion, and as a result, the spirits had managed to confiscate most of his faith.

Because of his parents' training and his willingness to listen to them, Walter only had one present spirit. This strongman, Anger, had a legal right to influence his actions as Walter freely chose to exhibit that response in many situations.

For Walter, being a teenager was harder than for the other kids as he was usually the odd one out. His color was one obstacle and the other was trying to obey his parents' wishes and not his classmates. He knew to be with the "in" crowd meant smoking, drinking, and cussing. He loved his parents and didn't want to hurt them, but the pressure was on to be one of the boys. All the standards his parents had set were slowly evaporating.

Being now thirteen and officially a teenager, he had purposefully discarded his boyish naiveté and traded it in for what was currently called "being cool". His personality was in conflict with what he knew to be right and what his peers said he had to do to be "in". The demonic stronghold resident inside rarely let him respond in gentleness when he was teased, which was quite often.

The once tender, shy boy was budding into an aloof and abrasive young man. His vocabulary widened and with each four-letter word he vented, his cooped-up anguish or prejudice and rejection.

As Martin Luther King continued his marches, the riots and fires became more prevalent in surrounding black areas. George had taken up his calling and was now a representative for the Civil Rights movement, trying to instill integration through peaceful means, believing God had initiated Luther's dream. As a result, Walter was bombarded daily by nasty threats and comments from local townsfolk and their well-meaning children.

One afternoon on his way home from school, a car drove by and some boys threw a couple of milk shakes at him yelling, "Tell your Daddy to take you back to Africa and quit stirring up trouble."

What once might have only caused hurt now intensified his prejudice and anger. The spirits would compound this by undermining Walt's relationship with his father. Thoughts would focus in his mind, sent from the ghouls to ruffle him. "Tell your father to quit". He's the cause of all your problems."

Walter embraced the suggestions, thinking to himself, "Yeah, it just isn't worth it. Someone else can do his job. If he really loved me, he'd quit."

By the time he got home, the milk shakes had dried to his clothes, adding to his aggravation. His heart begat immense darkness and Anger was ready to manifest. As he was about to enter the house, he reached for the doorknob and his hand made contact with a bumblebee. The pain added to his fury and at his mom's greeting he lashed out at her, something the power thrived on. "I hate this stupid town. Everything is going wrong. Tell Dad to butt out of this Civil Rights fight and let someone else do it!"

Mary was startled. Saying a prayer in her heart, she asked Walter what had happened to get him so cross and what was the mess on his clothes?

"Mom, since Dad started in this Civil Rights movements, I'm having more and more problems at school." He began choking on his words as he continued, "Kids even threw drinks at me today. That's what's on my shirt."

Feeling his hurt, Mary asked God to minister to him and Odessa stepped forward. Iridescent beams of light emanated from his breastplate.

As Mary's heart lifted her anguished prayer to God, it grew in brilliance too. The more her heart radiated this spiritual signal, the quicker her angel responded, calling for Regal to attend his charge. A brilliance at Walter's side. Regal stood, prepared to extinguish the darkness.

Reaching out and softly enfolding Walter in his loving wings, the shadow of hurt in his heart vanished. His emotions totally changed to one of peace and tranquility. Even the atmosphere in the room changed.

"Walter, honey. Slowly take a deep breath and smell the fragrance in the air. What do you sense?" Mary spoke in hushed tones, aware of the majestic presence.

"It's lovely, mom. It reminds me of how you smell when you're all dressed up. What is it?

She smiled. "That's the presence of the Lord."

Excitement rose in Walter's spirit. The demon in him quivered and shrank into a miniscule mite, settling into his flesh to permeate the Adamic nature.

"Walter," Mary said, taking him by the hand. "Can you remember the night your father was first telling you about slavery and that God would raise up someone to deliver our people?"

He thought for a moment. "No, Mom. I can't remember any of that."

"Well, you suggested that your father be another Moses and……"

Just then George walked into the room. Walter turned to his father and only love for him came to his heart. He walked over to him slowly and putting his arms around him, said, "Dad, you keep doing what God has called you to do." Then, before his parents saw his tears, he slipped away, holding in the grief and hurt from many cruel remarks, determined not to take it out on his family.

"Someday you'll be proud of me," he thought to himself. "Someday. You just wait and see."

Debbie had become withdrawn and dejected. The influence from the rejection she'd felt from her mother most of her life had brought her to the place where she had no self-esteem. She'd been told so often she was unwanted and worthless; it had now become part of her. At the emotional age of thirteen, she already had a crushed spirit. Her only protection from the pain was to escape anyway she could, often staying in her room for hours on end, pretending to be a famous recording artist. Watching herself in the mirror, she would sing and dance, trying to imitate the rock stars she'd seen on television. Her voice was very beautiful, and God desired she use it for His glory, not man's.

Self-rejection would emerge each time she looked in the mirror. All the anticipation and excitement she felt pretending to be a music star was jolted away as soon as she faced reality. Debbie was ugly. Her thick glasses, braces and boyish figure only added to the distaste she had for herself. The short hair she wore at her mother's insistence did nothing for her except expose ears that stuck out. So, with each glance at her reflection, the spiteful words she'd heard at school echoes in her mind. "Dumbo, Tin Grin, Four Eyes." Each one cut deep into her spirit. Self-rejection added salt to her wounds and increased her heartache. Her demeanor turned bitter and rebellious. More and more, she'd turned off her emotions and become callous.

Walking down the street one day, she found several firecrackers lying discarded in the gutter. Abruptly, the idea came to her to toss them off the bridge and frighten the drivers passing underneath. The only hindrance was where she could get some matches.

Sitting pondering the problem, the deviousness in her heart changed to a black luster. The ghouls fired on it and began granting her request. As she sat there, a man rode by on a bike smoking a cigarette.

"Hey, got a match?"

A demon swooped around his head and shot forth its dart. "Give her the box."

The man reached into his pocket and tossed her the half-empty container. "Here, you can have 'em!" he said and peddled down the street.

Debbie lit the perilous article and tossed it over the side of the bridge. "Where it stops, no one knows!" she cackled to herself.

Bang! She looked over the bridge, but there were no cars around. She cautiously waited for one to come into range, then spied one. Timing the firecracker perfectly and counting to herself, she threw it as hard as she could, trying to land it near the rear bumper. "Oh, just missed."

The driver slammed on the brakes. For a second, Debbie was frightened, wondering what the driver would do if he saw her. Her heart pounded, but in a moment the car sped away.

"Hey, this is groovy."

She saw another car coming towards the bridge. Immediately, she lit the fuse and flung the firecracker over, but in her excitement, she misjudged her timing. Landing on the windshield, it exploded, making a horrible noise and running the car off the road. A woman stepped out, visibly shaken and terror in her eyes.

Debbie quickly ducked behind the short wall, her heart throbbing loudly. She enjoyed the fear it created. A feeling of supremacy arose in her as she realized the potency of being able to control the fate of others. A car door slammed, and the motor started up, then she heard the car pull away. "I'll try it just once more for now," she reasoned. A trucked came into view. She counted down and then over the side the firecracker went. This time it landed in the back of the pickup, forcing it to pull over.

As Debbie peeked over the railing, she was horrified. A little dog was picking up the offensive weapon in its mouth when it detonated. The sight sickened her. Memories of her darling Chipper lying dead on the floor stabbed her mind.

She heard a door slam and looked over to see a young woman weeping hysterically as she embraced the wounded bloody dog. Debbie saw her face and the anguish etched there. She had just inflicted on an innocent stranger what her dad had done to her so many years before.

Fear and guilt flooded her emotions. Dazed, she dropped the match and remaining firecrackers and fled to a secret hiding place she often retreated to.

"God, I'm sorry. I'm so sorry," she sobbed. "Please forgive me."

How much did the Lord want to forgive Debbie? But seeing her heart, He knew these were only words of regret and embarrassment for what she had done not a heart cry to truly be forgiven by Him of all her wrong doings.

Weeks after the incident, Debbie regularly had nightmares of what she had done to that dog, which added to the self-hatred brewing inside her. Self-rejection continued contaminating her by polluting her mind with negative thoughts. "God will never forgive you. You're evil just like your mother."

But the Lord knew her potential in Christ, but would He have access to her?"

Joshua was a popular boy whose rugged good looks often made him the center of attention with the girls. Several coaches were also keeping their eyes on him for the school football team. Joshua was turning out to be a very competitive young man. His father had instilled in him that second place was only for losers. Therefore, he tried making up for it by being part of school clubs and sports teams so he could succeed at something to get noticed at home.

His relationship with his father was almost non-existent. Often, Sam offered to come to a game or take him bowling; but always at the last minute, he'd back out. Joshua didn't trust him and that added to his mistrust of others. His hopes were high of becoming a professional football player, and he made sure his school marks were above average. Basically, he was a good kid and endeavored to grow up and have a better relationship with his own children than he had with his father. Not too far behind was the second boy who took on his father's name, Sam Jr. He would have a very rocky start to life.

Esther noticed that Josh always enjoyed the police shows on television. It seemed that good triumphing over evil had been ignited in him through his Sunday school lessons. After all the Bible does say train up a child in the way he should go and when he is older, he won't depart from it (Prv22:6) Though Joshua wasn't raised by Christian parents, at least the teaching in Sunday School he received planted many positive seeds within him.

At his mother's urging, he enrolled in the debating club and public speaking classes. Although once there, he found much to everyone's surprise that he wasn't cut out to speak in front of people. The words seemed to get caught in his throat even when he remembered what to say.

The class was small, but one day in particular proved to be his most embarrassing moment. Standing in front of the class, ready to deliver a speech on President Lincoln, his mind went completely blank. Standing there staring at thirty pairs of eyes staring back added insult to injury, flustering him to the point that he ran out the door, swearing never to return. He kept the promise.

His father gave him a written letter of dismissal, along with dismal affirmation. "You'll never amount to anything if you keep quitting because things get rough."

Joshua absorbed the comment and stored it away in the vault of his subconscious along with all the other critical remarks stored there. Fear of failure and hopelessness posed serious threats to his personality and destiny.

Eva had retreated into her own intimate world of fashion magazines and movie stars. She kept her distance from her mother; and more out of fear than academic ability, managed to get straight A's in school. She was a bit of a loner and harbored a complete fear of others, including those her age.

Her independence had been fueled by a deceptive spirit who that came to her at night and penetrated her dreams, creating in her emotions the desire to be self-willed and aloof.

Flirting with the opposite sex helped appease her need for approval. Her platinum blonde hair was the envy of all the girls, and her crystal blue eyes mesmerized all the boys. As soon as she left her house, she would roll up her skirt and put on her 'Twiggy' eyelashes. She'd go from extreme introvert to almost whore-like in nature, leading the boys on and breaking many hearts before she was fourteen. Deep inside, Eva nursed a dream. From years of looking through magazines, she had coveted the fame and glamour of being a model and was determined that someday her face would grace the covers of top magazines. Whatever it would take, she vowed to do it.

Chapter Eleven
Contact with the Spirits

Janet Silverstone's contact with the occult was having serious consequences. Night after night, she would wake up aware of the presence of something in her room. She would call out hoping it was her mother, but the unyielding silence was cold and unnerving. Along with these occurrences, strange phenomena took place. Things disappeared around the house and appliances turned themselves on and off at will. Janet wanted to believe it was her mother's spirit, but somehow the assemblage simply felt too evil.

The fear this brought began to have repercussions. She became agitated, throwing fits of anger at minor things and talking to unseen voices. Even at the market, she was overhead talking in the vegetable department when no one was there. All in all, she was becoming quite neurotic.

Eva had become increasingly defiant towards her, rejecting her as a mother and authority figure. She had chosen to openly rebel.

Marvin, in an attempt to keep from wrongful thoughts towards his daughter, had opted for an on and off again affair with the waitress. She knew he was running for mayor, so the sly girl decided to blackmail him. She'd force him into paying her five hundred dollars a month to stay quiet.

It was a dire situation for him to be in, but one of his own making. He'd chosen to feed his own lusts as the deceitfulness of sin hardened his heart.

Over those next three years in junior high, all four teenagers gradually pulled away from the Lord and their Christian upbringing. That also left Sam Jr., Eva and her friend, Debbie, to find their own friends. The darkness had managed to infiltrate their minds so now they thought of Christian faith as childish and irrelevant for teens. The government was also doing its best to obliterate the word God from any federal property or building. For the pupils it had become nothing but a swear word.

During these years, life went on as usual in Cambridge. The townsfolk tried putting in an honest day's work and came home to share a few laughs around the television set. The demonic hosts were busying keeping residents badgered with incidents that would wreck relationships, destroy marriages and turn people away from God. Their most successful tactic was getting them beaten down, feeling helpless and isolated and to the point of desperation where suicide seemed an easy escape. The master planner of this was Satan, the prince of the power of the air, who worked in hearts and also created instances to strip away any purpose for living.

The suicide demon was one who had the ability to flit about, in and out of people at will. As situations warranted, the power would oppress its subject and then go on to someone else, leaving the victim to justify the urge.

Many of the residents were grandchildren of people who were alive during the Depression and as their relatives had opted for suicide to ease the trauma, unfortunately Cambridge had reaped what they had sown. A suicide curse rested on the land. Sam was an example of one who had inherited his grandfather's death wish. The spirit often oppressed him, keeping him drowning in self-pity.

His wife, Esther, usually stayed at home each day to take care of the house. She entertained herself with soap operas while the desire to know God that had been there years ago gradually faded away.

Yet in spite of this, the Lord, Commander of the Heavenlies, was preparing everything for Esther's induction into His army.

That Sunday at the local Bethesdian Church, Esther was detained by the song leader on her way out the door. "Excuse me, Esther, but I need your help," Mr. Dooley said. "I've heard you singing the hymns, and you're one of the few people who can reach the high notes and keep the tune. We're having a special next week, and I'd like to ask if you would sing a song for us."

Esther didn't feel intimidated as she agreed to do it.

Mr. Dooley handed her the hymn book and said, "I'll leave to you pick out something we all know."

As Mr. Dooley gathered his things to leave, so did the hand of the Lord withdraw, knowing His good pleasure had been accomplished.

That night at home, Esther propped herself up in bed and flipped through the hymnal.

"The Blood of Christ, Wash Me Clean." It didn't make any sense to her.

"Why was Jesus' blood so significant?" she asked herself. "What does it have to do with me now? God, if you're really there, help me to understand what this means," she prayed, turning the page to a song she had sung many times, but had never understood.

A ministering angel, sent by the Lord Himself, stood by her side. The brilliant being was there to fight off any spirits that would try to hinder God's work in her life. All he needed was her permission to allow it residence. The channel was clear, and the Lord opened her heart to understand the Scriptures.

"That's it!" she exclaimed loudly. "Oh, that's it! Once I was lost, but now I'm found. It's the amazing grace of God! Jesus shed his blood for me. Now I understand!" Before I was just walking around doing my own thing. Now Christ lives in me and does His thing through me. I give up my dreams and He gives me His.

For the first time, she felt how far away she really was from God. How pious she had been all those years when Mary and George had tried showing her, she must accept Jesus herself. She then threw the covers aside and slipped down on her knees beside the bed. Folding her hands in preparation for prayer, she was immersed in God's love. His presence engulfed the room.

Tears blinded her eyes as she petitioned God Almighty to forgive her. Things she had done over the years swiftly flashed through her mind. Hidden hates, lies, and complacency were now exposed so he could wipe them away. All the times God had tried to tell her the truth, and she had not listened assuming she already knew.

She was heartbroken at the depth of her rejection of Him, realizing all He'd ever done was love her and desire to have her love Him in return. One secret surfaced with conviction, but at that moment she heard Sam heading up the stairs. One look at her on her knees and his sarcasm would ruin the moment forever. He must be stopped from interrupting her. Nova, an angel given to her now by the Lord, engraved a thought in Sam's mind.

Halfway up the stairs, he suddenly felt hungry and decided to retreat to the kitchen for a snack. The angel saluted His Master, whose eyes shone down on His faithful creation.

A voice spoke deep in Esther's heart. Deep in her inner being, she heard Jesus say, "Let not your heart be troubled. You are trusting God, now trust in Me. There are many homes up here where My Father lives, and I am going to prepare one for your coming. Then I will come and get you so that you can always be with Me." (Jn 14:3) The Living Word had spoken. Esther sat there astounded. She didn't know what to say, especially realizing that the King of Kings was there in her bedroom desiring her to come into relationship with Him.

"Oh, God, I'm so sorry. I went to Bethesdian Church my whole life and never knew you."

God spoke. "They honor me with their lips, but their hearts are far from Me. They profess to know God, but by their deeds, they deny him." (Mk 7:6)

"Father," Esther began, wiping away a tear. "You have shown me how to know You, and I will show others."

In the quietness of the room, a voice spoke. It was quick, sharp and powerful. "Mark 1:17."

Esther excitedly searched for her Bible. She had hardly ever opened it. Most of it she couldn't comprehend, the language seemed so foreign to her. She turned to the content page.

"Now, where is Mark? Oh ... page 1504."

Eagerly, she flipped the pages until her gaze fell on Mark 1:17. Her eyes widened as she read the section which spoke to her heart. "Follow Me, and I will make you become fishers of men."

"Oh, yes, Lord! It would be my privilege!"

Week after week, Esther struggled through the sermons. It was always the same old thing. Repent, be good, and give your tithes so God can bless you.

Her singing debut had been postponed for a month, which she hadn't minded, but finally the day arrived. She had chosen Amazing Grace because it had become so real to her.

The minister settled everyone down with an opening prayer and then introduced her.

In the spirit realm, a real battle was beginning. Unfortunately, spirits of unbelief and deception had a legal right to be in the building whenever this pastor was there. The reason for this was because Reverend Edgeworth had never been born again. Like many others, he had been raised "Bethesdian", attended seminary college and now pastored a church. But it was all done in his own human effort. There was no special touch of the Spirit because his spirit didn't belong to Christ.

On the other hand, this was the day of salvation for Amanda Lawson. Her husband owned the local newspaper, and she would play a key role in God's plans for Cambridge. Her heart had been meticulously prepared over the years and now during Esther's song the Lord began moving on her.

Because she would have access to the media and could influence a lot of people in a positive way, Satan had sent a strong spirit of pride to inflict as much resistance as possible. Emerging through the roof, the spirit of Pride was encouraged by Deception and Unbelief, who stood guard at their normal posts. They stood in awe at the size of the mighty being now in their midst. Because of the power it was able to generate, Pride towered over the two other creatures. It was stronger than most and its very nature made it loom larger in appearances. The haughty presence automatically commanded attention, and they waited anxiously to see what would happen. Pride's outer covering gleamed a brilliant yellow, while its tail had the head of a serpent, out of which came darts of self-centerness, vanity and fear of man, its most effective snare.

As Esther sang, the words came alive to Amanda's inner man. All she had to do was admit she was lost.

Alter calls were not tradition in the Bethesdian church, so there was not a way for her to show her commitment to God unless she herself did something. Remembering a Christian program on television where the preacher called people to come forward to give their lives to God, she modestly slipped out of the pew and walked towards the front. The demon snapped its powerful serpent-like tail across her, leaving behind its stench. "Everyone will laugh at you. Get back to your seat."

Just at that moment, Mary, whom Esther had invited, slipped unobserved into the church. By her side stood Odessa. A demon turned and faced Odessa then, whipping his tail around, slashing into the angel's chest. Flickers of light flew in every direction. Mary, sensing a battle was in progress, slid into a back seat and began praying. Her concentration was interrupted as people simultaneously turned and stared, then whispered, "What's a colored woman doing here? She's got her own church to go to."

Mary bowed her head. "Lord, I pray for woman walking up to the alter. Open her heart to receive your Spirit. I bind all the demons in this building now in the name of Jesus."

With incredible force, rockets of crystal light plummeted down upon the ghouls in the sanctuary. As each made contact, the creatures became crystallized, and looking like pillars of salt, were unable to move. Mary softly spoke in tongues, concurring the exact will of God for the moment. Salvation had come to Amanda Lawson. It was her moment to meet Jesus Christ as the Father drew her to Him.

In heaven, an assemblage of angelic beings gathered around the Throne Room bringing their offerings of praise to celebrate the new birth of Amanda into God's kingdom. As her heart glowed with a brilliance awakened for the first time, Vala was given his first assignment as guard of this believer. The Word spoke, "I have reconciled her unto myself and now she will have a ministry of reconciling others to Me." (1Cor 5:18) The angel spread both wings; and in a flash, stood readily at Amanda's side.

Like a spider descending from the ceiling, a ruling beast untouched by her warfare prayer pierced the atmosphere with a chilling howl. Its pitch was so shrilling, the casing around the demons shattered, releasing them to scatter in all directions. A wicked smile curled the beast's parched lips and with a hideous laugh, they all disappeared from sight.

Even though the enemy had gone, two people under Satan's authority stood up and the first elder went over to Amanda and politely asked her to leave the building because she was drawing attention to herself. The second man strode up to Mary and disdainfully informed her that the church for 'her kind' was across town.

Esther finished the last verse; and noticing what was going on, placed the microphone back in its stand and then walked straight past the gaping onlookers and out the front door vowing never to return.

All three ladies stood outside hugging each other, laughing and crying at Amanda's salvation.

Determined to put the memory of what had just happened behind them and not give the enemy a place in their hearts by speaking slander against the elders, Esther turned to Mary. "Will your church accept white folks in it?"

Mary smiled. "Of course, we will; and if we leave now, we can still hear the message."

The ladies hopped in each of their cars and pulled away, leaving the Bethesdian Church and all of its hypocrisy far behind.

They arrived at the First Negro Church of Cambridge and quietly stood at the entrance looking in. A few heads turned, smiled and nodded greetings to Mary and her two guests, Esther and Amanda. Everyone was accepted and welcomed in this God-centered church, and the women lifted their hearts to God in gratitude.

The preacher continued his sermon convinced the ladies at the door had been brought there by God. Certainly, there was no other reason for two white women to be there. He quoted a passage from the Bible. "Can anyone keep these people from being baptized with water? They have received the Holy Spirit just as we have."(Acts 8:47) Amanda and Esther looked at each other as a warmth flowed through each of them simultaneously. Their spiritual companions stood silently by, awaiting orders. Mary prayed under her breath. "Speak to them, Lord."

At her request, the Watchers responded and deftly brushed their wings over both ladies as the Holy Spirit convicted them both of their need to be baptized. Esther wondered, "What is baptism?"

The pastor's next words echoed her thoughts. "What does it mean to be baptized? It's not the removal of dirt from the body, but the pledge of a good conscience before God." (1 Peter 3:21)

As he finished speaking, the pastor assisted an elderly lady into what looked like a large bathtub in the floor behind the pulpit. They stood together; their upper torsos were all that was visible to the congregation. Another man soon followed them and raised a hand to the Lord and then prayed for her to be baptized in the name of the Father, Son, and Holy

Ghost. As soon as they spoke those words, they gently lowered her back into the water until she was completely submerged and then lifted her out again. As the water streamed from her face, she raised her hands to God, a smile etched there which no power could erase, while the people watching clapped their hands and several called out "Hallelujah" and "Praise the Lord."

Mary turned to Amanda, contemplating her reaction. "Would you like to be baptized?"

Amanda smiled. "Well, I certainly would!" Without hesitation, she walked down to the front. Vala looked up to heaven as he strode beside her and smiled at the Lord. It was obvious God's Spirit had been birthed in this lady.

Esther reluctantly followed, unsure whether this was really necessary.

Following a hurried change into appropriate clothing, the pastor reached out his hand to Amanda. "Tell us your name, please."

As she turned around to see all those dark faces smiling back at her, years of her own prejudice melted away. "My name is Amanda, and I accepted Jesus today," she said, "so I want to be baptized to pledge myself to God." She went to the pastor's office and got a robe on.

Everyone stood and applauded as she stepped into the water and let them immerse her. When she came out, the glow and joy on her face was obvious. Eyes brimming with tears and love gazed back at her and encouraged her. She felt joy and acceptance. Now it was Esther's turn. The pastor handed her the microphone and asked her to share also. Cautiously, she began. "I went to church my whole life thinking I already knew who Jesus was. I was sure I was a good religious person, always helping and doing my part in church functions, but a few weeks ago ..." Tears coursed down her cheeks. "I realized I didn't know Jesus at all. I only believed He had lived. I didn't understand how His death on a cross affected me. Now I do, and I want to be baptized because as a child I was baptized when it wasn't my decision.

Today it is."

Esther choked on her words, and as she coughed, something left her through her mouth that only the angels saw. It was the spirit of Deception, fueled by religious pride. It left, for it had no foothold anymore.

God now had the beginnings of His army for Cambridge. As He was leading some to Himself, the enemy was busily working in the youth at Jr. High School to get them turned away from Christianity.

CHAPTER TWELVE
SNEAKING OUT

One night during Eva's last year at Jr. High, some friends sneaked out to go with some older kids across town and get drunk. There was going to be a drag race between two of the most popular boys in the senior class. Eva had a crush on one of them and wanted to be there cheering him on. Several girls in town were after Johnny Brown, but Eva was determined to get him to notice her even though she was only fifteen and he was almost three years older.

As the cars lined up ready to go, Eva readied herself, rolling up her skirt so it was a bit shorter and undoing the top button on her blouse the way the magazines had taught her. She sauntered over to Johnny's car just as he turned, and their eyes met. Reaching into her blouse, Eva pulled out a red carnation. "This is for you, handsome. A little good luck for the road."

Johnny took the flower and leaned forward to give her a kiss on the cheek.

"I'm Eva Silverstone." Eva's eyes hungrily took in his muscular form.

"I know," he said. "I've seen you around. Now move away from the car, darling, so I can win this race for you." He gave her a smile and a quick wink that would leave a lasting impression on her.

The call for the race began. "One, two, three, go!"

The cars sped down the boulevard to be stopped dead in their tracks by police sirens which came around the corner and blocked off the road. Everyone scattered and Eva, influenced by a few rums and Cokes, managed to fumble her way home without getting caught.

Her mother was sitting up in bed looking at an apparition which floated above her head when she heard a noise coming from Eva's room. As she entered her daughter's bedroom, she saw Eva climbing in through the window.

Eva didn't even attempt to act surprised or sorry. "So what?" she snapped. "Can't a girl have any fun?"

The darkness in Janet's heart was evident. The spirits that had influenced her for years were adding to it. The shadows in her heart were now deep and black, which indicated that evil had full rein to manifest.

At her attitude, Anger responded by meshing its nature with her emotions. It had been waiting years for a moment like this and reacted with a full blast of its purpose as Janet's face filled with madness. She grabbed a lamp, jerking it from a side table and smashed it over Eva's head.

After this violent and vicious outburst, Janet stood back and observed the scene as if she hadn't been involved at all. Her face was expressionless, as though she was watching a show on television instead of seeing her daughter lying unconscious on the floor.

Marvin, who had achieved his goals and was now mayor, ran into the room and panicked at the sight of his precious daughter with blood running down her cheek. Furious, he swung around and hit Janet full force, knocking her into the wall and then ran to phone for an ambulance.

With the commotion of the sheriff and the paramedics trying to find out what had happened, Eva regained consciousness. She looked over at her mother, hatred blazing from her eyes. Giving way to this sin, her heart befit blackness and the power within cemented its hold as Eva cursed her mother. "Damn you. I hate you. I'll always hate you!"

Janet lunged at her daughter, grabbing her by the throat. Anger was energized and compelling her to try to kill Eva. Frantically, the sheriff pulled Janet off and snapped a pair of handcuffs on her slender wrists.

As they were taking Eva out on the stretcher, the sheriff turned to

Marvin. "I'm sorry, Mayor, but I'm going to have to arrest Mrs. Silverstone for assault. She may be the mayor's wife but she cannot get away with attempted murder."

Marvin took Sheriff Beam into another room and whispered, "Is there any way to keep this out of the newspaper?"

"Well, sir, I'll do my best, but I can't promise anything."

Eva was admitted into a private hospital for stitches and a concussion. They wanted to keep her under observation for a few days. A private hospital was Marvin's idea. He thought that might keep the matter quieter.

Janet, rather than going straight to jail, was taken to a psychiatric ward for observation. The doctors felt it best to keep an eye on her to see what had caused an outburst that like this from a prominent citizen. Marvin added insult to injury by telling them what she was like at home, the voices she claimed to hear while meditating and her extra-curricular activities with the supernatural. Inwardly, he was hoping they would lock her up and throw away the key. His political career would be far better off if she weren't around. It was even worth the scandal of mental illness than having his backers find out about her midnight rendezvous trying to confer with her dead mother.

Esther, Mary and Amanda were meeting for their weekly prayer session. Amanda arrived with the morning paper and the Silverstone story was the main headline. With the women listening in astonishment, Amanda read the story.

Esther began the meeting with prayer and then asked for the ladies' attention to share something that was on her heart. "I believe God wants us to display pictures of townsfolk on a board so we can pray for them more effectively. We can start with Marvin's picture. As mayor, it is our obligation to pray for him so he can be born again. Then God can touch the town through him."

Mary, catching the vision Esther had shared, responded. "See who else's pictures is in there and we'll cut them out too."

"Well, here's a picture of Eva who is said to be in the hospital in stable condition."

"Okay," added Amanda, "cut that one out too. We have to pray for protection over her against bitterness and forgiveness. If she curses her mother now, she will bring a judgment down upon herself. The Old Testament states if anyone curses their parents he must be put to death, so I'm sure God takes it very seriously."

"Doesn't Eva go to the Bethesdian youth group?" asked Mary.

Esther's countenance changed. "Yes, but I went there my whole life and never met the Lord, so I doubt she has. In fact, I doubt any of them are saved. If they are, I can't imagine why they would stay. They certainly won't learn much. No matter how much I try to dissuade him, Josh, my son, still goes to their meetings and there is another girl, Debbie Olson, who needs our prayers. She has really been through a lot from what I've heard."

"Yeah, Walt has told me a few things that have happened to her. She needs to know God's love and grace."

"We'll put her on the list and. . . oh, here's Larry Olson, her dad, in an ad for his tire business. We'll add him to the list. He just became an elder at Bethesdian even though he's not saved, and he belongs to the Freeson's Lodge."

Amanda asked, "What's wrong with that?"

Mary began, "The Freeson's Lodge is a cover-up for men who want to feel that they are doing something worthwhile for the community. Now it isn't wrong in itself, but they have their own religion and beliefs that are a compulsory part of membership. In a way, they made their own religion. They believe God is the Master Architect and we are the builders. There is no such thing as seeking God's will. You just do what you want, and fate will decide if you succeed. All roads lead to God and as long as you try to be good, you will go to heaven eventually. They say the Bible is only partly truth since man wrote it, so you can't believe all of it. Most men profess to be Christians, but none are born again with Christ's Spirit living within them. If they were truly one of God's, they wouldn't be in that club because they'd see the deception. They also believe what Jesus did on the cross is irrelevant, and in fact, are not allowed to single Jesus out at all. Which means membership is open to all religions."

"Sounds like a cult to me!" Esther retorted. "They might say they're Christians, but how can they be if they don't have Christ in their lives. The very word means belong to Christ."

"But these men don't know or realize the deception involved. In fact, over a dozen American presidents have been in this club so there is great prestige in being a member. You even get a diamond ring when you memorize a lot of their stuff . Even when members feel odd about their rules they won't back out. And if they do, they get blackballed. That's what keeps them there." The first sentence in their 'Bible' is "To thine own self be true. Which of course is not the same as Jesus said "follow me" (Jn 14"19) "Well," declared Amanda, "I'd rather get blackballed here in Cambridge than burn in hell for eternity. Let's start praying for Larry too."

The hospital ward was unusually quiet. Because of the risk of patients escaping, the windows were always fastened shut, making the air stiflingly still.

Janet sat in one of the offices having her first interview with the psychiatrist, cementing her fate to be institutionalized with every comment she made. Preparing to take notes, the doctor pulled out his pad and uncapped his pen.

"So, why did you get so mad?" he asked. "Especially to try killing your daughter. Did you deliberately want to hurt her that way?"

Janet lowered her head. "I don't know what came over me, Doctor. This has been going on for years. Ever since my mother's spirit came to visit me."

Dr. Blake leaned forward in his chair. "What do you mean, your mother's spirit?"

"My mother is dead," Janet explained, "but her spirit used to come and visit me every week."

"I see. Did anyone else see her?" he asked, writing furiously, a frown creasing his brow.

"This is going to be a long session by the looks of it." he thought to himself. "My family knew about it, but never saw her." "Yes, go on." the Dr. moved around in his seat.

"A few years ago, after her death, her spirit came and was very rude to me; and since then, she hasn't been back. I was so hurt by it. But for many nights now, I've known there is another spirit that comes to my room. I've seen it float over the bed. But this one is very different, and I'm scared of it."

The doctor took off his glasses and looked at her intently. "Janet, are you scared now?"

"No, but it's daytime and you're here. I only get scared at night." Silent tears glistened from her eyes. "I get so upset after I feel the presence; I seem to take it out on Eva."

"Okay. That's all right. You go back to the ward and I'll prescribe something to help you rest. Then I'll see you in a couple of days." He showed her to the door. "By the way, did you love your mother?"

"I wanted to, but never could."

"Did the vision look like her?"

"Yes. It was definitely her, even the last time when she was so awful to me." "And the one that floats over your bed?"

Janet's eyes darted to the floor, and she scuffed her feet. Dejectedly, she raised her eyes to his, a look of despair in them and cried out to him, "I don't know her. She's just a lady."

The doctor walked back to his desk. He didn't have to think long at all to reach a conclusion. Scribbling across her file came the words "paranoid schizophrenic."

Janet shuffled down the hall, her paper-thin body barely making a shadow beside her. The once vibrant face was now drawn and chalk-like, bearing the consequences of toying with the powers of hell. As she passed other patients in the corridor, a little creature draped around her neck was busy waving to the others just like it in the ward. Greetings were exchanged in the unseen world. Janet's menace had a name, Insanity, and the ghoul had its purpose behind these walls. With the doctor's help, it had the power to keep her drugged and locked up for years.

The Lord grieved for Janet "Won't someone care enough to challenge these doctors and their philosophies and tell them Jesus died to destroy this work of Satan?"

CHAPTER THIRTEEN
STEPPING INTO A MANTLE

The kids were now in high school and trying all sorts of devious things as they tried to find themselves. Spring was in the air and the Sr. High prom was fast approaching. It was an occasion the girls dreamed about and the boys usually dreaded. The prospect of not having a date was now real dilemma in the lives of these teenagers.

Eva was a bit gross looking from 20 stitches reaching from the top of her head down across her forehead almost to her eyebrow.

Walter's problem was that there were no black girls at school for him to ask. He was still the only Negro in attendance, and it was out of the question for him to consider asking a white girl. Although much headway was being made with civil rights, they were still years away from that sort of fraternizing being acceptable. Walt decided to visit Ruxton County where most of the Negroes lived and went to church. Maybe he could find someone there to go with.

Joshua's problem was that too many girls wanted to be his date and he didn't want to hurt any of them. Poor Debbie didn't stand a chance of being invited. What boy would purposely dance with a girl who was three inches taller than him? Even if someone did ask her, she knew her mother wouldn't buy her a suitable gown, so she stated defiantly she didn't want to go even though inwardly it hurt when the girls discussed the prom around her.

One afternoon, Debbie was cutting across the back of the school grounds when she saw some of the other 12th graders gathered in a huddle.

"I wish I had a group to belong to." Unfortunately, Debbie had been called a nerd for so many years. Her glasses, braces, and elongated body were all targets for teasing, and the effects had forced Debbie to withdraw into herself. "If only I belonged to a group," she wished.

The demon hosts were ready to oblige. Peter Jenkins, the school rebel, turned around to her and smirked. "Hey, Debbie! Come over here."

The other kids snickered to each other.

"Shush!" Peter gave them a dirty look. "I'm going to get her hooked-on dope so she'll buy it from me. Be quiet or she'll know something is up."

Debbie walked over, longing to be accepted by this popular clique. All the other kids looked up to them because they were cool. They did what everybody else wished they had the nerve to do.

"Hey, babe, wanna get high with me?"

Those words pierce Debbie's heart. Someone accepted her. He'd called her babe. "Come on, doll. You can share my joint."

Doll. He'd call her doll. A demon landed on her shoulder. It resembled a locust, only its color was jet black and its wings were layers of scales. It whispered to her mind, "You said you wanted to belong. Go on. Here's your chance."

"Okay." Debbie smiled, grabbed the joint and sucked it hard the way she had heard you were supposed to. She coughed, but within a minute she felt light, relaxed, and giddy. It felt good, and Debbie enjoyed the sensation it brought. The intruder perched on her shoulder would remain there for a while, but further along that road of euphoria, Debbie unknowingly would give that demon the right to enter her body and reside. The spirit called Sorcery departed to go retrieve Bondage, and together they would enslave her and try to ruin her by enticing Debbie with different kinds of stimulants. Addiction was so easy to accomplish when they had a willing victim.

Once in control of her, the darkness could expand encompassing Suicide and anything else that might meet that objective. She could either be driven to overdose someday on purpose or accidentally. Evil didn't care, as long as she died not knowing the Lord.

* * *

April Fool's Day had arrived and was on Sunday that year. Walt asked permission to borrow his dad's car.

"I expect you're going to say April Fool because you know there's no way I'd lend it to you."

Mary saw the look of disappointment on her son's face. "Walt, why do you want your father's car? You know today is church."

"Yes. I want to go to church, but I wanted to go over to a Ruxton church to see if I can meet a girl to take to the prom."

Mary sat there for a moment, deep in thought. She knew it would be wrong for her to override her husband's decision, so she asked Walt to go outside and feed the dog. Once he had gone, Mary looked at George.

"Honey, there isn't any way for him to meet a Negro girl at his school —"

George cut her off. "Say no more. I understand. Of course, he can use the car."

Mary smiled. The Lord God was so good to me to choose you for my husband!"

George stood up and went to his wife, lovingly enfolding her in his arms. "Hey, He's been good to me too because just like Proverbs 31:10 says, 'An excellent wife who can find? She is worth far more than rubies.'"

Smiling at each other, they softly kissed, and Mary called out, "Walter, come here, please."

Walt knew his request had been granted by the looks on his parents' faces and the love that was radiating between them.

"Son, sit down." George looked at him earnestly. "Your mother and I have agreed to let you use the car, but there's one thing I want you to consider. Besides trying to meet a girl over there, I want you to make your peace with God."

"Okay, dad."

"Now don't say it if you don't mean it."

"Okay, dad" he said.

."Okay what?" his father asked.

"I mean God and I are okay." Walter replied

Mary looked concerned at his compliancy. "Walter, God has a purpose for you, and we want you to find it. You will never be fulfilled until you do."

"Okay, mom, I'll try. I got to go now or I'll walk in late. Oh, and thanks for loaning me the car."

"Well, listen for God to speak to you this morning," George added, handing him the keys.

As Walter pulled into the parking lot of the church, he heard the last strains of a song. Several heads turned around as he plopped into the back row. People sitting around him opened their Bibles. The minister glanced at him and continued with his sermon.

Walt sat intrigued, listening to the message and then the minister finished with words that cut deep into Walt's spirit.

"Dr. Martin Luther had a dream, yes, that's great. But did you know what? God does too. God has a dream. He has a vision and purpose for you. Ephesians says we were created in Christ Jesus for good works which he has beforehand prepared for us to walk in." (Eph 2:10)

"Amen!" someone called out.

"Now, what about you? Are you walking in that plan God has for you? Have you even asked the right questions to find out?"

A lady towards the front began crying, and the minister looked down at her with compassion. "Do you think God can't use you? Do you look at your appearance and decide no, not me?"

"Well, brothers and sisters, you had better repent. You need to repent right now." Taking a handkerchief from his pocket, the preacher wiped his forehead. "Finally, the Lord tells me right now there are two young people sitting here, and he is calling you to Japan, he wants to use you to bring Buddhists out of darkness and to the knowledge of Christ. You need to answer that call. That's all I have to say on that subject. Listen yourself for His voice.

The organ music began and people started walking forward and kneeling at the altar. Several were crying and the presence of God was very strong. Angels surrounded the building and flashes of iridescent diamond-like lights shot toward heaven as people prayed.

Walt noticed a beautiful girl in a red chiffon dress. Something stirred inside him as he watched her wiping away tears, she knelt down at the altar. He was stunned by her beauty.

"She's the girl I'm going to take to the prom," he said to himself. "There's something special about her." Faint flickers of love were already rising in his heart.

The minister stood up. "There is someone here who is slipping away from the Lord. You're getting yourself too concerned with the things of the world and way out of God's destiny for your life. I want you to come up here and make your peace with God."

Walt felt uneasy and shifted around in his pew. "I have something else to say," the minister declared. "Some of you were baptized as babies and you've been to church you whole life, but you're still on your way to hell."

A few more "Amends" rose from the congregation.

"You never made a personal commitment as an adult to Jesus Christ. You're trying to be good in your own strength and that's why you're not walking in victory. Because you don't have Christ's spirit, the Bible says therefore you don't belong to Him." (Romans 8:9) Walter sat silently; the Lord's Spirit touched him. "That's you, son," echoed in his heart. It sounded so real that Walt actually turned around to see where the voice had come from. "Today is the day of salvation. Do not harden your heart."(1 Cor 6:2) Agitated, Walt reached into his pocket, pulled out a piece of gum and shoved it unobtrusively into his mouth.

"Not me. I'm not going forward. I already know God. I've known who He is all my life. Feeling very uneasy, he quickly darted from the pew and out the rear door afraid to even glance back.

All the way home, even the music couldn't chase out the sound of that voice, the message and the feeling of closeness to the girl he had left behind. "Lord, someday I'll make a commitment, but not now. It's hard enough being colored without being religious too."

On the other side of town, the Bethesdian church was hot and stifling. Even with all the windows open, the air barely moved, and Larry Olson was having a hard time staying awake. The minister droned on as he did every Sunday, talking as if he didn't believe a word he was saying. And who did? Certainly, Larry wasn't getting any great revelation out of the morning's sermon. He had grown up in church and done everything expected of him. He'd sung in the choir and married there and now was an elder. "Still," he pondered, "I've heard all this for years, Jesus died for me. Surely there is something more. What about talking to God like George did the day he asked God permission to buy that truck." His mind wandered to the week's club meeting. The Freeson's Lodge, supposedly made up of Christians, but the men never once spoke about Jesus.

Who was Jesus and what does He have to do with my life now? Larry wondered.

As he sat there, the spirit of Deception that visited the Church each Sunday, saddled up to him on the pew. The depraved creature flung a thought at him, releasing its deception. "Oh, what does it matter? I'm going to heaven. I can figure it all out at the same time everyone else does."

He looked over at his wife, Rose. Age was beginning to show around her eyes, and there was a little grey in evidence around her temples, she was screaming out for something in her life to give it some meaning and frantically looking for a magical cream to prevent her aging. Her looks had always been her source of pride, and now the one thing she had always reveled in was evading her. With an unwanted pregnancy and early marriage, she felt life had passed her by and gripped her in the process.

As he watched her, Larry felt trickles of compassion for her. A new love was declaring itself. How could he help this woman he had once loved so much? What could he do to give her a sense of purpose in her life? The Holy Spirit engulfed him, causing the demon to disperse. He bowed his head to pray. "God, I don't remember every really asking you for anything before. I figured you were too busy for me. I ask you now to come into my life. Give me some purpose I can share with Rose. It's too late for her to undo the damage to Debbie's heart but maybe you could even undo that if You can."

Abruptly, Rose tapped him on the shoulder. "Larry, get up! Everyone is standing," she snapped. He obeyed, feeling as if a burden had been lifted. Slipping his arm gently around her waist, he grinned to himself and thought, "Maybe I can talk to God again someday."

Rose glanced at him in awe and then turned again to the front.

Down the corridor a little way, the youth group leader droned on while Debbie and Josh sat bored as usual. She was coming down off some pot she'd sneaked before church and sat staring out the window almost transfixed. Unbeknownst to her, every time she entered a drug-induced stupor, she opened herself up to demonic activity. There was no protection over her mind when the chemical ushered in a euphoric state. Her spirit was fair game to the prince of the power of the air, who used a bevy of evil creatures to inundate her with conflicting thoughts and emotions wearing on her self-esteem. The Lord had the answer, but Debbie didn't even know the question. (Eph 2:2)

Chapter Fourteen
A Perverted Spirit Attacks

Eva, propped up in her bed trying to get interested in her English homework.

At the sound of the doorbell Eva peered out the window to see Johnny Brown with a bunch of flowers ... She felt her face flush as the butterflies rose in her stomach. Marvin let him in and ran for the ringing phone. Eva skipped down the stairs. Johnny handed her the flowers, and she noticed a softness about him. He had a goodness along with his rebellious attitude-- and yet a kindness she wasn't used to.

"Both were startled when Marvin entered the room, so he quickly withdrew his hand.

"Dad, this is Johnny Brown," Eva said, making the introductions. "He's a friend of mine."

As they shook hands, she whispered under her breath, "And I'm going to marry him someday!"

Marvin, having witness the caress from this young man, retorted coldly, "Yes, I've heard of you and your drag races down the boulevard. Don't you know that's illegal?"

"Umm, Eva, I think I better go now. I'll be in touch." Glancing hurriedly at her father, Johnny mumbled, "It was nice meeting you, sir." Then he was out the door in a flash.

Eva sensed something and confronted her father with it. "Daddy, you're jealous. Why did you do that?" she snapped.

"Because you're the mayor's daughter, and I won't have you running around with hoodlums like him. Your mother's actions were enough to ruin my career. Don't you go and add to the list, young lady."

Eva, tired of his hypocrisy, could no longer contain her disgust. "Well, you're one to talk! All the kids know about you and Miss Roller-skates. So, don't act so high and mighty with me!"

Marvin flushed. "Know what?"

"I know she bought a diamond bracelet with some the hush money you gave her."

The fact that he had challenged her choice of boyfriends, this caused Eva's heart to grow harder. Hate became a flood tide in her emotions, and a demon released its poison. "No wonder Mother has been such a witch to me all these years. If it wasn't another woman, it was your work. Mom took her frustration out on me and I'm not going to let you take her place now to wreck my life." Just then there was a knock on the door.

Esther and Mary came in carrying a box of chocolates, having stopped by on their way home from church. Behind them, striding purposefully and with all their authority, were their angels so the demons in the room were rendered temporarily inactive. They huddled together in a corner, quivering at the magnificence of these mighty beings and their brilliance. The darkness hated the light.

"Hi," said Esther, "we've come to visit Eva."

Tension was heavy in the air as Eva and Marvin remained silent, her face still showing signs of her inward hate, while his showed hurt from her fiery comments.

"I'm Esther, Joshua's Mom," Esther continued. "And this is Walter's mother, Mary."

Marvin, ever the diplomat, extended his hand while Eva sat biting her nails.

"Hello, Mayor. It's an honor to meet you. Is there anything we can do while your wife is in the hospital?" Esther asked. We could help collect some of her clothes.

"Esther, you go along," Mary responded. "I'll stay here with Eva and we'll have a chat."

The Lord was already opening doors for these ladies to share all He'd done for them that they too could come into the knowledge of Jesus Christ and his saving grace.

On the way to Marvin's house, Esther had prayed under her breath. She bound the enemy and asked God to give her boldness to share with him. Studying his face, she noticed the look of distress created in his character lines. He was still a handsome man with his jet-black hair and dark eyes, yet there was an emptiness about him. Of course, Esther knew what that was and so began witnessing. "Mayor —," she began, but he interrupted her.

"Esther, please call me Marvin."

"Oh, okay ... well, Marvin, the Lord has asked our little prayer group to pray for you."

"What?" he cut her off again, this time with a chuckle? "Oh, my dear, I'm fine. I don't need any prayers."

This time it was Esther's turn to interrupt. "Well, actually, sir, it's important for us to pray for those in authority. And the Bible teaches that."

"Oh, really?" he questioned. "Well, Esther, I'm not really into all that. As far as I'm concerned, men wrote the Bible and also plenty of other good books. To tell you the truth, I prefer the other books because they aren't so narrow minded. Let's face it. Time and experience have given us more knowledge. The Bible was great for people who lived years ago, but we've gone beyond that now. Our thinking is too advanced to be locked into that anymore."

While he was talking, Marvin added we can chat more while we get my wife's things together. I enjoy a good conversation. Maybe I'll learn something." Thinking back to his youth he continued, "Although I used to know all that Bible stuff from Sunday school. But, after all these years, I'm afraid I've become pretty skeptical."

Esther nodded, but inside she prayed for wisdom for what she would say to this man to convince him of the truth of Jesus. A ray of confidence shone in her heart as she followed him up the stairs, whispering in her heart. "I can do all things through Christ who strengthens me."14 (Phil 4:13)

Odessa walked confidently by her side, shielding her from the attacks that could come from forces inside the house. As they walked eyes scanned the inside of this mansion, unhindered by any obstacles, it- could gaze into all rooms at once to see which demons might be inhabiting the premises.

Odessa spied Fear residing in a statue from Thailand, Violence, the ruler of a Tiki from the South Pacific and two demons in Eva's room. Their names, Rebellion, associated with her rock and roll record collection, and Idolatry, with her model magazines and rock star posters.

Under Marvin's bed where he kept his girlie magazines, Lust reclined, and suspended over the roof was the principality Antichrist, a demon that kept its influence over men in political positions. Its function was to make sure the laws of the land became less and less what God had first intended them to be.

This demon, with its innumerable eyes constantly scanning everything within its proximity, and many tentacles, managed to reach dozens of people at the same time building up their ego's while at the same time corroding their values. Looking around, Esther noticed the statues and experienced a check in her spirit as her eyes encompassed them all. "You have many beautiful things, Marvin, but I don't see anything which shows the Lord is welcome here." Surprised at her own boldness, she continued, "Do you consider yourself a Christian?"

Marvin was startled by her questions. "Yeah, of course I do! I believe there is a God, and I don't do anything too bad. That's what being a Christian is, isn't it?"

Esther reached over and picking up a photo of Janet on the table, took a deep breath before continuing. "No, sir, it's not. We are called to be followers of Jesus in all aspects of our life. We're not supposed to do things if Jesus wouldn't do them. Can you honestly say you've never done anything you felt guilty about?"

Look, I'm not perfect, but then no one is. I've made my share of mistakes, but God knows I try."

The Holy Spirit gave Esther a word of knowledge, and she knew she had to say it. Remembering that Jesus always dealt with the lost with compassion, she carefully worded her next sentence. "Marvin, committing adultery is breaking God's commandments no matter how hard you try to justify it. Also, everyone is separated from God from birth and can only be in right standing with Him when they make a union with his Son, Jesus. He is alive and will dwell inside you."

"Who told you I had an affair?"

The boldness God had birthed in her helped her answer truthfully. "God did just now. I don't know who it is, nor do I want to know, but you better repent and get yourself right with God, otherwise you're going to bring judgment upon yourself. So many people believe God is only full of wrath and wants to keep them from pleasure, but if they'd realize when they choose to do wrong there will be consequences and God won't intervene over their freewill. He doesn't want them to suffer but is restricted as long as they live their lives for themselves and not according to His will."

That moment, the phone rang again and Marvin went to the kitchen to answer it.

The Lord spoke to Esther. "Well done, good and faithful servant" (Math 25:23) the seeds have been planted, so that is enough for now."

When Marvin returned, much to his relief Esther changed the subject, obedient to her Maker, knowing His ways are perfect.

"Let's go collect Janet's clothes."

They were both silent while completing the task at hand. Marvin was pondering all he had heard, and Esther with the wisdom of God allowed the words to penetrate his spirit. When they closed the suitcase and Esther was leaving, Marvin looked at her in a new way. He realized she wasn't one of those religious fanatics who forced God on you. No, she was different and even though she had been blunt, she'd said her peace in a kind way rather than condemning. Her purity and right standing with God were obvious; and next to her, he felt his sin and uncleanliness.

"If you don't mind, I'd like to just walk home," Esther told Amanda. "It's such a beautiful day."

Marvin piped in, "thanks for your help. I'll think about what you said."

"I know," she said, smiling. "The Holy Spirit will help you." With that she shook his hand and walked out the door excited that God had used her to touch someone for Him. She smiled as she walked down the driveway and then looking up to her Savior, she whispered, "Thanks. I needed that."

While crossing the street, Esther saw a lady sitting in a car in the middle of the street with her head bowed. Concerned, Esther went up to her. "Excuse me, can I help you?"

"I'm not sure. The engine just conked out. I don't know why since I had it tuned up recently."

Esther, still with the boldness of God upon her, said, "This might seem a bit strange, but were you just praying?"

A smile instantly lit the woman's face. "Well, yes I was."

"I thought so. I'm a Christian too, so why don't we pray together? God knows two are better than one." At her consent, Esther hopped in the car and the woman informed her that her name was Patty." They reached for each other's hands and bowed their heads.

"Lord, you know what the problem is here and there is nothing that You aren't greater than. We ask You now, in the name of Jesus, to rectify the problem and have the car start for us. We thank you, Father."

Patty turned the key, and the car started up. Both ladies looked at each other and laughed.

"Well, praise the Lord!" they said in unison. Then, Patty added, "Can I give you a lift somewhere?"

"Oh, that would be great. Thanks." Esther smiled. "I just live down the street, number 46 Sherman Way."

Seated in the back in forms similar to men, sat two angels having a chuckle too. The whole episode had been arranged to enable the ladies to meet. There was a plan God was unfolding which had been birthed in His heart and would be for His good pleasure.

As the two women drove down the street, they began chatting as though they had known each other for years. Patty and her husband had met in bible school in the Midwest fourteen years earlier, both had desires to be used by God, but things had always stood in their way.

"Well, to put it frankly," admitted Patty, "my husband slowly went back to the cares of the world, to quote the apostle Paul. (Mark 14:9) He was more concerned with how to please me, and of course, himself! There was always an excuse not to get involved in missions. Then the baby came, and he said there was no way we could go with a child and then of all things she caught pneumonia here in the states, and we lost her a few months later. After that, he started to buy things to fill the void. He bought a motorcycle, new stereo, motorized airplanes, the list went on and on. It was always something else. Now, we're in serious debt with the bank hot on our heels to foreclose on our house. I lost my vision some time ago."

Esther sat quietly, unsure what to say. Finally, she asked, "Are you doing anything at all for the Lord now?"

"Well, we're both active in our church. I teach a women's Bible study once a week. The church we're with is of no particular denomination. We're just called Second Birth Assembly, and we meet down on Robin Way. Why not come and join us in our prayer meeting? We always welcome new faces. Oh, sorry. How rude of me. I'm sure you have your own church."

"Well, not really," Esther said, looking out the window, unsure of her new friend's reaction. "Lately, I've been attending a Negro church."

"You're kidding!" Patty exclaimed. "How did that come about?"

"I just wasn't satisfied with the teaching of the church I used to go to, and also I saw a side of their standards that I didn't like. So, the Lord led me to this one, and now I quite enjoy church. I love the way they worship. They have upbeat songs and use guitars and drums and even clap their hands in church! Can you imagine! Now, I understand these people more and it's great to praise the Lord with them the way David did in the Psalms. The only setback is there are only two of us white people who go, so sometimes we feel a bit conspicuous."

"Well, why not come to our next prayer meeting?" Patty suggested. "I'm sure you'd get a lot out of it."

"Okay, I might." Esther nodded her head. "Let me think about it."

"All right. I'll come by next week and see what you've decided."

As they reached the driveway, Esther added, "By the way, I can give your prayer group names of some people who desperately need some intercession."

"Sure, let me get my pad and pen." Patty dug in her purse. "Okay, who are they?"

"Well, Mayor Silverstone had just begun asking questions about God, so he's searching for something. His daughter, Eva, changed and hardened her heart after her mother attacked her and then was confined to a mental hospital for attempted murder. It seems all hell has broken loose on this family."

Patty interjected, "Demons from the sound of it."

"What?" Esther questioned; a bit puzzled.

"She probably has demons. Go on." Patty realized she had better tread lightly on that subject. From experience so many she'd met shied away from anything to do with the spiritual realm, preferring to avoid it. If only they would realize Jesus told us to go in His name and cast these horrible things from those who were bound by them.

Esther continued. "Also, my husband, Sam, is an alcoholic with a violent temper."

Patty turned to Esther. "Do you bind the demons in him and in your house?"

"What do you mean?"

"Never mind. Go on." Patty continued to write.

"Larry Olson who is with the Freeson's Lodge is an elder at the Bethesdian Church, and there's also my older son, Joshua. He seems to be getting further and further from the Lord as he gets older."

Patty thought for a moment, chewing on the end of her pencil. "How old is he," she finally asked. "Sixteen"

"Well, that's the age they often go off to do their own thing. We need to pray for his friends and also pray that God will protect him while he adjusts to some of the physical changes he will experience at this age."

Esther quipped. "You mean until he gets his wild oats out of his system?"

Patty's face turned serious. "He doesn't need to be sowing any wild oats.

They can produce a bad crop for years to come. His problem is his age plus pressure from his peers, but don't forget Ephesians says we wrestle not against flesh and blood. (Eph 6:12) Satan's hosts would love to trip up your son any way they can?"

"Why?"

"Apart from being able to destroy his life, what better way than to wreck your own walk and steal your joy? Pray for his protection from spirits and their evil schemes."

"I can't wait for my friend, Mary, to meet you!" Esther remarked, getting out of the car and then leaned through the window to thank her.

Just then the front door opened, and Samuel stumbled out, obviously drunk. "Where have you been?" he yelled. "I'm hungry. Where's my lunch?"

Patty looked at Esther, concern in her eyes. "Bind the demon of Anger before you go inside."

Esther looked at her, unsure of what she meant.

"There is a demon behind that anger and it's egging him on, so command the demon to be silent in Jesus' name."

"Okay. Thanks for your advice. I had no idea there was actually something compelling him to be that way." Esther turned towards her house and began praying as she walked, doing exactly what Patty had told her to do, expecting and awaiting results. As she approached Sam, she saw it immediately. His face changed, and his eyes lost that evil gleam, causing his countenance to radiate a much softer expression. Even his words were not the usual, laced with sarcasm and scorn. Instead, he apologized.

"Hey, I'm sorry I snapped before, but I'm really hungry."

"A feast awaits you, my dear!" Esther said, amazed at this new Sam, and as they walked through the door, she turned to wave good-bye to Patty. She thought, Wow! That lady sure could teach me a lot. I must keep in touch with her.

That night, she watched Sam closely, still amazed at the change in him. He certainly was different. Not so demanding, definitely more relaxed and he didn't even try to pick a fight. Esther was overjoyed with Sam's new responses and an excitement filled her as she thought about the possibilities with this type of praying.

When she went to her room to retire for the night, she was glad Sam had decided to stay downstairs a while longer. She wanted to ask the Lord about this new discovery. The Holy Spirit spoke, "Luke 4:18", and she opened her Bible eagerly. She read, "Set the captives free." Curious, she questioned, "Who, Lord?" Another verse came to her mind. Ephesians 2:2. As she searched for that verse, different people's faces flashed through her mind. She found the verse and read out loud, "You went along with the crowd and were just like all the others, full of sin, obeying Satan: the mighty prince of the air who is at work right now in the hearts of those who are against the Lord."(Eph2:2)

She heard His soft voice, "Set them free. Patty will show you how to use the authority in my name."

"It's amazing, Lord. If her engine hadn't stalled, I never would have met her. Did You set that up?" Esther giggled. "I bet You did."

Once Esther had shared with Mary what the Lord had given her about prisoners and spirits working in the hearts of those who are against the Lord, they were both eager to learn more and so decided to join Patty's prayer meeting. They were thrilled to meet some other Christians who enjoyed praying.

They discussed it on the way to the first meeting. "I must warn you, though," Esther added. "Patty really believes in demons being a major part of people's problems." Mary looked startled. "Christians too?" "Well, I don't know. We'll have to wait and see."

Once inside, Mary's face beamed to see Mrs. Kraus, the German lady from the rally, sitting on the couch. Glad to see each other, the two ladies hugged and apologized for not keeping in touch.

Patty tapped her pen on the side of her glass and said, "Okay, ladies, let's get this meeting started.

After introducing Esther and Mary to the others, she then began. "Ladies, I believe God has brought us together to share insights with each other as well as to bring some constructive and corporate prayer for Cambridge. The teenagers of this town are out of control. They are being influenced by this rock and roll rubbish they call music and by the powers behind it."

The angels guarding each one of the ladies stood around the house. Aware of the significance of this meeting, their strength increased with each show of unity emanating from their charges. Ready to do battle for the Lord, each stretched out one pair of wings, touching the tips to one another and echoing the sound of pounding waves throughout the heavenlies. Their forms, which towered over the house, radiated a brilliance no human eye could encompass and the glare kept the powers of darkness at bay.

"One thing I must caution you about," said Patty. "The evil spirits are going to try to disrupt our families even more now that we are united together in this fight. You will see it in the behavior of family members and incidents in your own life. Just remember that battle isn't ours, but his; and He has already won. So, let us cash in on that victory and in Jesus' name push back the powers of hell over our city."

As she finished, each lady proudly declared, "Amen. We can do it!"

CHAPTER FIFTEEN
A BRAND NEW HEART

For the last couple of months, Esther and Amanda Lawson had been attending Mary's church. They had enjoyed being part of the Negro church but felt in the Lord it was time to plug in someplace else. Even so, they still saw Mary once a week at Patty's prayer meeting.

Christmas was only weeks away and it was the one time that most families turned their thoughts to the Lord somewhere during the festivities. Sadly, the majority of people sang the Christmas carols with no real understanding of their meaning. They were part of the tradition and were sung repetitiously with no feeling for what lay behind the words.

During intercession at Patty's, the ladies had been challenged by God to order some gospel tracts and Christian magazines and place them wherever businesses had waiting lounges. Several members of different congregations had been challenged to display some in their own offices.

"How will they know unless they're told?" declared Patty. (Romans 10:14)

Larry had heard about the idea of Christian literature and decided to bring it up at the next lodge meeting.

"It might even give me a few extra points with God," he thought.

Most of the Freeson members were professional men with waiting lounges, so they had access to carrying out his suggestion; but their response left a bitter taste in his mouth.

"Brother Larry," stated Sheriff Beam, "leave that evangelism stuff to the ministers. Besides, everyone in Cambridge goes to church. We're American for God's sake, so we're already Christians!"

Larry sat in silence during the rest of the meeting. He looked at the men individually. "Christians, huh! There's Mike Taylor, who's dating the sheriff's wife. Ben Watson is charging legal fees for work he doesn't even do, and Jim, the mechanic, fixes one thing in your car and breaks something else so you have to come back. Oh, yes, and Tom Jennings, an investment broker, who invests people's money only where he knows he'll get a kickback. And there's Sheriff Beam who pockets the bail money and changes the paperwork. And they call themselves Christians!"

Deception spoke to Larry's mind. "So, then what does that make you? Do you think you are any better?"

"I suppose not," he thought.

At that moment, an angel appeared by his side. The glistening being silenced the powers of darkness from penetrating their blindness into Larry while God opened his heart. The memory of George talking to God sprang forth in his mind.

"That's what I want, but how do I get it?" he asked himself.

When the men broke up for coffee and donuts, Cronan, the angel, steered Larry towards the saltwater taffy bars which he hadn't seen in years. Spying them, his mouth watered as he popped it in, which was unusual since he didn't like sweet foods. He savored the bite, then suddenly clutched his jaw and gasped. Oh, darn it, there goes a filling.

The angel reminded him he was due for a check-up with Dr. Jones.

"Oh, well," he thought, "I'll make an appointment first thing in the morning."

Cronan looked to heaven and smiled. "Mission accomplished."

* * *

At Dr. Jones' office the next morning, Larry waited his turn, and his eye caught a magazine cover. 'Who is God and how Do We Meet Him' was blazoned across the front, announcing the feature article. Intrigued, Larry flipped through the pages eagerly searching for the article.

"What a coincidence," he thought, as his eyes scanned the page. Then his eye caught the phrase 'born again' just as the dentist called his name.

Getting up and replacing the magazine, he was determined to ask if he could borrow it for a couple of days.

Dr. Jones smiled. "So, how's your wife? I haven't seen you in a while. How's the tire business? No more talking. Open your mouth. Well, away we go!"

An hour later when he was finished, Larry couldn't remember what it was he wanted to ask the dentist. "Oh, well, I guess it wasn't important," he muttered to himself as he walked out the door.

A spirit hovered nearby Larry with an ugly smirk on its face, no one had prayed for him that day, and unfortunately the enemy was on the prowl.

Confusion retrieved its tail which was coiled around Larry's forehead, snickered and flew off to meddle in someone else's life.

On order from heaven, another angel, smaller than Cronan, came to rest besides the mighty being. "How did it go?"

"Well, we need to try something else, but at least he's interested. If only Christians realized the importance of praying every day for the lost, we could accomplish so much more."

The smaller angel gazed around. All over the heavenlies he saw battles going on for the souls of the people of Cambridge. Demons buzzing here and there, leaving their trail of destruction and frequently, brilliant beams of light shooting heavenward indicated the power of God was at work.

"So how much can we do for Larry without violating his own will?"

"We have free rein because so many are praying for him," Cronan replied with a triumphant note. "But their praying isn't consistent, which means the enemy will be a constant irritant."

The little angel added, "Let's maneuver him and George together. Then we'll have Gallant's presence too."

Eagerly, they sped off into the unseen atmosphere to set it up.

12TH GRADE

The teenagers were each one was trying to find a purpose. None wanted college   and the pressure was on to be 'hip'. Twiggy graced the cover of most magazines, and the girls were eager to look and dress like her. Pot was an everyday high for a huge number of teens and booze for their parents.

The opposite sex was the main topic of most discussions around school and many of the kids were at that awkward stage of trying to be grown up. The church was quiet on the issue of dating, and so the teens made up their own rules. Eva had been having a relationship with Johnny Brown behind her father's back. As she lied and manipulated him to continue her secret affair, a strain was put on their relationship which neither bothered to mend. Since Marvin's time was consumed with his job as Mayor, and Eva tried to avoid him, it seemed they only passed in the halls. Their lives were completely at odds. Eva was trying to find where she belonged but making friends was hard for her.

As Janet was stilled confined in the hospital, Eva's nightmares had become less frequent; but even so, she had this cloak of fear that constantly girdled her emotions. She wouldn't try anything for fear of failure and always waited for the worst to happen in any given situation. Johnny was the only person she trusted, nonetheless, he was making his first attempt at altering the status of her virginity. As though someone from above was protecting her, it seemed he was usually interrupted during his advances. Eva was grateful. She wanted to do it right in the confines of marriage.

Debbie, minus her braces, had traded in her glasses for contacts. Her appearance had changed remarkably once she'd rid herself of the hated items which had caused so much heartache through ridicule. She had turned from the ugly duckling into the beautiful swan almost overnight, and the guys were now lining up to see what else she had hidden away. Like Eva, it seemed both girls had a protection from above, and for Debbie the proof came the day Peter Jennings tried to appease his humiliation at her rejection in a most cruel way.

"Come on, Debbie. Why not go out with me Saturday night?" he'd demanded.

"Because you're not my type!" she'd snapped back, leaving his friends with a good laugh.

She'd become popular around school since the transformation of her looks that now she could pick and choose. Peter had no appeal, but she needed him for his supply of dope, so with the refusal a little unobserved wink followed suit. It wasn't enough, and Peter planned his revenge.

One afternoon, Peter had an idea to get even with the aid of a demon's sordid interference. The plan was to offer her some 'Mr. Natural,' which usually was quite a clean acid; but he would lace it with some rat poison, just enough to make her nauseous.

The next day at school, Peter sat down with her at lunch.

"I'm still not going out with you!" she hissed.

"It's okay," he responded nonchalantly. "I'm here for a different reason. I just wanted to give you a special deal." He furtively showed her the tiny piece of paper which had the face of a man engraved on it.

"Hey, it's a Mr. Natural! How much?"

"Since I've been hassling you lately, I'll give it to you for free just to show there're no hard feelings, okay? We'll just be friends."

Debbie beamed, her eyes hungrily drawn to the drug, contemplating the buzz it offered. "Okay, thanks. You're not so bad after all!"

Carefully, she wrapped the minuscule amount of acid in a tissue and stashed it in her purse.

Peter had no idea how lethal his gift actually was, but the force behind this scheme was fully aware of the danger, knowing that the combination of strychnine, acid and rat poison could possibly kill her.

The powers of the air snickered, hoping that soon another would leave this world and enter theirs.

A few blocks away at Patty's prayer meeting, Amanda quickly spoke up. "I just got a picture of a teenager who is in real danger. We must pray, but I don't know who it is." In unison the ladies bowed their heads. "Father, who is in trouble?"

Patty spoke up. "This may sound silly, but Deborah the prophetess just came to my mind."

Esther replied, "Well, there's only one Deborah I know, and that's Larry Olson's daughter."

"Well, let's intercede for her," said Amanda.

They called upon the Lord to send an angel to protect Debbie, and then they bound the enemy from trying to harm her until a peace had settled in their hearts.

Once school was out, Debbie raced to her favorite spot by the little lake nestled in the trees behind her house. Usually, she enjoyed the cool air and looking at the white sparkling snow dusting the lake's surface; but today she couldn't wait to sample this treat. She decided to drop the acid, go home and build a fire in the fireplace and listen to some Beatles.

As she prepared to unfold the tissue containing her precious friend, a heavenly being lingered by her side. Cherith drew his breath and for a split second exhaled over her hand. The blast of air blew the acid paper out of her hand and she watched it fly away down onto the embankment where it landed on the frozen pond. Without hesitation an evil force spoke to her.

"Don't waste it. Go get it. You're going to love the high it will bring. It's better than anything else you've tried."

At the command, the spirit of bondage residing inside her let off its power, and she willingly accepted its provocation. She craved that acid now and simply had to have it. Slipping and sliding, desperate to retrieve the tiny packet, Debbie climbed down the embankment and onto the ice. Common sense told her that ice often breaks. Fear abruptly overrode her craving and she hesitated, contemplating abandoning this venture.

Realizing what was happening, Bondage infused its power again, trying to override her emotions and connect with her appetite for a euphoric state. "Yes, I can reach it." Debbie determined. Moving forward again, she focused her eyes on the little piece of paper with Mr. Natural smiling back at her, his grin enticing her to partake of his pleasure. Purposefully, the demon of Death appeared on the scene, an evil hungry glint in its crystal eyes.

Cherith stood sill, then demanded, "Why are you here?"

"Me, you ask. Who sent you?"

"The Lord, the Host of the heavenly armies."

Determined to accomplish his objective, the demon reached out a distorted black wing, flicking it to navigate the acid a few more feet away. Debbie watched curiously as the package flipped along.

"That was odd," she thought. "It must have been the wind." From her very inside, Bondage pressured her further. "Go on, get it before it blows away for good." Distinctly, a voice called out, "Enough! Cherith, stop her!"

At this command, beams of light began falling down all-around Debbie, but they were invisible to her eyes. They seemed to form a shield around her as the angel ordered Death, "You must stop. Someone has prayed."

Just as Debbie took her next step, the ice cracked apart under her feet. She held her breath while her heart raced, wondering how she'd get back to shore.

How could she get out of this mess? She asked herself. Obviously, the acid was nothing compared to her life, so instinctively she called out, "Jesus, oh Jesus."

The powers stood in readiness for her cry to be answered, but which army had she entreated? Was she taking the Lord's name in vain or was she really crying out to him from her heart? A blast of light descended just as the ice opened up beneath her and she fell through. She fought the shock of the cold water and the fear, but it was too much, and she slipped underwater taking in a gasp of water into her lungs. The light was a signal to Cherith, telling him he could intervene supernaturally. The huge being stretched forth his arm straight through the ice and grasped her as she was swept several feet away, caught in a strong current pulling her to the place where the hole was, he lifted her carefully out and lay her gently on the bank. She lay there, almost blue. Death flitted around making abominable noises and shrills, hungry for its prey. The angel looked to heaven and the Lord gave a sign she was not to die.

From His throne, the glory of God descended upon Debbie and she stirred from her unconscious state. Gingerly, she sat up, shivering from head to toe, but curious as to how she had gotten to shore. The angel praised God for His mercy upon this human who willfully chose to ignore His love.

Chapter Sixteen
Fortune Teller Brings Curse

Walter and Josh had periodically been returning to Ruxton in hopes they'd find the lovely girl in the red dress. Every time they made inquiries, no one seemed to know who they were talking about, so Walter was mad at himself for leaving church that day without meeting her.

"It looks like I'll never find her," he concluded.

In desperation, he decided to go back one last time to see if he could glimpse her on the streets of Ruxton. He might just be lucky this time to catch her shopping or something. Joshua agreed to go with him. He was intrigued by Walt's obsession and wanted to see this girl for himself.

If Josh had only known the trap evil was devising for him as they set off in their quest, he'd never have taken that fateful trip. But as with all of the tempter's methods of destruction, the end result was sugar-coated.

It had begun subtly with peer pressure and then a few evil spirits had been successful in having him lose interest in God. Now these same spirits were ready to solidify their workings.

"If we can get him obsessed with girls, we've got him. Sixteen is the easiest age to divert him and once he's trapped, he'll be too guilty to go to church," the demons plotted.

As the boys walked down the sidewalk in Ruxton that day, an older man leaning on crutches signaled to them. "Here's a dollar. Would you go inside and get me a Coke? As you can see, it would be a bit awkward climbing the stairs with these things."

"Sure, I'll go," Josh volunteered.

While standing in line at the counter, his eyes were drawn to an adult magazine, strategically placed behind the register. The girl on the front cover was exquisite, and the thought of seeing her undressed fascinated him. As he contemplated the thought, a black mist appeared in his heart. In response, a spirit landed on his shoulder and eagerly jabbed its prickly feelers into his skin, releasing arrows of lust.

As Joshua fantasized over what mysteries were hidden behind that tempting cover, he was overcome by sensations he'd had before but never as strongly as this, and he relished it. Even while paying for the Coke, he couldn't stop staring at the cover and coveting the pleasure. Once outside, he contemplated asking the man if he'd buy the magazine for him.

The demon whispered, "Yes, ask him. He won't mind."

To hide his embarrassment, he took a deep breath and then blurted out "Excuse me, sir. I know you can't walk very well, but I saw a magazine in there I'm not old enough to buy. Would you mind getting it for me?"

Smiling in remembrance of himself at that age, the guy said, "Sure. I understand. Just give me a moment to get up those steps."

Joshua handed him the money and looked over at Walt who was sporting a big grin. Together they'd embarked on a journey God forbids.

Over the ensuing days, Joshua closeted himself in his room often, captivated by the images displayed in the magazine and the euphoric feelings it provoked. Esther, sensing something strange had entered the house, was determined to track down the source unaware that Lust now had a legal right to be in her home.

This same spirit was soon affecting her husband as well. His dreams were now similar to Joshua's. Alcohol had so controlled him it was rare for him to pursue Esther in a romantic way. But one night he came home high and demanded his rights as her husband.

In the morning after he left for work the next day, Esther got down on her knees and cried out to God. "Why?"

The Holy Spirit spoke, "I Peter 3:1."

She turned to it and read "... you wives be submissive to your own husbands so that even if they are disobedient to the Word, they may be won without a word by the behavior of their wives." Then her eyes fell on verse 6. "Do what is right without being frightened by any fear."

Another verse came to her mind. "Let no root of bitterness spring up and cause trouble" (Heb 12:15) as she pondered this, the Lord spoke in her heart. "Forgive him, Esther. He knows not what he does."

Well, God hadn't told her why it had happened but instead had shown her to obey which also confirmed that God knew her situation.

The next afternoon, Joshua missed the bus and decided to hitchhike home from football practice. The hosts of the air had a plan and Josh was about to walk right into it.

A fancy black sports car screeched to a halt in front of him and Josh ran up to the window. "Where are you going?" asked a husky female voice.

Joshua looked in and couldn't believe his eyes. "Um ... Oh . . . wherever you're going." He grinned as he sank into the soft leather seat astounded at his good luck.

"I was about to get something at the drive-in. Care to join me?"

"Far out." Josh couldn't take his eyes from her. She was the same girl from the magazine. The one he'd been dreaming about all week.

"My name is Ginger. What's yours?" Her striking hazel eyes swept his muscular form in a provocative way.

"I'm Joshua, and I've seen you before, haven't I?"

"Oh, I doubt it." She smiled to herself. How many times had she heard that line!

"Yes, I have," Josh insisted. "You're a model, aren't you?"

"Why, yes, I model in L.A. I grew up here and came back for a visit."

Becoming bolder with every question, Josh asked, "So, how old are you?"

Realizing where he was leading, she decided to play along. She'd always enjoyed flirting with the innocence of young boys. "Twenty-one. I graduated a few years ago. The year Kennedy was shot 1963", Joshua sat quietly. "I was still in elementary school," he thought to himself.

Between the two sat a strongman of lust, enjoying itself as it shot darts of its arsenic back and forth between the two. By the time they finished their hamburgers, Ginger was ready to conquer another young man; and he was more than willing to be conquered.

Just at that moment, Esther and Sam Jr. pulled up beside them. Sam had been pestering her all afternoon for a chocolate shake. The Holy Spirit wanted to give Joshua a way out.

"Joshua," his mom said, quickly finding a way to end this liaison without creating a scene. She tossed him her keys. "Here. Could you drive Sam Jr. home while I go across the street and see Mrs. Kraus at the hair salon? I'll get a ride home later."

Esther watched the two young people and Joshua's nervous reaction to seeing her and knew something was out of order.

The blonde sitting next to him was certainly too old to be a classmate. So, who was she?

Ginger called, "Okay, bye, Josh." Furtively, she slipped him her phone number.

Lust glared at Nova standing proudly beside Esther, always on the alert. "Well," it discharged, "Esther hasn't bound me, so I'm free to initiate my orders."

As Esther walked across the street, Nova ministered a thought to her.

"This is a battle."

Esther didn't quite understand but was determined to ask God about it once she got home.

When Joshua walked into the house much to his horror, his father was sitting with his girlie magazine displayed on the table in front of him. "Josh, where did you get this?"

Josh attempted to cover his guilt. "What do you mean, Dad? Where did you get it?" "Don't act all innocent with me, boy. You know very well where I found this. I was looking for the hammer you borrowed a week ago and found this under your bed." Joshua thought, "That'll teach me to return things in the future."

Unable to get around the issue, Joshua explained everything. It was almost worth it just to have some attention from his dad. They hadn't talked in weeks.

"Dad, see this girl on the cover? Well, I met her today," he said excitedly. "She even gave me her number so I can call her."

Sam remembered how he had felt at Josh's age. "It's about time you find out what life is all about, although I can't see what a doll like this would see in you." Handing the magazine back, he added, "Might as well let her break you in."

Esther stood silently in the shadow of the door. Intuitively, she sensed what they were talking about, although she only heard a few words. She was about to interrupt when the Holy Spirit prompted her not to intervene. "Wait, not yet. Talk to Josh alone."

After dinner that evening, Esther asked Sam if he would go get some ice cream, knowing that Sam Jr. would want to go along. Once they were gone, she would have her chance to talk with Josh without interruptions.

Hearing a knock on his bedroom door, Josh quickly threw the magazine under his bed and answered, "Come in." His heart thumped with the close call.

As soon as she entered, Esther felt something strange permeating the room and recognized an unusual aloofness from her son. She sensed he was hiding something. Granted, they hadn't been all that close, yet she loved him so much; and now he was all grown up and ready to become a man.

"Joshua, do they ever teach you Godly principles for dating at church?"

"You must be kidding! The pastor hasn't had a date in fifty years, and the youth leader wouldn't know what one was much less what to do."

Carefully, she approached the subject causing her so much concern.

"Honey, who was that girl you were with today? She seemed too old to still be in school."

A demon prompted him into retorting, "It's none of your business! I'm old enough to choose my own friends, in case you hadn't noticed."

Esther realized just how far apart they had become and recognized her mistake. "I forgot to pray before confronting him," she thought.

"Joshua, do you remember when Daddy started drinking years ago and you told me we should ask Jesus to help?"

He thought for a moment. "No, not really."

"Well, you did, and you were right."

Joshua turned away, reluctant to admit his need for Jesus' help. "So, how about we pray now?"

The demons trembled in the room as Nova prepared himself. "Father, help us to discuss Joshua's situation without an argument. I bind all demonic activity which would seek to hinder God's word in this situation in Jesus' name."

The angel grew in brilliance. The glare was almost blinding to the spirits.

In complete authority, he commanded, "The Lord rebukes you. Go at once!"

"Mom, that girl really liked me, know what I mean?"

"Oh, here it comes. Father, help me," she prayed.

"Honey, I know your Dad thinks its okay for you to go out and live whatever kind of life you want, but what do you think God has to say?" "Gee, I don't know. I'm not sure I care." "Is that because you're afraid the answer will be, no?" Shame-faced, he admitted, "Yeah, probably."

"I want to show you something in the Bible."

As Esther went to get her Bible, the angel stood by Josh observing the Holy Spirit prepare his heart to receive the word. Esther opened the Bible and began reading. "For this is the will of God, your sanctification, which is you abstain from sexual immorality, that each of you know how to possess his own vessel in sanctification and honor, not in lustful passion." (1 Thes 4:12)

"Joshua, I have always thought you were special, but once I became a Christian, I dedicated you to God, and I believe there is a call on your life."

"What do you mean?"

"I believe God has a special purpose or mission for you and Satan is going to try and stop you from finding out what it is and doing it. Is there anything you need to confess and get right with God about?"

The Holy Spirit convicted him.

"Yes, mom." He reached under his bed and sheepishly pulled out the magazine. "Here, you go ahead and throw it away. It messed up my whole week. I could hardly play football because I couldn't keep my mind on the game."

Esther's watery eyes filled as she left the room. "Thank you, Lord."

Walking down the stairs, she met Sam on his way up. From the smell of him, he'd hit a bar on the way home for a quick drink. His eyes fell on the magazine and turned cold.

"So, you're not content with your own life stuffed with religion, but you want to turn your son into a prude too."

"No, Samuel, I'm just trying to keep him from grief."

"Give me the magazine."

"No, Sam, I don't want it in the house."

"Tough!" he barked, snatching it from her hand. "If he doesn't want to act like a man, that's his problem; but I'm old enough to enjoy this, and this is my house, too."

He brushed past her and continued up the stairs. She turned dejectedly and watched them. Taking it all in was Sammy Jr who waited for someone to get him his bowl of ice cream.

Sam Jr. was eight now, and Esther hardly knew the boy. Somehow, she hadn't had the time or desire to really cultivate a relationship with him. She looked down and observed his resemblance to Josh. She was moved with compassion and asked God to forgive her neglect.

"Come on, sweetheart. I'll share some ice cream with you."

She found it hard making conversation with Sam Jr. What could they talk about? Her interest was learning about the Bible and helping to pray for the people of Cambridge. Somehow stories of frogs, spiders and Batman had long gone out of her repertoire. Esther had thought the television could be a teacher and companion for the hours he spent alone.

Unfortunately, she wasn't aware of what he was watching and the violence and rebellion that was creeping into the shows was also creeping into his life. She took this problem to the Lord the next day.

"Father, I can't run this home alone anymore. Please can you turn Sam's heart to you so he can become all you've planned him to be as a husband and father? Create a way for us to spend more time together. It's so hard for me to love him when he's such a stranger to me. We hardly talk unless there's a problem. I need your love for him while I wait for you to change him."

At the car lot the demons had been working on Sam's boss. Over the past few months, they had managed to whisper things to him to plant seeds of dislike toward Sam within him. The next afternoon the two of them had become embroiled in an argument which had led to Sam being fired. Now Esther would have him lying around the house all day. Could she remain faithful to the word God had given her about being submissive and not arguing with Sam, thereby ensuring her behavior would bring him to Christ? It was a tall order, but she was willing to try.

A couple of weeks later at the ladies' prayer meeting, Esther confided to the girls, "He's driving me nuts. All he does is complain and watch television. I'm afraid to even leave him alone with Sam.

As the ladies joined in prayer about her situation, Esther called out to God. "Father, do whatever it takes to change this situation."

Amanda rested her arm lightly on Esther's shoulders. "Now that you've prayed, don't get mad at what might happen. After all, you did ask God to be able to spend more time with him!"

Reaching up to pat her hand, Esther giggled nervously. "You're right. Sometimes the answers upset us more than the problem."

Sam and his young son were the only ones in the house, at least in the physical sense. Sam Jr. was playing airplanes and the sound effects were pushing Sam to the edge. "Go outside and do that," he bellowed."

Sam Jr., scared of his father, instantly obeyed and ran outside, grabbing Joshua's skateboard on the way. He knew he wasn't allowed on it, but in the furor of his father's blast, his subconscious pointed it out as a quick escape.

He jumped on it, picking up speed down the long driveway. For a brief moment, he hadn't a care in the world. He was no longer just an eight-year-old boy who had grown up with constant tension in his house and a family too busy for him. Now he was skateboarding for the first time and it felt great as the breeze whipped through his hair.

At the bottom of the driveway, a man started the engine of his car. He checked his rear-view mirror and seeing it clear, put the car in reverse and back up. Suddenly, there was a loud crack, a scream and then a dull thud. The driver jumped out of the car and ran to the rear. Sam Jr. lay in a heap and the skateboard was wedged under the back tire.

Samuel heard the commotion and casually wandered out the front door, only to be confronted with a strange man carrying his unconscious son up the house, yelling, "Call an ambulance!"

"No," panicked Sam, "There's no time. Just put him in my car and I'll take him." The episode sobered Sam up quickly, and in a matter of minutes, they were at the local hospital.

He finally tracked Esther down at Mary's and the two ladies prayed on the drive over.

"I can't believe God would let this happen," cried Esther. "Why my baby? Why my family?"

Mary noticed the anger rising in her voice. "Esther, be careful. Listen to yourself. We can't see God's purpose in this, but we must trust him and not grumble or accuse."

Once they arrived at the hospital and were anxiously pacing the waiting room, the doctor came and asked for the family of the boy to follow him. Mary followed a few paces behind fighting off confusion and praying in tongues.

Leading them to a window, they saw Sam Jr. lying in a bed with tubes attached to different parts of his body and bottles of colored fluids suspended on both sides of him. Esther gasped in shock and reached for Sam's hand. The trembling hand interlocked.

""He's in very serious condition," the doctor warned in a somber tone. "We're doing all we can. It will take a miracle to bring him out of this without some permanent damage."

Sam stifled his tears. "My wife believes in miracles, doctor. She fully trusts in God more than anything. He'll give her a miracle."

Glancing at each other in astonishment, Mary and Esther realized what was at stake here. Esther's faith and also God Himself were working together on Sam.

"Oh, Lord," Esther prayed silently, "turn this disaster into a reason for celebration."

Mary hastened away and called the other ladies to join them at once at the hospital and relayed to Patty what Samuel had said. On the way over, Patty bound the demons in him and asked God to loosen His Holy Spirit to open Sam's heart."

Despite the current trauma, when Esther introduced Sam to the ladies, he noticed something different about them. They seemed to radiate a joy that brought a calmness and peace to his turmoil. Sam was touched that they had come to pray for his son, although he was skeptical something would happen. Still, he tried to imitate Esther's hope.

It was during this trying time that Sam realized his neglect of little Sam Jr. and how he never had been much of a father to either of his sons. He vowed he'd changed if Sam Jr. pulled through.

Family and friends took turns at the hospital. For days, Sam Jr. remained in a coma, and Esther's faith was severely tested. Since becoming a Christian, she had tried to do everything right. Now she began withdrawing from God because she didn't know what to say. Her emotions told her that God had let her down, to feel betrayed and the spirits were busy piercing her mind with the unfairness of God.

Esther pulled in the driveway and walking through the back door, she held her tears in check. Her pain turned to fury. "How could you, God? Why my son? Why did you let this happen?"

She went to the den and sat silently in the dark. Tears surfaced as she ached for all the time lost she had not spent with Sam Jr. She felt guilty and ashamed. The Lord planted the thought to get her Bible and led her to Job. "Shall we indeed accept good from God and not adversity?" (Job 2:10) Why does your heart carry you away and why do your eyes flash, that you should turn your spirit against God and allow such words to go from your mouth?" (Job15:12)17 Behold you have admonished many and have strengthened weak hands, your words have helped the tottering to stand and strengthened weak knees. But for now, it has come to you and you are impatient. It touches you and you are dismayed. If you would seek God and implore the compassion of the Almighty, surely now He would raise Himself for you."(Job 4:3) Esther sat, stunned. The Lord had spoken. A beautiful peace settled over her. God would make good out of this disaster so she mustn't get bitter. Her angel awaited her response. She dropped to her knees and raised her arms toward heaven. "Father, forgive me for I have sinned."

A luminous light emanated from her body. The praise in her heart sparkled like diamonds, releasing a spiral of fragrance into the heavenlies.

CHAPTER SEVENTEEN
SHORT PRAYER WORKS WONDERS

George and Mary were just finishing their Morning Prayer time together when George looked at his watch. "Oh, no! I have to get going." Quickly, he kissed Mary and headed for the shower. He knocked on the door. "Walt, are you almost done?" "No, Dad. I just got in here." "Okay. I'll go and use the other shower, but in the future this one is for us. You have your own."

"But, Dad, yours is a lot better," Walt replied.

George was just about to find out why. It took him almost five minutes to regulate the water temperature, and once that had been accomplished the pressure kept changing, depending on what Mary was doing at the kitchen sink.

Hard, soft. Hot, cold. It was beginning to irritate George. Eventually, he simply turned the hot off and rinsed himself quickly under the cold water. The whole ordeal had made him ten minutes behind schedule. Then he couldn't find his watch. He looked all over the dresser with no success and aggravation enshrouded his soul.

"Mary!" he shouted. "Where's my watch?"

"Don't you remember you gave it to me yesterday to get a new battery?"

Another five minutes wasted. Finally, he was ready to leave when halfway down the stairs the phone rang. Certain it was a call he'd been waiting for, he raced back up into the bedroom and grabbed the receiver.

"Hello? Hello?" No one was there. That was all he needed, another delay.

Once in his car, George mellowed out a little and turned on the radio. The deejay was interviewing Mayor Silverstone who was talking about the town bazaar to be held at the town hall in a couple of weeks. Anyone wanting to set up a booth could, and all the profits would go to charity.

"Yeah, and I know which one. Your pocket!" The words were out before George could stop them.

"Oops," he thought. "I'd better be careful not to judge him. I need to pray for him instead."

Suddenly, George remembered a prescription he was supposed to pick up at the drug store. He turned around and drove back the few blocks to Dr. Kelp's pharmacy, muttering to himself. "I hope I don't have to wait. I can't afford anymore hold ups." There ahead of him in line was Larry Olson.

"Morning, George? How are you?" Larry smile, extending his hand in greeting. "Just fine, thanks. How's the tire business?"

"Well, not fantastic, but we're surviving. I really could do with some bigger contracts though. Got any connections?"

"Well, yes, as a matter of fact I do," George replied, looking up to heaven.

Larry swallowed. "Um ... actually, George, I really would like to talk to you. Do you have time today?"

"Oh, no. I'm sorry, not today. Not for a few days. I'll give you a call next week." Larry felt disappointed and so did the Lord.

Back at Larry's tire shop, the demons were holding a conference. "Look, he's starting to get too close," Antichrist snarled. "We need to join ranks to discourage him from wanting to know God."

"How can we persuade Larry he doesn't need Him?"

"I know," Anger said sadistically. "We'll get him mad at God. I've got a plan that works every time. I'll have to get a few of you to help me set it up, but it's a sure way to put all the blame on God and we'll have achieved what we wanted!"

The despicable group huddled together as they plotted their evil. As they conspired, a pyromaniac demon joined their midst.

George was waiting in line at the post office when the Holy Spirit convicted him. "George, you put yourself ahead of Larry's needs. That isn't the attitude I desire my children to have." A scripture came to mind, pricking his conscience. "They seek after their own interests, not Christ Jesus." (Phil2:21) George prayed under his breath. He remembered how he'd treated Larry and whispered, "He needs contracts, Father. Please bring him some contracts. Amen."

"A very short prayer," was Gallant's first thought, but at least he had his order and immediately called for assistance.

A ministering angel at once went to Bill Butler, the owner of the local cab company. The angel moved on him to realize he needed new tires for all his cabs and a contract with someone for repairs and future services. Especially, the angel reminded him, snow tires.

Bill pulled out the yellow pages and saw several companies listed. His eyes scanned the advertisements until they came to rest on Larry Olson's halfway down the page. "That sounds like what I need. I'll try them," he thought.

The men met for lunch and once the papers were all signed, Larry went into the cocktail lounge to celebrate. While he sipped his vodka, he remembered mentioning to George how he needed contracts.

He glances towards heaven. "God, you must have heard." He finished his drink but didn't think to actually thank the Lord. In the unseen dimension, one angel remarked to another. "God answers the desires of their hearts, but they never stop to thank Him."

"Yes, you're right. But remember, it's the goodness of the Lord that leads men to repent. (Rom2:4)

We haven't finished our job with him yet."

Summer vacation came and most families were out having fun. All that is, except the Evans. Sam Jr. was still lying in the hospital in a coma. During her long, silent vigil watching over her son's prostrate form, Esther would pray to God Almighty to his hand to be guiding all their lives to bring glory to Him and for Sam to come into a relationship with God. She had tried her best to continue to believe God that good would come from this tragedy. Her husband had stopped drinking completely during the week and it was only on the weekends that he would "tie one on." His excuse was that it was his way to cope with the stress. "The only thing," she pondered, "was that when he was sober the aloofness and mocking was still there."

This whole ordeal had undoubtedly brought Sam and Esther much closer. Even though he never admitted it, Sam was grateful in his heart that Esther had an "in" with God. He was hopeful that the combination of Esther's faith and his smaller booze consumption might inspire God to heal his son. Neither of them had given Sam Jr. the affection he needed, and they were both desperate for a second chance.

Joshua was working as a lifeguard so he could earn some spending money. He would most likely get a football scholarship to whatever university he chose. But he wasn't really interested

One Sunday after Esther had left for church and Joshua had gone to a football game, Sam decided to watch television. He was looking for a baseball game, but as he flicked the dial, he caught tidbits of sermons from a couple of stations. "And God's Son died," said one. "He died for you," said another. Abruptly, Sam shut off the television. He sat in silence, except for the whisper of singing wafting from across the street. "Oh, come let us adore him."

"What do they mean about God's Son dying?" he asked himself. "Adore him? Why must I worship Him? Why did He die?" He couldn't get the phrases out of his mind.

Bondage, being in residence for so long inside him now, began getting perturbed. "Forget this rubbish. How about a cold beer instead," it whispered? "Turn the set back on and find a football game."

Sam sat somewhat detached from the coercion going on in his mind. He really didn't feel like doing either suggestion; but the thought kept niggling at him until finally, for something to do, he got up to go to the refrigerator. After he'd only taken two steps there was a knock on the door. Esther had been praying for him that morning, so Nova had the authority to take matters into his hands. Sam changed direction and opened the door, but there was no one there. Puzzled, he looked around, and heading down the street he saw a line of cars following a hearse. Slowly, they passed by. The Holy Spirit spoke to him, "Where will you go when you die, Sam?" The thought was disconcerting, so he quickly went back and closed the door and went to the refrigerator to get a beer, but his eyes were drawn to a bottle of brandy.

Bondage responded, "Just relax. You deserve it."

Sam grabbed the bottle and poured a tall glass. "I'm sure God understands what a trial I'm going through. After all, He caused it," he murmured to himself.

He eased himself comfortably into a chair and hit the remote button to control the television. Nothing happened. He tried it again, but still nothing. His eyes were drawn across the table to Esther's Bible which she had forgotten on her way out the door. Without thinking, he went over and picked it up.

Then settling on the couch, he took a sip of brandy, and it burned his throat. In fact, it didn't even taste good. Grimacing from the taste, he looked at the Bible. He was slightly fearful of it because it was like looking at all the world's questions with answers you couldn't comprehend.

"I just don't understand it," he mumbled, casually flipping the pages open. His gaze fell on a verse. "It was through what His Son did that God cleared a path for everyone to come to Him. Christ's death on the cross has made peace for all by His blood." (Col 1:20)

Sam was startled. It was like those words were speaking straight to him. He read it again. "So, that's why Jesus died for me. This means I can't go to God without Jesus."

A spirit of unbelief flew into the room. Its presence made the house almost unbearably cold. Sam noticed it and went to check the thermostat.

Nova appeared and immediately confronted the evil force. "Who sent you?" it demanded with absolute jurisdiction.

"Antichrist!" came the snickering response. Then the demon disappeared as fast as it had arrived.

The angel knew that it was following some ghastly plan, so he decided to pursue it. It landed over Sheriff Beam's house and placed the thought in his mind to call Sam to make a wager for the day's football game, anything to keep him from reading the Bible.

Nova realized it was more important for him to be with Sam and returned. The Bible lay open on the couch. He softly exhaled, opening the pages to the book of Acts. Sam sat down and began reading. "What must I do to be saved and they said ..."(Acts 13:12) Just at that moment the phone rang. Of course, it was the sheriff.

"Hey, Sam, the Dolphins are going to be on television playing the Steelers in ten minutes. Wanna make a bet?"

Everything else fled from Sam's mind and he was transported back to the worldly realm. The men made their bets and Sam rushed to get a beer and turn on the set. The Bible lay where it had been left...forgotten.

When Esther returned home, the first half had ended and Sam was back to his nasty self.

"I'm hungry. Go make some lunch!" His voice disrupted the inner peace she had gained while being at church. She walked towards the kitchen but was caught short seeing her Bible lying on the couch. Assuming Joshua had left it, she picked it up and without much thought placed it on the shelf and went to make lunch.

The seed had been planted in Sam, but would it have the opportunity to grow? The day ended with him losing two hundred dollars to the sheriff and then passing out in his easy chair.

The next morning, Esther woke early and went to the den. Sitting in the dark, she cried out to God for comfort. This had been such a drain on her with little Sam Jr. being in the hospital. She wanted a word from God that her son would be well, a word that she could hold on to, something to build up her faith. With her eyes closed, she quietly waited.

All at once she sensed brightness in the room. She was aware that her body felt warm, it felt joy, it felt a peace that filled every part of her being. Slowly, she opened her eyes and saw a figure standing before her. It was bright and shining, like nothing she'd ever seen before. "Lord, is that you?" she whispered.

"Trust me." The words wafted over her and then the figure vanished.

Esther rubbed her eyes and shook her head in disbelief. "Oh, my goodness! Was that Jesus?" So many thoughts ran through her head. She was so excited. But, who could she tell?

She ran upstairs to wake Sam but pulled back just as her hand touched his shoulder. "No," she thought. "I'd better not share this with him. He'll think I'm nuts! On second thought, did I really see that? It happened so fast!" A scripture came to her mind. "And he believed God and it was credited to him as righteousness."(Gen 15:12)

A song of joy in her heart for the first time in months, she quickly went downstairs to make a special lunch. At last, she had a reason to smile. She put flowers on the table and then called Joshua and Sam. Both were pleasantly surprised at the beautiful layout on the table. Joshua gave her a hug. "What's this all about, Mom?"

Esther smiled slowly and chose her words carefully. "I had a visit from the Lord this morning."

Sam looked over at Joshua and raised his eyebrows.

Esther caught the look passing between them, but she remembered the scripture from that morning and steadfastly continued. "He told me Sam Jr. would be healed, and I believe Him."

Sam put down his coffee cup, spilling some of its contents. "If that's true, I'll become a Christian too!" he said sarcastically, shaking his head and snickering to himself. He picked up the newspaper and turned straight to the sports page to see which horse he could bet on that day. Joshua glanced uncertainly at Esther, she understood his look and smiled, her eyes filled with hope, endeavoring to reassure him.

Just then the phone rang. She snatched the receiver from its cradle before it could ring again. It was the hospital calling. Two sets of eyes were on Esther as she nervously twisted the cord around her finger.

"No!" she snapped. "That's impossible. No! I don't believe it!" She started shaking uncontrollably and Joshua knocked over his chair as he rushed to support his mother as she continued listening. Sam stared transfixed at his wife's face, sensing something was terribly wrong.

"When?" she whispered, trying to hold back the tears. She looked at Joshua and Sam's frightened faces staring at her and then she slowly replaced the receiver.

Forcibly pushing past Josh, she mumbled, "Sam Jr. died fifteen minutes ago." Then she ran to the den, unconsciously returning to the scene of comfort which she'd experience just hours ago. "No! No! It can't be true!" she moaned unceasingly, clutching her stomach as though nauseous. Her angel stood by her, sharing her pain and anguish. It ministered a thought to her. "Pray, Esther. It's a battle. "It's a spiritual warfare".

Then she remembered what Patty had said, that demons are man's problem and that we wrestle not against flesh and blood, but against principalities". (Eph. 6:12) A new strength flowed through her being as angrily and confidently she came against Satan. "Demon of Death, I rebuke you in Jesus' name, for you have no power to hold my son. God said he would be healed, so take your grip off my son right now. I command you in the Name of Jesus."

Sam had crept after her and stood at the door watching, not daring to interrupt as she continued praying in tongues for several minutes. He had no idea what power she was invoking with her prayer, but he couldn't deny the authority in which she spoke. So, he waited silently in the shadows, knowing he could do nothing for a mother fighting for her son's very existence in a realm he had no knowledge of.

Suddenly, the phone rang, breaking her concentration. Sam rushed to answer it and reappeared at the door within a few seconds. "Come quickly," he called to her. "We have to get to the hospital. The doctor said Sammy Sam Jr.my isn't dead. He's alive!"

Esther looked at him with the assurance of knowing her God had heard her prayer. There were tears in his eyes. Maybe he would believe through this.

She took a step towards him, compassion flowing from her eyes to his. He swept her into his arms, and they clung to each other tightly. It was the most contact they'd had for a long time and it felt good. "Come, let's go to him quickly," said Sam.

All the way to the hospital, Esther praised the Lord, and in the heavenly realm, so did Nova. In fact, the heavens resounded with joyful acclamations for God Almighty as a host of heavenly beings joined Esther's angel in loud praises.

Once at the hospital, the small amount of faith in God that had risen in Sam was dashed when the doctor explained away the situation. He blamed the mistake on faulty equipment that registered Sammy Sam Jr. had died when in fact he hadn't. Esther was just so happy that Sam Jr. was awake, she wasn't swayed from giving God the credit. Nothing anyone could say would discredit what she'd seen and heard that morning.

A young intern beckoned her over to a side alcove. "Esther, I've seen you at our church and heard your prayers for Sam Jr.'s healing. I know, with no disrespect to the Chief Pediatrician, your son was dead. I came into his room and saw what looked like a black mist over the top of him. He was blue and had stopped breathing, then a few minutes later that mist vanished, and his breathing started again."

"That must have been just after I prayed this morning," Esther said confidently.

"I'm convinced there was heavenly intervention. There can be no other explanation for what I witnessed," said the intern. "Don't let this doctor who doesn't believe in God explain it away. The fact that the Lord answered your prayers because one of the nurses on duty said she saw it too, and you know what? She asked Jesus into her life just a few minutes ago."

"Thank you for sharing this with me. It helps to overcome the loneliness and the question 'why' that I've had all through this situation. God used this to bring an unbeliever to Him, someone who may never had found Him if she hadn't seen this miracle with Sam Jr."

The intern put his hand on her shoulder and looked squarely in her eyes. "Yes, we need to let God be God, in the good times and the bad, because we never know the whole story. So, don't doubt Him or His ways anymore. Your son is going to be fine."

CHAPTER EIGHTEEN
YOU'RE IN THE ARMY NOW

For months, Larry Olson had been prospering. Word of mouth as well as heavenly help had provided him with some good, solid business. God had been blessing him in answer to the ladies' and George's prayers. Unfortunately, Larry hadn't been seeing it as coming from God's hands. The spirit of deception had him blinded and any need he might have had to rely on God had dissipated along with his debts.

His wife, Rose, was also getting her share of heavenly activity. Every week when she went to Mrs. Kraus's hair salon, Mrs. Kraus would lay hands on her and bind the spirits that controlled her mind and kept her from wanting to know the Lord.

But Rose already had a god. Its name was money, and it meant she and Larry were getting along better because she liked the fact that there was more money to spend. As long as Larry kept supplying her with her desires, a false sense of harmony was established between them; but unbeknownst to either of them, Greed had its talons embedded deep in her heart. With each new purchase it had tightened its grip until her whole world centered around her shopping expeditions. Larry was unwittingly the source of this control as long as he kept feeding this monster the more power he gave to the demonic spirit. The vicious smile on Greed's face became crueler with each purchase.

Larry had been given six months from above to change his ways. God in His mercy continued blessing him even though the angel's had little success in having him acknowledge where his source of supply was coming from. In fact, the prospering only added to the self-deception that he was all right with God, which unfortunately is often what happens. Oh, he prayed occasionally, but only when he wanted something. He even prayed on the golf course for his ball to go further or for the weather to stay clear, that sort of thing. That wasn't exactly what the Lord had in mind, but often the demons would answer the prayers because they wanted Larry to think he knew God. That suited their purposes perfectly.

For several weeks, Rose had been contemplating a move to Florida, with or without Larry, she didn't care. She liked the sun and the surf and was determined to get there one way or the other. Her only concern was ensuring she had enough money to finance the increasingly selfish desires.

One evening as she was watching television, she saw how easily insurance companies would pay off an arson fire on company property. As she watched the show, it sparked an idea and a desire in her to take matters into her own hands. "That's it!" she thought to herself. "If Larry's business burned down, we'd have to go some places else and start over. Maybe we could move to Florida or California with the insurance money." She toyed with the idea, conceived it and gave birth to darkness in her heart. The pyromaniac demon had found its vessel.

At last, the perfect opportunity had come. Larry was on a Freeson's Lodge retreat so she could sneak into the place, pour some gasoline around and set it ablaze and no one would suspect her. After all, they already had enough money to live comfortably with no major worries. At least to most people's idea of comfort — but Rose's obsession with wealth had completely taken her beyond reasonable behavior.

That fateful evening, Rose made herself a few drinks to bolster her courage, then late that night, she sneaked out of the house and rode Debbie's bike across town to Larry's tire shop.

She had Larry's spare key which she'd swiped from his desk drawer and let herself in the back door having parked the bike out of sight behind the building.

After dousing the place thoroughly with gas, she threw a match on it, unaware she had spilt some of the liquid on her dress in her hurry to complete the job. The pyromaniac demon upon her was transfixed by the flames. She stood there staring, entranced by the soaring yellow and purple colors lighting everything around her.

Suddenly, she remembered where she was and ran to the stairs, but as she did, she slipped on a patch of grease and tumbled down the stairs. She lay there unconscious as the flames swept all over the budding and then, licking at her lethally sprayed clothes, the flames consumed her in a matter of seconds.

The demon hurried off to his commander to report what he'd accomplished. It wasn't part of the plan for her to die so soon, but the host laughed venomously. "It doesn't matter. She belonged to Satan anyway. It was her choice."

"Yes!" added Deception. "Kraus had been praying for her for months, but she chose not to respond."

Anger interjected with a villainous grin. "This certainly should get Larry mad at God!"

Deception asked, "Where do the demons assigned to Rose go now that she'd dead?"

The spirit of Antichrist stepped forward, Pride and Bondage leaning over its shoulder, hanging on its every word. To the other demons they seemed to be part of his character. "They're going to work on her daughter, Debbie. We're going to do the same thing to her that we did to her mother. Force her into a marriage where she's bored and uses stimulants to entertain herself, have her strive for material things that her husband can never provide. In essence, we're going to wreck her marriage just like we did her mother's and her mother's before that."

"But she isn't married."

"That can be arranged."

There was a rumble of diabolical laughter as each demon assigned to Rose realized their potential hadn't been cut short because of her Rose's untimely death. They now had a new victim to pillage and weave their web of evil around, just so long as she didn't learn the secret to retard their control. But Deception would take care of that, as long as he had no interference from God's kingdom. Their eyes flashed as they looked from one to the other, contemplating the strategies and intrigue they'd be allowed to command over Debbie's life.

Deception cautiously moved forward. "Excuse me, but since I'm new on this team, could you please tell me how long you've been with this family? How many generations?"

Antichrist answered in a voice laced with pride and dominance. "This is our fourth generation. Unless she gets saved," he shuddered at the idea, "we have the right to continue on down the line."

"What happens if she gets saved?"

"The demonic control in her family will be broken, and then," it laughed, "you're all going to have to find a new home!"

Deception shuddered at the concept of being without a body to dominate, even for a little while. Then Jezebel spoke. "I'm the strongman and no one seems to know that. As long as I'm in control, Debbie will never follow Jesus. She'll be too busy getting stoned and living out her fantasies."

At that they all snickered, aware of how powerful Jezebel had been to all previous generations when they had opened that area to be influenced. With one last ghastly roar of triumph for their next victim, they vanished to do as they were bid.

George woke up suddenly and shook Mary. "We have to pray for Larry. I just had a dream that he was on fire," he said urgently.

Mary reached over and turned on the light and they immediately prayed. Mary went first, praying in tongues like she never had before. Her heavenly language was summoning extra angels to go and prepare Larry for the phone call he would get in the morning.

Larry lay fast asleep as the angels surrounded him, shoulder to shoulder, at the retreat. They were ready to counter-attack the forces which they'd been alerted were on their way. In his dream he was standing in a field and all around him were charred plants and burning branches. A man in white walked towards him in the dream and slowly extended His hand. "All you who are heavy laden come to me and I will give you rest,"

(Matt. 11:28) said the figure softy with eyes of compassion which seemed to see into Larry's innermost being. Larry reached for his hand in the dream and asked, "Who are you?"

"I am that I am, and I shall replace the years the locust has eaten."(Joel 2:25)

The phone ringing startled Larry and he reached for it savoring the lovely feeling and peace that he had from his dream. It was Sheriff Beam telling him that his tire business was in ashes and that they had found the body of Rose. It was believed that she had set the place on fire which meant that there would be no insurance. "I'm sorry to say this, Larry, but you've been wiped out."

Stunned and unable to fully comprehend it all, Larry mumbled that he would leave in a few minutes. He asked the sheriff to call Debbie and tell her he was leaving and would be home in a couple of hours. He knew he wouldn't be able to deal with talking to her until the full realization had hit him, so it was better for the sheriff to break the news and he would face her with the horror of it after he'd had some time to think.

When Debbie received the news, she hung up the phone and lay quietly in bed. She had mixed emotions, mixed thoughts about the situation. All the years of bitterness and hatred towards her mother seemed to melt. Then, quickly it all rose to the surface once again as she realized what this would do to her father. "How could she have done this to him, to us?" she thought bitterly. "Serves her right. She got what she deserved."

Beside her on the bed sat Jezebel, a rather large demon, resembling a man with its wings and with blackend legs draped across Debbie. It was the same spirit that had controlled her mother and her mother before her. In strategic positions around the prostrate form were the rest of the demonic host which had been given permission to taunt her. They had quickly assembled at her bedside when the sheriff had rung. They each knew this was their moment to inflict their dominance if she opened the door to their suggestion, their entrance was inevitable. It would be Debbie's choice. She could react in love and forgiveness towards her mother or she could increase in her spirit hate and bitterness, allowing darkness to find a place to dwell.

An angel appeared in the room. The demons froze. They knew they could only use the power of suggestion until Debbie made her choice. The angel also had this ability; and as Debbie lay there, her memory was jogged by a coloring she had done in Sunday school. It was a picture of Jesus on the cross. Beneath Christ on the cross it said, "Father, forgive them."(Lk (23:34)

Unforgiveness quickly and deliberately stuck its feelers across Debbie's face and then slithered across her back, chanting, and "Good riddance." Debbie hardened her heart, sighing out loud, "Yeah. She got what she deserved."

The angel grieved.

Debbie had made her choice.

✱ ✱ ✱

At the funeral parlor two days later, Larry was surprised at how many people were there that he and Rose hadn't known. The more he talked to people, the more he put two and two together. George, Mary, Esther, Mrs. Kraus, Amanda — all of them were Christians. Larry walked over to where they sat on the couch. They all stood as he approached, shook his hand and softly offered their condolences. Their sorrow was real because they were under no disillusionment as to the kingdom Rose had chosen to spend eternity in. Larry, unaware of the depth of their grief for his wife's spirit, thanked them for their words of compassion and then added, "All of you are Christians, aren't you? How did you know my wife? She certainly wasn't religious."

Esther spoke first. "We didn't really know her, but we've been praying for both of you for a long time."

George, attempting to justify why he hadn't spent any time with Larry, added, "I've been praying for you to get some contracts."

A sense of comfort enveloped Larry. He liked these people. He looked across the room to his Freeson Lodge buddies and there seemed to be such a contrast between them. All of his lodge buddies were sitting around with drinks in their hands, gossiping and telling dirty jokes. It was obvious they weren't here for compassionate reasons -- more than likely it was just a good excuse to get together and tie one on. "They certainly haven't been of any comfort to me," Larry thought, his gaze returning to the group he was with. "Yes. There's definitely something different about these Christians."

Just then a demon of unbelief landed on his shoulder. It glared defiantly at the angels standing behind their respective charges. "No one's bound me," it said and then shot a comment into Larry's mind. "Look what these Christian's prayers did for you. They brought down the wrath of God!" With that it flew out the door.

Debbie sat off in a corner by herself. For a girl of sixteen, she had been through a lot. She pulled a compact from her purse and checked her makeup. Glancing around the room, she eyed the different people gathered there. Her gaze fell on her father's lodge buddies. "What a bunch of phonies!" she thought to herself. Then she looked over at the Christians. "Now Esther, she's certainly been through a lot, yet God came through for her, didn't He?" Then she remembered her own incident, the close call she'd had on the ice. She knew she'd fallen through the ice, but how did she get back on the shore? Did God send an angel?

"Oh, it's all so confusing," she mumbled and sighed loudly. "If I believe in God, I'll be bored right into heaven. I might as well go to hell! At least then I'll have a lot of good memories to take with me." She went over to the wine glasses and downed a couple of drinks, unaware that Unbelief snickered over her shoulder.

"She'll be easy to ruin!" laughed Jezebel to Unbelief. "Between you and me, she'd got no chance!"

Two angels stood off in a corner, silently observing both the earthly and heavenly activities around them. Reminding themselves of all Debbie had been through and the catalysts for her dark heart, a messenger was summoned to go and report to the Lord. "Raise up an intercessor for Debbie." The angelic being extended its wings and in an instant, vanished.

Just then the mayor and Eva came in. The two girls grabbed a couple of glasses of wine and sneaked out the back. Debbie looked at her old friend. They'd grown up together, but now they had grown so far apart. "You don't look very happy, Eva. What's the matter?"

"It's Johnny Brown. He's been drafted into the Army. He's going to go to Vietnam and I'm sure I'll never see him again."

"You don't know that!" retorted Debbie and she downed another glass of wine which someone had forgotten on a nearby table.

"Yes, I do! There are protests and riots going on all over the country because so many have died there."

"Maybe you can resurrect some of those old prayers from youth group. If anything could keep him from getting hurt, that might," Debbie offered and burped.

Eva shrugged and gulped down her stolen wine. Just then her father walked in. "Okay, girls, you're under arrest!"

"Oh, Daddy," Eva laughed nervously, uncertain of his true reaction.

Marvin slipped an arm over the shoulder of each girl, thinking how each of them had lost their mothers, one way or the other, so maybe he could just let the drinking slide this time. He looked at them fondly, so grown up now. Where had the time gone? "Debbie, I want you to know you're welcome at my house any time," he offered.

As young as she was, as soon as he said it his motive was obvious to Debbie. Poor old Marvin still had a thing for little girls.

The lust spirit assigned to him was absolutely determined to get him into some kind of trouble.

The Lord looked for someone to stand in the gap and fortunately there were several in town who could help pray him into the kingdom. But would Marvin let them, or would the god of this world keep him blind?

Six weeks later Johnny was taken out of Eva's little world. He was off to boot camp. Her heart was crushed and the loss of identity for her was overwhelming. Suddenly she was nobody's girlfriend and in her school that was devastating.

Eva had grown into a very introverted young lady. The scar across her forehead was partially hidden by her hairstyle, but the damage that had been inflicted so many years ago by her mother had left a permanent scar on her heart. Her father and she needed each other even more so now, but the demons were determined to pervert the father and daughter relationship any way they could.

Marvin struggled with loneliness as he lay in his bed. He figured the only alternative he had was to divorce Janet, who was still in the asylum, and find someone else he could share his life with. It was obvious Janet would never be well enough to come home. The asylum was all the home she'd known for so long and the doctors said there had been no improvement in her mental state. In fact, the last time Marvin had gone to see her she had hardly recognized him. She lived in her own fantasy world, one she and the spirits shared and there was no room in it for him. Eva didn't care one way or the other what happened to her mother. She couldn't really remember a time when she'd felt close to her and any happy memories she may have had had slipped into the dark recesses of her mind. If her father wanted to get a divorce and find somebody else, that was fine with her.

Chapter Nineteen
Backsliding

In early autumn as the four teens began their semester in high school, the pressure was on each of them to decide what careers they wanted and which college they would attend.

Marvin took Eva off to the side one day and sat her down. She knew he had something serious to say. "Honey, I can't live this way anymore without a wife. But as a married man it's not proper for me to date while your mother is alive--"

Eva interrupted. "It's also against the Ten Commandments."

"Um . . . yes . . . that's true. Anyway, I've thought about it and I've decided I'm going to divorce your mother."

"But the Bible says God hates divorce," (Mal 2:16) Eva added bluntly, refusing to let him off easily.

"Since when do you know so much about the Bible?"

"You're the one who forced me to go to church all these years. You expected me to learn something, didn't you?"

"Yeah, and I certainly think it's done you some good." Marvin was grateful to change the course of the conversation. Her words had convicted him.

"Dad," Eva continued, "I'd really like to go to a Christian college. I've always wanted to be a model; but in case it doesn't work out, I better have something to fall back on. I have a better chance of learning around people who aren't taking drugs, and I think I will find that at a Christian school."

"I'm proud of your decision," Marvin said, placing his arm around her shoulders and squeezing tightly. As he looked at his child now all grown up, fatherly affection bloomed in his heart. He loved Eva so much and was determined it wouldn't become twisted. She was so pure, so lovely. "Honey, you pick the school and I'll gladly pay for it

Antichrist lingered nearby, fidgeting. It called out into the heavenlies for Deception. "You need to try and see to it she never gets to a college."

"My pleasure," Deception responded. "Leave it to me. I'll go get some accomplices."

For Joshua this was to be his most crucial season in football. He wanted to earn a scholarship through his sports achievements as a quarterback and attend a good college where he could get picked by the pros.

The ghouls had a plan, too, of course. They wanted him forced into a marriage that would end bitterly, like his own parents, Sam and Esther. The perfect choice to lure him into this trap would be Debbie, the spirits went to work maneuvering these two to meeting, knowing if they succeeded in bringing them together, Lust could interject in the relationship if they opened a door.

One thing about Josh was his single-mindedness about his future. He avoided the wrong crowd, aware trouble could follow and concerned himself with keeping his record clean. He kept his body in perfect shape and health, and so far had stayed clear of tempting ladies as his mom had so warned him. Lust had a bond on him due to the magazines and the darkness wouldn't let up. Josh was torn between what his mother had said God forbid and what his body was demanding. "I just can't disobey that scripture," he reasoned. "God won't let me get a scholarship if I do."

After practice one day, Debbie went to get her bike and found her back tire was flat. A spirit hovered nearby, waiting for the performance to begin. Debbie was bending over the bike in her gym outfit just as Josh rode by on his bike. Lust, residing in him, released its evil as Josh encompassed her long shapely legs. Pictures from the magazines flashed through his mind and his feelings intensified. All her fatness had melted away and she looked good from the backside. Lust gave birth to sin.

His bike headed straight for a board which had a long nail protruding upwards. Because his eyes were on Debbie, Josh failed to see it until it was too late. It made a deep puncture in his front tire. Josh stopped and gasped, "Oh, great! Looks like I've got the same problem you do."

As Debbie turned around, she was captivated by his handsome looks. She began coveting him immediately, thinking mainly how a date with a quarterback would boost her popularity. Jezebel, her ruling charm, and Lust in Josh were ready for a uniting.

We got a long walk ahead of us Debbie moaned.

He watched her jogging over to the telephone booth, her long legs clearly defined under the bouncing, little skirt. His heart began beating faster. His body reacted in a way that was becoming more frequent. Jezebel acknowledged the spirit in Joshua. "So far, so good!" it tittered. No one answered the phone at home.

As they pulled into her driveway, sounds were emerging from the house. Crash! Bang! Smash! It sounded like the house was being torn apart. Larry Olson's car was parked in the driveway. Joshua left his bike and crept up to the window to peek in. Larry was throwing dishes and glasses at the ceiling. He was yelling, "I hate you! I hate you, God, for wrecking my life!"

The Holy Spirit, who already had placed a call on Joshua when he was a young boy, moved over him. Suddenly, he was embraced by a compassion and a love for Larry. He ached for the things this man had been through and wanted to help. Slowly, he walked in and Larry turned around, his eyes blazing with anger. In the spirit realm, demons of Hate, Bitterness and Anger were everywhere. In fact, Anger had fastened its cruel grip on Larry and wouldn't let go.

Joshua knew Larry's life had been turned upside down, and Joshua understood Larry's loneliness. Purposelessness had strangled both of them. Joshua approached him cautiously. He had no protection from the spirits that were in the room. He wasn't born again, and he wasn't reconciled to God. He already had Lust in him, and so the struggle began.

Larry growled, "Get the hell outta here!" It reminded Joshua of his own father, Sam. Larry lunged at him, knocking him to the floor and Joshua became mad, and anger welled up in him.

"Hey, man, what's your problem?" he asked, standing to his feet.

Just then the Holy Spirit moved upon his spirit to have compassion. Joshua thought for a second as the anger subsided. "Mr. Olson, I know you've had some major tragedies. I only wanted to help."

Larry sank slowly to the floor and began weeping helplessly into his hands. His shoulders shook uncontrollably with the force of his grief. Tears came to Joshua's eyes too. He really hurt for this man. He spoke softly, "I heard you say you hate God."

"I do. I can't believe he did all this to me."

Joshua chose his words carefully. "Can my mother come by sometime and talk to you? She's a committed Christian and knows how to talk to God. You know, I'm sure it was her prayers that spared my brother Sam Jr."

Joshua's mom was across town right at that moment, chopping the vegetables for dinner when Larry's and Joshua's faces came to her mind. She had learned that whenever someone's face popped into her mind the Holy Spirit was prompting her to pray for that person. So, she immediately put the knife down and began praying. She asked the Lord to move into Larry's life and to soften his heart towards the things of God. "Lord," she added, "If Larry and Joshua should be together at this time, let your Spirit guide their conversation."

That was precisely the prayer Joshua needed, because now he had to tell Larry his daughter was high with a flat bike tire. "Mr. Olsen . . ." he started and faltered.

Debbie needs you. Larry said sarcastically. "She's hated me for as long as I can remember. I've never been able to figure out why. The only thing I can think of is that it might have started the night her dog died."

"Sir, she's out in the driveway and she's pretty drunk -- bourbon from the smell of it. Will you help me bring her in?"

Cronan, sent from the Celestial City, sublimely appeared. His four faces shone in resplendent crystal. His two wings stretched out far from his back, sounding as the pounding surf with each movement. Two arms stretched out towards heaven, ejecting myriads of lightning rods. This was a sign to the surrounding demons to desist.

As Larry went out the front door, the evil in him squirmed, obeying the command not to manifest. His blood pressure shot up as he saw Debbie weaving her way up the path towards him. He raised his arm, ready to strike her, but Joshua quickly interrupted his thoughts. "Mr. Olson, tomorrow is a new day and I'm sure it will be better."

It wasn't very spiritual, but there was some truth to it. Cronan stood beside him and softly brushed gossamer wings across Larry's eyelids. In an instant, love surfaced. Tenderly, he carried Debbie into the house, promising to call Joshua's mom.

Once inside Debbie sobered up quick. Josh looked at Debbie, he had a desire to be held by her. Just a comforting hug, nothing sensual; but instead, he leaned over and gave her a quick kiss on the cheek. You'll be all right he said and settled into the couch. Thankful he wasn't in Larry's shoes.

To Debbie that kiss meant much, much more.

As football season came into full swing, Joshua's chances looked fairly promising for a scholarship. Girls made several attempts to get his attention, but he was content to forego their stimulation and enjoy his own little world. Also, he didn't want God mad at him for disobeying his mom's words concerning the bible and fornication. "Anyway," he reasoned, "what do a few pictures hurt?"

Walter Smith wasn't doing very well, but nobody seemed to notice. For him, every day was a setback as the powers of hell took shots at him through the lips of other students. He held the tears in check, but his spirit received the wounds. As his heart hardened to compensate, he began forgetting the love of God and drifted away, becoming more spiteful and callous. Even his parents had become too busy to notice the chip on his shoulder since conversation around the dinner table rarely involved him.

Martin Luther King had been assassinated and George, who worked for the Civil Rights Movement, was becoming skeptical. He too had to fight bitterness and prejudice.

Walt rushed as fast as he could to make sure he got to the bus stop on time. Today he had to sit for his SAT test to see if would qualify for college; and he knew if he was late, Mr. Jefferson, the principal, would have one more reason to taunt him. No, he couldn't afford to miss out on sitting for that test, but when he ran out the front door, he saw that the bus was closing its doors. The driver looked over, stared coldly at him and deliberately pulled away from the curb. Anger tightened its grip, whispering into his mind, "You see, Walter. It's the white man's world. You don't fit. You're never going to amount to anything."

Light rain fell as he started his three mile walk to school.

Walt knew his dad would soon want the name of his choice of college. "What's the point?" he thought. Then he remembered a dream he'd had -- he was the first black driver in history to win the Indy 500. He savored that dream as he walked down that wet, lonely road, hoping someone would come along and pick him up, fantasizing how he would someday win the trophy at Indy.

The demon of Deception walked alongside him. "I'll make him covet it. I'll make him want that trophy so much, but ensure he never gets it." He laughed wickedly.

Just as Walt rounded the corner, his eye caught a car coming straight for him. Purposely, the car had swerved into a puddle next to Walt, splashing him with its contents. Walt's favorite beige pants were soaked with muddy stains. In the spirit realm, the demons laughed at him. That was one more incident which could enable them to strengthen their influence if he allowed it.

"He sure puts up with an awful lot, doesn't he?" Anger quipped.

"That's his Christian upbringing, but it won't last long if I have my way." Resentment replied.

He was forty-five minutes late by the time he arrived at school. Mr. Jefferson saw him walk in and demanded an explanation. Walter lost his temper. He threw his books against the wall and ran down the hall to the boy's locker room. The principal followed. "You get down to the cafeteria now. That SATs started ten minutes ago. You need to take them right away or you won't be able to take them at all."

As Walt crept into the room, most of the students looked up. He was splattered with mud and felt humiliated by the looks his appearance invoked. The Lord had compassion on him and sent a ministering angel to him. Deception objected. "Who sent you?" he demanded.

"The Lord!"

At those words, the demon took a step backwards, knowing he had no authority once the Lord had decreed something. The angel of comfort continued, "Esther's and Mary's prayers have granted me permission to do anything in Walt's life that will draw him to Jesus. Now stand aside. You can't influence him anymore today." The angel swept his mighty wings in an arc, knocking Deception from Walter's presence. The angel hovered over Walt while the fruit of God's Spirit, peace, was released. It descended on Walt and enabled him to take a deep breath and begin the exam. He still wasn't able to complete it, so his score was lowered, but at least the demonic host couldn't work on him for a while.

That night in bed, Covetousness hovered over him and filled his mind with the dream again. He would win the Indy 500. "It must be a prophecy," Walt decided upon wakening the next morning.

In reality, the demon was dangling a carrot for him to pursue.

At breakfast that morning, Anger shot a thought into George. The demon was hoping to get the two mad at each other before the day had begun. "Walt, what college do you plan to go to?"

"Oh, no, here it comes." Walt's thoughts were racing as to what to say. "Then he blurted, "I don't plan to go to college, dad."

"What do you mean?" George roared across the table.

"I took my SATs yesterday and I know I didn't do too well." Walt raised his voice in defense at his father's reaction. "Look, I don't want to go to college. I want to race in the Indy 500."

His father rebuked him. "Where did you get such a silly notion?"

"I watched the race on TV years ago; and I've dreamed I won the race twice now, so there isn't any need to go to college. Especially now that I'm not going to get in anyway." With that, he jumped up and stormed out the back door, determined not to miss the bus again.

Mary and George looked at each other. Mary straightened her glasses. "He'll be all right, honey. You know how boys are, but maybe we should pray about it together. You know Jesus said if two of you on earth agree concerning anything they ask; it will be done for them by My Father in heaven."(Matt.18:19)

George stood up. "It will have to wait. I've gotta go. I'm late." He bent over and gave her a peck on the cheek before rushing out the door.

Mary sat and silently prayed. "Lord, we never seem to pray together anymore. It's as though we're drifting apart as a couple in You. George is slowly drifting away from You too. He's becoming prejudiced and critical and everything seems to center around his work. He doesn't have any time for me or for You, Lord. Please reveal Yourself to him again. I commit this situation into Your hands, Father. Amen."

As she stood up to go about her housework, Odessa delicately wrapped its wings around her form and she hummed to herself softly, knowing God was in control.

* * *

As Thanksgiving passed and Christmas drew closer, Eva began thinking more about the Lord. The Holy Spirit had been touching her heart and had been able to have her recognize there was a void in her life that Johnny hadn't filled, but now that he was gone, her life seemed redundant. She missed him terribly and because she'd been spoiled by the affections of an older guy, the boys her own age left her cold.

Her dream of becoming a model seemed to be fading and her true calling was beginning to surface. Using her spare time after school, Eva had become a candy striper at the local hospital. She embraced the feeling of being needed.

Patty's group of ladies came regularly, bringing flowers and magazines to the patients. Eva admired the hospitality they had shown while sharing about the Jesus who heals.

It had been a long time since she had been to the youth group but remembering how boring it had been, she seriously doubted whether she should go back. Each day, though, she asked God to protect Johnny and bring him home safely.

One lunchtime in the cafeteria at school, Eva was walking to find a seat when a gust of wind blew her napkin off the tray and right onto Walt's plate. As she looked down at him, memories flooded through her mind of the day they had met, and she couldn't help smiling.

"Will you join me?" invited Walt. A sense of acceptance was awakened by her smile.

"Sure! I'm not prejudiced," she stated, aware of the rejection he received from the other students. "In fact," she added with a chuckle, "You're one of the most stable guys around here." It was just the reply he needed, and he joined in her laughter.

"Thanks. But frankly, I think I owe that to my parents and God," he said.

Eva paused and slowly sipped her milk. "Walt, I've been wondering about God lately. I mean, I know there must be more than just the youth group and the choir. I'm looking for a Christian college to go to. If I'm going to know God, I'd like to do something for Him or at least with Him. Do you understand what I mean?"

Walt thought seriously for a moment. "Can't you just know Him?"

"Mumm . . . I guess so, but it's not enough. I mean, what's the point of learning all those Bible passages over the years. When do I ever use them?"

"Then what are your plans for a career? Maybe you should go to a Christian college and learn how to teach Sunday school or something. That'd make you feel useful, wouldn't it?"

Eva thought for a second. "Still, that's only a once-a-week thing. If I'm going to commit myself to this Christian business, I want to do something every day. I want to have a purpose, something that will make a difference for Him."

"I've heard of this Christian missionary group, Reach Out, which takes anyone over sixteen on short mission trips all over the world. That might be what you're looking for."

She pondered this silently as she slowly ate her lunch. "Yeah. Maybe that's the answer," she thought.

Walt watched her as she ate, his mind crowded with his own thoughts as to his future and what place God had in it. Complacency rushed its sinewy antennae near his ear and as the thought settled, he shrugged his shoulders and sighed. "You know, Eva," he finally added, "my parents made me go to church my whole life. I've seen God answer prayers, so I know He's real, but I don't see how he fits in my life anymore. I believe He's there and I know that Jesus died for me and all that, but what more do I need to know? What's the purpose in knowing more? I wanna race cars, not preach the gospel."

The Holy Spirit whispered into Eva's mind and she accepted the thought. "Yeah . . . but I'm sure there's gotta be more. At least for me."

Chapter Twenty
Evil Spreads Like Fire

It was the last week of high school for the young adults. They certainly weren't kids anymore. Walt continued following his dream of being in the Indy 500; and meanwhile, his parents prayed about it. He read everything he could find on cars and racing and had even been given a job on weekends in the pit at a local raceway. He was good with car engines and his reputation was getting quite well known. Walt's problem was that he wanted to be behind the wheel, not under it. His dad was upset at his son's choice of careers. The two had obvious tensions, and it was affecting the usual tranquility at home.

One Sunday they had an argument. The demons in the house were whizzing frantically around, and the words Walt and George were stabbing at each other were so obviously not their own. Mary was so upset by it, she declined to go to a special service at the Ruxton Church with her husband and retreated to the bedroom to be alone. Walt had a race to go to, and he walked out the back-door mumbling that his father should stay out of his life. In less than an hour he would severely regret those words.

The powers of hate and prejudice had been active in Cambridge for years, which is why most black families stayed in Ruxton and wouldn't cross the Cambridge line. The Smiths had felt directed by God to live in Cambridge, and so far, its incidents had been minor. The Freeson Lodge also had another special club. Some members weren't of this lodge, but they could be in both clubs if chosen. This other group also claimed to be a church but felt their duty was to get rid of what they thought were cursed people--the Negroes. They burned down their homes and businesses and beat up many of them, all in the name of God. They called themselves the AFW which stood for All For Whites and that Sunday they were after one man in particular--George Smith. They knew today where to find him in a small Ruxton sanctuary.

The organ music played softly, and George was on his knees. "Oh, Father, forgive me for the way I talked to Walter this morning. Maybe it is Your will for him to drive race cars, and I don't want to interfere."

Drifting in and out of the sermon, George thought of all the ridicule his son had endured. He remembered that mealtime when he explained to Walt about slavery and prejudice. "Father," he prayed, "no matter what happens to me, please keep your hand on my son, and protect him from the powers of darkness who want to shipwreck his faith."

George felt overwhelmed. He was in great pain in his back from arthritis, and he was very tired. "God, I am tired of the hate, the jeers I get, not for being a Christian, but for being colored. I don't know how much more I can take."

There was a crash and a loud explosion. Suddenly, flames were everywhere. The roof was falling in and the screams were horrific as people turned to run out of the building. George saw a young girl in a red dress trapped beneath a fallen beam. He ran over and lifted it to free her and she ran out of a side door just as George's world came crashing down. Suspended above him was a large beam and as the flames engulfed it, the reinforcement gave way, killing him instantly. Ironically, the same girl whom his son had admired was safe.

Mary lay on her bed listening to the sounds of sirens rushing past. She looked out the window and down towards the town where she saw huge flames shooting in the sky and a thick cloud of smoke funneling upward. Her husband's angel came by her side and touched hands with Odessa. As the two touched in the heavenlies, a peace came upon Mary. She knew her husband was dead and now was with God. "Father, you spared me today. Don't let me ever forget that. May George rest in peace."

Mary grabbed her sweater and hurried to the car. Within minutes, she was in Ruxton. People ran towards the church. When she rounded the corner, she was shocked, caught off guard to see the little white church gone. All that was left was a pile of smoking ashes and there were people crying all around. One of the elders was walking towards her. She knew what he was going to say. She nodded and turned around and drove straight home. As she went through the door, her house seemed deathly quiet and unusually empty. It would seem that way for a long time.

Later that evening on the way home, Walter was eager to share with his mother the victory he had had that day. It seemed they were one driver short and Walt got to drive, and much to everyone's astonishment, he won the race. This reinforced his decision to race for a living, and he hoped for his father's support. As he walked up the driveway, he formed the words in his mouth, apologizing to his dad for his behavior that morning. When he came into the kitchen, he was baffled to see his mother sitting there alone with her Bible and her eyes swollen from crying. He approached her reluctantly, fearful of the circumstances.

"Where's dad?"

Mary signaled him over and tears streamed down her face. "Son, daddy's gone to be with the Lord."

Stunned, Walt could only whisper. "What happened?"

"The AFW set the Ruxton church on fire, and your daddy didn't get out. I got a phone call later from a young girl who said George helped save her life, but several died, including the pastor."

Walter's grief was compounded by the fact that he couldn't take back the angry words he had spoken. He retreated to his room and begged God for forgiveness.

The funeral was held in Ruxton where most of George's friends lived, and the service consisted mostly of black people. Esther was surprised when Sam offered to drive her, and both were surprised to find Larry Olson already there. The two men sat together on the couch reminiscing of the day they had joked about George asking for permission to buy a car. As they sat there, the Holy Spirit convicted each man of his distance from God. They both felt outside His love.

Larry told Sam about the day his son Josh brought Debbie home drunk. "He should be a pastor, your son. He did a really good job settling me down."

"Pastor! Heck, he's going into the pros as a quarterback!" Sam grinned.

Larry's eyes followed Esther around the room. He so much wanted to talk to her but didn't know what to say. Something about her intrigued him.

Joshua was coming down the road driving his mom's car when suddenly he had a blowout. The car slowly came to a stop in front of the funeral parlor. Larry looked out the window to see Joshua jacking up the car and decided to go out and offer a hand.

Esther noticed the two outside and decided to join them just to see if she could witness to Larry. Most people were open about the Lord at times like this.

"Hi, Mom," Joshua called. "I'm sorry. This wasn't my fault."

"I know, son. These things happen, don't they, Mr. Olson?"

"Not if you buy my tires," he replied, grinning.

Esther and Larry shook hands, both remembering the day they'd met at Rose's funeral. "What brings you to the funeral?" Esther asked. "Did you know George?" "Not really, but I heard something about him I've never forgotten." "Oh? Good things, I hope."

"Oh, yes!" Larry smiled. "He asked God for permission to buy a car from your husband Sam!" "Oh, yes, I heard about that. You know, it's partly because of his wife that I'm a Christian now. What about you? Are you a Christian?"

"Probably not in the same way as you," he replied.

"What do you mean?"

Just then Pride landed next to Larry, raising its fellers to shoot its foul venom. It was caught by surprise by Nova, Esther's angel landing on top of it. Nova was brilliant and the light was so strong that Pride disintegrated into a vapor. The angel waved its arms over Larry, clearing the way for God's Holy Spirit. A hunger for righteousness came upon him.

"Esther, I want what you have," Larry said, almost choking on his words. "I want to know God like you do."

The demons weren't giving up. As he spoke, the car fell off the jack, nearly crushing Joshua's hand.

"That was a close call!" Larry said, walking to the back of the car.

Sam wandered towards them; a bit tipsy as usual. He put his arm around Larry and winked. "Since you're one of the Freeson's, you didn't have anything to do with George's church burning down, did you?"

Larry felt his face flush. Esther, embarrassed by her husband's insensitivity, retorted, "Sam, don't be so rude!"

"What are you doing for work since your tire company burned down?"

"Our president from the Lodge has offered to sign me up with his company to sell insurance. It's not too bad, and if I sell a lot of policies, my commission will keep me going. It's just Debbie, and me now. I have some money saved for her college, but I don't think she wants to go."

Sam interrupted. "You should be able to sell a lot of policies to your brothers at the Lodge."

"Yes, that's one of the plusses of being a member. We all scratch each other's back. But I have a different job offer next week at the bank. I'll just wait and see which one works out."

Joshua slammed the trunk of the car, indicating his tire fixing mission was over; and the three of them went back into the parlor. People began gathering their belongings and getting in their cars for the drive to the cemetery. Larry was watching Esther as she comforted Mary and admired the two women praying in such awkward circumstances.

Once at the grave site, the eulogy was said, and Larry began thinking how uncertain life is. Larry read the tombstone. George Smith, 1921 Born, 1947 Born Again, 1969 Gone Home. Rain began falling and everyone scrambled for their cars and left in somber moods.

George's death had a bitter effect on Walter. His attitude towards God grew even colder. In fact, it borderline on anger. Whenever he would think about his father' death, Anger, already in him, would manifest; and often the end result would be Walter slamming a door or throwing something against the wall. His decision to win the Indy 500 changed from one of delight to one of "I'll show them." Racing cars was nowhere in the plan God had for Walter, and as he continued working at the track and dreaming of his victory, his relationship with the Lord became non-existent. He, like Joshua, felt careers were too important and therefore, always refused any drugs when offered them, but instead got high on the challenge of their prospective destinies.

Debbie, on the other hand, popped, smoked or swallowed anything she could get her hands on. Finding her allowance was insufficient to sustain her growing habit; she had begun stealing at the big department store and then later returned the items for a cash refund.

One afternoon during the rush of Christmas shopping, she slipped a pair of earrings into her pocket unaware the store security guard was watching. The normal policy in apprehending a shoplifter was to approach them before they left the store and show their credentials. In this instance, the man followed her down the hall and through the exist.

"Excuse me," he called.

"Yes?" Debbie turned around, eyeing the stocky frame and acne scars on the man behind her.

"I think you have something that doesn't belong to you," he said, flashing his badge. Debbie tried to bolt, but he grabbed her arm and began walking beside her on the sidewalk. Debbie felt nauseous with fear. "Can I sit down, please? I feel faint," she said.

Keeping a tight hold on her, they sat on a small wall. Debby eyed him, wary of what he might do. "Let's see the earrings you clipped," he commanded harshly. Debbie reluctantly reached into her pocket and brought out the offending articles. The guard took them, turning them over to reveal the price of $3.45.

"That's what you owe me not to turn you over to the cops."

Debbie's biggest fear wasn't the fact that she'd been caught stealing, but that there were several joints in her purse. Carefully, she tried to get her wallet out without him seeing the pot. He pushed her hand and said, "I don't want cash, honey. I want some of you!"

"What? What do you mean?"

"I want some of you. Either you fix me up or you're spending the holidays in Juvenile Hall." The spirit of lust was pulsating in the man. As usual for this type of demon, it had a peculiar odor. Debbie noticed it and assumed it was the man. He noticed the look of disgust on her face. He raised his voice. "Either come with me or go to jail. Take your pick."

Debbie drew a breath and answered, "I'm a virgin, but I don't want to go to jail."

With a devilish grin, he stood up, pulled her to her feet and walked her to his car. Grabbing her purse, he threw it on the back seat, blindfolded her and demanded she lay down on the floor. All sorts of thoughts began going around in her mind and fear seized her. After some time, the vibration of the car stopped, and she realized from the smell around her that she was in a garage. Pulling her out of the car, he dragged her up some stairs and threw her onto a bed. The whole thing was bad enough but being blindfolded made it that much worse. The man grabbed her right hand and tied it to a post on the bed. She heard him unbuckle his belt and was caught off guard when he thrashed it across her face. She screamed and was shocked by a brutal punch.

"Shut up!" he yelled at her.

She saw stars and bit her lip at the impact. Blood was dribbling from Debbie's nose and down her chin. With one hard yank, her blouse was ripped. She lay frantic with fear. Then a sharp excruciating pain traveled across her stomach.

"Oh, my God," Debbie thought, "he's stabbing me!"

In fact, the man was slashing her with a razor blade. Any physical confidence Debbie had would soon be destroyed as this man and the demons in him slashed the razor all over her chest and stomach. The cuts weren't that deep, but Debbie couldn't tell because of the blindfold.

Suddenly, light blinded her as he removed the cloth about her face. Debbie looked at her chest and stomach. It was a mass of blood. The memory of that day at the pond when she had been miraculously saved from drowning arose in her mind. "Oh, God," she pleaded, "please get me out of this too." A peace settled on her and the fear stopped. An angel had entered the room and moved over her. At the same time, Violence came out of the man and manifested itself to the angel. Its long tentacles swaying all around as it reached out to contaminate anything it touched. The angel, in contrast, stood with its arms folded and myriads of light shot at the demon. The angel continued to get more brilliant. The light was too strong and Violence vanished.

"I'm going to make a drink. I'll be right back," her assailant barked.

Debbie sat on the edge of the bed repulsed, yet with total peace. Somehow, she knew she would be okay. She saw some lighter fluid on the table. Maneuvering herself, she stretched as far as she could with her left hand and grabbed it, purposely squirting some on the carpet below. "Oh, God, get him to untie my hand," she prayed.

When the guard came into the room, he didn't notice the toxic smell. The angel put a thought in his mind, and he came right over and untied Debbie, figuring she wouldn't run away.

Looking her up and down with a grin he lit a cigarette, taunting her.

"Please, can I have one too?" she asked.

He reached into his pocket and lit one for her. She watched as he undressed and began to walk towards her. She lifted her feet up off the floor and dropped the cigarette, igniting the carpet and then hastily jumped back as the flames scorched his legs and he let out a horrible scream. Because at that moment she was in a trance-like fear, one of his demons was able to enter her.

Lust now had a new home. The smoke set off the detectors on the ceiling and a loud alarm shrieked. Knowing she had to act fast, Debbie saw her chance to run and only partly dressed, shot out the door and down the stairs.

Realizing he wasn't following her, she ran through the kitchen and out the back door, straight into the yard of the neighbors, screaming for help. A lady heard her and came to let her into the house. Immediately, she called for an ambulance. Debbie looked out the window and wondered why the fire had gotten so out of control. The angel of death hovered over the house. Its mission completed, the man had fainted enabling the flames to spread and engulf him. The lighter fluid bottle helped feed the flames and within minutes the whole house was ablaze. In answer to a call, the fire department was there, and Debbie was safe in an ambulance on her way to hospital. This was the second time for her. The angels wondered if she would give the glory back to God.

Across town at Mary Smith's, the dinner table was unusually quiet. After thanking God for the food, Walter blew his top.

"Mom, how can you still thank God after what He has done?"

Mary swallowed and put her fork down. "Walter, we have to trust God in these kinds of trials."

Walt snapped, "I don't, and I'm not going to ever again." With that he picked up his plate and stormed out to finish dinner on the porch.

Mary couldn't hold back the tears. First George's death, and now this aggression from her son towards the Lord and toward her for believing.

For days now she hadn't had the desire to talk to God. Her bible was collecting dust on the table. She left the dishes and went upstairs, brushing the dust off the book and sitting in George's favorite chair.

"Father," she prayed. "So many times, George sat here and talked to You. You gave him comfort. You gave him wisdom. Now I need that comfort and wisdom, and I need a vision for Your will in my life."

Gently, the Holy Spirit entered the room in all His fullness. That sweet powdery smell filled the room, and Mary breathed it in. The peace of God came over her, and a supernatural infilling of the Holy Spirit engulfed her. "My dear precious child, listen to Me."

Tears welled up in her eyes, and she knew God Almighty was communing with her, taking away the aggression and tension.

She felt God's loving presence knowing He was in the room in a different way, and she relaxed. A quiet voice spoke deep in the depths of Mary. "Isaiah 57: 12."

Heart pounding, Mary fumbled through the pages of her Bible and turning to it she could hardly hold back the tears as she read, "The good men perish, the godly die before their time. No one seems to realize that God is taking them away from evil days ahead. For the godly who die shall rest in peace." (Is.57:1-2)

Mary lay the book down. It was a revelation to her. The most perfect answer to why George had died. The evil of the AFW was spreading, and prejudice was everywhere. Again surprisingly, she heard the voice. "Isaiah 4: 3-4." She read, "Others died that you might live.

I traded their lives for yours ... you are precious to me and honored and I love you." (Is 43:4) Closing the Bible, Mary gasped, recalling how that was the first time she hadn't accompanied George to Ruxton. "You really did spare me, God, didn't you? But for what purpose?"

Unconsciously, she opened the Bible again, and her eyes were drawn to these words. "Don't be afraid. I am here to help you. You shall be a new sharp toothed threshing instrument to tear all evilness apart, making chaff of mountains you shall toss them in the air, and the wind shall blow them away. And the joy of the Lord shall fill you full." Is 41:15

"I want you to return to the Bethesdian Church."

Mary swallowed hard. "Go back there?" she thought. She couldn't deny the Lord had commanded her. It wouldn't be easy, but she would obey. Could she get the other ladies to go back? Amanda and Esther were enjoying the fellowship at Second Birth Assembly. Attending a church that didn't welcome you almost seemed to defeat the purpose. But Mary knew God would have a reason and His word stated, "God shall supply all your needs... that in time should include what a real church is meant to offer. And all those who believe were together and had all things in common." (Act 2:32)

CHAPTER TWENTY-ONE
ENEMY WORKS OVER TIME

The Evans family life tried to get back to normal after Sam, Jr.'s accident and months spent in a coma. A new nightmare was about to begin but it would take years to really come to light. It seemed Sam Jr. had been invaded by a very strong perverted spirit during his coma. Esther first noticed that the television shows he watched had changed. He wasn't interested in violence of any kind, even in sports programs, in fact it seemed anything macho didn't interest him. On the other hand, he enjoyed the Jetsons and Little Betty Boop. My Three Sons was his favorite. Esther was caught by surprise one day when she came into his room to find him dressing up a Barbie doll.

"Where did you get that?" she asked.

Sam Jr. didn't even wince. It was as if he delighted in his toy. "Eva gave it to me, and look at the pretty dresses, Mom."

Esther shrugged it off, happy to have him alive and well and suggested a trip to the ice cream parlor. Maybe there they could find something to talk about.

On the drive over, the engine began spluttering and the car jolted to a stop. Esther's first impulse was anger, but then the Lord quickened to her the scripture she had read that morning, "All things work together for good." (Romans 8:28) She smiled to herself and got out of the car and lifted the hood. Of course, she knew she wouldn't be able to even tell what was wrong, but it seemed like the right thing to do. A few seconds later, a car pulled up behind her with none other than Larry Olson behind the wheel.

He grinned. "Well, well. What a surprise."

"Hi, Larry. I was driving along and all of a sudden it just died on me. Would you have any jumper cables?"

Larry maneuvered his car to face her side and set up the cables. The car started immediately.

"Did you buy this from your husband?" he asked, chuckling.

"As a matter of fact, I didn't. It belonged to my mother who died a couple of years ago. It was part of the estate left to me."

Larry paused. "Oh. Is that why Sam didn't need to get another job?"

"Yes, I'm afraid so. I can't find anything that interests him. He just stares at the television all day knowing the inheritance will last a while yet"

Esther prepared to leave, and Larry fumbled for words to keep her there. "Where are you off to?"

"The ice cream parlor. Care to join us?"

That was all he needed to hear; and as he followed her, he tried to picture their conversation. Did he want to talk about God or tell her he was lonely and attracted to her? Lust appeared to make sure it was the latter. Larry noticed a strange odor. He thought maybe he was low on oil.

It was getting late and Esther ate quickly, making small talk because she didn't really know what to say. "So, Larry, how's it going at Bethesda?"

"Well, the prettiest lady left," was the quick reply. He sat watching her, enjoying the picture she created with the auburn tints in her hair capturing the sunlight that filtered through the window.

Esther blushed. "Is that the only reason you go to church?" She was wary, knowing this was dangerous ground. The perverted spirit arose in Sam Jr., causing him to become restless. Flittering about the table with his hands, he knocked over Esther's sundae, and it landed in Larry's lap. The conversation came to an abrupt stop, and Larry quickly cleaned himself off.

The enemy had succeeded in diminishing the pursuit of spiritual things. As they walked to her car, she remembered she'd forgotten to bind the demons being able to influence their conversation and actions. Larry handed her a card belonging to a dealership of her make of car. "The Ponto's Car Company is across town. Ask for Edward, and he'll get your car checked quickly."

They shook hands and got inside their cars, both wishing they had said different things.

Larry's singleness was taking its toll on him. "Where do I start looking for a lady?" he asked himself. "I guess the best place would be a bar."

He turned the car for the nearest one and the powers of darkness were ready to comply by finding an atheist woman to be his new friend. That night he met Wanda and began an affair that robbed him of the seeds planted. He lost all interest in God as temporarily and intimately his needs were being met by this new lady.

Esther rarely crossed his mind anymore. But he remained in hers, aided by the Holy Spirit encouraging her to see him through God's eyes, she faithfully prayed for him daily, committing him to the Lord. He still put his time in at the church and at the elder's meetings but was indifferent to the gentle work of the Holy Spirit convicting him.

A few weeks after the encounter at the ice cream parlor, Esther and Mary were together shopping and her car barely started so she decided to give Edward a try at Ponto's Car Company. She was surprised to see an older man who was colored. For whatever reason she hadn't expected a Negro.

"Well, hello, ma'am. Can I help you?" he asked, passing right by her and fixing his eyes on Mary. Mary was surprised too, but more surprised that she reacted as a woman. "Oh, Father, please forgive me."

Esther noticed too, but it was obvious the black man was handsome, and he had his eyes on Mary. Edward lifted the hood and fiddled with a few things then closed it, stating, "I thought so."

"What? What's wrong?"

"Lady, this car is on a recall list. Ponto's is giving new engines to all who have this model.

"Really? So, what do I do?"

"Leave it with me, and in a few days, it will be like new. No charge."

"Well, praise the Lord!" Esther exclaimed with a smile. Mary grinned too, trying not to make eye contact with Edward, but the attraction was too strong, and their eyes met. An awareness of the sensuality in each of them was present between them.

Over the next four days, Edward couldn't stop thinking about Mary. He also was a widower who had lost his wife in the church fire, but he had never gone to anything religious himself. If Edward had said his last name, Mary would have recognized his wife, a dear Christian lady who had sung in the choir. His daughter, Tayna was the girl in the red dress who had become Walter's obsession and also the one George had rescued before losing his life.

The following Saturday night it occurred to Edward that if he wanted to find Mary, he had to find the church she attended. Calling his daughter, Tanya, to dinner, he started asking questions about different churches.

"Daddy, since when have you gotten religious?"

He became defensive. "I'm only asking. I heard this lady say, "Praise the Lord," the other day. What kind of church would she go to?" "Is she black or white?"

"Both!" he stated matter-of-factly. "What?"

"One lady was white and the other was black. They both seemed to know God intimately. Would she go to Bethesda?" her father inquired.

"No, I doubt it. They wouldn't say "Praise the Lord" like that. Certainly, no black lady goes there."

"Where are the ones from your church that burned down?"

"They're all scattered about now." Kissing him on the cheek, she finished with, "Look, dad, I gotta go." She disappeared out the door.

Edward pulled out the phone book and started looking at the names of churches. "This looks interesting. Second Birth Assembly. I'll try that one."

As destiny would have it, just the Sunday morning Edward went to Second Birth Assembly, Esther and Mary returned to Bethesda. Slipping into the back pew and praying like never before, the women waited expectantly to see what would happen. The demons were buzzing the church, angry that those spirit-filled women were back on their turf. Standing next to them were Odessa and Nova, their angels. Because of their prayers, all demons were bound from doing anything during the service. As a result, several people cried during the hymns and for a change. People slept during the service because they were tired and bored, not because they were influenced by outside forces. When the service was over, no one greeted the ladies. Only glares or quick glances were their welcome. Even Mr. Dooley, the worship leader, walked right by without a word. Going out the back door, Reverend Whitcliff nodded stiffly to Esther. "I thought you were through with us."

"The Lord told Mary to come, and she called me. I asked the Lord if I should come back, and He said 'yes'. So, here we are."

He pulled Esther off to the side. People filtered out of the church and stared at them. "Esther, you can't just waltz in and out of churches! You decided you didn't want to be a Bethesdian when you left so definitively that day. You made your own bed." Esther cut him off. "Are you telling me that I'm not allowed here?" Defiantly, he looked her straight in the eyes. "In a word, yes." She was shocked. "What about Mary?"

The Reverend paused for a moment. "They have a church for black people." "God told her to come here," Esther interrupted. "Wherever her kind go, that's where she should go."

Esther felt her blood pressure rise and dislike for this man permeated her being. A scripture came to her mind. "They profess to know God; but by their deeds, they deny Him." (Titus 1:16)

Meanwhile, Mary couldn't have felt more humiliated standing off to the side. The looks and jeers from people who claimed to know God were a nightmare. It was like a breath of fresh air when Larry walked purposefully up to her.

"Hello, Mary. Welcome to Bethesda," he stated determinedly, glaring at Reverend Whitcliff.

"Hi, Larry. It doesn't look like either of us are welcome here," Mary replied sadly.

Odessa and Nova raised their wings toward the heavens. Bullets of light rocketed through the skies. No words were spoken, but the Lord knew what to do. The Holy Spirit enveloped Larry and convicted him of his separation from God because of his fornication with Wanda. He suddenly had compassion for Mary, also remembering her recent tragedy. Underneath he was very glad to see Esther wanting to return to the church he attended. To him, she was very different and much needed in that congregation, maybe even as a good friend to him too.

"Leave it to me, Mary," he said, patting her on her shoulder. "I'll have a talk with the Reverend."

With that, Mary signaled Esther with a look that said, "Let's go!"

Esther complied, backing away from the minister and extending her hand politely. "I hope you will take this situation back to the Lord, sir. His will always prevail, one way or the other. I wouldn't try stopping it if I were you."

"Is that a threat?" he retorted defensively.

"No." She added with a smile, "Just a fact."

Wednesday morning at the ladies' prayer meeting, Amanda came in looking somber. Once everyone was settled, all eyes turned to her. "You'll never guess what happened. Reverend Whitcliff had a heart attack last night." The ladies gasped and looked at each other. "Is he okay?" Esther asked, concerned. "No. He's dead," Amanda replied.

Immediately, Patty took over. "We need to pray that God's will can prevail and Esther and Mary can go to Bethesdian Church and bring some light there."

Marry nodded. "I think Larry Olson is prepared to stand for the truth."

"I'm sure his demons aren't!" interjected Patty. "We better pray for him right now."

Amazingly enough, across town the elders of the church had met to discuss funeral arrangements and the new leadership for the church. None of the elders were born again so the communication was definitely demonically controlled. After ten minutes of debating why this one or that one should be "top dog", Larry lost his temper.

"Listen, just shut up, all of you. You sound like the disciples arguing over who should be greatest in the kingdom."(Luke 9:46)

Next to Larry stood Cronan, poised and ready. The Lord had commissioned Cronan to Larry, and the angel was determined to bring him into the Kingdom of God as prayers were lifted for his salvation. Cronan birthed a thought in Larry's mind. "Gentlemen," he stated, "I'd like to know which one of you are born again."

The men were stunned. No one said a word.

Then Sheriff Beam arose. "How dare you? That's private between God and me." "Then tell me this. Why does the Bible say we should confess Jesus before man?"(Matt 10:32)

Mr. Dooley turned red in the face. "The Bible says we aren't to judge. Are you judging us?"

"In a way. I've read we are to judge the household of God. If I'm going to be in this church, I want to know if the men running it know God." Larry felt a surge of confidence. "For example, did you ask God's permission to buy that new carpet at a tune of $3,500?"

Sheriff Beam slapped his hand down on the table. "Look here, Larry. You're getting out of place." "Excuse me, Sheriff, but I ask you men to think about something. Do you know the Reverend refused to let Esther Evans return here? And Mary Smith isn't allowed at all. What is this? We are supposed to love each other. Why do you think the Reverend had a heart attack?"

"Too many donuts," Mr. Dooley retorted sarcastically.

Everyone went silent. Larry swallowed, a thought going through his mind. "Father, please give me the right words," he prayed.

"Gentlemen, Jesus said you must be born again to enter the kingdom of God. (John 3:3) I want to know which one of you is born again." He looked at Sheriff Bean. The sheriff stared back coldly. He looked at Mr. Dooley. Dooley lowered his head and stared at the floor, saying nothing. "Gilbert, what about you?"

"I've always known God. I've been a Bethesdian ever since I was in grade school. I've never missed a Sunday yet," he added proudly.

Without even a forethought, Larry announced, "Being a church member and being born again are two very different things."

With that, he walked out the door. Cronan followed, leaving the elders and the demons to hash it out.

Once in his car, Larry felt like crying, yet he also felt triumphant. There was a feeling of gain, but also one of loss. He pulled the car out of the church parking lot and began driving, uncertain as to where he was going. His eyes were drawn to the side where he saw Esther's car.

He recognized it from the night he followed her to the ice cream parlor.

After all, how many yellow Ponto's had a sticker stating, "Smile, God Loves You"? He pulled into the driveway behind it. With Cronan motivating him, he strode up to the front door and rang the bell.

Patty answered. "Well, hi, Larry. Come on in. We were just praying for you." Her friendliness and warmth relaxed him, and he felt only slightly uneasy with the group of ladies.

"Hello, Mary. Hello, Esther."

Patty spoke up. "This is Amanda Lawson."

"Oh, yes. I know your husband from the Lodge."

Each lady reacted inwardly when they heard the word Lodge. How that club had deceived many a man? Amanda smiled. "Yes, I'm trying to get him to quit."

Patty interrupted, knowing this wasn't the time to bring that up. "So, Larry, what can we do for you?"

"I've just come from the church. I guess you heard about the Reverend."

The ladies' faces were somber. "Yes. What a terrible shame," Esther said. "I tried warning him from preventing God's will be done."

"Esther," Larry said, taking a seat, "I want you to come back to Bethesda. I know you are born again and that's what we need."

The ladies were surprised at his choice of words. Inwardly, they praised God.

"Mary, you might as well come too. If we're going to shake that church of its hypocrisy, now's the time to do it."

Patty interrupted, cautiously choosing her words. "Larry, what about you? Do you want to be born again?"

"To be honest, I don't really know what that means."

Amanda popped in. "That which is flesh is flesh ..."

Patty interrupted. "Come on. Let's not talk religion; we need straight talking."

"You need to accept Jesus into your heart," Esther spoke softly.

"What does that mean?" Larry asked again. He was starting to feel anxious, almost concerned, like a cornered fox. The demons in him were getting restless. Deception and Antichrist let off their power. In a second Larry lost the humbleness to listen anymore. "Excuse me. I need to use the bathroom."

All were quiet as Larry left the room.

"Pray," Patty instructed. "We bind the demons in him in Jesus' name. Father, open his heart. Save him, Father."

In a few minutes, Larry returned. Patty stood up again. Larry, come and sit down here. In a nutshell, I will try and explain to you what it is to be born again. I'll try and use words that you know. Sometimes we Christians have our own lingo, and we use it too much."

Esther realized he needed encouragement from someone he knew. "Larry, I know God is working in your heart. Thank you for encouraging us to come to Bethesda."

Patty put down her coffee mug and looked straight at Larry. She could almost see in his eyes a spirit looking back. "I'm going to pray first, Larry, that God will help you to understand all this. All of us have been where you are."

"Okay," Larry whispered, bowing his head and to the ladies' amusement he folded his hands like a little boy saying his bedtime prayers.

"God, we ask..." The phone rang and everyone jumped. As Patty went to get it, she realized the demons were trying to divert this meeting. It was Amanda's husband asking her to pick up his laundry. What timing!

"Okay," stated Patty, "let's try it again."

"Father, we ask you in Jesus' name to open his heart to understand and to receive You."

Larry began to sniffle. The power of God encompassed him, and he softly cried. Only he knew the things he was ashamed of, but it seemed he was ready to make his peace with God for it all. He felt guilty for the years of hate towards Rose and cried violently as he thought of her burning alive at his tire shop. He kept crying, burying his face in his hands as he thought of being wiped out financially. Now he was forty-eight years old with nothing to look forward to. His daughter, Debbie, was moving right down the wrong path. Patty went over and softly placed her hand on his shoulder. Her eyes also filled with tears. "Father, we ask You to heal these hurts and make Larry whole and give him a future and a hope. Give him a purpose in You."

A peace infiltrated him, and he took out a hankie, wiped his eyes, blew his nose and then took a deep breath. His face had a new softness, almost a glow about it.

"Boy, do I feel better!" he said, smiling.

Amanda offered him a glass of water. "So, do you want to ask Jesus into your heart?"

Larry beamed, stating, "I sure do!" The ladies laughed with joy.

Patty signaled to Esther and she began to speak. "Larry, I'm going to pray with you to receive Jesus. The Bible says in John that all those who receive Him, to then them He gave the right to become the children of God." (John1:12) Amanda interjected, "Yeah, and the Bible says if you don't have His Spirit, you don't belong to Him." (Romans 8:9)

Patty cleared her throat. "Larry, are you ready to repent?"

"From what?" As soon as he said it, he thought of his wandering lustful incidents.

"You have to stop doing the things God shows you are wrong. Ask Him to forgive you for doing those things, and tell Him you won't do them anymore."

Esther folded her hands across her chest. "Larry, you need to admit you don't know God and that you were not on your way to heaven. Can you do that?" But most important is to know nothing you do will get you in Heaven. It's a gift. Just take it; and also, all the things you thought about God, forget and start a fresh walk.

As Larry looked into Esther's eyes, he went limp inside. He had a real draw towards her and then realized he was attracted to her. He looked at her. "Yes, I realize I need to be born again."

Patty spoke up. "Do you mind if I ask where you heard the term 'born again'?"

"I saw it in a magazine at the dentist's office."

The ladies looked at each other and Mary praised the Lord. It had paid off. Larry got down on his knees, folded his hands and closed his eyes. Esther was touched by his humility as were the other ladies.

"Jesus," he began, "Please forgive me for all that I've done wrong. I..." He went quiet. A tear fell from his eyes, trickled down his cheek and hung from his chin. No one moved. "Oh, God, how I want to know you like George did. I want to have your permission for everything I do. I ask Jesus into my heart and ask You to do Your will in my life. I'm so sorry, God, for the way things have turned out, especially with Rose and how mad I was at You. Please forgive me. I didn't know that You loved me, but I do now because I can feel it. Amen." He opened his eyes and looked at Mary. She had tears in her eyes too. "Mary, I want you to know it was George's comment years ago that showed me there was more. Since I heard, he could talk to God, I've always wanted that too."

Mary nodded. "There's one more thing, Larry. From now on you can end your prayers with 'in Jesus' name' because now you have the right to go into God's presence because of what Jesus did. Do you understand?"

"Not really."

"Prayers that aren't done through Jesus' name don't get past the ceiling. Jesus said ask anything in my name and if it's according to the Father's will, it shall be done." "But how do you know if it's His will?"

"It will take time, but we will show you; and as you learn to communicate with God, He'll show you too."

"Oh, great! This is like George asking permission, isn't it?"

"Exactly."

Breaking the ice, Amanda jumped out of her seat and hugged Larry. "Well, you're my brother now!"

One by one each lady hugged him. It was the most love Larry had felt all at once. Taking a sip of his water, Larry let out a sigh. "So, can I join your little group?"

"Sure!" Patty laughed. "Welcome aboard."

In the heavenlies, the angels rejoiced. Cronan was now able to work with this child of the Father to enable him to know God through Christ. The demons on the other hand were furious and setting up ways to wreck Larry's new-found faith. His first obstacle would be a confrontation with his daughter.

CHAPTER TWENTY-TWO
ANGELS ABOUND WHERE EVIL GROWS

In the morning, Debbie was reminded of her encounter by the fresh wounds on her body. She glanced in the mirror and self-rejection settled on her as she took in the scars which defaced her blossoming figure. Going to her stash box, she downed a couple of pills which had a bad effect once she reached school. The headmaster caught her stumbling down the corridor and sent her home. She was temporarily suspended.

As soon as she arrived home, her father's booze cabinet became her companion for the afternoon. When Larry walked in, he found her slumped on the couch and the stereo going full blast. His joy quickly diminished seeing the bourbon bottle on the table.

Being a brand-new Christian, his heart had been changed. God had taken out his heart of stone and replaced it with a soft new one. The darkness was gone, but his own emotions came into play. Blackness seeped into his heart. A spirit of anger flickered next to him.

The foul thing winced upon seeing the presence of the Holy Spirit in him. Appearing in the room was a sparkling light. It grew and grew into a figure. Huge in stature there stood a warrior, Cronan, Larry's new companion. The gleaming angel raised his shield and hundreds of bolts of light beams encircled the demon.

"He's the Lord's now. What authority have you to antagonize him?" "Look at his heart," the ghoul drooled.

"Yes, there is slight darkness, but let's see what he does in response to Debbie."

Larry lost his temper. "What the hell is going on here?" He grabbed

Debbie by the arm, pulling her across the table as she lost her balance. The glasses and bottle tipped over, spilling their contents.

"Why should I tell you?" she snapped.

"Because I'm your father!"

"No, you're not. You're a man I lived with for sixteen years, but you've never been a father."

She jerked away, stumbled out the door and up the stairs.

Larry sat down, stung by her words. Anger responded to the darkness in his heart, slashing its tail across his face, besetting him to keep holding onto his wrath.

He jumped up, ready to go and finish this confrontation with Debbie. Cronan retaliated with a bolt of light bursting from his chest, rendering the demon immobile. Then the Lord whispered for Larry to get his Bible.

He was so surprised, he froze. "God, you can talk to me!" He had to think about where his Bible would be. He never even took it to church. Slowly, he turned around and saw it by the fireplace on the shelf. As he walked over, eager to hear what God had to say, his eyes were drawn to the table where the booze and the ice cubes dripped onto the carpet. His immediate impulse was to get something to clean it up. The Lord spoke again, "Do it later."

Larry sat quietly, and then Job 15:2 came to his mind. Having no idea where Job was, he looked it up in the contents. As he was turning the pages to find it, a new sensation overcame him. Suddenly, this book was precious to him. Now he wanted to know everything it said, immediately, he realized a new strength in himself. His eyes gazed straight down on "for vexation slays the foolish man, and anger kills the simple."(Job5:2) He looked up as the words rang in his head. Anger kills the simple. Looking back his eyes lay on a verse. "As for me I would seek God and I would place my cause before God." "Yes!" he exclaimed. "That's it!" (Job 23:4)

Raising his face to the heavens, he prayed, "God, Debbie needs to know you too. Help me to bring her to you." The demon's influence in the home started a campaign. Jezebel, Debbie's companion, flew upstairs to her and along with Anger began stirring her up against her father. It was easy because of the alcohol and the drugs already in her system. She lay looking at the posters displayed around her walls and began rationalizing that her father needed to be mellowed out. Jezebel moved across her chest, placing the idea in her mind to put some of her acid in his vodka bottle. The more she thought about it, the more she liked the idea. She would sneak downstairs and drop it in later, figuring within a day, during his cocktail hour, it would be consumed.

The next day Larry had a job interview in town down at the Savings and Loan. A couple of demons assigned to antagonize him hoped to wreck his first day as a Christian so he would return to the bottle of vodka for comfort. The first thing that went wrong was the alarm didn't go off, thus making him late and leaving no time to pray before leaving the house. As a new babe in Christ, he did have a certain protection now, but still the demons could and would try to provoke him.

He rushed out the door just in time to see someone clip the side of his car, knocking the side mirror to the ground. This made him furious, and without thinking he blasphemed loudly. The demons clapped, proud of their ingenuity. The single road into town had a street cleaner on it, spraying soapy water on both sides making it impossible to pass. Anger sat next to him shooting its tentacles into Larry's temples, causing his blood pressure to rise as he let himself get more and more agitated by the machine in front of him.

He arrived at the bank and in his hurry to get inside, didn't lock the car and left his keys inside. Racing across the parking lot, he didn't see a puddle of ice cream and slid a couple of feet, scaring him more than anything else. At the door he grabbed some composure and strode in. An angel hovered by his head. "Pray," was his command?"

Larry responded. "I need this job. Please help me get it." He walked over to the Loan Department, noticing a rather pretty secretary picking up the telephone.

"I'm Larry Olson and I had an appointment for..." he glanced at the clock above her head, "for forty-five minutes ago. "I'm sorry I'm late."

"Please take a seat. The managers on the phone at the moment."

Larry glanced at the phone with one button light glowing, then it went off. He waited, knowing he'd be called any minute. Fifteen minutes later the manager's door opened. A short, stocky man rushed out shouting over his shoulder, "I'll be back after lunch."

Larry jumped up. "Excuse me. I realize I was late, and I apologize; but we have an appointment."

The man stared at Larry, looking flustered. "I'm sorry, but after half an hour of waiting for you, I got a call from my father-in-law and they suggested I hire their nephew. So, I'm afraid there's no vacancy left. I hope you understand. They'll be a pain in the neck if I don't hire the boy. Maybe some other time." he picked up some envelopes and kept walking.

Larry stood there slightly crushed. Antichrist came by his side, planting its noxious suggestion. "Some God you've got! Can't even get you a job."

Slowly, he walked across the bank and out the door. His heart hardened and disappointment towards God came into his emotions. Anger stalked him, shooting its power. He was receiving it. He came to where his car had been parked, but it wasn't there. The curse words flew, and the demons laughed spitefully. To make matters worse, Gerald Simpson, who owed him two hundred dollars for a bad check he wrote to pay for new tires, drove by and ignored him?

"Every time I see that guy, I want to punch him!"

The Holy Spirit spoke. "Is that a way a Christian would talk?"

Anger shot its poison and Larry didn't answer God, choosing to hold onto his feelings. Walking down the street, he ran into Sheriff Beam.

"Hey, Larry, you look like you lost your best friend."

"Someone swiped my car."

"Sorry to hear that. Come into my office and we'll get the particulars."

As he was leaving, the sheriff asked, "Have you found a job yet"

"No." he took a deep breath.

"Something will turn up."

By the time Larry got home that night he was exhausted. His first day as a Christian had been a nightmare. "Although." he admitted, "I got my car back."

He strolled through the door and thought of his nightly cocktail. As he went to the liquor cabinet and opened it, the heavenly host waited in anticipation. What would he do? If he drank the vodka with the acid in it, anything could happen.

Esther had an overwhelming urge to call him. She went to the phone but couldn't get a dial tone. She tried again. Nothing. She bowed her head. "Father, I lift Larry up to you right now for discernment, wisdom and protection."

Cronan stood by and Nova materialized next to him in answer to Esther's prayers. "What should we do?"

"He needs to get a word quickened to him not to partake in strong drink."

"You start."

The angels stood with wings interlocked and began worshipping the Lord. "Praise you, Jesus."We praise you, Jesus." Luminous light beams expelled from their breastplates toward heaven.

Larry began pouring the vodka into his glass and the tiny pill of destruction flowed with ease from the bottle. The acid was planted. As the lights skyrocketed through the ceiling, God spoke to his heart. "Read your Bible."

"Was that you, God?" he asked the air. There was no response. Larry would have to learn obedience on the first command. One day it would be a matter of life or death.

He kept standing, waiting for another word. The house was quiet, and all the ghouls were frustrated. They could do nothing. It was up to Larry to choose.

He remembered George's comment. "You too can have an in with the boss." Walking slowly to the bookshelf and reaching for his Bible, excitement flowed through his being. God had spoken to him before in Job. Would He do it again?

Doubt filled his mind. What if He didn't? Holding the Bible, he retrieved his drink, a familiar comfort in times of uncertainty.

God spoke. "Proverbs 23."

After a few minutes of searching, Larry found the scripture. His eyes were drawn to certain verses. "Who has woe, who has sorrow, who has bloodshot eyes? Do not gaze at wine when it is red, when it sparkles, and goes down smoothly. In the end it bites like a snake and poisons like a viper ... Your eyes will see strange sights and your mind imagine confusing things. You will say they beat me up, but I didn't feel it. When will I wake up so I can find another drink?" (Prv.23:35)

"Wow!" Larry exclaimed. "I can't believe this is in the Bible. How did they know all that years ago?"

God spoke again. "For you were once darkness but now you are light in the Lord. Live as children of light." (Ephesians 5:8.)

Gripping the glass tightly in his hand, Larry went to the kitchen and poured it down the sink.

The angels rejoiced and God gave him another talent.

Chapter Twenty-three
<u>Jailed for Life</u>

Graduation Day arrived and all four kids, including Debbie, graduated. Walt decided to forego college and begin his career dream at the local racetrack. Unfortunately, he was usually under the car, not driving it. He'd have to get his own car and his own sponsor if he wanted to be a driver.

On one of the first scalding hot days of summer, Mary realized that she had better get the car tuned up, after all George wasn't there anymore to do these things for her. She remembered Edward from Ponto's Dealers and reluctant to go herself, she sent Walt.

Pulling into the garage, his eyes were drawn to a souped-up Mustang being worked on. Walt's eyes sparkled as his inner dream to race was nourished by the elegance of the vehicle. Sponsors' names were emblazoned all over it, and he coveted the idea of being sponsored as a black in this white man's sport. Deep inside, he had a longing to show that colored people were equal.

"Hi!" Edward called. "It sure is a beauty, isn't it?"

"Yes." Walt smiled.

Wiping the grease from his fingers and tossing the rag, Ed extended his hand. "Do you like racing cars?"

"It's my dream, even though I've only done it once. But I won!"

"What if I give you a try-out? I'm looking for a driver this season. I'm too old and with my daughter going overseas on a mission, it's just me left to raise my little boy; so I haven't the time. What's your name, son?"

"Walt Smith. I've brought my mom's car in for a tune-up."

"If you pass my test and I think you're good enough, I'll back you. We'll split the earnings sixty-forty and I get the sixty. My daughter, Tanya, is going to be a missionary in Japan; and I'd like to send her as much money as I can."

Walter was overcome. "Sir, I'll make you proud of me. I'll do the best I can."

The two shook hands and it seemed that for a moment Walt's loss of his own father wasn't so severe. Within hours, Walt's dream would be crushed. His hopes shattered. The US government had different plans for him.

Running through the kitchen door, Walt was caught short by seeing his mother crying at the dining room table. She was holding a letter and fear gripped her as to its contents.

"Mom, guess what?" he exclaimed, attempting to stop her tears. "I've got some great news for you. Edward, over at Ponto's is going to sponsor me to race cars."

Mary wiped her eyes and slowly shook her head. "I don't think so."

"What do you mean? Come on, Mom. I've been waiting my whole life for a chance like this."

She signaled him to sit down. "Walt, I'm going to pray, and I want you to pray too."

Pulling a chair out, he flashed back to the afternoon when Mary told him George had died. He braced himself for the worst.

"Father, we come to You in Jesus' name and ask You to be present with us right now. We know that Your Word says, 'all things work together for good to those who love You and are called according to Your purpose'. I love You and Walt is called so maybe between the two of us You can make good in this situation. Amen."

"Mom, what's the matter?"

"Son, you've been drafted into the Army. You leave in two weeks for Fort Benson in New York to go through Boot Camp. After six weeks, you'll be sent to Vietnam."

Mary began crying and Walt sat there stunned. Anger stirred inside, releasing its toxic vapors and in response, Walt got up, grabbed his chair and threw it across the room.

"Why, God? Why did you have to do this to me? I hate You!"

"Walt, no! Please!" his mother begged. "God can turn this into a blessing if you let Him."

"Sure, just like He did for dad!" With that, he stomped out the door.

The darkness in his heart increased and the demon invaded his soul with the injustice of it all. Hate coiled its ugly presence around Walt's heart and penetrated through the darkness a murderous anger. He ran to combat the intense emotion he felt which was demonically fueled. Running, running, he didn't care where he went. Remembering an old favorite spot by the lake, he went to a place of familiarity. There by the water was Josh. His good friend could console him at a time like this.

As Josh lifted his head, Walt saw that he was not his usual self. Slurring his words, he sang out a familiar line from a song. "Hey, Walt, it's all over now!"

"What are you talking about? Wait a minute. You're drunk! What are you doing drunk? You can't be a football star and drink!"

"I'm not going to be. I've been drafted! Can you believe it? After all these years, following the Bible rules, God nails me in the end. What a dirty trick!"

Sitting beside him and popping the first beer he'd ever had, Walt washed away his anger with the soothing liquid. The two boys once again united, reminisced on the years gone by and the dashing of their hopes and dreams. As the sun went down and the beer was all gone, they did have one good chuckle. Both would be trained at the same place.

While stumbling home in the dark, Josh came across Debbie sitting under a light pole. "Got another beer?" he asked.

"Sure," she said, pulling one from her purse.

Taking a big swig, he belched and then blurted out, "I've been drafted into the Army."

"Are you scared?" she asked.

"I think I'm angrier because I wanted to play professional football."

"Yeah," she said after taking a sip of beer. "And I wanna be a famous singer like Cher. So much for dreams."

As Debbie entertained the effects of the alcohol, Jezebel stirred in her and Lust commenced instigating her emotions. She looked at Josh. He'd always been so handsome, so clean cut. Debbie coveted him for herself and leaned over, drawing close to his lips. "Let's go someplace and make love," she whispered enticingly.

"I've never done it," he said uncomfortably.

"Me, neither, but everyone thinks I have, so I might as well."

Crushing his beer can in one hand, Josh swung the other over her shoulder. "I always held back so God would answer my prayers, but it doesn't matter now." Then he kissed her.

The spirits of lust in both of them joined and pulsated. The night would end with Josh and Debbie becoming one. (Mark 10:8)

***

As that week rolled on, both Mary and Esther prayed for God to touch the hearts of their sons. "As a king's heart is in God's hand like channels of water," they prayed, "so let God maneuver them and keep both boys safe."

Proverbs 21:21

Memorial Day weekend came, and the ladies decided to call a special prayer meeting. A new roster for choosing soldiers was coming into effect and the women wanted to ward off any more boys from Cambridge being abducted into this senseless war.

As Esther and Mary drove over to Amanda's for the meeting, she was caught by surprise to see a big tent going up. In huge black letters across the top was written, Magical Carnival. "That's all we need, more deception!" she retorted.

"What are you talking about?" Mary asked.

"I guess if the carnival is advocating magic, it will have palm readers and clairvoyants reading crystal balls and such."

"What does that have to do with deception?"

Mary slowed down and looked through the window, pointing to another sign. "Authentic Gypsies, Tell Your Future, By the Stars, By your Palm or Tarot Cards." "Just as I thought," reiterated Esther.

"I was just reading this morning in Isaiah how God cursed those who went to astrologers to know their future, in fact it even said they were calling upon demons when they went."

"What do the demons have to do with it?" (Isaiah8:19)

"My guess is they go and make the predictions happen, so you end up coming back for more."

Sitting at Amanda's, Esther brought up the new irritant in town, and the ladies prayed. They asked God to release more angels to the area to push back the powers of darkness. As they prayed, pillars of light reached heaven and entered the throne room of God. Angels dispersed and fought off the principalities using the same light shafts as weapons. The angels were permitted to intercede in unplugging electric cords, jamming the lighting systems, cutting a rope on the tent so it collapsed and in essence wreak havoc. The purpose was that God cared for these people too; and while the enemy was ducking light shafts, the Holy Spirit could work in the lives of the employees, encouraging them to turn to God in their time of need. After all, they didn't know they were children of darkness.

That night when the carnival opened, not much had been accomplished in drawing many to God. They'd had a chance, just like those who later would pay financially to come into their web of deceit.

Esther's angel spoke to Odessa. "There are two coming tonight who will cross forbidden lines."

"I know and the freedom of choice God gave man can be manipulated by demonic influence. They can be persuaded or deceived. After all, the demons were here long before man. This is their turf."

Up the path came Debbie and Eva, talking and laughing, celebrating the finish of high school. Principalities over the carnival stood ready. Witchcraft, towering over the tent began flapping its wings slowly as his dark, leathery skin sent off a fume. Only the angels saw its vapor, like a rainy mist floating down on those coming into the tent. Both Debbie and Eva were open to its deception as both had the curse of witchcraft over their lives. Debbie had inherited it from her father's involvement in the Lodge, whose sin was idolatry and heresy, and her own involvement in drugs. Eva had the same attachment to witchcraft because of her mother's dabbling in calling up the dead." Sins reach the third and fourth generation" Numbers 14:18.

Both had a particle of darkness indicating to the spirit world they were fair game.

Once in the tent, Debbie's eyes were drawn to the singsong, "Know Your Future." She grabbed Eva by the arm and excitedly pulled her over to investigate.

Devouring her last morsel of cotton candy, Eva scoffed, "You don't believe all this stuff, do you?"

"Come on. Let's try it; and if I, do it, you have too also."

They each paid a dollar and walked through some black curtains with long strands of beads dangling over the doorway. The clicking sound caused an eerie effect which added to their anticipation. Emerging from a doorway a lady came in and immediately offered Debbie a chair. Dressed in a typical Gypsy outfit, complete with a handkerchief tied around her head and one round gold earring, her piercing eyes mesmerized them. She looked deep into Debbie's eyes, making contact with her demon. In the spirit dimension, Debbie's demon shot information into the Gypsy's mind. She looked into her crystal ball. A puzzling look crossed her face; and she reached for her cigarettes, offering one to Debbie.

"I don't smoke," Debbie replied, thinking she doesn't even know the present, how can she know my future!

The lady raised her eyebrows. "You will, dear, you will."

"So, what do you see?" Debbie asked with a smirk.

"I see a death many years ago. Someone you loved, someone close to you. "Debbie's countenance changed drastically. Flashing back to Chipper, a hardness came into her heart as she remembered the little dog lying crushed from the weight of the door.

"You recently lost something that will give you something. You also will lose something which will not be returned."

"A bit vague, don't you think?" Eva quipped.

The light went out underneath the crystal ball. The lady turned to Eva. "Your vibrations are very strong. Quickly, sit down. I'm getting a message." Odessa whispered to her mind, "Don't do it!" Eva hesitated, feeling an uneasiness she couldn't understand. "Quickly!" commanded the Gypsy.

In response, Eva sat down as the light returned to the ball, fading in and out until eventually becoming brighter.

"I can't see anything," the fortune-teller exclaimed. The demon of witchcraft stood intimidated by Odessa. It feared the angel and didn't move.

"Give me your palm."

Odessa began to glisten. "Eva, no! Don't do it!"

The lady reached for her hand; and as if Eva was compelled to obey, she extended her arm. The lady ran her fingers into the etched lines in her palm.

"This is a year for decisions. The school you want to go to, don't go! It will mean death for you."

Straight away, Eva thought about the Christian college she'd contemplated attending. The spirit of fear lodged in her and pulsated. After years of lying dormant, it was given its cue. It had to scare her from entering that college. Squeezing its bristly tentacles around the vertebrae, it released a decaying cancer which was dispensed into her soul. Fear, the enemy of faith, now had its opportunity and her emotions responded by yielding a trauma to her spirit.

Thoughts came to her mind. "You'll die there. You'll cease to exist."

The Gypsy knew she had her pawn as Eva swallowed hard and added, "Anything else?" "You must go back to your dream of being a model. I see the name 'John'." Eva's eyes widened. "No one could have known that!"

"Okay. I'll do it!" she thought. I'll model until Johnny comes home from the war." Her spiritual strongman laughed diabolically. Odessa's armor diminished and with a flash was gone to recoup.

As the girls left the carnival that night, unbeknownst to them in each of their hearts a small mark was visible to the spiritual inhabitants, stating both had willingly participated in an evil forbidden by the Word of God. Each was seeking their future which is witchcraft or in another word, necromancing.

When Debbie got home, Larry was sitting in his favorite chair about to read the Bible. As she looked over, the message came to her the Gypsy had said, "You will lose something which will not be returned. You lost something that will give you something." She had to figure out the puzzling message. "Does that mean that Dad will remarry?"

Pointing to his finger, Debbie questioned Her Dad "Is that a new ring?"

"Yes." He displayed it proudly. "I received it today from the Freeson's Lodge."

Deception and Witchcraft greeted the new member of the Olson's household. Debbie had been followed by a curse spirit, which some call a 'jinx', who wouldn't live in her but simply assist the others in the house to disrupt Larry's walk and endeavor to prevent Debbie from meeting Jesus.

Giving him a hug, she apologized for her behavior the week before and said, "Let's go out to a movie and have a good time!"

Larry looked at the Bible. "It could wait," he thought. So, the two went out, uncovered by prayer.

Fortunately, Larry had the special grace and hedge of protection which comes from being a new Christian. Although he was in the flesh watching the movie, he was safe for now.

CHAPTER TWENTY-FOUR
HEALINGS STILL HAPPEN

Fourth of July fireworks seemed to be far behind as three of the teens boarded the same bus for New York City. It was a sad scene at the depot as Mary, Marvin and Esther all said goodbye to their offspring.

Eva had the most optimism, after all she was going to the Big Apple to have her lifelong dream come true. It was bound to happen now that the Gypsy had seen it in her palm.

Mary and Esther held hands to say a prayer over Walt and Joshua. Marvin, sitting over to the side, felt left out. Turning to him, Esther smiled. "Come on, Marvin. Why not join us?"

Cautiously, he came over and joined hands, leaving Eva who had declined their offer. She listened intently to Esther's plea and wondered if the two boys would really come back alive. The prayer was ended with an Amen and the honk of a horn. The bus was ready to depart.

Both women stood silently, reaching out to God in themselves, with their own petition of mercy. Odessa and Nova watched the streams of light emanating as the unspoken words touched heaven and God Almighty placed a mark on each boy that only the angels could distinguish. They couldn't affect their freedom of will but could minister to them and arrange circumstances to keep both alive. That's all the mothers could hope for right now.

The bus ride proved to be the beginning of a new way of life for each one. Walter was going to run straight into the worst prejudice he'd ever imagined, and Joshua would have his morals and Christian values depleted. Upon arrival at the NYC bus depot, the three hugged and kissed goodbyes, promising to keep in touch.

Eva halted a taxi and asked to be taken to the YWCA. Little did she know the cabbie figured her as an easy mark and went several miles out of the way, diminishing what little funds she had? While checking in, she commented, "You certainly have a lot of rivers here, don't you?"

The little bald man behind the counter chuckled out loud. "Not you too!"

"What do you mean?" Handing her the receipt and key, he grinned.

"You've been shafted, my dear! The cabbie must have taken you in circles a few times because there's only one bridge between here and the depot!"

"I hope I have better luck finding a job." Eva felt stupid and angry as she gathered her belongings and got into the elevator, realizing just how alone and naive she really was. The room was small and dingy, and her view faced the back of a building. While she was unpacking, Fear tightened its spiteful grip. "What if I don't make it?" she wondered.

Startled by the phone, she ran to answer it. It was Mr. Beasley downstairs. "I have a job opportunity over at the dance hall if you want it."

"No, thanks. I'm going to be a model."

"Sure, kid!" he stated derisively. "That's what they all say. Remember, it's there when you need it!"

Boot Camp

Walt and Josh were horrified when reality hit in the first drill at Boot Camp. The sergeant in charge was a cross between Frankenstein and King Kong. Immediately, he had his digs into Walter. "Just because you got your freedom, boy, don't think you're going to get any promotion around here!"

"Yes, sir," he answered fearfully.

"Say it again!" the sergeant bellowed.

"Yes, sir!"

Much to Walt's relief but disgust, the sergeant had another whipping boy. "Epstein!" the commander shrieked. "We don't like little Jewish boys around here either. Got it?"

"Yes, sir!"

"You and the black boy go take a shower and scrub off some of your heritage," he hissed.

Joshua hurt for his friend as he watched the sergeant hand each of the boys a box of toilet cleaner. He remembered the day when Walt had saved his life in the pool and all the barbs he had endured over the years. "Stop it," he demanded. "Who do you think you are? You can't do that!"

"Yes I can. You'll find out fast enough. MP, arrest this man for insubordination."

Two military police stepped forward demanding, "Put your hands behind your back."

Hate darkened Joshua's heart and the ghouls stood ready to activate it. Placing handcuffs on him, the MPs took him away to a small cell. As the door locked behind him and the guards left, he sat in the darkness choked by the tears he struggled to contain. Only weeks ago, he was on top of the world with hopes and dreams. Now he was under arrest his first day in the Army.

Lunch hour came and went without a sign of anyone, and then Josh heard a door open and footsteps coming down the corridor.

"Thank God, they're coming to get me."

Epstein stood there with all his hair shaved and blood on his nose. "Evans, you're next for the haircut, military style," the MP jeered. "Then off to KP duty where you'll be for the next month."

A gloom settled into Joshua's spirit, a helplessness. Apprehensively, he followed him down the hall. "God, why are you doing this to me?" he whispered. His eyes watered. Even God, it seemed, had turned against him.

The month raced by quite fast, and the two boys were almost ready to be shipped overseas. Troops had already started to withdraw and there were high hopes the boys wouldn't have to go at all. Josh had put in to become a helicopter pilot. He wanted to help retrieve those coming home. If accepted, over the last two weeks he would be trained to fly the big machines.

The day came for the lieutenant to go over the applications. Joshua's was next in line and visible from the top of the pile.

Stirling, a striking and powerful angelic being sent to lead Joshua into his calling, appeared that morning to begin his task. With the window open, he turned around visibly in the material world for just a split second. The wind created blew Josh's paper into the trash. It would remain there and later be dumped and burned.

A malicious opponent appeared. "Who gave you the right to do that? He's fair game."

Stirling replied, "Did you see the mark on his heart."

"I see darkness, but no mark."

"Look again. He has a hedge around him in answer to his mother's prayer of protection to Jesus. To be a pilot now is too dangerous, and God has plans for this boy."

A week later Joshua felt lonely and gave Eva a call. "How's it going?" he inquired.

"Oh, Josh, hi! Everything's great."

"Did you find a job?"

"Yeah, and I'm making heaps of money!" she lied.

"I just called to say goodbye because Walter and I will be out of here in a couple of days." "Good luck. I hope God takes care of you."

Sitting at the foot of Eva's bed, a demon snickered. "That prayer didn't even get past the roof!" Reaching over with one of its tails, the ghoul excreted a fungus of depression.

Fear inside her increased its purpose. "I'm never going to make it here," she whimpered.

Unfortunately for Eva, it had been a depressing month. She went from one agency to another to begin her modeling career and they all said no. "I'm sorry, but you're not versatile enough. We can't afford to have your scar seen; and with the type of shots we need, there's no way around the problem."

The ever-present anger and hate for her mother surfaced and as she dwelt on it, a thought came to her mind. "You're eighteen, so you're of legal age. Why not go to a bar and have a relaxing drink?" It was a brilliant idea, and so she spent the next half hour getting all dolled up. After all, she never knew who might be there.

On her way out, Mr. Beasley called to her. "Where are you off to all decked out?" "I'm going to get a drink at a nearby club."

"Why not go over to the ballroom I told you about? There are plenty of guys and the drinks are cheap."

An ogre landed by her shoulder and issued a thought. "Go ahead. You'll enjoy it!"

"Okay!" Eva smiled, reaching for the address. The web was spun, and she was walking into it. This so-called ballroom was a hangout for hustlers and working girls on their beat. The enemy was ready to corner Eva like a fly in a silken trap.

When she arrived, her eyes drifted from face to face as she took in the leers sent her way. The club consisted of a counter with stools lining most of the room and a huge dance floor. Suspended from the ceiling hung two round balls of mirrored glass which dispersed hundreds of flickers of light in all directions. Eager to hear some good rock and roll, she was let down by some old geezer from her father's generation singing about moonlight on a river. An older looking man sporting a goatee strolled over. "Hi, doll! Can I buy you a drink?"

"Sure, why not?" she said flippantly.

He made eye contact with the bartender, confident he'd found his pigeon, who created a mixture bound to affect even the most experienced boozer.

Eva took the glass tentatively. As she took a sip, the liquid burned her throat. She turned hastily away so he wouldn't see the reaction on her face. Once she'd regained her composure, she asked, "What do you do?"

"I own this establishment and help new girls in town get started in different careers. Modeling is one that's close to my heart. You look like a model."

Eva's face lit up and she bravely took another sip. The ornery spirits in the room began chanting, calling up an increase of their loathsome intents. They knew Mr. Beasley had called and given the low-down on her, hoping to lure her into their plan.

As Eva finished the drink, she felt lightheaded, almost giddy. Her host winked at the bartender and asked, "How about a dance while my friend makes you another drink?" "Fine, but not so strong this time, okay?" "Sure, honey!" replied the villain behind the bar.

While they were dancing and her back was turned, he reached into his pocket and dropped a pill into the waiting drink. Even though Eva felt relaxed, she still had a hesitancy towards this man. God was initiating a warning, but she rationalized, "I'll be nice to him and see if he can help get my career going."

He certainly had a career in mind, but it wasn't the same one she did.

An hour later, Eva passed out. The patrons in the bar were used to seeing young girls carried out, and so with no resistance, the bar owner took her upstairs to a private bedroom. He quickly undressed Eva and then called to the barman through an intercom to send Casey up.

A muscular Negro appeared at the door and handed a camera to the owner while he proceeded to undress. He then crawled into bed with Eva and then assuming different positions, the camera clicked away, and each flash brought delight to the demons in the room.

Once the photography session was over, the men gathered together their blackmail equipment and left abruptly. It would be hours before Eva would wake up. They went to the front desk and exchanged some money for Eva's home address.

The hustle and bustle of the city began at it usual time and Eva awoke, startled by the loud traffic noise. Looking at the unfamiliar ceiling, she cried, "Oh, God, where am I?" Then she realized she was undressed. A deep sense of shame came over her. Had she had sex? How could you know? And how had she gotten here?

Suddenly, the man's face came back to her memory. Fear tightened its choking grip. "What if I had sex and now, I'm pregnant?" Fear gripped her even tighter. "What if there was more than one?" Fear stung her eyes. She felt so dirty and so used. "Where was Johnny?" she thought, "He's the one I'm saving myself for." Now she'd ruined everything. She saw her purse and the contents spilling over onto the floor. The wallet lay empty, her last fifty dollars gone.

While trying to wash away her guilt in a steaming hot shower, she contemplated calling her father and asking him for a ticket home. No, her own pride wouldn't let her do that. She had to make good, she had to prove herself.

Once she was on the sidewalk and the bright sunlight embraced her, Eva felt even more unclean. The clothes she had on made it obvious to those around her that she was a girl who stayed out all night. She could almost hear them saying it with their eyes.

Just then a jogger flew around the corner and bumped straight into her. As she retrieved her fallen purse, her eyes were drawn to a sign beside a soup kitchen. "Jesus Cares. Come and Have a Meal on Us."

She stood looking inside. It was empty except for a young man. She began thinking just how far away Jesus seemed. In fact, the name Jesus had little meaning for her.

With a crack, the doors flung open and the boy motioned her inside. "Come on in and have some eggs," he invited.

That was the best proposition she'd had in a while.

Eva sat quietly while the boy made breakfast. "My name is Trevor. What's yours?" The two made small talk while Eva inhaled the scrambled eggs and bacon. "We don't normally fix such a fancy breakfast, but I figured you would be used to this and a long way from mom's cooking."

Just the word 'mom' stirred the darkness in Eva's heart.

"My mom's dead, thank God," she retorted. Pushing her hair back, she pointed to the scar. "She cracked a lamp over my head, and they put her into a mental hospital." Trevor looked concerned. "Did she die there?"

"No, but she's never getting out so she might as well be dead. As far as I'm concerned, she already is."

"What did you do to make her so mad?"

"I got caught sneaking in my window late at night." The spirits in her were getting restless. They didn't want her getting too close to this guy.

Trevor sat next to her. "My mother's really dead, but she lives. She was a Christian, so I know she's with Jesus."

The demons winced. "I joined this group right after. That was two years ago."

"What's this organization called?"

"Reach Out."

Eva remembered Walt telling her about them. "Oh, yes, I've heard of them. A friend of mine told me about you."

Choosing his words carefully, Trevor asked, "When were you born again?"

"What's that?"

"When did you accept Jesus?" Trevor asked.

"Oh, I grew up in a church. I've always known about Jesus."

"Yes, but knowing about Him and knowing Him are two different things."

Fear inside her seethed and expanded, causing pressure on her spinal cord. Its stingers penetrated the nerves, depositing a residue. The poison seeped into her system and her response was fear that Jesus wouldn't love her either. She didn't want to get close only to be hurt again. The thought of being 'born again' sickened her. Once had been traumatic enough.

"Well, Trevor, I've gotta go!" Promptly, she retreated out the front door.

* * *

When she got back to the hotel, Mr. Beasley looked concerned. "Where have you been all night?" he demanded.

"I don't wanna talk about it," she sighed and slowly walked down the hall, entering the elevator.

Once in her room, the phone rang. "Miss Silverstone, the housemaid just quit. Do you wanna job?"

Fresh in her mind was the empty wallet and she replied. "I'll take it, but I can't start until tomorrow." Discouraged and disgruntled, she crawled into bed and eventually drifted off to sleep.

Chapter Twenty-Five
Beams of Light Shine in Darkness

Back home in Cambridge, the city was bustling over with winter just around the corner. The air was getting quite chilly and the sky was often grey. Second Birth Assembly had increased its members by a few, and Mary and Esther were still hanging in at Bethesda.

Larry Olson was caught between being a Christian and a Freeson member. The women had explained to him that he couldn't remain in the Lodge, which denied Jesus as the only way to God, and still grow as a Christian. There was a spiritual side to this compromise.

"Look, Larry," Patty remarked one day at their prayer meeting. "The Bible says you can't sit at the table of the Lord and partake with demons. We are trying to warn you that you're in something which has spiritual repercussions even if you can't see it."(1Cor 10:21)

Esther interrupted. "The situation is this, Patty. Larry's new job selling insurance is with the president of the local Lodge, so he can't really bite the hand that's feeding him."

The women understood and had compassion for him. Maybe God would let it slide for a while.

There was a knock at the door. Amanda went to open it and was taken aback to see Mayor Silverstone standing on the porch. The women had been praying for him regularly. What could he want?

Removing his hat and jacket, he was astonished to see Larry among six women. Especially as one of them was black.

After the introductions, Marvin stated his purpose for being there. "I'm running for reelection and just doing some home visitation. Are you all having a party here?"

"No, Marvin," Esther said. "This is a weekly prayer meeting. We've prayed for you many times."

"Thanks, but I hope it's for my re-election."

"Not quite!" Amanda chuckled. "It's for your salvation."

"Even though I don't get there too often, I've been a member of Bethesda for twenty years."

"So was I," said Larry.

"Me too," replied Esther. "But neither of us were Christians."

Marvin looked puzzled. Hadn't he heard this from her so many years before. "Ladies, what would you like to see done in Cambridge that I could do in trade for your votes? I'm sure you know a lot of people between you."

Amanda bluntly stated, "Take evolution out of the schools. I don't want it being taught to my grandchildren."

"I'm sorry, but that's a state matter. Anything else?"

Esther interjected. "I want the girlie magazines out of view in the stores. Better yet, take them out altogether."

Marvin thought to himself, "What did I come here for?" Hastily, he replied, "Esther, I'm sorry, but did you ever hear of freedom of speech? This country was founded on the fact that people can read or look at whatever they want. That's the law."

"Ten years ago, you'd never see those types of magazines out in plain view for any kid to see, and we had the same law then."

Amanda broke in. "Marvin, the morals of this country are deteriorating and you politicians are letting it happen. You're too lenient. We want it stopped."

Larry sat quietly, thinking of his own questionable literature at home. The Holy Spirit spoke to him. "And let no wicked thing be before your eyes in your own house."(Psalm 101:3)

Amanda's words also spoke to Marvin as he recalled his own stash under the bed.

Esther spoke up. "I want prayer back in schools."

"Ladies, that's a state law too."

"Are you mayor or not?" snapped Patty. "Did you try to prevent any of these laws from being passed? We want you to go to the governor and at least tell him. Then we'll vote for you."

"Okay, but it won't do any good."

"I hope you'll try," said Amanda. "God puts men in authority and also removes them." (Romans 13:1)

"Now, girls," Esther cut in, "You're starting to sound like a lynch mob. Marvin, we know you will do what you can to help bring Godly principles back to our town."

When the meeting ended, Larry stopped Esther outside the door. "How about having a cup of coffee with me?" Esther thought that maybe she could have some input in his life and agreed. "I'll meet you at Roxy's Restaurant."

Following behind her, Larry formed his words. "Esther, I'm attracted to you. No, I can't say that" he muttered. Esther felt like a schoolgirl. Surprised at her own flirtations, she wondered if this was such a good idea after all.

Nova saw the danger and grew in stature as he prepared to fight the aversions about to come. He released a verse into Esther's mind. "Flee youthful lusts." (2Tim 2:22) As Larry dwelt on the idea of knowing her more intimately, a slight darkness appeared in his heart. The Holy Spirit convicted him. "Be holy for I am holy." (1Peter1:16) Larry felt the warning and his desire dissipated. "You're right, Lord. I'm sorry." The darkness disappeared.

Esther thought of all the trials and rejection she was having with Sam. The thought of being held by Larry was tempting. She pictured him in her mind. "Yes, he certainly is handsome!"

Each time she thought of his face, an inviting warmth crept over her. She pictured him kissing her. Lust entered the car and sat beside her, confident of his reception. "Get rid of Sam, and you can have Larry," it snarled into her mind.

She imagined the two of them as one and the possibility of marriage. Then she thought of having Debbie as a daughter.

"Oh, Esther, stop this! You're getting carried away."

"You're also in sin," spoke the Holy Spirit.

Suddenly, she felt embarrassed, like a child caught with its hand in the cookie jar. "I'm sorry, Lord. Please do something about Sam."

"Like what?" was the answer?

Esther was surprised at God's response. "Like change him!" Fully expecting God to confirm He was changing him, the answer she received surprised her. "Can you praise me for him being the way he is?"

Esther went blank. She didn't want to answer the question. Grateful to have reached the restaurant, she purposely ignored God and joined Larry. "We'll go Dutch," she said, not wanting to be indebted to him.

"No, I can afford to buy you a cup of coffee," Larry said with a smile.

Nervously biting her lip, Esther squirmed, searching for something safe to talk about Larry stared lovingly into her green eyes and allowed himself to slowly become enticed. Lust stood by waiting, unable to intervene until the cue was given from Larry's heart.

"Larry, speaking of affordable things, this job which you have, can you afford to lose it if you quit the Lodge?"

"Not really. They're going to want to know why I'm getting out, so you tell me why I should quit."

"Think about the things you've heard at our meetings."

The Holy Spirit recalled the words to his mind, and he thought out loud how the Lodge believed 'all roads lead to the same God.'

Esther slowly sipped her coffee. "What does that tell you?" "They're liberal," he said trying to make light of it.

"No, they're in deception."

Lust shivered and shrieked in the spirit realm. A call recognized by the demons that more comrades were needed. In an instant two more appeared. Both immense in size and looking half-man, half-beast. Their skin was sleek and smooth, almost wine colored. Their faces resembled owls, with eyes citron yellow glistening across the atmosphere. Antichrist and Deception demanded to know what was going on. Lust brought them up to date so they could join forces. Nova waited expectantly by Esther's side, summoning her to use her authority to silence the enemy's works in the room. "'Larry, Jesus said, 'I am the way to the Father, no one goes to Him except through Me'." John 14:6

The waitress sidled up to the table. "Want some more coffee?" she asked.

"He looks like a big tipper, be friendly," she thought to herself.

While the waitress made small talk, Nova counter-reacted the situation by reminding Esther she should bind the demons.

Esther thought, "What do demons have to do with it? Larry's saved."

"You don't understand. Just do it."

She prayed, asking God's presence to be over them, and in the name of Jesus she silenced any demon trying to interfere.

Nova became fluorescent, while Esther's prayers released flutters of light heavenward. In an instant they returned, strong and fast, ricocheting off the mighty angel's chest. Like darts, they were fired straight into the demons. Faster and faster, they came until the creatures couldn't repel them anymore; and with a squeal they disintegrated.

The Holy Spirit brought to Esther's mind, "There is one mediator between man and God, that is Christ Jesus" (1 Timothy 2:5) she quoted it to Larry.

Cronan laid hands-on Larry and brought clarity to his thoughts. "No wonder my prayers haven't been getting through. I've been praying to Virgin Mary."

Looking perplexed, Esther asked, "Where did you learn to pray to her? Certainly not at Bethesda."

"I learned it at the Lodge. One of the members is a priest from Ruxton, and he says it's better to ask her and she'll ask Jesus and then He'll ask God. After all, Jesus turned the water into wine for Mary when originally He hadn't planned on doing any miracles."

Esther put down her mug. "I rest my case. Can't you see the deception? We've got to get you out of that Lodge."

"I know," Larry said a bit dejected.

"Go home and read Colossians 2:9-10, and then I'll see you in church on Sunday."

Right then Larry felt so peaceful he was ready and willing.

The two parted with a handshake and then went their separate ways. A ghoul of deception followed Esther home. As she sang praises to God in the car, beams of light rose to heaven and the angelic host reformed them as mighty arrows of truth, piercing the demonic spirit's intentions and causing it to shrivel.

Realizing it could not win in this situation, the demon halted in its dimension allowing the car to continue while it darted ahead to wait for her at home.

Nova wondered what Deception was planning and sped to ask the King. "Lord, have you given Deception permission to do something to Esther?"

The heavens thundered as the Lord God Almighty declared, "She's beginning to crumble. This test will show what she really has in her heart. I've told her to praise Me for the way Sam is. Now the demon will challenge this."

Esther walked in the door to find the television blaring and little Sam Jr. lying asleep on the floor. Her husband was nowhere in sight.

Clicking off the set, she gently woke Sam Jr. "Where's Dad, honey? Is he home yet?"

"I dunno," he lied, knowing full well his father was upstairs.

"Did you do your homework?"

"Yes," he lied again. "Mom, I wanna stay home tomorrow. I feel sick," he lied once more.

"Sure, sweetheart. I'll call the school in the morning."

Assuming she was on her own again for the night, Esther went to the den feeling anticipation in her heart to hear from God. Conviction for her actions that day came over her. The Holy Spirit reminded her that she was to praise Him for Sam.

"That's a tall order, but I'll try."

As Esther closed her eyes, a brightness seemed to come into the room. She thought it must be the Lord again, but unlike before, a fearfulness enshrouded her, almost as a warning. Deception was manifesting into an angel of light.

Nova stood to watch as a witness in the hope that Esther would try the spirit as the Bible teaches. (1John4:1)

"Esther," a voice whispered. Opening her eyes, she took in the gleaming form of a striking man-like creature. His skin was like polished porcelain. He had high cheek bones and piercing violet eyes which seemed to look straight through her. Standing at attention only a few feet from her, she took in his features, mesmerized by the glow emanating from his being. She was consumed by it. It was intoxicating.

"Esther, Larry's the one for you," it whispered enticingly. "Larry needs you. I'll take care of Sam Jr. and Sam myself. They'll find the Lord quicker that way."

In an instant, the room was dark, the visitor had gone. Outside the house, rain poured down from the sky. Suddenly, there was a crack of lightning that lit the room and then a thunderous boom split the air. "Okay, God. Thank you for revealing that to me."

Deception looked at Nova, ridicule in his eyes. Dispelling a diabolical guffaw, he disappeared, leaving a noxious mist which settled on Esther's head. Its deception seeped into her mind and took root. She would easily accept this because she wanted it.

Over the ensuing days a critical spirit followed Esther around the house. Every time she looked at Sam the demon slung negative thoughts into her mind to help extinguish what love was left for him. The critical demon could be most effective, human nature being what it is and our human heart so evil. (Gen 6:5)

It didn't take long until Esther developed the habit of being critical. The demon had done its job and departed.

As Esther received the negative notions, her once soft heart grew harder; and she found herself picking on Sam Jr. as her personality embraced the poison.

One afternoon while cleaning his room, Esther came across a skateboard hidden in his closet. Waiting for him to come home, she let her anger simmer but when Sammy, Jr. walked through the door, she exploded. "How dare you ride that skateboard after what happened to you! You know I've forbidden you. Why, Sammy? You promised me you wouldn't." Sam Jr. was becoming quite the liar.

Defiantly, he declared, "I had my fingers crossed so it didn't count."

"Don't you understand that is the same as lying? In fact, you've been lying a lot lately. Go to your room and stay there until dinner."

Looking smug, he walked away without a word, thinking how glad he'd be when he left school so he could move away with no one telling him what to do. Very common in kids his age.

Larry's Lodge night came, and he was mustering up the courage to withdraw his membership. Right now, pleasing Esther and God, in that order, seemed the best thing to do. President Tonkin came over and greeted him. "Larry, we have a surprise for you. We're moving you up in the organization. It's very prestigious and at this level, we all agree to buy each other's products exclusively. It's advantageous to you because you'll get some good commissions on those insurance policies you sell.

The thought of the extra money was tempting so thoughts of leaving were shelved for the moment. "We're going to have our initiation time upstairs in ten minutes. It's now or never."

The men filed into the elevator and Larry stood deep in thought. Esther's words came back to him. "We've gotta get you out of there." Deception stood nearby. "Just do it for a little while, then you can leave."

"That sounds good," Larry thought so he turned and followed the men.

Arranging them in a semi-circle, the Grandmaster stood forward and donned a special hat. It seemed to be a hood with holes cut out for his eyes and mouth. He handed one to Larry, indicating he was to put it on. Larry felt uneasy. The Holy Spirit spoke to his heart. "No! Don't do it!"

Larry cast his gaze over the men looking at him. The pressure was on. Sheriff Beam sneered, "Come on. Don't be a prude." The men laughed. Succumbing to the jeers, he pulled the hood over his face, unaware that sewn in the back in gold thread were words of blasphemy against the Holy Spirit. It was written in Latin so only the Leaders knew what it said.

"Now repeat after me," the sheriff said. "I, Larry Olson, swear by the gods …"

"The what?" Larry asked.

"Just say it!"

"I, Larry Olson, swear by God." "No!" snapped Beam. "By the gods!"

Suddenly, Larry felt sick, almost faint. He knew this was wrong. Conflicting thoughts penetrated his mind. Coward! Don't do this! Don't! Don't!

Beams' voice broke the confusion. "Just say it, Larry."

With a stammering voice, he whispered. "I swear by the gods I will not share the Lodge's motto." He then stated the words written on the back of the hood, unaware of the repercussions those words would have on him spiritually. "<u>Sesincerd Contigo Niso</u>" means "To thine own self be true"

Antichrist stood proudly and defiantly, surveying his unwitting servants eagerly carrying out his plans. He resembled a man in his stance yet had hooves instead of feet and a head like a goat. This spirit had had access to Larry ever since his involvement in the Lodge and now because he didn't renounce this involvement, it had a legal right to remain and block his walk with God.

Chapter Twenty-six
Cupid Is Busy

At the ladies' weekly meeting, their previous unexpected guest returned. After all the greetings, Marvin stated his reason for coming. "I've thought of what you said last month about how God appoints leaders and removes them. (Dan 2:21) I realized the other day that even though I'm a Christian, God hasn't been part of my life. Everything I do, I do for what seems best at the time."

Amanda spoke up. "Marvin, who told you you're a Christian?"

"I believe in God."

The ladies looked at each other and Patty chuckled. "I used to talk just like you." The Holy Spirit spoke to Esther. "Now is not the time."

"Mayor, how's your position against the display of magazines going?" she asked.

"I sent out letters to the shops that carry them and asked for them to keep them behind the counter out of public view. My secretary followed up with phone calls, and they've all agreed."

"We don't want them at all!" Patty retorted.

"Ladies, this is a start. There are men who enjoy that kind of thing. It adds spice to their marriages."

Abruptly, Patty put her glass down. "Hogwash, Marvin. It adds to the men's sin. It does nothing for the marriage."

"Incidentally," Esther added, "we have a speaker this Sunday who's talking about God's laws in romance. Why not come."

"That sure sounds different. Maybe I will."

The next Saturday night, Marvin's house was full of little visitors. Crass little creatures cruised in and out, trying to persuade him not to go to church in the morning. One angel had been commissioned to watch over him for the night. Its purpose was to ward off a badger of poisonous missiles.

Embracing an impulse to find a Bible, Marvin's eyes roamed the bookshelves. "Do we even have one?" he wondered. "Yes, there it is," he stated aloud, taking it from the shelf. It was a new paraphrased version which someone had left on the doorstep only a few months before.

Sitting in his lazy-boy chair, he was uncertain of what to do. "Where do I start?" He glanced at the words in gold lettering which read 'The Living Bible'.

"What does Living mean?"

Instantly, an unclean spirit released into his mind his latest issue of 'MISS' magazine stashed under his bed. Suddenly, he didn't want to talk to God; and laying the Bible on the table, he went to make himself a drink. The angel was struck with a light shaft. Someone had prayed, and the bolt ricocheted off his shield and made direct contact with the unclean resident. The prayers had bound the enemy in Marvin's house and the demon temporarily froze.

The Holy Spirit spoke to Marvin. "Open the Bible!" The gentle persuasion compelled him to leave his drink behind and return to his seat. "Now just read." The voice seemed to resound in the room and Marvin quickly turned to see where it had come from.

In obedience to the command, he opened the book near the end looking at the title, Ephesians. He could hardly pronounce it. The words leaped off the page into his spirit, and immediately he knew what God was saying to him. "But when you expose them, the light shines in upon their sin and shows it up, and when they see how wrong they are some of them may even become children of light" (Eph 5:13)

Marvin sat in disbelief. The words had pierced his heart. God was telling him to come against the evil of perverted literature. As if supernaturally led, Marvin went to his room and got out his latest issue. He flipped through the pages admiring the beautiful girls with perfect figures.

"This isn't so bad," he thought. Darkness gave way and birthed a supernatural cue. The unclean spirit appeared next to him and signaled Lust already resident in Marvin. They enfold tentacles and choked out the word he'd received. Marvin retrieved his drink, and the next morning he was too hung over to go to church. The demons had succeeded, but the Lord wouldn't be swayed.

Something malicious was coming Marvin's way but would become a catalyst to help push back the degrading values and mocking of God's word in Cambridge.

The next day Marvin was back to his usual shenanigans in business and promising favors to those who would vote for him as Mayor. The election was only a week away and an envelope arriving at his office could cancel his chance of winning.

"Excuse me, sir. This just came for you," his secretary stated, handing him a large envelope.

As she went out the door, he followed her with his eyes and picking up his opener he smoothly slit the corner of the envelope, his mind still on the girl. Spying the handwritten message, "Photos - Do Not Bend" and no stamp or return address, his attention turned to one of curiosity. Who could this be from?

Nausea gripped him as he gazed at pictures of his daughter's form being embraced by a black man. They appeared to be making love. "This Will Do Wonders For Your Career" was pasted in untidy cut out letters on a separate sheet.

Just then the phone rang and Marvin jumped. It was Larry Olson. "Hey, we missed you at church yesterday." Marvin didn't respond.

"Hello? Marvin? Are you there?"

"Yeah, I'm here."

"What's the matter? Cat got your tongue?"

"Larry, listen. I can't talk now. Can I meet you after dinner at my house?"

Larry noticed the quiver in his voice. "Is something wrong?"

"I don't want to discuss it on the phone. I'll tell you tonight."

It occurred to Larry, this would give him an excuse to call Esther. He could ask her to pray for Marvin and his meeting with him.

At the sound of his voice, butterflies fluttered in Esther's stomach. Deception smirked viciously.

"Esther, something's happened to Marvin and he wants to meet with me later. He sounded worried so I thought you and I could pray together first before I go."

Do you mean over the phone?"

Larry pondered that for a second. He so much wanted to be near her, to see her and touch her.

Before he could answer, the words leaped in his spirit. "Lead me not into temptation but deliver me from evil." (Matt 6:13) Pushing the warning aside, he justified it, remembering that where there were two gathered in His name, the Lord is in the midst of them. (Matt 18:20) "No, I think we should meet in person."

"Okay," Esther replied. "You can come over here."

"What about Sam?"

Nova whispered to Esther. "What about avoiding all appearances of evil?" (1 Thess 5:22)

She felt confused. Thinking for a second, she rationalized that Larry and she were meant for each other so there was nothing to feel guilty about. "It's okay. Sam's at the track."

When she hung up the phone, Nova shook his head in disappointment. The Holy Spirit came upon her. "Thou shalt not commit adultery." (Ex 20:14)

"God, is that You? Make up your mind. Can I have him or not?" Deception expanded in size and circled vigorously around her, stirring up her emotions to cause a counterfeit peace. "It feels right when I'm with him," she said aloud. Deception cackled with self-satisfaction.

Hurrying to get changed and put something attractive on, Esther felt like a teenager. It was a wonderful sensation to feel young again and to have a reason to look feminine. She missed being admired as a woman.

✱ ✱ ✱

By the time Larry arrived, she was in an emotional tizzy. She'd let her feelings, desires and fantasies play havoc with her heart and was ready to fall into Larry's arms as soon as he walked in the door. She was radiant and Larry absorbed it, stating, "You look beautiful."

As their eyes met. They both crossed a barrier, that attraction that comes from desiring someone for yourself. They had both committed adulteries in their hearts.

At the racetrack Sam won some but lost most of his money. On his way out, he noticed a pamphlet tucked under his windshield wiper. It was a leaflet that read "A New Life for You." Sam knew it was about God and started automatically to crumple it in his hand. An angel came by his side and whispered, "Open it." Sam obeyed the command and read, "God has a miracle waiting for you."

The words spoke to his heart and came alive, cutting deep into his spirit. "God," Sam choked back the tears. "If you can give me a job, a purpose, I'll believe. I'm so bored with my life and my family. I want a new chance, a new life."

While he drove home, he hummed a song he'd heard Esther sing often. "This is the day that the Lord has made." (Psalm118:24)

After several stops in traffic jams, Sam turned to corner to Sherman Way. He spotted Larry's car parked outside and assumed a Bible study or something would be taking place inside.

A demon flew by. "Sneak in the back door." It was just enough ammunition to get Sam's thought stirring; and so, he parked down the road and crept in the back, quietly skulking into the kitchen.

On the sofa the two had just begun to pray. Larry gently reached for Esther's hand as he'd seen done in other prayer meetings but his time it didn't help them to unite their prayers or purpose. Instead, it stirred up their flesh.

The Lord spoke to his spirit. "This is wrong!"

Esther's heart raced and her skin tingled as she felt his strong hand resting in hers.

As Larry prayed for Marvin, she opened her eyes and watched him. His innocence in the things of God, his humble spirit and gentle manner, touched her.

She gazed upon his dark eyelashes, so long and intriguing. Her eyes travelled down to his lips, taking in their perfect shape and velvety texture. His soft, clean-shaven face, with only the hint of a wrinkle to mar the surface, added character to his features.

Lust was birthed in her heart and the demon didn't have to touch her, but instead spat a verse into her thoughts. "Do not be unevenly yoked." (2 Cor 6:14) And then added the line Deception had told her. "Larry's the one for you."

Yes, it seemed right. She was unevenly yoked to Sam.

With these thoughts dancing through her mind, she hadn't noticed that Larry had finished praying. He looked up and their eyes met.

The physical sensations emanating from each of them cause Larry to automatically respond to the desire in her eyes and he gently leaned forward and kissed her waiting lips tenderly. She couldn't suppress a small moan. This was what she'd dreamed of. She also didn't hear Sam come in the back door.

Alarm beds rang in both Larry and Esther, but the draw was too strong. Their hands unclasped and sensuously they embraced.

Like a wounded bull, Sam flew into a rage. Slamming the door into the wall, the vibration knocking a china dish off the mantle. The crash startled Larry and Esther, causing them to separate abruptly.

Anger entered Sam as his heart was charcoal black from the sin he had entangled himself in. Grabbing a marble and gold bookend as the demon let off its force, Sam responded by bringing it down full force on Larry's head. He threw the off ending article to the other side of the room as Esther tried to take it from him and then he grabbed her by the throat, choking her with supernatural strength.

Esther attempted to scream but couldn't. Her breath was being cut off. Fear gripped her and she cried out to God in her heart. Beacons of light flashed towards heaven and angels were released to come to her rescue. Three huge cherubs appeared and commanded the demon to release Sam. As they vanished, he came to his senses and realized his hands were around Esther's throat. Repulsed and bewildered, he shoved her away and then noticed Larry lying with blood all over his face. Esther ran to Larry and cradled his head in her lap, moaning. "Larry, darling! What has he done to you?" There was no response.

Sam Jr. came in the front door and as soon as he saw Larry, sped across to Mary's house. Screaming, "Help! Come quickly!" he frantically raced inside.

Mary came rushing down the stairs. "Sam Jr., what's the matter?"

"Dad's had a fight with Mr. Olson and he's bleeding from his head. Quick, call an ambulance."

While dialing emergency, Mary sent up a prayer. "Lord, please help Larry." But it was too late.

Within ten minutes the ambulance and police had arrived. One young officer escorted Sam into the kitchen and another sat on the couch with Esther, observing the marks on her neck and waiting for her explanation. She was sobbing and not making much sense.

The ambulance attendant felt for Larry's pulse and then looked at the policeman and slowly shook his head. Esther caught the look and wailed, "No! Not Larry! He can't be dead. God, don't let him be dead."

Unable to pacify her, the policeman realized by her reaction there was more to this than a disagreement. He'd seen enough cases in his time to recognize a crime of passion.

Eventually, Esther calmed down and then stared blankly, unwilling to believe that her husband had killed someone. And her one chance for happiness had just been killed.

She spied Mary and rushed to her, sobbing hysterically. "It's all my fault. God will never forgive me."

While the two ladies wept, the forensic men began to snap their photos of the prostrate form. Then the ambulance attendant lifted Larry's body onto the stretcher and slowly covered his face with a white cloth.

When the rescue squad carried Larry's body out, the reality hit both ladies. They went silent with mixed thoughts. Here was the man they had prayed so hard for and so long for him to know Jesus, the man who had folded his hands like a little boy and had asked Jesus to come into his life. The man they had nurtured and, as a baby Christian, they had watched him grow. Now in a moment's madness, his life had been snuffed out; and he would never know the joy of growing in the Lord.

Esther felt nauseous and asked to be excused. She went upstairs to her bedroom and knelt by the bed. Her memory was jogged, and she remembered the night Sam had come home with lipstick on his sleeve. Now here she was feeling so dirty and so wicked for much the same sin. Anger rose in her heart.

She fell across the bed and slammed her fists into her pillow. "How could you do this, God? You said Larry was right for me, and now You've taken him away. Sam was supposed to get saved, and now I hope he rots in hell!" The vileness spewed from her mouth, and her heart grew dark.

Recognizing their opportunity, the evil forces grouped together, eager to inflict more sin to her heartache. Esther's anguish was interrupted by a knock at the door. She turned to see Sam standing there handcuffed to a policeman with his eyes red from crying.

Her first impulse was to run to him and apologize, but she stood her ground, determined he would pay for what he'd put her through. It was easier to hate him.

The officer broke through her thoughts. "Excuse me, ma'am, we're taking your husband to the station now."

A tear trickled down Sam's face, and he brushed it off on his shoulder. "This is what I get for praying! I should have known better."

As all the visitors left, the house was still. Esther's eyes were drawn to a pack of Sam's cigarettes; and without any thought she lit one, her first in almost ten years. It was comforting, more comforting than prayer. Nova gave a sigh and his eyes pleaded into the heavens, indicating to the Watchers that he was sad, very sad.

At the funeral four days later, Esther was about to receive some startling news. Debbie walked over to her standing by the open casket. She looked down at her father lying lifeless, yet his face still seemed as handsome as always.

She bent over and kissed him lightly on the forehead. As her lips touched him, the coldness startled her. Even though they'd had their ups and downs, Larry was all that she'd had, but now he was gone.

Into her mind came the words she'd yelled at him so many years ago. "I hope you die!" Guilt consumed her and she struggled to hold back the tears. Esther gently reached over and slipped her arm around Debbie's waist.

Debbie stared at her. "You know," she stated, "he was attracted to you from the first day you met. He saw qualities in you that made him want to know you better. Right or wrong, you brought a ray of sunshine into the life of a man who had no vision or purpose."

Esther sighed deeply and wiped her eyes. "Debbie, is there anything I can do for you?"

"Mrs. Evans, there's something I need to tell you."

Seeing the anguish on her face, Esther questioned, "What is it, Debbie?"

"Have you heard from Joshua?"

"All I know is his Boot Camp ended, and he's someplace in Saigon helping to evacuate soldiers."

Looking uneasily at Esther and wondering how she'd take the news, Debbie mumbled, "I'm pregnant and Josh is the father."

Suddenly, Esther felt compassion for this girl who was carrying her grandchild. She embraced her in a hug and replied, "Honey, we'll take care of you and the baby. Don't worry."

Esther walked over to the large room at the funeral parlor where many of the Freeson members were standing. The men stared. She knew they knew the truth behind Larry's death. Her Christian witness was lost, so feeling condemned and useless, she went and made herself a bourbon and downed it in one swallow.

The demon of heaviness stood nearby. It would have plenty of opportunities to attach itself to her if her shield of faith continued to deteriorate.

The court case was very messy. Even the Christian women who had been so close to Esther were shaken by what they felt was treason. For Esther to entice a baby Christian brother was inconceivable.

Amanda was quite blunt. "I'm ashamed of you, Esther!" she reprimanded her outside the courtroom. "Your husband's going to spend life in jail, and all the work we've done in town for the Lord has been ruined because of you."

Naturally, Esther tried defending herself and her emotions, so instead of receiving the rejection from her good friend, she hardened her heart and allowed bitterness a small place. Despair stood by with Heaviness and Suicide kept a watchful eye for its chance.

Over the next few weeks, Esther began to succumb to the loneliness in the house. Sitting in bed one night, a thought came to her. "Call Amanda and ask to be reinstated."

"God, was that you?" Waiting in the darkness, Esther pictured making the call and then she could see Amanda hanging up on her.

"No! I don't want to give her the chance to do that. I'll write instead."

The Lord quickened to her. "No. Call her." Putting pen to paper, she ignored the prompting and began to explain how the emptiness in her life and lack of direction had helped add to her need for Larry. She explained about the angel and how it had assured her Larry was the one.

Esther now questioned whether it had been an angel of the Lord at all.

A gnawing, emotional scar was slowly being brought to the surface.

Rejection, so deep in her inner man, had opened the way for her to be deceived. Now that same rejection was keeping her from God's love and forgiveness as well as her closest friends.

Optimistically, Esther posted the letter at the post office the next day and then sat in front of the television for the rest of the afternoon. Bored with her life now, the only relief was when Sam Jr. came home from school each afternoon. At least then she felt useful for something. She looked forward to hearing from Amanda. She missed her friends so much.

That afternoon while the mail was being sorted down at the post office, Mr. Jackson the postmaster, had just lit up a cigarette when the phone rang. He placed the cigarette into the ashtray and went to answer it. Just then a gust of wind flipped the cigarette into the tray with Esther's letter lying on top where it smoldered, slowly obliterating the address.

When he returned to his desk, he saw the damage to the letter and selfishly tossed it into the wastebasket. "Who'll know?" he thought. "I can't risk losing my job."

The trial was quick, and Sam got life. Esther back slid and did nothing to encourage Sam Jr. to be a Christian. Debbie had a girl she named Lilly which Esther took care of while Debbie finished 12th grade and then got a job at a pizza place.

CHAPTER TWENTY-SEVEN
SHAKE WHAT CAN BE SHAKEN

Both Joshua and Walter were weary after their long stints in the Army. Most of the troops had been withdrawn, and the boys were counting the days until they could go home. Joshua was aware that he had a daughter named Lilly from his rendezvous with Debbie. Going by the picture, she was very tiny because she'd been born premature but still had fully formed features with reddish wispy hair and green eyes like his.

Whether he would marry Debbie was beyond his reasoning now, for even though the war was fading out, according to the press, Joshua knew daily in the village where they were stationed anything could happen.

Near the end of their field mission, Joshua's group entered a village several miles from base. The people lay motionless all over the dirt road. No animals, no children, no indication of life.

The sergeant eyed a small shack with its door ajar. "Private Evans, go and see what's inside!"

Obeying, Josh carefully crept towards the old building when suddenly the Holy Spirit spoke. "Don't go in there."

It was so fast, quick and strong, Josh couldn't ignore it and he stopped, then turned back towards the group.

"What are you doing?" the sergeant whispered fiercely.

"I can't go in there."

"Why the hell not?" The veins on the sergeant's forehead stood out. "God just told me not to."

"Oh, really? Well, I'm God around here and I'm telling you to go!"

"No, sir. I won't," Josh argued, remembering what Esther had said about how God speaks quickly and sharply.

The sergeant abruptly turned towards Epstein and commanded him to go in Josh's place. He glared at Josh. "I'll deal with you later."

Hesitantly, Epstein entered the shack while the others lay hidden on the lookout for any movement.

Without warning the building exploded into flames and Epstein, totally engulfed in fire, ran outside and threw himself on the ground. He rolled frantically, trying to smother the fire, screaming with every turn until at last all was still. It was over. Josh turned away as tears filled his eyes, realizing that would have been him if God hadn't warned him.

When they returned to their base, the men withdrew into themselves. It had been a horrible incident. The softness and innocence had long been crushed in Josh. His whole personality was changed as he had been severely wounded in his emotions. The last straw came the next day .

The compassion which had been placed in Josh's heart by the Lord had been put to good use in assisting the villagers. He helped them in many practical ways in farming and health care, teaching the children and even playing games with them.

After months of gaining the trust of the villagers, the commander suddenly went crazy and a horrific tragedy took place. When the word was given for them to pull out, the commander and some others began a wild killing spree, raping the young girls and setting fire to their homes. The shock of it turned his compassion to anger; and without thinking, Josh grabbed one of the soldiers and beat him senseless.

As Josh ran from the ugly scene, a young Vietnamese boy with a bayonet stopped him short by shoving the lethal blade into his leg. The child's eyes radiated pure, unadulterated hate. Josh knew the boy would kill him just to get even.

"Joe! Traitor!" the boy sneered at him.

"No! Not me! I didn't set the fires!"

Josh slowly reached for his wallet. He had no money because cash wasn't issued to the soldiers, but the boy didn't know that. Carefully, he slipped out the picture of Lilly and made like he was cradling a baby. "Please, I want to see my little girl."

The boy shoved the blade deeper in his leg and Josh reeled backwards to the ground. With an evil look on his face, the child cocked the gun and repeated, "Joe! Traitor!"

Stirling appeared by his side, an immovable force ready to call the hosts of heaven, bringing to Josh a word in due season. "Ask God to help you."

Instantly, Josh remembered the day his mother had reached for his hand and the two had prayed, asking Jesus to help them.

"Jesus!" Josh called. "If You'll save me, I'll do whatever You want. Please let me live to see Lilly."

Myriads of light ricocheted from Sterling's chest like arrows darting in all directions. Several hit the boy and the hatred in him was rendered powerless. In response, the boy dropped the gun and retreated into the field.

Gunfire echoed around him, but Josh was so full of gratitude he lay there and thanked God for sparing his life while tears streamed down his face. "Jesus, I know I've grown away from You over the years, but this day I give You, my life. I thank you for a new chance. I'm sorry for the resentment I had towards You for letting me get drafted; and when I get home, I'll marry Debbie and raise Lilly to know you too."

The angelic watchers cheered with joy and praised the Lord, the God of all heaven and earth. Josh had been born again. (John 1:12) God took out his heart of stone and replaced it with a new soft and clean one. He put his sins as far as east is from west; and marking him for ownership, God placed

His Spirit inside. To them who received Him, He gave the right to be called the children of God. (John 1:2)

One hundred miles away, Walter was about to walk into what could seem to be his worst nightmare, but God would ensure it turned out for good. The division he was with was rounding up and finishing their assignment. Explosives went off all around the areas; and as Walt was running for cover, he stepped on a snake which turned and bit him. He saw the men in the distance piling into the truck and then begin to pull away. His call went unheard.

The faster he ran, the more the poison was pumped throughout his bloodstream. Stupefied from the toxin, he stumbled and fell down a hill, breaking his leg when he smashed into a large boulder. Laying there in the rain, he heard the truck fading in the distance, oblivious to his cries for help.

Hours later, as darkness crept over the earth, fear paralyzed him. Delirious from the poison still in his system, Walt cried out to the only one who could help him. "Please, God, help me!"

Regal noticed the flicker of light evident in Walt's heart as he pleaded to God. He grew brighter and brighter. All of the praises sent up for Walt now could be released. Beacons of light showered the patch of ground he lay on the seargent back at base had a thought. "One of your men is missing and he's still alive."

Walt's face came into his mind and compulsively he beckoned to two soldiers, telling them to go back to the place where they'd last seen Private Smith. Once there, the soldiers were guided by a heavenly messenger to Walt's body lying unconscious in the dark.

Immediately, he was flown to Saigon for treatment and then a week later transferred to an Army hospital in Tokyo where he would spend the next few weeks recuperating before being honorably discharged.

The days passed peacefully, and Walt was becoming increasingly bored. One day a group of missionaries came to visit the men in the hospital and perform some songs and dramatic Christian plays.

Walt lay there watching as different thoughts went through his mind. His own belief in God had disappeared so many years before, and the death of his father had caused a mistrust in God's goodness and character. He also had resentment towards God that his plans to race cars had been snuffed out in lieu of the Army.

"Your life was almost snuffed out too!" reminded Regal.

Walt had been given a pair of crutches and so he was able to walk around. The team invited him to the main dining hall where they would be having a special banquet paid for by church donations. Anger, which had been in Walt for so many years, released its toxins; and Walt declined their offer, preferring to lie in bed watching television.

Regal gazed towards heaven. God's plans for his life were about to be thwarted if he didn't go to the banquet. But how could Regal maneuver him there without breaking his will?

Strategically landing on the roof, the magnificent angelic entity raised his gossamer wing and delicately tapped the television antenna, sending it hurling to the ground, then returned to monitor his charge's reaction.

The picture blurred and Walt snapped, "Oh, great! That's all I need!" He lay there for a few moments while the sound of laughter drifted up from the dining hall. Grabbing his crutches, he muttered to himself, "I might as well go to the banquet. There's nothing better to do now."

Sitting as politely as possible, he made small talk with the missionaries. Walt was stunned when the guest singer turned out to be the beautiful girl in the red dress, the one he'd dreamed about for so long. He studied her beauty while she sang *How Great Thou Art* and felt the same flicker of love welling up inside that he'd felt the first time he'd seen her.

As she was singing, she noticed Walt and her face lit up. She inclined her head in welcome. Overwhelmed by her response, he grinned, a feeling of acceptance rising in his heart. This was the girl his father had saved during the church fire.

When the girl finished her number, she came directly to his table and patted him on the shoulder. "What a surprise! I'm so glad you're safe. I've been praying for you."

Shocked, he exclaimed, "How do you know me? And what in the world are you doing in Japan?"

"Do you remember that day in church?"

Walt cut her off. "Wait a minute. What's your name?"

"I'm Tanya and my father is Edward Frazer. He told me his protégé had been drafted, and I knew he was talking about you by the description he gave. Anyway, do you remember that day when you came to my church in Ruxton and then left so abruptly?"

"How did you know I was there?"

"The Lord spoke to me as you darted out the door. He told me that I'd see you again and that I was to pray for you."

"That's amazing because I wanted to meet you."

"Now you have," she said, grinning.

"Yeah, but I wanted to take you to the prom."

Tanya slowly sipped her tea. "There'll be more opportunities like that."

Walt glanced at his watch. "I'd better go back to my room. The head nurse is a tyrant, and she'll have me for breakfast if I don't get back in time for lights out. Then in a few days I'm being shipped back to the States, so I won't get a chance to see you again. When will you be back there?"

The smile left her face, and she sat deep in thought. 'Do you remember what the minister said that day about Japan?'

He thought for a second, then shook his head. "No."

"He said that God was calling two people to bring the Gospel to the Buddhists in Japan."

Walt's face beamed. "You mean you and me together?"

"Who else is here from Ruxton?" She eyed him smugly.

Regal stood behind Walt and laid his hand on Walt's shoulder. "She's yours, Walt, if you serve the Lord."

"Tanya." Walt asked nervously. "Would you come back with me to Cambridge and raise a family? I wanna race cars, and I know it would be an exciting life for us. I'd be a good provider."

She fidgeted with her earring then looked seriously at him. First of all, Walt, God is my provider. He also spared my life years ago in a church fire, and I promised I'd serve Him wherever He took me."

Tears came to Walt's eyes as he realized Tanya had indeed been spared and God was now bringing them together.

"Tanya, how did you get out of the fire?"

With compassion filling her heart, she slowly responded. "Your father. I knew he died saving me; and I told God that I would pray you into salvation so when you died you could go and be with him."

Suddenly, the room filled with noise as the crowd started leaving and the organizers signaled for Tanya to join them. She slipped her phone number to Walt and added, "God has told me you will be my husband, but only if we stay here and serve Him as He planned for us. We have to be in His will if we want the marriage to work."

With a loving smile, she disappeared into the crowd, leaving Walt sitting there, thoughts crowding his mind and Regal there to help him.

Across the world in New York City, Eva struggled to find her niche. She'd been from one job to another and never seemed content. The big break in the modeling world didn't come for her; and over the past couple of years her heart had grown cold as she endured city life. Marvin had paid off the bar owner for the pictures of her supposed sexual encounter and had tried unsuccessfully to woo her home.

One hot summer night she decided to go for ice cream; and when she entered the restaurant, her eyes fell on Trevor, the guy from the soup kitchen. She hadn't seen him since that day. Sliding into the booth next to him, Eva exclaimed, "What a nice surprise! How have you been?"

"Hi, Eva. I'm fine. It's great to see you."

"I can't believe you remember my name."

"I've been praying for you all this time."

"You can't be praying hard enough because I've had a lousy time here in New York."

He ordered two sundaes from the waitress and reached over and took Eva's hand and seriously added, "Eva, you should thank God. It could've been much worse. Girls have all sorts of weird things happen to them in this city."

Remembering her encounter at the bar, she nodded soberly. "I guess you're right."

"Listen, we have a speaker coming tomorrow night who has an incredible testimony."

She interrupted, "What's a testimony?"

"It's each person's personal story of how they met Jesus."

Eva thought, "I don't have a story. I don't really know Jesus."

Her countenance changed, and Trevor knew she had been convicted. A ministering angel waited by her side and began to glisten. As Trevor prayed under his breath, the prayers that had been stored up in heaven turned into light shafts that penetrated her heart. A peace came over her. "Yes, Trevor, I'd like to come."

"I'll meet you at the soup kitchen at seven tomorrow night."

When Eva returned to her hotel room that night, the ghouls sat nearby discussing how to keep her from that meeting. There had been many prayers stored up for her; and as the demons thought up different schemes, bolts of light flashed into the evil villains causing the ideas to be forgotten.

Lying on her bed, Eva's heart began to soften. A tear rolled down her face as she remembered all that had happened to her over the past decade. She was grateful her father had paid off the hoods and forgiven her for being at the wrong place at the wrong time.

Still, she had that unclean feeling and haunting doubt. What had really happened that night the photos had been taken? "I feel so alone, God. I don't even feel like you care."

She entertained doubts and then border lined on anger for God not helping her dreams come true to be a model. Fear inside her enlarged form a small ugly particle to become a strong dart, piercing her heart with its arsenic. Eva responded vehemently. "I've never felt Your love. I doubt I can trust You."

Unbelief in the room flapped its wings and expanded its chest, setting off a murky vapor which settled in the room.

Carras, an angel sent to minister to one who would inherit salvation, raised his wings, worshipping the Lord; and then like a vacuum, inhaled light shafts raining down from Heaven. (Heb1:14) With a mighty breath, these same shafts were expelled like rockets directly into the demon's eyes, causing it to disintegrate.

Carras tenderly gathered the tiny parcels of light in its arms, and then, standing over Eva, sprinkled them a few at a time like gold dust showering her in the love of God. The darkness in her heart subsided, and impulsively, she slipped out of bed and knelt before the Lord.

The ogres in the room stood bound and helpless as she called upon the Lord of Glory. "Jesus, I don't know you. My heart has so much hate in it, and I want to be able to love, but I don't know how. Will you please come and change me so that I can have a testimony too?"

While Eva buried her hands in her face and sobbed, the atmosphere in the room became a dazzling light and all-consuming fire, yet nothing was burning. She felt her face flush and continue to rise in temperature, almost as though it was burning. Opening her eyes, she saw the words 'erased' in front of her, then she heard, "Open the Bible."

She knew the hotel had placed a Bible in her drawer which she had long since discarded to the back of the closet. Eagerly searching for the book, she heard, "Amos 3:3." She flipped the pages vigorously until she found Amos and then excitedly used her finger as a pointer, scanning the pages until she found the correct verse. "Do two walk together unless they have agreed to do so?"

The voice spoke softly again. "Turn to Romans 1:21." 'For although they knew God, they neither glorified Him as God nor gave thanks to Him, but their thinking became futile and their foolish hearts were darkened.' "Oh, God. I agree to walk with you. My heart is full of darkness. I'm sorry. Please forgive me."

The room was still. Eva sat in anticipation of God's next command. Deep in her spirit, her inner man, like a tiny seed, God's presence had been birthed. Thoughts of the death of her father and mom who was still locked away quickened in her mind bringing some hardness to her heart.

Immediately, Carras was assigned to be her Watcher and the Lord whispered, "(John 12:25)." 'If you despise your life down here you will exchange it for eternal glory.' "What does that mean?"

The Lord was gentle. "Eva, my precious child, have you had enough?"

Conceiving the thought, she cried and laughed at the same time. "Yes, Lord. I've had enough of my life this way. You take over."

"There's one more thing, Eva," added the Holy Spirit. "Read Acts 2:3." 'Repent and be baptized, every one of you, in the name of Jesus Christ so that your sins may be forgiven.'

I will ask Trevor!" she exclaimed excitedly. A thought came to her and slowly she walked over to the mirror. Unsure of what to expect, she gently pushed back her bangs, exposing her once marred forehead. She blinked and with overwhelming joy, cried, "It's gone! My scar is gone!"

That night Eva slept with the Bible open next to her. For the first time, its words had come alive. God had spoken to her through it; and now she wanted to learn what it said over again, but this time walking with God.

In the morning, the spirit of Antichrist had been doing its dirty work. The best way to block her commitment to God was to give her what she really wanted, a modeling career. The phone rang. "Hello?"

"Eva, this is Mr. Kylie at the Star Agency. I have a job for you if you're interested." Forgetting what had happened the night before, Eva rose to the occasion. "Oh, great! What is it?"

"It's for shampoo and they want an exclusive representative to advertise their product all over the country. They like your hair style and want you to keep it that way so no one will see the scar."

At his words, Eva gently stroked across her forehead where the ridge had always been. Just then she remembered her reflection in the mirror the night before and that God had erased the scar. Part of the verse penetrated her mind. "Exchange it for eternal glory." In the next few seconds, the silence was deafening. Eva had to decide whether to follow her dream or follow Jesus. Which would it be?

CHAPTER TWENTY-EIGHT
WOMAN HAVE SAME VISION

Much had happened in America. Eighteen-year-olds could now vote, capital punishment had been eliminated and the Watergate scandal had just begun. Even though abortion had been legalized, the angels fought hard to keep young girls from terminating their pregnancies.

God's Spirit was moving across the States. Some thought it was the end of the Jesus Movement, but its purpose would be much more lasting than a movement. God's Word said that young men would dream dreams and see visions; (Acts 2:15) and although many were seeing pictures through hallucinogenic drugs, there was a God-consciousness coming into effect.

The local churches didn't know how to handle it. Tradition said women had the long hair, not men. You dressed up for church, not wearing dirty jeans and barefoot. Yet, thousands of kids were seeking the truth; and if the church wouldn't let them in, they'd find their enlightenment someplace else. Some of the top rock stars confused kids by adding Eastern philosophies to their music and implying any god would do. Little by little riots began taking place. People were rising up against the government; and with Jimmy Carter as president, not much was going on.

Six months before, a pastor named Burrows had started a small church called Real Life to disciple these Jesus 'freaks' into salvation. With his own money, he rented the town hall each Sunday and all were welcome. Long hair on boys, beads, and even girls could wear pants if they wanted. After all, he knew that even though the Bible forbade women in men's clothing, that when that had been written, men's clothing didn't include pants, they wore robes. So, if a girl wanted to wear slacks that was fine by him as long as they came.

Being a widower didn't help the controversy surrounding him, but the townsfolk observed he had a well-mannered son Sam Jr.'s age. Esther hoped the young boys would hit it off.

Esther had moved a long way in those years; unfortunately, it was backwards. Because she had started smoking again, she didn't want to be around Christians in case they smelled it. Consequently, she withdrew from church. Obviously, Larry wasn't there for support at Bethesda and Mary had it tough enough without stirring waves to get Esther reinstated, so it was easier to simply stop attending. Esther still made sure Josh went. She wanted him to have some stability in his life after everything that had happened and realized that God was the only reliable One, she could entrust him to. Patty and Amanda had written her off because, with all the witnessing they'd done, they couldn't afford to be connected with an adulteress. Sam, serving his time in jail, refused to have visits from Esther; and as her whole existence had been turned upside down, she sadly became a companion for a bourbon bottle.

Lounging at home one day and allowing the booze to agitate her feelings, Esther grumbled how much she felt like Job. "God, it isn't fair. I feel stripped."

In the presence of the Lord, Nova stood in humble servitude. "Lord, may I go to her now and bring her back?"

The mighty voice of God reverberated across the heavens. "It will be her choice to come back, but you can do whatever you can to help."

Eagerly, Nova went to carry out his task, starting at the ladies' weekly meeting. Five women were present and having their usual prayer time. Like incense, as the women sang, beams of light were lifted, wafting through the house and then ascending to God's throne room.

Sitting down to begin their intercession, Patty prayed, "God, what do you want to say to us today?"

"Restore one in gentleness lest you too fall." (Gal 6:1) The words came softly to her spirit, and she repeated them to the others.

Amanda spoke up. "He's talking about Esther. She's totally backslidden. I don't know if I can forgive her."

Mary interjected. "It says in John 8 that if any of you is without sin, let him be the one to throw the first stone."(Jn 8:7)

"What makes you think she wants to come back to Jesus?" Patty asked.

Mary's voice held a note of mercy. "Because she loved the Lord so much, but she let her flesh get in the way of God's commands, the result was disastrous. Her guilt for Larry's death was overwhelming, and she started smoking and then she turned to liquor. As the church, including us," she looked at each face in turn, "alienated her, she gave up." Ladies, I don't blame her for her reaction. I think we've been too hard, and Jesus said we would be known as his disciples by the love we show to each other. We haven't shown her any love, and I think we owe her a deep apology."

Patty reached for her Bible. "Well, it says in I Corinthians 5 that we are to judge strongly church members who are in sin."

"That's right," interrupted Amanda. "It says throw them out of the church because if one is allowed to go on sinning, soon all will be affected."

Mary cut in. "All Christians sin."

"They don't have to," Amanda stated. "Especially when they're breaking the obvious like fornication and adultery."

"Look, churches are full of people, especially the youth, who are fooling around," Mary stated. "Why are they allowed to stay then?"

"Because the leaders of the church would rather compromise and keep the numbers and finances up than deal with it!" one of the women quipped.

Amanda suggested, "Why don't we all pray about it during the week; and if any of us agree to reinstate her, then we will."

"A lot can happen in a week," Mary reminded them.

Patty smiled. "Esther's strong. She'll be all right."

Esther wasn't as strong as Patty thought. The feeling of emptiness had robbed every ounce of joy she had once had in the Lord. The alienation from her Christian friends and lack of vision, purpose and calling had plundered all God had done over the years. The worst blow came when Amanda didn't respond to her letter. That crushed her.

For many months, the demons had added fuel to the fire by letting her engulf the idea that she had done the unpardonable sin and wouldn't be forgiven. She carried out her homely duties, but sometimes in her intoxicated state. She often did them again, unaware she'd already done them before.

One afternoon, Esther felt a little more hopeful as she received a letter stating that Josh would be home soon, and he would do the right thing by marrying Debbie and giving Esther more grandchildren. She and Debbie had become close, leaning on each other and the bottle to keep them company and entertain them.

The demons lurked around the house eager to see what they could plan.

The Holy Spirit interceded for Esther and sparkling gold rays of light plummeted from heaven, summoning Nova to do God's bidding. The Lord spoke to Esther, "Ezekiel 16:62." She wasn't sure it was God and turned to it gingerly, expecting a rebuke. "I will reaffirm my covenant with you, and you will know I am the Lord. (Ez16:62) Despite all you have done I will be kind to you again ... when I forgive you for all that you have done."

Esther gasped. Her spirit emanated a dazzling light which showed Nova she was receiving God's mercy and was truly sorry for all she'd done wrong. It was a sorrow that led to repentance, not death.

God spoke again. "Turn to John 8."

As Esther read, she recognized this as the story where a woman had been caught in adultery and the law said she was to be stoned. She skimmed the Chapter, knowing basically what it said; but when she read the last section, the words leaped into her heart, Jesus declared, "Neither do I condemn you. Go and sin no more." (John 8:11)

Tears slowly trickled down Esther's face. The years of built-up guilt were being released. "Oh, God, thank You for forgiving me. The weight was too much for me to bear."

The powers of darkness would not give up easily. Deception had its own plan. Intertwining with Bondage, a demon who had the right to influence her as long as she smoked and drank, the two compelled her to go to her usual comforts.

Esther decided it would be her last time. Near the end of her drink, she looked down at her Bible lying open to the verse God had quickened to her earlier, but this time she only caught part of it. "You will know I am the Lord."

Deception moved its stinger across her eyes, compelling them to look on the next page. "If a righteous person turns to sinning and acts like any other sinner, should he be allowed to live?" (Ez 18:24)

Esther's eyes widened and Deception secreted its nature into her mind. She conceived the thought, "God has forgiven me, but must I die for my sin."

The demons began laughing. They knew full well that only Jesus' death could atone for sin. Esther made herself another drink, toying with the idea of suicide. As the hours went on, more and more heaviness settled into her heart.

She began reminiscing just how stupid she'd been, allowing Larry to get infatuated with her. Her mind drifted back to the years she was married to Sam. How she had let her family down, not knowing how to relate to them, and now she had brought ridicule on the family's' name. "Yes, my penalty is due."

As if compelled by some inner force, she weaved her way to the garage, closed the door, got in the car and turned on the engine. Rolling down all the windows, she breathed in the exhaust fumes. "Soon, Lord, I'll be with You and I won't have the guilt anymore."

Nova immediately called upon Odessa to summon Mary to go to Esther's house right away. It was an urgent call across the spiritual sphere.

As first, Mary hesitated, remembering Amanda's strong recommendation that they wait a week and also Patty's comment, "She's strong."

"No, she isn't. I must go to her," she adamantly declared.

Pulling into Esther's driveway, Mary heard the car engine and quickly opened the heavy garage door. Esther lay unconscious in the front seat and Mary tried pulling her out but didn't have the strength. Turning off the engine and choking on the fumes, she cried out desperately, "Jesus, help me!"

Odessa and Nova linked together in a circle around her and a new strength arose in Mary, enabling her to pull her friend to safety.

On the lawn, she began mouth-to-mouth resuscitation and as Esther coughed and sputtered, Mary cried in gratitude to her Lord. Wrapping her arms around Esther, Mary begged her forgiveness for deserting her when she needed her the most.

As the ambulance pulled away, Mary thought of a title for her next Bible study. "Don't shoot the wounded. Some day you might be one!"

CHAPTER TWENTY-NINE
OPERATION MATTHEW 25

The anticipation was mounting, and Joshua could hardly contain himself. Today would be the day he would see his daughter Lilly for the first time. At three years of age, she was slower than most kids her age. The drugs Debbie had been taking when she was pregnant and also the booze, she slipped into the bottles to help Lilly sleep had a lasting effect on the child.

Esther's ordeal was long past; and although she now was walking gingerly with God, she knew she was forgiven for trying to commit suicide and for the encounter that had led to murder. She realized she must press on towards her higher calling and to not forgive herself would bind her in self-pity. God's Word said there is now no more condemnation for those in Christ Jesus. So, if God could forgive her, Esther must too. (Romans 8:1)

In gratitude and indebtedness to God for returning Josh safely home and bringing him into a relationship with Jesus, she determined to serve the Lord single mindedly.

The future looked promising as Joshua prepared to go and see his child. Esther had high hopes that Debbie would eventually be born again herself and then raise her granddaughter in the ways of the Lord.

She was standing on the verse 'you and your household shall be saved', but was forgetting that with Debbie's will, this just might not happen. (Acts 16:1)

As he was leaving, Esther stopped Joshua in the kitchen and motioned for him to sit down. "Honey, I think we should pray before you go over there."

"Okay, mom. Great idea!" he said, reaching for her hand. "Father, thank

You for bringing me home safely from the war. Please work on dad in jail that he would put all the tragedy behind him and come to know You. Please help Lilly accept me as her father."

"I think you should worry about Deb first," Esther added softly, concerned for the way she was so reliant on the bottle.

Squeezing her hand and looking deep in her eyes, Josh took in his mom's face. The character lines were obvious and the streaks of grey mixed in her auburn hair had increased. So much had happened while he was in 'Nam; but now that he was home, Josh was determined he would fill the role of head of the family.

Once at Debbie's, Josh felt nervous. Even though the two had known each other for years, they were like strangers. Debbie's hand shook as she reached for the vodka bottle and asked him if he wanted one too. She was apprehensive as to his reaction to their daughter and waited for him to speak. Although he had changed much in the months he'd been converted, now wasn't the time to tell her about becoming a Christian and that he didn't drink, so he gave a casual, "No thanks," to her offer.

While they waited for Lilly to wake from her afternoon nap, Debbie sat Indian style on the sofa and then looked nervously towards Josh. "So, how was the Army?"

His eyes clouded over. "I'll never be the same. I've never seen so much hate and useless killing. It was a nightmare." he shook his head despondently as the memories lingered.

Slowly twirling her ice cubes with her finger, Debbie cautiously asked, "Are you going to try again for a career in pro football?"

Josh realized he had to make a decision in himself and then relay to her what he desired for their future. Looking her straight in the eyes and aware of the liquor in her hand, he said slowly, "No, Debbie. I have other plans."

"I heard you were a Christian."

Stirling released flutters of light and God's presence touched His precious son. Confidently, he exclaimed. "Yes, I did."

"If you became a Christian in 'Nam, what were you before?" she asked smugly.

"I was nothing. Just a church goer."

Debbie moved uncomfortably in her seat. "What's changed?"

"The Bible says Jesus died and rose again so that all those who live, and that means those who are alive in Him, shall no longer live for themselves but for Him." (2Cor 5:15) I'm going to live for Him. I'm going to serve Him.

Downing the dregs of her drink, she said, "What does that make me?"

Calmly, Josh responded. "Debbie, now is not the time to get into this. I came over to… "

Just then a child's cry broke through the tension; and grumbling to herself, Debbie went to get Lilly.

While he waited, Josh surveyed the room. It was obvious his would-be bride wasn't much of a housekeeper. "God, I hope You'll help me with this," he prayed.

Stumbling around the corner came Lilly, a huge smile lighting her face. Her dress was covered with smears of chocolate, while in her chubby, little hand a candy bar was being gripped tightly. As she took another suck, a morsel slowly dribbled down her chin. The candy was the only comfort the child had known. Her mother didn't realize she needed to be touched more than to have her appetite satisfied.

"Here's your daddy," Debbie said, with a twinkle in her eye.

Joshua reached over and lifted her into his lap, carefully trying to avoid the sticky substance making contact with his new white shirt.

As God birthed a special love in his heart for her, a deep sense of wonder encompassed him, and he realized that this little girl was part of him.

Choosing his words carefully, he looked across at Debbie who was calmly rolling a joint. Aware of how different they really were, he sent up a desperate prayer. "Lord, help me." "Debbie, I want to marry you and help raise Lilly."

I'm showing the house for sale. After all that, I intend to go to Hollywood. Lilly can stay with you & Esther. She sat there staring at him as she lit a match, then almost as if someone had whispered the words to her, she relayed, "That's nice, but no thanks." I'm not really into getting married.

He cuddled Lilly to him and she nestled under his neck, relishing the contact of another human being. "What do you mean, no thanks?" Jezebel shot forth a thought to Debbie "You don't want to live with a Jesus freak."

"Just what I said!" she snapped. "My life is fine the way it is."

Aware that the drug and alcohol were influencing Debbie's mood change and she was unlikely to listen to reason, he said softly. "Will you think about it?"

Not wanting to hurt him too much, she nodded, drawing on the joint." I finally have no one to tell me what to do."

After spending an hour playing with his daughter, Josh headed for home. He felt dejected and extremely confused. Esther greeted him with a loving hug, expecting good news.

"When's the big day?"

"She said no, mom," Josh stated sadly, leaning his chin on her shoulder. "Oh, honey, I'm sorry. "We'll just keep praying and ask for God to intervene. It will all work out, you'll see."

"Even though I don't really know Debbie or approve of the way she lives, I still love her, like she's part of me."

"Josh, the Bible says that will happen . . . "

He interjected, "You mean when people are married, don't you?"

"No. It isn't necessarily marriage that joins two people together. It's the uniting of their spirit. Go get my Bible and I'll show you."

Watching her son climb the stairs, she remembers their last talk on sex. "Had it really done any good?" she wondered.

Esther turned to I Corinthians 6 and began reading. "Don't you realize that your bodies are actual parts and members of Christ? So, should I take part of Christ and join Him to a prostitute? Never. A man joins himself to a prostitute, she becomes part of him, and he becomes part of her. God tells us in scripture that the two become one." Shifting nervously his position, "What does that mean?"

"That your spirit became one when you made love. You and Debbie became one. Because you were joined, your spirit longs for her. There will always be that unity since she has part of you and you have part of her. Listen, Josh, we'll just keep praying for God's will in this situation. Both Debbie and Lilly need to be saved too."

"Okay, Mom, thanks for your wisdom. I'll be up in my room if you need me."

Settling back in her chair, Esther read into Chapter seven where it spoke about whether or not it was good to be married. She read it with little concern; but incredibly, as she came to verse thirteen, she read it out loud just to be sure it said what she thought. "A Christian woman who has a husband who isn't a Christian ... she must not leave him."

She sat there quietly remembering the night the apparition had enticed her with the words that she could have Larry.

The Holy Spirit engulfed her and opened her heart to this scripture. Sadly, she admitted, "That wasn't You that night, was it, Lord? I should have known better. It was a contradiction to Your written Word."

Softly, tears flowed. "God, I sure made a mess of things, didn't I?"

"I told you to go your way and sin no more." (John 8:11)

Receiving God's words, Esther felt reassured, but still deep in her heart were the pangs of bitterness, anger, and resentment against Sam. Three evils which would affect her in due process.

At Mary's house, Odessa waited expectantly for the forthcoming phone call. As the familiar jangle echoed through her house, the angel gleamed with the knowledge of who was calling.

After the operator connected them, a much-loved voice spoke. "Hi, mom! It's Walter."

"Walter! Thank God you're safe!" Mary responded. "What happened? I expected to hear from you long before this. Where are you? The operator said collect call from Japan."

"I'm in Tokyo, mom. I got married."

Joy rose in Mary's heart, but then just as quickly, she felt betrayed. "You got married and didn't even wait to come home so I could share it with you?" "Mom, I'm not coming home," he whispered. "What are you talking about? I've become a missionary."

Mary was unsure what to think. God's presence descended on her; and as she breathed in, she smelled that now familiar scent, indicating that the Lord was present.

A voice spoke gently to her spirit. "He's mine now, Mary. He's in my will."

Tears cascaded down her cheeks; and Mary was so overcome, she cried with joy. "Who did you marry?"

"Mom, it's a miracle! It really is God! Do you remember Edward Fraser from Ponto's Dealers?"

"Yes."

"It's his daughter, Tanya. She's also the girl that dad saved when the church was burned." Mary sank into the chair near the phone. She hadn't thought of George for a while, but now that loss surfaced again.

"Mom, there's more exciting news," Walt added. "She's pregnant!"

"Walt, speak up. I can hardly hear you. What did you say?"

"You're going to be a grandmother!"

Elated, Mary raised her hands and her eyes to heaven. "Praise Jesus! He's so good."

The atmosphere changed abruptly when Walter added, "We won't be coming home for a while, though. We're part of a group here called 'Reach Out'. We live by faith, and it's amazing to see how God supplies our needs. Even our whole wedding, reception and Tanya's wedding ring were given to us. God didn't forget anything."

"Walter," Mary replied lovingly. "I'm so glad to hear what you're saying and even if it means I won't see you or my grandchild for a while, that will be fine with me. Let's let the Lord's will prevail in your life."

"I gotta go now, mom. I'll be in touch soon. "I love you."

"I love you too, my son, and I'm proud of you."

She hung up the phone and then dropped to her knees. "God, thank You for Your faithfulness. Not only did you keep Walt safe but you saved him, gave him a Christian wife, and called him into Your service."

Springing into her memory came the dinner table conversation when Walt had just started school. Yasha, the little Japanese girl, who the kids had teased turned out to be a seed planted to give Walt a foregoing burden for the Japanese people as a whole. God had planned this from the beginning.

An assurance came over her, a peace that Walt and his new family were in God's hands. Now Mary could persevere in the things God had planned for her in Cambridge

Eva was getting restless. Although Trevor had baptized her and the kids from Reach Out begged her to stay, she knew God was calling her home.

As she thought about her options, inevitably she was always led to Cambridge and a peace would come into her spirit.

Chapter Thirty
Rejection is a Powerful Foe

Eva, during her lunch hour one day, she picked up her Bible and decided to go to Central Park, hoping that in a setting of God's creation, she would be able to clearly hear what he wanted her to do.

Sitting by a huge pine tree, she bowed her head and prayed for Him to guide her as she read His word. A scripture was given to her mind. 2 Timothy 4:6, and eagerly she looked it up. . . the time for my departure has come.

The word had been very clear, so with only a few people to say goodbye to, Eva returned home. According to scripture, a prophet is not usually welcomed in his own hometown; but Eva had a special call and God was going to use her in many ways. (Lk 4:24) Upon returning, the Lord had directed her to Pastor Burrows at his Real Life Church, and she was growing quite fast and steady with the Lord.

God needed to do a penetrating work in her heart, cleansing her from those things that would defile her flesh and spirit. Because of years of rejection from Janet, the scars were very deep, and her habit of hate needed to be broken. Her mind had to be renewed. The main obstacle which had to be dealt with was the embedded ill feelings still lodged against her mother. In order for God to forgive her completely, she had to forgive Janet. If she chose not to forgive and forget, the Lord's healing process would be stifled.

There was much healing needed in her emotions and most of all, God wanted to release her spirit from fear that bound her even now in her Christian walk. She simply couldn't trust people, and there was deep-seated fear that God was not the loving God she'd always heard about.

Physical changes needed to take place too. Her platinum hair, which had always been long and tantalizing to men, was now cropped off shag style, and gone too was the usual heavy makeup.

Since her selfish desire to be a famous model was now exchanged for God's dream, Eva was determined to put all influences of her past life behind her. This included trying to attract men by how she looked.

The spirit of witchcraft which had influenced her for years and had claimed her during her palm-reading adventure, was always hanging around, trying to frustrate her walk. Between witchcraft, fear and rejection, God had his work cut out for Him in keeping her strong in the faith. He was going to shake everything which could be shaken and cut off the branches that didn't bear fruit. (Jn 15:2) All this included the demonic strongman who had restrained her for so long. Jesus was setting this captive free. The healing of her facial scar had been a good start. For the first time in her life, Eva didn't wear bangs and actually felt good about herself.

She now had something to share. How God had come into her life and was removing those wounds which had held her captive for so many years. The Lord was preparing her for the baptism of His Holy Spirit, to give her a new boldness to be a witness for Him; but she did have one needling thorn that kept haunting her. What had happened with the bar owner in New York?

In fear one evening, Eva asked God point blank. "As you are my Father now, please tell me. Was I raped that night?"

Softly into her spirit came the verse. "Luke 1:34."

Apprehensively she turned to it. "How will this be ... since I am a virgin?"

Tears flooded her eyes and much anguish was released as relief was instilled. No, she had not had that stolen from her. Eva cried; the Lord ministered to her crushed spirit. As God touched her, her own self-rejection dissipated and the power behind it was broken.

Suddenly, a warmth like melting wax descended upon her. Her body tingled and her tears changed into joyous laughter. The baptism of God's Holy Spirit was a gift being given by Jesus to His daughter who was so willing to obey and walk in righteousness.

Opening her mouth in glorious adoration, Eva started to thank her Father. Much to her astonishment, she began speaking in tongues. Mercilessly, the old fear strangled it.

"That's weird! I sound like an idiot," she exclaimed to herself.

As though echoing in the room, she heard, "Turn to I Corinthians 14:39."

Had that voice come from inside her? Her eyes widened and joy returned to her spirit. "Forbid not the speaking in tongues."

"Okay, God, it's in Your Word. I don't understand it, but I'll do it."

As she prayed in her unknown language, God was setting up a divine appointment which was part of her destiny.

Esther had become a member of Real Life, and she and Eva seemed more like mother and daughter as they talked and debated the things of God. Esther also wisely offered advice so Eva would not make the same mistakes that she had.

One day they were together having coffee and Esther spoke something deep in her heart "Eva, honey, just some advice I wish someone had shared with me. It's very dangerous to disciple the opposite sex. A couple of witnessing times with a man is all right, but you must be careful not to get emotionally involved. Also, it's easy for a man to be drawn to you, married or not, when he has bared his soul and shared his deep secrets in repentance." Softly, Eva said, "Is that what happened with you and Larry?"

"Yes. Little by little, over quite a period of time, we began to reach out to each other very subtly, to fill the voids in our own lives. I know in my own heart I began coveting him. God warned me more than once, but I wanted what I wanted and that was some special affection. You must make the Lord number one instead of going to other people to fulfill you.

Remember, Satan will use every trick he can to deceive us into thinking wrong can look right, so we must be always on the alert for his schemes.

Being single, Eva, God will probably not bring you a husband until you walk fully depending on Him. The enemy will probably send you someone who offers your love but has no real heart for the Lord. It's an old trick which pulls many a young romantic away from God's inheritance for them."

Esther had no idea as she spoke that was exactly what lurked around the corner.

Now that Joshua was back in town, he too had joined the ranks of Real Life, and the three were about to embark on God's special assignment for them. Esther, at long last, was stepping into her mantle.

"Guess what?" Eva exclaimed as she waltzed into the chapel one day. "God does have something for us to do here."

Excitedly, Esther asked, "What is it?" She eyed a huge book Eva carried.

"I found this book which is over one hundred years old, and it's apparently what the church taught for years on kingdom principles in an evil world."

"Sounds heavy!" Josh laughed.

"It is! It states that the earth is the Lord's and all it contains, and He has given dominion over it to His children. But Satan, who is the god of this world, has taken that right and has cornered every aspect of the world's system to implement his wickedness and cancel out God's purposes. It seems that in the church, Christians got off the track expecting Jesus to come any day and they stopped doing anything for Him to help increase His kingdom."

"What's the point?" Josh interrupted.

"Some teaching infiltrated the Body of Christ, saying that God has already chosen who is to be saved; and since everything is supposed to get worse in the last days, we might as well let it and not do anything to prevent it. Then God will save those He's destined to."

"So?" Josh asked, trying to grasp what she was really saying, for even Josh believed in predestination. Just then he remembered a verse he'd heard at a young people's rally years ago. "But how can they know unless someone tells them." (Romans 10:14)

Confused, he thought, "So how can they be predestined? We have to tell them for them to be able to choose Jesus."

Esther picked up Eva's train of thought. "I get it! No one is implementing the Kingdom of God in their everyday lives and businesses. They're just waiting for God to come zap them and make them all perfect. After all, Jesus said, "Go, disciple nations, and so all nations must be witnessed to before He can return." (Romans 10:14) We're a long way from that now. There are over three thousand different people groups who have never heard the name Jesus."

"What do you think we can do?" Josh asked. "Do you want us to Christianize Cambridge?"

"In a way, yes. We need to push back the powers of darkness in the different areas of the world's system so that people actually switch the ruling principles behind the government, businesses, the media, the health care programs and agriculture. God's standards need to be implemented in these areas, instead of the enemy molding us into his character and oppressing us, so that in the end God gets criticized. What we really need to do is return to the greatest commandment, to love God with all your heart and your neighbor as yourself. The Lord spoke to me, suffer the little children to come unto me."

Josh was puzzled. "Do you mean the children of Cambridge?"

"It's a good start. Josh, I know how much you love children. Pastor Burrows has given us access to his building to set up an afternoon playground for working mothers. Most of it would be financed through the weekly offerings, but a small fee would be charged for each child. We need to start planting some good seeds since some of these kids will never have the opportunity to go to church. This way we kill two birds with one stone. First, we provide a service for the parents and keep kids off the streets; and then using the Sunday school materials, we build a Godly foundation." Esther was intrigued. "What can I do? What about me?"

"Just go home and pray and see what God shows you; then we'll meet again next week and discuss the possibilities."

At home Josh made a weak cup of coffee and grabbed his Bible. Going to the den, he left Esther to make dinner and think over what had been said.

He pondered over the different rendezvous his mom had had in this room over the years. How in that very seat she had cried out and received from the Lord a miracle for her son? How also she had sat there and been clearly tricked by an angel of darkness. "I guess we're all vulnerable," he sighed.

Gently, Josh began praying. "God, I'd love to do something for you, but frankly, I'm not good enough. I don't know enough and what happens if I fail?"

Stirling looked on. Josh had deep seated strongholds that would take some time to eliminate and then for his emotions to be healed. Because of Sam's relationship with him, or lack of it, it would take a while for Josh to love his heavenly Father and gain some confidence himself.

He had so much self-rejection and criticism compounded with his fear of failure, he was afraid to try anything. His misconception of God was blocking and grieving the Holy Spirit.

Josh mistakenly felt that God, like his dad, would only love him if he performed. So, reluctantly he decided to get involved in Christianizing Cambridge.

In the morning when Esther had her devotions, a new challenge occupied her spirit. A sense of anticipation and her old joy in the Lord was back. She felt the Lord close by, and it was wonderful to have a purpose with Him again. "God, what can I do?"

Expecting Him to drop an incredible plan out of the sky, Esther was surprised when all she heard was "Mary." Instinctively, she called her old friend, stating that she would be over in a minute as she had to talk to her.

Mary, her usual polite self, didn't want to offend Esther, but needed to forewarn her that they wouldn't be alone. "Of course, you can come, but my son's new father-in-law is coming by for a cup of coffee."

"I can come another time."

"No, it'll be fine. Actually, you know him. Remember Edward from Ponto's Dealers?" "You're kidding. Wow, isn't God incredible! Is he saved?"

"He's raised a Christian daughter who's a missionary, but that's all I really know about him. "His daughter was the one George saved in the church fire."

"Okay. I'll be over soon, but I won't stay too long because you'll need to have time with him."

As it turned out, Esther arrived before Edward. The two friends embraced, then sat down to cement in prayer whatever God wanted to do.

Once Edward arrived, he stood in amazement as he realized that Mary was the lady, he had tried unsuccessfully to track down a few years before.

"I can't believe it!" he exclaimed. "I looked for you and eventually wound up at Second Birth Assembly the week after I'd seen you. I made a fresh commitment and was baptized and still attend there on Sunday nights."

Esther looked at Mary and gasped. "That must have been the same week God told us to go back to Bethesda, and we haven't been back to Second birth Assembly since."

"And now we're related." Edward chuckled. "What a small world."

Odessa and Nova began to sparkle. The Holy Spirit interjected a thought to Esther and then another and another. Before she knew it, Esther realized divinely why God had brought the three of them together.

Sitting at the kitchen table and sipping steaming coffee, Esther revealed her thoughts. "God is speaking to His children, to quit being so apathetic and letting the devil destroy Godly principles in society. I have an idea I think is from Him. Tell me if you'd like to be involved. In the city of Greenlane, a few miles away, there's a state penitentiary. There are boys there from all over this part of the country. Many left their towns to try their luck in the 'big city', but a lot of them ended up in crime as it was profitable."

Mary and Edward glanced at each other, unsure where Esther was going with the conversation.

"Ed, would you be willing to recruit men from church on a volunteer basis and begin teaching mechanics at the prison?"

"What for?"

"Besides teaching the inmates a trade, you could witness to them at the same time."

"That sounds like a great idea, but why us? Why not let the church do it?"

Mary looked blankly at him. "Who do you think the church is? It's you and me and Esther, the people in the church."

Esther added, "I'll go to the State Board of Correction and see if they'll agree to what we propose. If we give the inmates some love and hope, they should be less likely to return to crime and end up back in jail."

Much to Esther's joy and surprise, but confident that God goes ahead, it was obvious the Lord had prepared the way. Mr. Sullivan at the bureau was a born-again Christian, and God had already been working on him to find a plan which would disciple those prisoners who were willing.

With his full blessing and supervision, he proposed to set up a hall in the prison grounds for Ed to use twice a week after dinner. The first half hour would be in teaching God's word and the next hour would be training in mechanics.

His future hope was to add other electives, such as printing, carpentry, farming, plumbing and electronics. Any man who enrolled in this program would have the possibility of a reduced sentence. With the help of local Christian businessmen, job placements for when they were released would be found, provided they continued attending the half hour discipleship time. But if they decided to quit the Christian study, they lost their jobs and would have to finish their sentence.

"Do you think we'll be able to find other businesses prepared to hire them?" Esther asked, concerned.

"Leave it to me. I have a very persuasive friend, and he'll go into each of the churches asking for help. What's the initiative for businessmen to help in the first place?"

"They'd be getting workers who are grateful for a second chance and unwilling to blow it who also will be on minimum wages. But best of all," he added with a smile, "it's a chance to serve God in a real way. I mean, what are most Christians doing with their lives anyway to serve God instead of themselves? After all, we're destined to rule and reign with Jesus; and if we can't be bothered to do anything here, we can't expect Him to put us in charge of anything up there."

They shook hands, sealing what had been established and then Mr. Sullivan compassionately placed his hand on her shoulder. "I heard what happened to you and your husband."

Esther looked away, embarrassed by his words.

"I want you to know I don't hold it against you. It's obvious you're back in right standing with God, and who am I not to forgive you."

"I was so stupid," Esther mumbled.

"You're also human. We make mistakes. We don't often cause the loss of another's life, but Christians make wrong choices and sometimes have a demonic help in carrying out those decisions."

"I can't blame demons on my own lust," she replied despondently.

"That's true, but until we get to heaven, we'll never know how much instigating demons really did behind the scenes to try to ruin our walk, how much they actually enticed us and tempted us knowing our hearts are deceitful and our flesh is weak."

CHAPTER THIRTY-ONE
SINS RUN IN THE FAMILY

God spoke to Amanda. "Restore one in gentleness, lest you too fall." (Gal 6:11)

"Ladies, I have to confess something," she stated. "I really need to release forgiveness to Esther. I just got so upset, worrying about our reputation in town, it was like I threw the baby out with the bath water. Frankly, I miss her."

Mary looked around at the ladies with their eyes glistening with tears. "Girls, Esther has repented. She and some others from Real Life are beginning to set in motion plans for discipling Cambridge. I'm sure there's plenty of room for us in what they're doing. Did you know her son got saved while he was in Vietnam and the mayor's daughter accepted the Lord in New York? Our years of praying paid off. They've come back to help influence our town in the ways of God."

"I've been having a vision," Amanda stated. "I keep having the same dream. There are always pregnant girls around me, and I certainly know it isn't a vision for myself. I'm too old." "What about Abraham and Sarah?" One of the ladies chuckled. "No!" Amanda laughed. "It must be someone else."

"Anyway, they're having a meeting in a couple of days," Mary offered, "for those Christians in Cambridge who want to do something about instilling righteousness here. Why not come and see what God may have for you to do to increase His kingdom's principles?"

The following Monday Esther, Josh and Eva were quietly waiting on God. Esther spoke first. "I have a picture of a pregnant girl in my mind."

"That's interesting," said Josh. Turning to Eva, he said, "What did you get?"

Just then footsteps could be heard coming down the hall. Appearing in the doorway were Mary, Patty and Amanda. Esther quickly glanced away, her old feeling of rejection surfacing as she heard Amanda approach.

"Esther," she said, kneeling humbly in front of her. "Can you ever forgive me for the horrible way I've treated you?"

The usually compassionate Esther disappeared. Her emotions lay dormant and her heart harbored coldness. After a few moments, she shrugged dispassionately. "I forgive you, but it really hurt when you never responded to my letter."

Confused, Amanda asked, "What letter?"

Reluctant to give up the long-sedated bitterness, she assumed Amanda was lying and had received the letter, but spitefully hadn't responded. "You know what letter I'm talking about. The one where I asked your forgiveness and tried explaining why I sinned."

Just then the Lord brought back to Amanda's mind the verse he had placed in her heart. "Restore one in gentleness lest you too fall."(gal6:1)

"Esther, I promise you I never received a letter like that; and if I had, to be honest, I don't really know what I would have done. But it's only the proud who think they'll never fall, and God opposes the proud. It says in Isaiah that it is only in a humble and contrite heart that the Spirit of God rests. I don't want to block Him out by being proud and assuming that I'm better than you since I could make a wrong choice too."

Immediately at her words, Bitterness hovered nearby and attempted to infiltrate Esther's reaction, then releasing its vile slime it spat the thought, "It's her fault you backslid for three years."

Staring blankly at Amanda, she contemplated the truth behind the statement and then in her heart she pushed the suggestion away and lovingly, she reached over and hugged her old friend.

They were suddenly aware of the others in the room as applause and cheers sounded all around them. It was wonderful to have unity restored.

Over coffee a little while later, Eva inquired, "Amanda, Patty tells me that you've been dreaming about pregnant girls. Have you got something to tell us?"

Esther gasped, astounded at her words. "I just had the same vision."

"That's right! I guess God is trying to tell us something," Josh stated.

"I have a thought," offered Eva. "An organization called Reach Out in New York used to run a home for women with an unwanted pregnancy. It was an alternative to abortion. Maybe God is asking us to set up some sort of clinic."

"Where would we get the finances to do that?" asked Esther.

"Welfare is forking out money all the time for these ghastly operations, so maybe we could get funds from them for those girls who otherwise qualify for their program."

"Okay. Seeing my dad is mayor, I'll start with him. Maybe he can do something," Eva replied.

"Anyone else with any inspiration as to how we can influence Cambridge for Christ?" Mary looked around eager to hear what Christ desired. Several angels stood shimmering and standing guard against the demons outside the building. This meeting was being maneuvered from the very throne room of God.

Patty excitedly spoke up. "I had a vision a while ago. I left it on the back burner, but I sense now is the time to cook it up. My husband and I called it 'Operation Matthew 25'. One of the few times Jesus was angry was when His servants didn't use what had been given to them to do something for God and called them useless, wicked servants and threw them into outer darkness. Interestingly enough, that is also a description of hell, so that means He sent His unfaithful servants there. He went on to say that when we deny others, we are denying Him; and when we did it to others, we did it unto Him."

Amanda sat forward. "What was your plan?"

"First of all, the local church would have a directory including Christians from all denominations and their field of work. Those who are members of churches could get a discount when using these services. That would help bring the business to each other."

"Yes," Amanda added, "and it would be a great door-knocking opportunity. Those we recommend could get a discount too. We could go into peoples' homes and offer them the church directory. Part of this operation could be to rotate members of the church in helping the townsfolk with other duties not covered in the list. For example, yard work, laundry and baby-sitting, or even making meals for the incapacitated. As examples, the Christians would have the lowest prices in the area, advertising that it was being done for the glory of the Lord. No matter what the competition did, we would always keep our price lower. It would be a six-month procedure, ending on New Year's with an evangelistic rally at the church. People will have been touched by this, seen what being a Christian is all about, and want to become one too. I really believe God would honor this and everyone would be blessed."

The group was startled by Pastor Burrows' voice coming from behind the door. "I'd like to do my part. For years I've been putting aside money, both individually and from the church, which I thought was to go for a new building once our membership doubled, which it has. I believe God is telling me, that instead of erecting a new building, I need to add a second service and use that money towards 'Operation Matthew 25'."

All went quiet in the room and then a burst of laughter and hallelujahs were forthcoming. They had a long road to go, but God's faithful little servants were developing into a mighty army that would really cause an impact on society. God was proud of His children and the angels rejoiced at the mercy and goodness of God who hadn't given up on the people of Cambridge any more than He had given up on the people of Nineveh.

The following day, Eva was elated as she walked down the street. Her morning quiet time had prepared her. God was planning something special. So strongly the words from 1 Peter 3 came to her, '. If anybody asks any of you why you believe what you do, be ready to tell him and do it in a gentle and respectful way.'

Abruptly, Eva was shaken from her thoughts when a rock pelted her in the back. She turned around to see three scruffy looking teenagers standing there. Immediately, she realized they were mocking her shirt, which had emblazoned across the back the words 'Jesus Changes Lives'. Giving them a deliberate smile, she slowly turned around and then continued on her way. Suddenly, anger rose in her as another rock stung her shoulder blade.

In the spirit realm, demons were playing havoc, hoping to steal her witness. Determined not to react, she slowly counted to five and while turned said, "Listen, guys, Jesus really does changes lives. I'm proof of that."

The spirit behind the aggressive one exploded at the sound of that feared name, instigating an immense hate into the boy and he responded by running straight towards her, shoving her in the chest and knocking her onto the ground. Then with a devilish grin, he viciously spat in her face and roared with laughter.

Her first response was to retaliate with the same hatred he'd shown, but God's hand was heavy upon her and her new purpose was fresh in her mind. She didn't want any reaction she could show to be a hindrance to the vision He'd given her from being fulfilled. She was an ambassador for Christ and would not let Him down.

"Leave her alone!" a voice demanded. The boys scattered when they heard the authority behind the command then with a gentle hand softly helped her to her feet. Eva's eyes met the stranger's and immediately she liked him.

"Hello," he said softly, wiping the saliva from her cheek. "I'm Bill Butler."

"I'm Eva Silverstone. Thanks for coming to my rescue."

"Are you the mayor's daughter?"

"Yeah, but don't hold that against me." They both laughed.

"Can I buy you a cup of coffee?" he asked.

Eva was surprised. She had expected him to say drink.

They walked together to Roxy's, and as he brushed the dirt from her back, she turned to him. "What do you do in Cambridge?"

"I own Headway Taxi's. What about you?"

Slightly embarrassed, Eva stated, "Oh, I've got my fingers in a few pies."

"Like what?"

Figuring her stand on Christianity would probably scare him away, she was reminded of her morning scripture. "I need to witness to him, not worry about dating him," she thought.

Taking a deep breath, she declared, "I live at home and basically my father supports me so I can do volunteer Christian work."

"I knew you were a Christian by the words written on the back of your shirt. I'm a Christian too. I grew up in a boys' private school, and in my last year I accepted Christ as Lord of my life. Then my dad died last year, leaving me Headway to run."

Eva smiled. "I've been a Christian for six months. What church do you go to?"

"I go to Second Birth Assembly," he said as they entered the restaurant, but I don't seem to be doing anything for God. I feel so useless."

"Maybe I can help. At Real Life we started a little project we call

'Operation Matthew 25'."

"Sounds fascinating. What's its purpose?"

After ordering their coffee, she continued. "We want to push back the powers of darkness over this town. They've controlled us too long. We're going to stand up for our rights, not to be forced to endure such ungodly and demonic influences all around us. We want to disciple inmates and place them in jobs. We want to help pregnant teenagers through their term and then into adoption as an alternative to abortion. We're also going to set up a preschool for working mothers. It could even develop into a playground for kids after school. Basically, we want to instill Christianity and truth into them before everything around them fills their mind and body with deception."

"That sounds like quite a job! How can I help?"

"I know what you could do. Part of our plan is to offer decreased prices for all Christians and anyone they refer to those involved in it, as a sacrifice unto the Lord for all He has done for us."

"I could do that, no problem. I could even play Christian music in the taxis and use your logo 'Jesus Changes Lives' in bold letters over the ashtrays. Those who are interested could take the free literature, which I place in each cab, having the names of churches printed on the back."

"Just make sure it's a church where the pastor is saved."

Together they laughed and clinked their mugs to seal the plans. Bill liked Eva and she liked him. Maybe God was doing more here than either one realized. Only time would tell.

Chapter Thirty-Two
School is the Devil's Territory

Over the next few months Operation Matthew 25, as it was nicknamed, began to unfold. There were obvious hostile reactions by some in the area. Headlines even in Lawson's newspaper stated 'Born-again Go Fanatic'. One article claimed that the local church had become a cult, brainwashing its subjects into believing they could create a perfect world. Then the names were bandied around - deluded, irresponsible, un-businesslike and childish were thrown at them in print.

But the Lord can turn everything for good. Amanda decided to become more involved in the editing of her husband's paper and vetoed all stories that were in opposition to their plans. Her husband, Frank, gave the go ahead for Amanda to write her own editorial; and with the help of God's Holy Spirit, she brought out consistent declarations that opened up all sorts of replies to her articles. She was able to take advantage of the freedom of the press by answering each letter personally, using the Bible standards and then printing them in her column.

The youth were screaming out for some purpose and the powers of darkness were amply ready to fill the void. A new man came on the scene claiming to be the Messiah. By the thousands, youth flocked to Reverend Star. So, it was important for Amanda to explain to her readers just exactly what Real Life was trying to implement, and in no way were they a cult harboring a bunch of devotees that would try to force others into their philosophy.

Her June 20 edition quoted the following. "To my readers, once and for all I want to state in my editorial our goals as Christians in this community. For a decade our youth have fought for freedom through sit-ins, fasting, riots, streaking and even burning our flag. What are they actually trying to be free from, or to? This is the most violent century in history. As we've strived for peace, we've found conflict. As we demanded love and physical satisfaction, we ended up in lust with our passions turning into bondage. The world has bombarded us with sex and stressed that the beautiful people smoke, drink, swear and make love to a bevy of different partners. One in two marriages ends in divorce, hence commitment is nonexistent. Television has systematically and purposefully degraded the moral fiber of this country, a country founded on Christianity. The earliest settlers came here seeking freedom. Freedom to worship Jesus away from mans' rules and dead traditions in their home countries. That was the whole reason the First Amendment was written ~ to obtain freedom to worship the one true God. Cleverly, Satan has taken this and twisted it, so that freedom to worship anything or anyone is now law. But even so, the name of Jesus may not be lifted up in any school or on any government property. Very soon it will be illegal to display Jesus in a manger; and before we know it, 'In God We Trust' will be banished from the dollar bill. What the Christians are doing in Cambridge is a conscious united effort to claim their rights as citizens and to fight for reinstating the original Biblical values which this country was founded on. Personally, I'm tired of looking at naked bodies on billboards, buses, magazine stands and television. What about my rights and my children's rights? With Operation Matthew 25, which unfolded last week, this is our way of saying Christianity is not a religion, it's a relationship with the living God through Jesus who is alive in Spirit, and we want to restore His righteousness in all spheres of society. Beginning with this newspaper, we're going to censure the articles and we're not going to publish anything which is contrary to Christian principles, which includes the abolishment of the daily horoscope which God expressly forbids in His Word. Christians have united and will not shop any longer in stores that carry girlie magazines at all. We are circulating speakers and petitions to hundreds of churches across the Midwest, and we're going to fight the media and Hollywood for the constant blaspheming of our Lord. The prophet Isaiah was told to lift up a standard over the people and that's exactly what we're putting into motion now."

Much to Frank's surprise, his paper had doubled in sales. Readers wanted to see how Amanda handled the critical letters. It was great -- God and Amanda were ready to take them on.

The Chamber of Commerce rose its ugly head, claiming the religious were using God as an excuse to butter their own bread cheaply, and equal rights groups protested that non-Christians were being discriminated against. The Hosts in heaven were ecstatic.

Bill Butler had done exactly what he said he would and more. He rose at the challenge to implement his convictions. His desire was to please the Lord, and so he went full out with his commitment.

He changed the name of his cab company to 'He Saves' and placed the logo 'Jesus Changes Lives' on the back of each seat and above the ashtray. So as not to discriminate and end up in court, he hired any applicant, forewarning them that morning devotions were mandatory. Legally, that was his right. Christian music tapes were supplied daily to the drivers for their riders' listening pleasure. They were encouraged not to slander the attempts of the employer in his purposes for God.

Because Bill's rates were so much lower, he was able to get most of the business, and God honored him as he as touched many through his music and the free tracts given with the change.

Eva and Bill had become good friends but were careful not to place themselves in any compromising situation which could lead to temptation. Eva felt good about herself; and although she was kept busy, there were a growing desire in her to be loved by a man. Her father, who was in his last year as mayor, had gotten in on the action too. He didn't know Jesus, but God was turning his heart, like channels of water, to meet His purposes.

It was now illegal to have more than one point of alcohol in your blood stream while driving a car. That meant even one beer would put you over the limit. Consequently, those who went out socially were too afraid of getting arrested at the constant check points, so they didn't bother drinking at all.

The police noticed that violence in the home had dropped. Speeding and fender benders decreased, and the angels glowed as more fathers spent time with their families.

Eva helped bring this new law into effect. One night she watched her dad and other politicians with civil servants at her home for a cocktail party. Quietly she listened from the den when much to her horror she realized that the majority of the city's ordinances were being discussed and finalized by men with minds befuddled with alcohol. How easy for spirits to influence these men who were supposed to be God's appointed authority.

The next evening very meekly she read to Marvin from her Bible. 'It is not for kings to drink, for they may lose their judgment' and then they stumble when making decisions'. (Prv 31:4) Eva carefully worded her sentence. "Dad, do you remember Amanda's editorial where she tried explaining about the project our church is undertaking?"

Glancing over his glasses frames, Marvin then straightened up. He knew his daughter had some Godly wisdom for him. Over the many months, he'd seen her change from an introverted, purposeless girl into a woman of strong character, conviction and vision. She radiated love and joy, and Marvin was conscious of the fact that she had come back from New York different. He'd attributed this to her encounter with the hoods and thought it must have scared her back into religion.

"Yes, honey, I read that article with great interest. My office has been bombarded with threats, claiming I'd be fired if I aided you in any way."

Carras slowly folded his wings and then extended them just as rays of light, similar to the moon shining on a lake, descended in pillars upon Marvin. The sovereignty of God was at work.

"I remember some time ago," Marvin began, "one of your little renegades so bluntly informed me that God puts men in authority and God removes them. With a chuckle he continued, "I've remembered that, and I have in my own way thanked God for this position I've held longer than any other mayor in this area."

Eva slowly knelt at his feet "Do you remember in the article that Amanda stated from Isaiah 'lift up a standard over the people?' Well, dad, that's your responsibility."

"Really? Have you ever heard the phrase 'You can't fight City Hall'? All of these so-called irritants you want to change are now law and it's very difficult to reverse them. And do you really think you can make people become Christians be forcing them into your mold? Kings have tried to do that for centuries, but it doesn't work. You Christians are supposed to be the light, the salt. You're supposed to show the heathen the way by setting an example."

Raising his eyebrows for added emphasis, Marvin continued. "The church and the state must stay separate. There is no government capacity to instill morality or righteousness. Our laws concentrate on the safety of people. We aren't an organization to prevent moral degradation in society." Even as he uttered those words, he knew something was wrong. If they were responsible for people's well-being, weren't they also responsible for the values in society? It was almost like a baby sitter telling the five-year-old, "Okay you can play with this loaded gun, but you must be bathed and in bed by eight-thirty."

Eva saw a side of her father she'd never known, and she was relishing this conversation even though he appeared to be resisting her point. "Dad, what if I wasn't quoting the Bible for my ammunition for the lack of values in this city? The Ten Commandments just happen to make good sense. Besides, what about the environmentalists screaming for the injustices against plants and wildlife? You officials readily listen to them. What if I were Spanish or Black insisting on my fair share of the pot? Equal rights are in the Bible; in fact, Jesus claimed it was the greatest commandment - love your neighbor as yourself." (Mark 12:30)

"Very good, Eva. You've got me on that one."

"Why is it dad that Christians aren't allowed to scream for their rights to a moral society?"

"They are, Eva. They just don't bother."

"Dad," she said respectfully, "let me remind you that since they lowered the drinking age how much trouble the youth have been into. How many more unwanted pregnancies, drunk driving, vandalism and suicide? The men who helped lower the drinking age made that decision while stumbling themselves."

"I see your point."

With that, Carras removed his wing from Marvin, leaving in his mind the idea of dropping the alcohol consumption level. Gazing up into the heavens, the angel smiled. "It's a start, Lord."

Josh and a few ladies on rotation from the church ran a preschool which had close to fifty children each day in attendance. Many children were coming home full of faith in a heavenly Father; and, in their own innocence, they were bringing a witness to their relatives. The Holy Spirit was moving in Cambridge, much to the delight of His Army and the angels who now had many others aiding them in the heavenlies.

Even though some people got fed up, after a lot of hooting and hollering, they simply packed up and moved away. Thanks to a magazine reporter from New York, whose purpose was to ridicule the Christians' efforts, he became an instrument for blessing with an article about what was happening in this Midwest town. Almost a hundred families moved to Cambridge and Ruxton, which had now joined the planned outreach. Marvin had cracked down on the All for Whites movement and sent them scattering so blacks and whites were working side by side and gleaning from each other culturally.

The powers of darkness were regrouping and sending in new recruits. If this heavenly plan caught on, little towns and cities would catch the vision too. Principalities and rulers were shifting gears; a new stronghold was being let loose. The rest of the eighties would be a time of uncertainty in people's lives. There was no strength or trust in leadership, nothing to believe in or hope for. It was a time of emptiness, and recession was an added oppression.

To further contradict the Bible and get people's thoughts off Jesus, the demons resurrected an old deception -- UFOs. Little lights, big lights and colored ones, began streaking the sky. Those who claimed to have seen them became more defensive as they were mocked and called crazy. The clergy had to try and explain what they really were, but no one wanted to talk about demons, especially the church. The villainous forces were ready for even this.

Hollywood was about to turn out the most destructive thriller of its history. A little possessed girl was going to shock people nationwide. Hospitals filled as the weak fainted while watching this film. Mental hospitals sedated and nurtured the fearful who had freaked out by the grossness portrayed on the screen, while those who were intrigued, set out for their libraries and bookshops to learn how they could meet their own personal spirits.

Occult toys, songs, books and fashions infiltrated society; then right in due season the enemy released the movie in Cambridge. The spiritual repercussions would go deep. To some, the ineffective exorcism during the last scene stole credit from the church; and it made a mockery of the name of Jesus Christ. To many, the whole thing was so absurd, so unrealistic, that they could never imagine a demon affecting them.

Little did they realize you don't need to levitate or do a hundred and eighty degrees turn with your head to have demons inhabiting and manipulating your body? It's possible because Satan, the god of this world, holds us captive to do his will. We live in his domain. He is the god of this world. (2cor4:4)

Debbie sale of the house had fallen thru, so she was raising Lilly, in a house she thought was haunted.

On one of the hottest evenings of the year, Josh had a phone call in the middle of the night. "Josh, its Debbie. Please come and help me."

"What is it?" he asked, signaling Sammy, Jr. to go back to bed.

"Please, just come quick!"

"Is Lilly okay?"

"Yeah, but I need you, please. Something weird is going on in the house. I need you now." Then the phone went dead. She had hung up.

Joshua quickly dressed and as he ran down the stairs, Esther came from her room, flinging a bathrobe around her shoulders and called him back. "What's going on? Where are you going?"

"It's Debbie! She's in trouble. I've gotta go to her."

"Do you want me to come?" Esther asked.

"No, mom. Its better I go alone. I'll be all right. Just say a prayer while I go over."

Esther stood watchfully by the window, peering out through the Venetian blinds and saw her son run across the road. She prayed in tongues and her spirit commanded the enemy to be bound in Jesus' name. This battle would not be easy, for Debbie's strongman, Jezebel, had legal right to her body, soul and spirit.

As soon as Josh opened the door, he saw her frantically rushing from cupboard to cupboard and then looking under the couch as though searching for something or someone.

"Where are you?" she demanded. "Stop it, stop it!" Just shut up!" She clutched her head as though blocking out a loud noise.

"What is it, Debbie?" he shouted, grabbing her hands from her head.

Trying desperately to free herself, she yelled, "It's here! It's here somewhere.

It followed me home and I can't get rid of it."

Josh grabbed her shoulders and shook her. "What's the matter with you? Are you stoned?"

Just then her eyes stared blankly at him and without a word she brushed his hands aside and walked as though in a trance to the couch, lighting a cigarette as she went, "When did you start smoking?"

"I don't."

Horrified, she looked down and saw the cigarette smoking between her fingers. Turning back to Josh, her eyes glazed over again. He noticed there was a coldness emanating from them into his spirit. It was deathlike.

"My date left these here tonight," although she hadn't smoked for years. Calmly and with obvious experience, she inhaled the smoke and then expelled it through her lips.

Suddenly, she choked and her eyes returned to their normal clarity. "Josh, I'm scared. I saw this movie tonight and something happened to me while I watched it. It was like something entered my mind and began talking to me in the movie, saying 'We're going to get you'."

Taking another drag of the cigarette, she began crying. "God, help me. I don't know what to do."

"Let me pray for you."

As Josh approached her, a voice spoke through Debbie. "No! We don't want you to." Chills rushed up Josh's spine while the hairs on the back of his neck prickled. The voice echoed in his mind.

"That was a demon," he thought. "What do I do now?" Instinctively, he went to Debbie and placed his hand on her head just as he'd seen Pastor Burrows do so many times in church.

Debbie winced away as the voice spoke again through her. "Leave us alone. You've got no right to touch us."

"In the name of Jesus Christ, come out of her now," Josh declared boldly.

"No, she's ours! We don't have to."

Debbie's face turned to anguish, then turmoil and hate flashed in her eyes.

"Debbie," Josh said authoritatively, "look at me! Say this after me. 'Jesus died for me'."

There was no response.

"Jesus shed His blood for me." He shook her. "Come on, Debbie. Say it." All was quiet. "Jesus died" for her.

"No! Shut up! We can't stand that name."

As Esther was praying across the street, her requests and praises to God's glory were entering the presence of the Lord and filing back to Earth from heaven. Missiles of light bombarded the spirits in Debbie, and suddenly she went limp.

Gently, Josh shook her. Her dazed eyes constricted. "Hi, Josh," she said surprised. "What are you doing here?"

Without thinking, she reached for her cigarette in the ashtray. Then again, as though fully experienced, she smoked it without any odd reaction.

"What do you mean?" Josh realized all of this was beyond his understanding. She had heavy demonic control and there was nothing he could do until she was ready.

"Debbie, I'm going home, but can I pray for you first?"

Just then a demon of Antichrist spoke to her, snarling into her mind, "Get that Jesus freak outta here!"

She captivated the thought. The word 'pray' reverberated in her mind. "I hate that word 'pray'," she thought.

"No, I'm fine. You just go ahead and go home. I'm goanna go to sleep now. By the way, why did you come over? If you're trying to persuade me to marry you, I still haven't changed my mind." The person that was going to buy my house backed out, now am stuck with Lilly for a while.

Angered and hurt, Josh sighed. "No, I just wanted to say hello." Then turning, he dejectedly walked home. What a defeat that had been.

"It's a battle and she must choose herself," the Holy Spirit whispered. It's a spiritual battle. (Eph 6:12)

The following morning Josh called Eva, immediately telling her what had happened and how strange the whole thing had been. Quite intrigued, Eva promised to go and visit, but right now she was too excited. Johnny was arriving in Cambridge that day. He was a hero and had done two tours of duty and was coming home to claim his woman.

As they hung up, the Lord quickened to Josh to pray for Eva. Johnny could very well be a temptation she may not want to avoid.

That same morning when she went to have her devotions, Eva was too excited to really listen. Hurriedly, she prayed for her old friend Debbie but without much love, compassion, direction or purpose. God wasn't interested in how many times she'd prayed or how long her prayer was, but whether or not there was compassion behind it. That's what added the power.

Eva brushed past her devotions calendar, oblivious to the Chapter from the Bible written for that day. In bold letters were the words 2 Corinthians 6 and this was God's warning to her. "Oh, I've read that Chapter so many times before, what could I possibly learn from it today?"

God had planned to pierce her heart with the words, 'Do not be unequally yoked,' but Eva missed it. (2Cor6:14)

Carras set out to try and do battle so Johnny would be prevented from pulling her off course. Appearing before God Almighty, he stood in humble submission and said in a concerned manner, "We can't let him near her, Your Majesty."

The Lord uttered in a loving tone, "What do you propose to do?"

"He is an angry young rebel. He likes driving fast and drinking hard, and we both know what a deadly combination that is. I need to have the authority to counteract the persuasion he may have over her life."

"Yes, Carras, you go and do what you can to spare my daughter the pain that comes with love birthed in the flesh." Because Eva was one of the key witnesses, the forces of evil were desperate to get her sidetracked. Spirits were assigned to both her and John to manipulate their thoughts, emotions and bodies desiring each other.

As time went on, the inevitable happened. Oblivious to the alcohol law, Johnny drove after drinking too much and ran off a curb which put him in a serious condition in the hospital with a head injury. Eva was constantly by his side; and instead of using proper judgment, she let sympathy rule her emotions.

Pastor Burrows and Esther warned her that she was in deep water, but deception had clouded her discernment and was drowning out the voice of God

Visiting Johnny one frosty morning in December and clutching a posy of flowers, Eva was reminded of his own visit to her when she was in the hospital so many years ago. The thought came of how Johnny had supported her and hadn't been concerned by her scar or black eyes but had loved her for herself.

She desperately wanted Johnny to know Jesus too and decided it was time to press him for a decision. "Eva," he said plainly, "I'd be a hypocrite if I asked Jesus for help now. I never prayed in Vietnam, so why should I now? I don't need a crutch, only messed up or weak people call on God."

"But what if I said I can't marry you unless you're a Christian?" As he was thinking, a demon released its poison. "Tell her okay for now. Then you can do what you want." With a smile on his face and a smirk in his heart, Johnny said the sinner's prayer and then proposed.

With all the pressure that God could place on her conscience, it came to no avail. Eva's witchcraft prediction was going to come true. She would soon be Mrs. John Brown.

Everyone at Real Life tried to counsel her. Pastor Burrows refused to marry her and even Bill offered his name in efforts to detour the pending disastrous union.

Over the Christmas holidays, Eva shelved all her projects putting them on hold in lieu of her upcoming marriage. Her father wasn't impressed at all while her family in God was shocked and the heavenly host was in mourning.

"Oh, Righteous and Holy One," Carras beseeched. "My little charge had ignored all the warnings. We know how unevenly yoked marriages seldom work, especially when it's out of Your will and done in rebellion. May I have another partner to try and combat these forces that will try and steal her walk with You by living with an antichrist husband?"

With heaviness in His heart and tears in His eyes, the Lord issued a warrior. "So be it," declared the sovereign King.

❋ ❋ ❋

As Operation Matthew 25 came to a close on New Year's Day 1975, the project ended with 332 new converts and a new reverence towards God in Cambridge. The angels were rejoicing; but on the other hand, that day, instead of Eva enjoying the fruits of her labor for God, she was sharing her honeymoon with a man who had a devilish destiny — to pull her away from God.

Chapter Thirty-three
Change for the Worse

A new decade had begun and with it an all-out war against God's creation was letting loose for time was running out for the evil deities.

The music and movies spoke loud and clear about that which was already happening in many lives. Pink Floyd was adding bricks to the wall, and many people were adding bricks to the walls of their hearts.

Kramer vs. Kramer, the top grossing movie, put audience in tears as the reality of the destruction of divorce was displayed in vivid display.

Both The Wall and Kramer vs. Kramer showed that man was becoming hard, callous and building their own walls, while the church in Cambridge tried to proclaim there was someone who cared.

In the heavenlies, principalities who ruled over fashion were having their annual meeting. One ugly demon spoke first. "What's left?"

Lust announced with glee, "Let's go back to the mini-skirt. Only this time we'll make them so tight that no girl can sit in them properly."

"Christians won't wear them," sneered Complacency.

"Yes, they will. We'll put them everywhere, flooding the markets and adding peer pressure and fear of man. They'll bend eventually."

Rebellion cried out, "What about hair-dos? We need something really wild now!"

Deception replied, "We'll bring in the Eastern look, you know, like Buddhist monks!"

"Oh!" the ghouls all giggled. "You mean shaved heads! That should flip out a few parents."

"But what girl would cut her hair so short to look like a man, or even shave it?"

"I know! Send a delusion. Weird is beautiful, weird is better! That'll get them in."

Jezebel stepped forward, towering above the other ogres. "I'm going to raise up a female singing star, empowered by me as her strongman. I'm going to fill her with deception. The dirtier, the messier and the weirder, the better. Unnatural will be sexy. Black lipstick, black nail polish and black clothes to add to the depression."

Witchcraft sauntered forward. "We could get her to bring in Satanic emblems as part of the fashion of the times."

Antichrist's tongue spat forth. "We're going to use my plan this time."

All eyes were fastened on this malicious beast who had effectively brought in trends for centuries which had helped to decay Godliness.

"She's going to do the ultimate mockery." With a shudder and repulsive growl, he declared, "The crucifix will become an insignificant world-wide trinket, a common piece of jewelry, even made of plastic and tin to be dangled from the ears and necks of this godless, rebellious generation. Send out hordes of Self-rejection, so when people stare at these kids it will make them feel unwanted and add to the growing hate in their hearts. Rebellion, you and Deception starts moving on the hairdressers."

"Okay!" They roared with wicked glee. "Let's go make skinheads!"

* * *

Debbie Olson was the first to fall into the plot. Always wanting to be a singer, she was led right into the ploy dying her hair jet black with one long purple streak down her left side. She began painting her lips and nails deep purple and wore her clothes inside out. The years of rejection that so deceitfully gripped her spirit, continued to bear fruit and her heart stayed dark and vexing as people laughed at her wherever she went.

Lilly, now 12, was forced to endure the jeers and the taunts of other school kids. "Your mother's a witch. Your mother belongs in the Adam's family," they taunted her. Lilly, who had never known love, had found her consolation in food. She'd always go to candy to console herself and the pounds kept adding up.

For Debbie, the spirit of witchcraft never gave up on her. It seemed to come and go as it pleased. It had total right to be in her life because of the dope she smoked and because of the palm-reading at the carnival. Debbie was frustrated with her life and bored as a mother. The government sponsored her as a single parent on welfare and her long-buried dream to be a singer seemed out of the question. Her consolation was to get stoned on anything.

One night she took some sleeping pills, and then forgetting how many she had, went back and took more. The double dose caused her to pass out on the living room sofa with a lit cigarette dangling from her fingers.

Awakened by the alarm, Lilly sleepily stumbled downstairs and stood staring at her mother as the flames engulfed the throw rug in front of the couch. Realizing what was happening, she panicked and screamed until a pyromaniac demon swooped down beside her, wrapping one of its tentacles around her shoulder.

Then just like her grandmother, Rose, she stood there transfixed gazing into the flames, and remained there almost wishing her mother wouldn't wake up.

Suddenly, there was a pounding at the door. It was Josh, coming by for an unexpected visit. Lilly was unable to move and then Josh, smelling the smoke, hurriedly broke the window, unlocked it and climbed in.

His first thoughts were for Lilly so he ran straight to her and tried to shake her back into reality. He grabbed the unfinished drink sitting on the table and threw it in Debbie's face in an attempt to bring her out of her stupor. Thankfully, he heard the fire truck pull up. The alarm had signaled them as the smoke had hit the detector on the ceiling.

In the end, everyone was safe and only the carpet had been damaged. But Lilly had been bewitched. She had purposely not tried to save her mother and a seed of hate weaved its way into her heart.

Over the ensuing weeks, Lilly often woke up with what her mother called nightmares.

"No, Mommy!" she pleaded. "They're ugly little creatures that jump around on my bed at night. Their eyes are a shining yellow and they look right into me."

"Have you been smoking my pot?" Debbie snickered as she walked out of the room leaving her daughter to fend for herself.

The little girl lay on her bed and the loneliness of her empty room invaded her. Deep hurt was festering which added to the dark hate already present.

There were barely any toys and only one doll she'd had for four years; which Joshua had given her for her fifth birthday. It was a Ken doll and he thought it might give her some manly figure to relate to when he wasn't there. The spirit of rejection passed on from Josh at conception was amply fulfilled. Soon, she began playing with the little ugly creatures, for at least they gave her some attention.

One evening, Lilly was trying to do her homework when in the spirit realm, demons tried to block her mind and bring a heaviness upon her eyes so she couldn't concentrate or finish her assignment. It was an old scheme of the enemy, often used against children to destroy their desire to read. That way they wouldn't venture into a big book called the Bible.

Lilly had an idea. "Little gremlin, would you please help me read?"

For the moment, the demon removed the scales from her eyes and she clearly read with ease. "It works!" she exclaimed, and soon this became a habit as she called on her little ghoulish friends to help her.

Months later at the Fourth of July fireworks, one of the children was teasing her about how fat she was. Hate emerged from the recesses of her heart. "Gremlin, I want you to hurt her for me."

When the last firework display was sent up, it fell back to earth unused, apparently a dud. The little girl who had teased Lilly ran to pick it up; and just as she approached it, the explosive went off, spraying hot ashes across the child's face.

As it turned out, she only had surface burns that eventually faded; but as far as Lilly was concerned, she had found a new way for vengeance.

As usual on Saturday morning, Lilly sat down to keep herself occupied with cartoons. A new show had started about a family called The Puffs; and over a period of weeks, this cartoon was showing how to put spells on wicked people. It was okay to do it as long as you only hurt those who were awful to you, and Mr. Puff encouraged his children on the show to stamp out evil with these spells and the secret power they all had hidden away.

Josh had started to come around more often and becoming insistent that Debbie stop her teenage shenanigans and give Lilly the father she so desperately needed. Each time as he would leave the house, Debbie would go; and with a demon speaking through her, convince Lilly that Josh was evil. The spirits had plans for Lilly and they didn't want a born-again Christian around to hinder them.

In mid-August, Josh came over to find Debbie crashed on the couch. He quietly sneaked upstairs to see what Lilly was doing. He heard her talking through the door and gently pushed it open just enough to peek in. His eyes widened in horror as he saw a pentagram drawn on the wall and his daughter standing on a box clutching the Ken doll in her chubby hand.

"You're a bad man," she yelled, hitting it hard. "Mommy says you're evil. My gremlins told me not to talk to you, so now they are going to make you go away. I have Mr. Shadow to talk to. I don't need you!"

Josh slammed open the door; and Lilly, surprised by the intrusion, tumbled off the box onto the floor.

"What are you doing?" he demanded.

The Holy Spirit quickened to him, "Stop! Don't yell at her."

Meekly, she turned to him, her eyes blankly gazing into his just the way her mother's had at him so many times before. She calmly replied, "What's wrong, daddy? I'm just doing what I saw on T.V."

"Oh, Jesus," he prayed, "help me. My daughter is possessed." 'Pray for her,' were the words that came to his spirit.

Josh began crying out in prayer to Almighty God and suddenly broke into tongues, which he had never spoken before. Tears stung his eyes as he wept for mercy for this pathetic little girl.

Stirling and three other angels began doing battle. This time swords of light were drawn and the many prayers stored in heaven by Josh and Esther came into effect. Light beams darted and shot all over the room. The demons were hit, one after another, with these arrows of light, letting out screeching cries with each wound.

Running to the door, Lilly declared, "Look! Look! The gremlins are going out the door. Stop it! You're sending away my only friends."

Joshua swooped her up in his arms; and holding her tightly against him, he demanded the power of witchcraft to be broken over her life.

The Holy Spirit descended upon her; and the presence was so strong, every demon vanished. "Lilly, I want to tell you who your special Father is," Josh whispered, stroking her hair. "He lives in heaven and loves you more than anyone else does. These gremlins you think are your friends and this stuff that you've learned on television makes God very sad. Do you really think I'm evil?"

The innocence returned to her and Josh stayed another hour, pleading the blood of Jesus and a protection over her until she could understand for herself how to know the Father through Jesus.

Over the years, Operation Matthew 25 had proven to be a great success. Although it had been officially ended years ago, the theme behind it had endured. People were loving God and loving their neighbors. As recession hit America hard, the people in Cambridge and Ruxton prospered. No one had too much, and no one was in need. Even those who weren't Christians but thought they were added to the spirit of the project and brought honor to God.

Marriages in Cambridge seemed to be running smoothly. Bill Butler had married a divorced lady who, with her four-year-old daughter, had come to Cambridge and sought refuge in Second Birth Assembly, away from her traditional church which stated she must never marry again. The Lord had brought them together and blessed them, and Bill Butler couldn't have been happier.

On the other side of the coin, Eva had made a serious mistake. In the beginning, John consented for her to attend church functions and continue the volunteer work she was involved in, with little Becky only eighteen months away from starting kindergarten, Eva decided that would be a good time to go back to serving God. She began praying for the Holy Spirit to change Johnny's heart.

Once their daughter, Becky turned 4 and was eligible for preschool, he insisted she get herself a job.

He'd always wanted a ski boat; and with his job at the railroad, financially it was impossible unless his wife had an income too.

Eva had refused Marvin's help and Johnny was reluctant to live with his father-in-law, so they had borrowed money from the town's largest bank and bought a small cottage in Ruxton. For his thirtieth birthday, John had bought himself a royal blue Corvette, which only added to the mounting bills and helped force Eva into getting a job at the telephone company.

Obviously, there was no way to do evangelism as a long-distance operator, and as Eva stifled her gift and calling, her walk seemed to stagnate too.

A letter came in the mail one morning. The handwriting resembled Esther's, but she couldn't be sure. It was a small pink card with a verse meticulously written in calligraphy. "Those who live should no longer live for themselves but for Him who died and rose again on their behalf . . . we are Ambassadors for Christ - 1 Corinthians 5."

As she was committing a dream to God, a burden for her mother gently surfaced. Janet was still locked away in the institution and Eva was surprised at her thoughts as it had been years since she had seen her mother. Because of the mental deterioration, Janet couldn't even remember who Eva was.

God whispered, "You must forgive her to enable me to answer your prayer."

"Yes, Lord, I forgive her," she sighed.

But God knew her heart. The particle of bitterness was still embedded there.

Esther and Joshua were dealing with their own nightmare. On the evening of Sam Jr.'s twentieth birthday, Esther sat in stunned unbelief when her son paraded down the stairs in a dress. Because of all his lying, he allowed a perverted spirit in. Swallowing hard, Esther exclaimed, "Sam! What on earth are you doing?"

She stared in shock at his flawless makeup. It looked as though he had been applying it for years. "I'm going out. David Bowie is playing in Salt Lake, and I'm meeting a boyfriend there."

Overcome by a rush of nausea, Esther snapped, "I can't believe what I'm seeing. You're dressed like a woman!" With a feminine wiggle, he sauntered to the couch, sat down and delicately crossed his legs. Then fluffing the skirt over his knee, Sam Jr. sat watching his mother with a smirk on his face,

Bewildered, Esther leaned forward and gasped when she noticed his clean-shaven legs. "Mother, I've been dressing like this for years, but you wouldn't know. You and God didn't seem to have any time for me."

Pain pierced her heart. He was right. She had neglected him; and as a mother, she had failed miserably.

"But God saved your life! Why are you trying to be someone you're not? God made you a man."

Sam Jr. fidgeted uncomfortably. "Years ago, when I first realized my tendency towards being feminine, I went to my counselor at school and talked it over with her."

Esther sat back, repulsed, and waited for the next bomb to drop.

"Mrs. Radcliffe told me to be what I wanted, that I make the rules. If I wanted to be a woman, then to be one. I could even get an operation to alter my physical appearance. She told me that God had saved my life so I could start over. He'd made a mistake and now I had the chance to be what I wanted."

Esther silently cried. She didn't know what to say.

"I've gotta go, mom. My boyfriend's waiting."

"Do you mean boyfriend or just a man who is a friend?" Esther asked, afraid of his answer.

"I mean boyfriend." he said with a smile.

Sam Jr. saw the look of anguish on his mom's face. For a moment, he had compassion for her and deep inside wanted her to help him. He wasn't happy, he was only wanting to be loved. But the perverted spirit which had been with him for years, squeezed his heart, choking out any affection he might have for her. Then with the swish of a scarf over his shoulder, Sam Jr. strutted out the door in Esther's best evening dress.

In complete desperation, Esther burst into tears and instinctively got her Bible. "Father, you must tell me what to do."

A verse rose in her spirit from years before. "You have forgotten My laws and I have forgotten your children." Truth was in those words. She wanted to read the verse in context and turned to Nehemiah, thinking it was there.

While turning to it she wept bitterly, realizing it was during her backslidden years that Sam Jr. went to the counselor instead of to her. What Esther didn't know was that the perverted spirit that had come in while Sam Jr. was in the coma, compelled him to lie and then taken him to the extreme of perversion, feeding his mind with the lie that he was a woman trapped in a man's body.

Through her tears, she focused on a verse. Nehemiah 4:14 — "Don't be afraid, remember the Lord who is glorious. Fight for your friends, your families and your homes." Esther cried and just shut her Bible.

Esther too had a root of bitterness which needed to be removed before God could move fully in her family in answer to her prayer. Buried deep within her was resentment towards Sam for being an incompetent, uncaring husband. Added to this was the knowledge that he had taken away Larry, a ray of sunshine in her otherwise unromantic life. She now wanted to blame him for the way Sam Jr. had turned out. What Esther didn't know was that her bitterness and the evil behind it was poisoning her.

As she harbored these feelings, she was releasing cortisol, the fight or flight enzyme, because of Sam Jr. and his rebellious ways. It had been established by many doctors, that people with Sam Jr's problems and diseases, such as ulcers, also were unforgiving and bitter people. Would Esther be another casualty? The choice was hers.

Mary had decided to find a job. There were always homes that needed to be cleaned; so for the last four years, Mary had been the housekeeper for a family of four. The children, aged ten and eight, helped to be a replacement for her longing to see Leroy, her grandson. She enjoyed playing games with them and reading stories from the Bible.

At home one Friday afternoon, she went directly to the medicine cabinet. For months she'd been bothered with regular headaches, but fear had kept her from going to the doctor. "I'll be all right," she told herself. "Maybe it's menopause. I've just turned fifty-one. What could possibly be wrong?"

She slowly rubbed the back of her neck and prayed. "Father, I can't stand this pain anymore. Why won't You take it away?"

As the weekend dragged on, her headache became worse. Nothing she took made any difference. While getting dressed for church, she snapped, "God, why won't You do something and stop the pain?"

Sitting in Bethesda, looking out the window, she listened to the minister give the announcements. Softly, the Holy Spirit spoke to her, 'Job 15:12'. Embarrassed by her earlier outburst, she apprehensively turned to the scripture. 'Why does your heart carry you away and why do your eyes flash that you should turn your spirit against God and allow such words to go out of your mouth?'

"I'm sorry, Lord," she humbly prayed. 'See a doctor,' penetrated her spirit.

The following Wednesday, after a day of thorough examinations, Mary silently dressed and waited in Dr. Buckner's office. Looking somber, the doctor shuffled some papers, then pulled out an x-ray and displayed it so she could view it. He pointed to the edge of her cranium and stated, "I regret to inform you, Mary, but there seems to be a small tumor in this area of your brain."

Gasping at the word, Mary sat bewildered. A mocking spirit flew by, fling the words, "Some God you have!" at her. She paid no attention to it, remembering the word God had given her at church. "I must not blame God," she thought.

"Is it serious?" she asked, worried.

"Yes, I'm afraid it is. We're going to have to operate as soon as possible."

"What are my chances of recovery?"

To be honest, with the location of the tumor, you may lose your sight. We can't be certain until we see what we're dealing with."

"Blessed be the name of the Lord," she stated. "No matter what happens, I'm not going to blame this on God."

Gathering up her belongings, she added, "Doctor, I'm going to go and talk to my Lord about this, and then I'll let you know what I'm going to do."

Smirking, the doctor said, "Whatever you say, but don't leave it go too long. Personally, I don't believe in miracles; but if you can conjure one up, then go ahead and try."

On the drive home, Mary's head was aching, but it was nothing compared to the anguish in her heart. A sense of distance from God crept over her. After so many years of a loving God blessing her and guiding her, was this how it would all end? Blind or dead?

When she entered the house, she couldn't contain her tears any longer and fell onto the couch, weeping with great sobs of despair. Odessa stood nearby, listening. "Praise Him, Mary," he whispered. "Just praise Him." Reaching for her Bible, the tears stopped completely, and she turned to her favorite book, Job. So often God had consoled her through the words written there.

As though detached from the circumstances, she opened near the end of the book. Reading from Chapter thirty-three, the words leapt into her heart. 'Why do you complain against Him, that he does not give an account of all His doings?' (Job33:13) Quietly, she turned the page. More words convicted her spirit. 'Don't let your suffering embitter you at the only One who can save you.' (Job 36:11) "Father, I'm not bitter. I guess I feel rejected by You to allow a disease to be in me makes me think You don't love me anymore."

Letting the pages flip through her fingers, it opened to the book of Joel. There in the second Chapter, Mary read out loud, 'Praise the name of the Lord your God, who has dealt wondrously with you.' (Joel 2:26) "Yes, Lord, you have dealt wondrously with me, even though my trials and heartaches. Please tell me, what is this test You're putting me through? Is it really necessary?"

There was no reply.

Mary sighed and put her Bible calmly in the dresser. Maybe tomorrow God would speak, but for now the best medicine seemed like an early night in bed.

Chapter Thirty-four
Crusade Comes to Town

Joshua had been fairly fulfilled in his part-time role as a father and very fulfilled in his full-time role at preschool; but he too was getting restless for someone he could call his own. Long ago he had decided if he couldn't walk in righteousness without a woman, he wouldn't be able to walk in righteousness with one.

With only the occasional fall and making a real attempt to block out unclean pictures in his mind, Josh had pleased the Lord in his walk as a single man of God. There was a young woman Josh's age who was coming to speak at a combined church rally on New Year's Eve. Her life story was in paperback, and Josh had sent away for it.

As he read the truth behind this lady's demonic infiltration and her subsequent release as a Christian, he wondered if maybe his unclean thoughts were being demonically fueled. Marcia Miller, the evangelist, may hold the answer. In fact, maybe her coming to Cambridge would release a lot of pent-up problems that Josh and others had.

On the outside, everything seemed okay; but on the inside many Christians were still captive in emotional and sinful bondages. Those with some spiritual maturities were meeting at Second Birth Assembly to prepare as counselors for the crusade.

Patty was elated. "I've been telling you all for years how much demons can wreck a Christian's walk, and now we're going to see God move in a mighty way."

Mary questioned, "Are you trying to tell me demons need to be delivered from Christians?" Thinking how great it would be if her tumor was just a demon that needed to be cast out. Before Patty could answer, Mary spoke again. "But the Bible says that light and dark can't be together. How can I have the Holy Spirit and darkness at the same time?"

"I want you to open your Bible to 2 Corinthians 6:14." Eagerly optimistic, the little group turned to the scripture, waiting to see what new revelation God had for them. Even though they'd been Christians for a long time, they were still open for God to teach them new things from His Word.

"Mary, you read verse 14."

'What fellowship can light have with darkness?'

Patty looked at her seriously. "What is that talking about? It's saying Christians aren't to be yoked in fellowship with unbelievers. It goes on to say that we're God's temple and to come out and be separate from unbelievers. It's not saying a demon, which is 'darkness', can't affect someone who's 'light'. God tells us our battle is against spirits and evil forces. We don't wrestle against flesh and blood." (Eph 6:12)

Glancing at her open Bible, she went on, "Now what does the next Chapter say in verse 1, assuming he's still talking about separating ourselves from ungodly people?"

Mary read, 'Let us purify ourselves from everything that contaminates body and spirit.'(2Cor 7:1)

"Stop there," Patty said. "See, God separates body and spirit as two different things, and we are to purify ourselves from those things which can defile them. That could include ungodly people or books, music or even television. Now turn to James 4:8. Again, we're told to purify our hearts. James was talking to Christians and he called them double-minded and sinners. He told them to submit to God, resist the devil, which means stop falling into temptation and then the devil will flee. Repent and stop being double-minded. Only a Christian can be double-minded because the heathen doesn't have anything to do with God's kingdom."

Joshua broke in. "So, what you're saying is that demonic spirits of darkness can compel Christians to sin."

Amanda spoke. "Remember what Peter said to Ananias, 'why has Satan filled your heart?'"

The room was still as each person sat, deep in their own thoughts.

Josh decided to come clean, even though he risked being rejected and condemned because he knew God gives grace to the humble. There it was in James. "I have a problem I just can't seem to shake. Horrible pictures come into my head and I know it's from the days when I read my girlie magazines, but I don't own any anymore. In fact, it's been years since I even picked one up."

In a motherly tone, Patty asked, "Is there anything else you're doing wrong?"

Unbelief came to his mind and he added, "I don't trust God enough; and when He tells me to do something, I don't do it because I'm afraid it won't work."

"You're in the sin of fear and disobedience; and because of that you're double-minded so the unclean spirits have access to your mind," Patty gently replied.

Eva slowly raised her hand. "Besides the obvious deception I had by my marriage being unevenly yoked, I find I just don't want to read the Bible or pray anymore, even when I have the time. It's like something is blocking my walk with God."

"Have you ever been involved in the occult," Amanda asked. "Like having your fortune told or being involved in a séance, or even following astrology?" Alarm bells rang in Eva's conscience. Besides the palm-reading, she'd had all sorts of demonic activity in her life. Taking a deep breath and then exhaling loudly, Eva felt anguish in her spirit. "Do you know why my mothers in that mental hospital?"

Everyone looked at each other, but no one dared to speak. It had all been speculation and gossip that her mother had just gone crazy.

Eva continued, "After my grandmother died, mom began calling her back from the grave. It went on for quite some time. I know now that even though she thought it was her mother, it was a familiar spirit which used to come into my room scaring me with nightmares for years. As a Christian, the dreams have stopped, but I always seem to be a little afraid when I lie in the dark. In fact, I seem to be afraid of many things. I even have a fear of God as well as the fear I have of darkness and death. I'm really frightened of being left alone. To be honest, I think I married Johnny out of fear that I would never get married. Now I live in fear that if I don't do what he says, he may leave me and take Rebecca away."

Patty poured a cup of coffee and then sat next to Eva. "It says in Deuteronomy (18:11) that those who go to mediums or spiritists or consult the dead will be detested by God. In layman terms, there's probably a curse on your family and it may even go back to your grandparents."

Fear tightened its grip. "I don't believe all this. I'm going home and you can debate it out between yourselves about voodoo and Christianity!" With that, Eva rose, grabbed her Bible and purse and then mumbled quick good-byes before rushing out the door. It was obvious she was fearful of what she could learn.

Patty continued, "Even though we are seated in heavenly places spiritually with Christ, our bodies are still here and susceptible to lusts, corruptions and demonic persuasions."

Amanda nodded, catching her train of thought. "Do you all remember that family from Minnesota who moved here last year? What was their daughter's name?"

"I think it was Maureen, and she left for college last fall," Esther answered.

"Do you remember she came to the Lord at our New Years' service and then was baptized? During the next couple of weeks, she stopped getting high on pot and beer, broke up with her boyfriend and did her best to quit smoking. The following month we had a message on repentance from bitterness and she came forward to the altar, crying hysterically as she forgave her dad for abusing her."

Esther added, "I remember. Didn't she start groaning and then with a shriek she went quiet? She looked so beautiful and peaceful and from what I heard, she never smoked again. Obviously, the key was forgiveness."

Shyly, Mary asked, "Who did Jesus send his disciples out to cast demons from?"

Patty replied, "Anyone who repented and wanted the name of Jesus to set them free. Some, however, have decided that the only people we're allowed to cast a demon out of is an unbeliever. You tell me someone who doesn't believe in the name of Jesus who will let you cast a demon out of them in His name. It's Jesus who sets the captives free, those who call on Him. But sometimes we must confess the sins of our ancestors as well as our own. God punishes those who don't love Him, right down the family line." Deuteronomy (5:9)

As all the little warriors got into their cars to go home, each were in their own vigil of prayer. A few knew they needed to fast and seek God for possible strongholds the enemy had in their life.

Christmas passed and the New Year's rally was a day away. For many in Cambridge, this season would bring them to a closer relationship with God depending on whether or not they responded to God's call for holiness the night Marcia preached. After reading her book, Josh felt a closeness to Marcia, and in fact, had been praying for her and her ministry.

The opening night the auditorium was packed. The advertisement had declared that through the name of Jesus people would be healed and set free. Even the skeptics turned up to watch.

Eva's fear had convinced her it was not the place for her to be on New Year's; so instead, dragging little Becky along, she and Johnny went to a private party in another county with one of his work mates. But all night she had a little nudge that she was in the wrong place.

After the worship and praise time had ended, all eyes followed the tall brunette onto the stage. She was immaculately dressed in a white tailored suit with a pink rose in her lapel. Her hair was long and dark cascading down past her waist; and as she moved across the platform, it flowed behind. She was even more beautiful than Josh had anticipated, but even more so, she radiated a joy and holiness that touched his spirit and many others in the hall.

Her words were bold. "You must repent from all your deep dark secrets," she pronounced. "God's Word warns us to give the devil no opportunity. What are you giving the enemy the opportunity to do through your secret sins? What relationship do you need to have reinstated that's keeping you in bitterness?"

She took a sip of water. "Turn to Acts 8"

Now Simon was a magician who along with many others, decided to become a believer and be baptized, so he was. Now he had become a brand-new follower of the Lord and decided he wanted to do miracles too and offered money for the power, but Peter turned to him and declared, "No! Your heart is not right before God."

Now why would he say this to someone who has just become a believer? Simon was a baby Christian, and that's a very harsh thing to say to a baby Christian. But then Peter turns to him and says, 'I see you're full of bitterness and captive to sin.' (Acts 8:23) So he had repented from his obvious sin of fooling around with the occult, but he was still bitter at somebody and the enemy still held him captive in that area. Have you repented from everything or are you still being held captive in your heart by areas you're hanging on to? Now's the time to leave it here at the altar."

The musicians quietly played and over a hundred people filed down to the front, tears streaming down some of their faces, while Patty's little prayer group had all their eyes fastened on one couple as they went forward.

Joshua and Esther slowly made their way to the front, holding hands. Watching them, Amanda began to weep. "God, please do all You can while Esther's down there. Don't let pride stop her."

As Marcia prayed, some of the people let out shrieks and groans while some fell over, immersed by the power of God. Many dropped to their knees, begging God's forgiveness and making a new commitment, apologizing for their complacency.

In the heavens, the angels were in full warrior defense. Missiles and shackles of light were hounding the demons until not one was left standing victoriously. Esther buried her head in her hands and cried loudly while Josh rested his hand lovingly on her shoulder. Marcia made her way over to them brushing the hair from her neck for a second so that a breath of air could cool her down. Then, placing her hand tenderly on Esther's head, she asked, "What do you want the Lord to do for you?" She glanced at Josh, indicating she would deal with his mother herself.

"I have stomach pains so I live on antacids."

"There must be more to it than that." Gently, Marcia asked, "Who are you mad at?" Again, she looked at Josh. Releasing his hand from Esther's shoulder, he stood back.

Josh only just caught the words. "I hate my husband. I've resented him for years." "Are you ready to repent?"

"Yes, I am."

Placing her other hand on Esther's shoulder, Marcia stated, "In Jesus' name, we break the powers of Satan. We command the spirits of bitterness, anger and hate to leave now in Jesus' name."

Suddenly, Esther coughed several times. Just like she had the day she got baptized. Surprised, she clutched a hankie and tried to compose herself.

"This isn't the time to be ladylike. Lift your arms and praise Jesus. He's setting you free."

As Esther obeyed, her face contorted and she bent over, grabbing her stomach. Josh started to reach for her, but Marcia shook her head.

"There's another secret that you have which is eating you up inside," Marcia declared. "What else haven't you been honest about?"

"I am still carrying bitterness towards the ladies' prayer group. I probably got rejection too.

"I break the power of deception over you in Jesus' name. And spirit of suicide, leave at once."

Esther couldn't stifle a yawn. In the spirit realm as each creature was forced to yield their ground, Nova sliced them with his sword of light, dispersing the ogres. "I'm free!" Esther cried. "Praise God, I'm free."

Marcia placed her hand on Joshua's head and prayed in tongues.

Esther reluctantly tapped her on the shoulder and whispered, "I'm his mother, and I need to say something to him first. It might help his release."

"All right," Marcia replied. "Thank you for your honesty. I'll come back in a few minutes."

Mother and son walked over to a bench and sat down. Josh noticed a difference in her eyes and a softness in her face which had been missing for years. "What happened back there, mom?"

"I repented of years of hating your father, which meant that even as a Christian, I gave demonic powers access to myself. But I've kicked them out by repenting and asking God's forgiveness."

Taking a deep breath, she laughed. "It feels great!"

Then, patting him on the hand, Esther's face became serious. "There's something I need to tell you. We've always celebrated our wedding anniversary on the wrong date. The fact is, we got married because I was pregnant with you."

Josh turned away, shocked at this disclosure. "It seems to run in the family, doesn't it?"

"Even more than that," Esther stated," Your father was adopted as a baby, his mother was only a teenager when he was born and gave him away, so he was determined you'd have both parents married when you were born. I guess both of us felt all along like we'd started on the wrong foot."

A tear rolled down Josh's face.

"But I've always loved you and I'm very proud of you. My little sex talks with you years ago was to prevent you from ending up in the same predicament as your dad and me."

Josh leaned over and embraced Esther. The two held onto each other tightly, while God's Spirit released a new measure of grace and faith over both of them. Stirling and Nova rejoiced. "Maybe you should go and let Marcia pray for all this so that God can heal the wounds."

"Okay, mom," he said, affectionately giving her a peck on the cheek; but as he walked over, Josh just couldn't humble himself enough to admit the lust that was running in his family line. Instead, he shared only about his fear of failure and mistrust of God.

Marcia discerned he was holding something back. "Is there something else you want to tell God you're sorry for?"

Josh so much wanted to be honest, but he couldn't bring himself to admit that his thoughts weren't pure. He shook his head and said, "No, I'll be all right."

The day came for Mary's operation. God had spoken very clearly for her to not be afraid. There was a peace over her. Even the doctor noticed it.

Walter had been alerted by the Holy Spirit to leave Japan and go home. He wanted to be close to his mom in her hour of need. He paced worriedly up and down the waiting lounge while Tanya sat quietly in the corner and prayed. Leroy, their son, sat across from his mother playing with a karate doll which the stewardess had given him on the flight home. The Smiths didn't really approve, but figured that at his age, a toy was a toy.

Th e doctor signaled for them to come to Mary's room. Her face lit up as her eyes were drawn straight to the child. For seven years of age, he was small; but then he took after his mother. Edward peeked around the corner and Tanya went to him and wrapped her arms around him tightly when he entered the room. "Dad, let's pray," she suggested.

Mary reached for Leroy's hand, and they all bowed their heads in reverence except Leroy who was fascinated by the hospital machines with their blinking lights.

"Father, we commit Mary to You for Your will to be done. We ask for You to keep her safe from pain and to guide the doctor's hand."

Walt softly cried. It was almost as if he was wishing he'd had this chance with his father at least to have said goodbye in prayer. But no one was thinking the worst for Mary. They were optimistically praising God that he was going to see His daughter through this dangerous surgery.

There was some shuffling by the door. Much to Mary's astonishment, about twenty people from Bethesda were lined up in the corridor. One by one they filtered in, reading an encouraging verse and then leaving a little bouquet of flowers. Reverend Rowlands was last, and he read a small speech he had prepared. "All of us want to say thank you for the example you have been in behaving like a proper Christian. You never stopped believing in our hypocritical bunch; and as you prayed for us through the years, many had their spiritual eyes opened. We owe you a lot and pray that God will bring you safely through this."

Mary reached for a tissue and wiped her eyes. All the rejection she'd felt there had been turned to good. Softly, God spoke to her spirit, "Well done, good and faithful servant. Come, share your Master's happiness."

The doctor came in and informed the group it was time to leave. Walter lifted Leroy to kiss his grandmother, and then as they disappeared out the door. Mary sighed. "It's just you and me now, Lord. Thank you for letting me see my grandchild. I'm ready to come meet You if that is Your will." A tear trickled down her face.

Four hours later the doctor came to the waiting lounge. He walked slowly, with his head hanging down. It didn't look good. "I'm sorry, Walter," he said sadly, squeezing the black man's arm tightly, "but we lost her on the table. There was nothing any of us could do. The tumor was just too big, and it was almost as if she wanted to go."

Walter held back his tears, then swooping Leroy into his arms, walked briskly down the corridor. Tanya and Ed stayed behind to make arrangements for the body to be transported to the funeral parlor.

Three days later at the burial service, many from Cambridge and Ruxton gathered together to pay their last respects. Flowers and wreaths lined the walls of the room. With a heavy heart, Esther made a note of who had sent each one so she could send a thank you letter later. There was one small, obviously inexpensive arrangement. It looked like the cheapest one could buy when ordering for a delivery. She guessed it must be from some poor black family Mary had known from Ruxton. "How thoughtful," she sighed.

Esther reached for the message and then read it in a stunned whisper. "Forgive me, Mary. I knew not what I did." It was signed, "Sam Evans."

She gasped and then broke down in tears. People turned and Joshua ran to her, wrapping his arm around her. She placed the card in his hand and he silently read the words.

"I don't believe it," Josh mumbled. "Mom, God touched him because you released and forgave him last month."

Just at that moment, Edward walked up. "I thought you might like to know who turned up in my carpentry class last night after participating for forty-five minutes in a Bible study."

Josh and his mother looked at each other. "Sam?" Esther smiled.

"Yes, apparently something happened to him this past week; and the warden has permitted him to attend, even though his sentence won't be reduced."

"Good, he's stuck there!" a demon spat into her mind as it whizzed by. Esther didn't even grasp the words. They darted in and then darted out. She was just grateful that God was touching her husband.

Josh had been trying to decide about seeing his father.

Sam had refused visits by his son after Josh had shared about his conversion in Vietnam. After that, they didn't have much to talk about, so it had been years since Josh had seen him.

That night, sitting nervously, he waited for the prisoners to be brought in. There was Sam. He looked well. Definitely pale from lack of outdoor activity, but physically healthy. The shock was written on his face when he saw his son, and then hesitantly he walked over and reached out his hand.

Josh shook his father's outstretched hand and thought, "Couldn't he just hug me once?" But rather than offend him, Josh sat down and contained his compassion.

"Son, this is a surprise! What brings you here? Me?"

Josh was happy to say the word "yes"

Sam shrugged. "On New Year's Eve I had a dream about my father. He wasn't my real father, and he always let me know that."

Josh listened intently. Was his dad about to bear his soul?

"I don't know if your mother ever told you this, but I'm adopted. My mother was a little floozy who got knocked up and then had me adopted out. Thank God they didn't have abortions then, or I'm sure I wouldn't be here."

Taking a drag from his cigarette, he looked around and quipped, "Although, maybe that would have been better."

"Don't say that, dad," Josh said kindly, as his eyes were drawn to a petite redhead clasping a Bible and talking to another prisoner. "Hey, who's that?"

"Still got your eyes on the chicks, eh, son?" his father replied lightly slapping him on the cheek. "That's Stephen Hanks and his daughter, Sharon. She's one of you. She's a Christian too. His cell is next to mine, and I always hear her coming and preaching to him."

"Sorry, dad. I interrupted. Tell me about your dream." Josh realized time was running out, and it was more important to hear what Sam had to say.

"There was a man in a long shiny robe. I assumed it was Jesus. He told me I'd been released to forgive my father and then I woke up. I couldn't stop thinking about it for two days. Then I overheard Sharon saying, 'God only forgives those who forgive others.' Then Edward told me about Mary's death. I couldn't apologize to her in person for being so rude, so I sent some flowers."

Josh choked as he said, "I saw them, Dad." He placed his hand carefully on his father's calloused one. "Mom showed them to me. That was very thoughtful."

"It was guilt that motivated me to send them. I don't understand all this Jesus stuff, and I don't know how to trust God as my Father."

Stirling brushed his wing over Joshua. "Neither do you," the angel whispered.

"Dad, I've been a Christian for eight years, and I still have trouble trusting God sometimes."

"That's my fault. I read a book that Sharon gave to her father. It said if we didn't trust our earthly father, we'd have a hard time trusting our heavenly one."

Squeezing his dad's hand, Josh said tenderly, "I've always loved you deep down, but you wouldn't love me back. You only shot me down."

"I know, son. I did to you exactly what my father did to me. Will you forgive me?"

With a quick hug, he whispered, "I already have." Then with a wink, he added, "Will you become a Christian?"

They both laughed. "Yes, I want to know God as my Father. I want to talk to Him like George Smith did so many years ago."

And so, among a room filled with vessels Satan had commandeered for his evil purposes, Josh and his dad knelt while tears were spent unchecked.

Reverently, Joshua prayed his father into the kingdom of God.

Chapter Thirty-five
What's the Lord Up to?

Much had happened in five years not only in Cambridge but all over the world. The Greenpeace Ship, which sailed as a representative of nature citing a symbol of protection, was bombed without warning or mercy. Mexico was hit with one of Mother Nature's worst disasters, an earthquake measuring 3.1 on the Richter Scale which killed thousands, and the death of John Lennon sent a fearful message to us all that the States weren't safe for anyone.

In the media, there seemed to be a struggle going on as new attempts to stretch censorship were being taken to the limit in the name of freedom of the press.

In 1981, the best picture award went to <u>Chariots of Fire</u> where a man's Christian principles were put to the ultimate test. While the next year, the world looked upon an Indian leader in the movie <u>Ghandi</u> who for all the good he stood for, had denied Christ because of the behavior he had seen in a church. Ironically, he was assassinated two years later.

1983 took our eyes to the stars and the possibility that other creatures had 'evolved' in this so-called 'accident' called the universe. Music went from seductive to demonically inspire. Many began to align themselves publicly with the powers of darkness, attributing their success to Satan. Sex symbols came and went, luring young people by the thousands to live fast and die young. In a bid to do something humane and worthwhile, Live Aid, a satellite-beamed concert seen in one hundred and sixty160 countries across the world, raised eighty 80 million dollars to be sent to Africa for relief. The principalities and rulers didn't mind as long as Christian missionaries didn't present the money and stay over there to administer it.

What some called 'God's judgment', AIDS' was now an ever-present thorn that didn't seem to want to go away no matter how hard the scientists tried to find a cure. Only certain people were supposed to be the victims; but as time went on, it seemed the evil cared not whom it infected.

1984 brought the Olympics to California; and while sports contenders from around the world demonstrated their prowess, committed Christians from eighty nations endured the heat and smog to share their faith all over the city for two weeks. According to the Los Angeles police, there was a ninety percent drop in violence and crime during those fourteen days and incredibly, not one murder.

At the beginning of this half-decade with seven hundred million people watching on television, Prince Charles married Dianna Spencer. While in Cambridge, and with only a guest list of twenty-five, there was another marriage; and the angels rejoiced with God as two of his servants took their vows. It seemed not only had Joshua been destined to pray for his father that day in prison, but he also had been led there to meet his future bride.

Sharon Hanks was soon to become Mrs. Joshua Evans. The two had worked side-by-side in many of the church projects while courting. God had waited over a year before he spoke the word 'yes' to both of them simultaneously.

Thus, it was on Valentine's Day 1985 that Pastor Burrows united the two in holy matrimony. When Josh and Sharon returned from their honeymoon in Florida, an unexpected letter awaited him. It was from Debbie and stated she had moved to Hollywood to join a band and that Lilly was now his, free and clear. She had left her with one of her neighbors, Esther, and all he had to do was go and pick her up. Obviously, Debbie felt she would be a hindrance to her plans in L.A. After all, who wanted a tubby teenager as an encumbrance when so many doors might open up to her? Before she left, Debbie had sold her home finally; and with the little left after paying off her mortgage, she halved the balance with Josh. His share had been given to Esther, and he could collect it once he picked up Lilly. She had hoped it would be incentive enough for him to be willing to finish raising the child.

"Sharon!" Josh called to his wife as she was unpacking. "You'd better come to the den. There's something we need to discuss."

Observing her walking down the stairs, he realized how grateful he was to God for this fine Christian wife whose main aim was to please the Lord and her new husband.

"Sweetheart," Josh announced warily, "you've become a mother."

"What do you mean?" she asked, coming and sitting on his lap and entwining her slender arms around his broad shoulders.

Softly kissing her neck and brushing the silky locks from her cheek, Josh realized Lilly was bigger than she was and wondered how Sharon would manage taking on this child.

He carefully worded his sentence. "Debbie has left the state and is legally pursuing to have Lilly become ours. There's no way I can let my daughter be adopted out to a home, so we're going to have to pick her up and bring her back to live with us. I know this is a big shock, honey, but there's nothing else I can do."

From what Sharon knew of Lilly, she realized that her job wouldn't be easy, but she figured that with a lot of love and God's grace, together they could nurture her out of the deep emotional problems that Lilly was hounded by.

Hence, Lilly joined their family and in 1986 became a sister to Rhonda, a seven-pound little charmer with green eyes and curly red hair.

With the new baby on the scene, Lilly slipped into the background. Now all the attention was on her sister. As a teenager, she was soon to be the odd one out because of her obesity. It was as if history was repeating itself since Debbie had once been unattractive and teased; now her daughter was also fat and being left out, having to endure cruel jokes just as Debbie had.

Lilly's rejection was very deep-seated, and this had many inroads into her life. Being dumped by her mother when she went off to Hollywood was the ultimate slap in the face, and the enemy was now given a wide-open door as she cultivated her rejection and resentment to harden her heart.

Now with little Rhonda in the house, her feelings went on into jealousy and then into anger until finally, a mocking hate was born towards life and all it had to offer. Even more so, she inwardly rebelled at all the extra chores put on her to help run the house.

Sharon had formed a committee and had gone on the rampage against the video shops, picketing and screaming out for justice to stop the infiltration of R and X rated movies being so freely available in town. She also formed a censorship committee at the local movie theater, not only to veto some of the films, but also to censor the advertising which was shown before the movie actually began. It seemed the commercials were advocating cigarettes, alcohol and premarital sex as the normal way of life.

Second Birth Assembly's youth group would monitor the films for those movies that they felt it appropriate, they would stand outside and hand out gospel tracts as the audience left the cinema, especially after those movies which would leave the patrons wondering what really happens after death.

With his work at the preschool, Josh had delegated some of that to others. Now he and Bill Butler were running a men's fellowship. Its purpose was to bring non-Christian businessmen to an evening with 'the boys', with the exact opposite intentions to the Freeson Lodge. Their idea was to enhance family life the way God intended. Often times a testimony would be shared and the men would pray for each other and talk about things that God was doing individually in their lives.

So, Josh was busy, and Sharon's time was occupied, which left Lilly to take care of Rhonda. Emotionally, it was good for Lilly to have someone to love if she would let herself do it. There was a hunger in her to feel needed somewhere. She was riddled with rejection and also, like her father, had that feeling of never being worthy. Each glance in the mirror added to her own self-hate and gave the ghouls distorted delight. Even though Josh had prayed a prayer of protection over her, the enemy was still seeking strongholds so Lilly would never be redeemed.

At this time there was a new philosophy being unleashed over the heavenlies. It was controlled by the principality Antichrist and would in time, be deemed 'The New Age'. Satan was strategically placing vessels of his own choosing into the public school system where slowly, over a period of time, this 'god within' delusion, would surface in all areas of modem society and even be table talk at local cocktail parties.

All in the name of science, teachers began flooding schools looking for kids with ESP and other special gifts. Telekinetic, moving objects with your mind, and bending metals became a spectacular way to gain special attention; and Lilly decided she wanted to do something to be noticed, so she entreated God to give her some of that special power.

It had taken Josh many months of prayer and teaching to undo the demonic damage in Lilly's mind about the use of God's gifts versus calling on demons to aid you, now unknowingly, she was calling to the Lord to bestow on her forbidden power.

The school's mandatory course in minor psychology had subtly deadened her Christian foundation but had encouraged her that' yes, there was a god, it is a force within all of us, we must simply tap into it. That force is our inner strength that helps us to live; it gives us life.' So eagerly, Lilly tried to encounter this 'god', but the result would cement deception.

In the grammar school of Cambridge, the powers of darkness were Releasing the same delusion, and Eva's and Johnny Brown's daughter Amy named after her Aunt, was about to be ensnared in the trap too. The school bell rang and the third graders sat down quietly, eager to hear what the substitute teacher was going to teach them.

Lilly sat fascinated, even though a little confused, as the teacher explained to all the children that god was within, only instead of calling him 'god', for now we'll call him our guide. Lilly thought this all sounded familiar from Sunday school but hadn't he forgotten something? Curiously, she raised her hand and stated, "I learned we can't know the Father unless we know Jesus. (John 14:6) David over there doesn't know Jesus because he's a Jew. They don't even believe in Jesus."

"Young lady," the teacher growled, "let me ask you this. Do you believe God is a loving God?"

"Yes, sir, I do!" She smiled as she thought of the God her step mother, Sharon, had talked about.

He looked over his glasses disdainfully at her. "Then do you think a loving God would stop David from talking to Him just because he doesn't believe in Jesus who isn't even alive anymore?"

Lilly sat there deep in thought, unsure of what to say. "Would He?" the teacher barked.

Shyly and uncertain of the answer, she replied, "No, I guess not."

"One other thing, miss. The police can arrest you for speaking about Jesus on school property so you'd better keep that stuff to yourself!"

Lilly's eyes widened as she slid down in her seat, embarrassed and confused.

Every day that week the children were to go home and try to reach their inner guide. Once they found him, they were to ask his name. The second part of the exercise was that once they knew his name, they were to ask him to do something for them.

When Lilly arrived home, she quietly walked past Sharon, still deep in thought, at what she'd heard in class.

"What's the matter, honey? Is everything all right?"

A demon flew by and deposited into her mind the thought, "Don't tell her or she'll call the school and complain. Then you'll really get it!"

Conceiving the thought, she turned to her step-mother; and with her heart aching to cry in her arms and explain how that mean man had embarrassed her, instead she softly answered, "No, mom. Everything's okay. I'm just tired."

"Okay, sweetie. You know what? I'm going to see your grandmother, Janet, as soon as daddy gets home. When she gets better you can come and meet her too. Would you like that?"

"Yes," she called back as she trailed her school case behind her up the stairs.

As Lilly settled in to do her homework, she decided to make the atmosphere just right. Sneaking downstairs to the dining room she stole two candles and some matches from the kitchen. Remembering how the older kids in gym class participated in yoga, Lilly decided to copy them and sat Indian style on the floor. Then, folding her arms across her chest, she began to hum. She felt stupid as she tried to relax and let herself go with the mood. She was also distracted by the flickering lights of the candles, but just as she was going to give up, it happened.

"Lilly!"

"Who was that?" she stammered, scared but excited. "I am your guide!"

Lilly sat still. She heard her heart pounding in her chest.

Moving her eyes in a circling motion, wondering where the voice had come from, she whispered, "But, you're outside of me!"

The spirit merged inside her and spoke to her mind. "No, here I am! I'm the power inside."

"What's your name?" Lilly asked, intrigued by what was happening.

There was no reply.

"What's your name?" she insisted.

'Satan' was whispered through the canyons of her mind.

Suddenly, the candles blew out, yet there was no breath of wind. Scared, Lilly jumped up quickly to turn on the light. Looking around the room she felt a presence but was unsure whether it was real or not. At least she'd made contact with something.

Glancing at the picture of Jesus hanging over her bed, He seemed so insignificant at that moment, too far away; and when it came time to go to sleep, Lilly didn't bother to say good night to Him, something she'd done many times before.

Sitting reverently in her car, Eva said a small prayer asking God to help her with her meeting with Janet, the long-lost mother she hadn't seen in years. Her thoughts returned to the day of her grandmother's funeral and how devastated Janet had been. "She must have loved her very much," she thought sadly. "Why didn't she love me?"

Sensing the old thoughts of hate were surfacing, Carras laid his hand tenderly on her shoulder and released myriads of light to follow her into the demon-riddled hospital. Waiting nervously in the lounge, Eva tried forming her words, but it was too late. A haggard-looking woman shuffled up and then sat beside her.

"They say you're my daughter," she blurted out. "What do you want?"

Her mother's tongue was harsh and cold. The demons in her were igniting their poison to ensure this Christian didn't feel any compassion rising up which could cause her to pray for their vessel and their home. They couldn't take the chance.

"Yes, I am." She smiled, determined to overcome this rejection and then leaned forward to slip her arm around her mother. The demons in Janet became agitated and she drew away.

"Don't touch us!" a voice commanded.

Eva sat stunned. "Did she say 'us'?" A verse came to her mind, quickened by the Holy Spirit. 'We are Christ's ambassadors as if God Himself were speaking through us." (2 Cor 5:20)

"That's it," Eva thought. "The demons see Jesus in me."

Desperate to break down the barriers, she responded, "Here, mother"

"Janet! Call me Janet!" she demanded.

Eva relented. "Here, Janet. I brought you a present." She smiled, handing her a box of chocolates. Her mother gave a tiny grin and then, resembling a little girl on Christmas morning, she eagerly ripped open the box.

Eva's heart melted and tears welled up in her eyes. She had always wanted her mother's approval and love, but instead all these years Janet had hated her. Now her mother, almost fifty years old, was acting more like a child. Would Eva ever know her mother's love?

Her visit was brief, and the nurse agreed it would be good for her to return to visit Janet again in a few days. Meanwhile, Eva would get the church together to pray. As she left, Eva sent a prayer to God to minister to Janet and open her heart to a revelation of who Jesus really was.

Walter and Tanya couldn't have been happier back at his home. Tanya was busy working at the preschool with Joshua and Walt had been able to return to his first love, car racing. Edward had kept his promise and given him a car and, so the hunt was on for sponsors. God was now willing to give him the desires of his heart as long as Walter never let the thrill of victory impair his vision with God. He promised the Lord, he would give Him the honor and had painted on the side of the car the words 'For His Glory'. Walt proved himself to be a competent driver, in fact, a very competent one; but God's words were very clear to him one day during devotions. 'Do nothing from selfish ambition.'

"Okay, Father, I won't," Walt promised.

Leroy, their son, was now eleven and was fascinated with violence. It had started subtly years before, watching Kung Fu movies on television while they lived in Tokyo. Then with his model of a karate boy, the gift from the airline stewardess, he would spend hours upon hours making up karate moves and sound effects as if in actual combat. In Japan, the children were usually very polite to him; but once in America, the formality of consideration towards others didn't seem to be present in the local young people of Cambridge, and of course, kids will be kids.

Because Leroy was rather small, he was often picked on by bigger boys, including black children who now were about 30 percent of the school. He began having a complex about his size and decided fighting would be the best way to defend himself. Borrowing books from the library over the months on karate and Kung Fu, he had taught himself quite sufficiently. It seemed soon he would have the unwitting opportunity to prove it. There was a club at school which gave students protection and leadership among the school body, and there was a status that went with it. Any member of the Bad Boys was not to be messed with, and Leroy envied their loyalty to each other.

One day some sixth graders ran by, grabbed his books and threw them into the air. The wind caught the papers and scattered them all over the street as the kids ran off laughing. There was something about sixth graders that made them think they were better than anyone else. Although Leroy was old enough to be in sixth grade, he'd lost a year in the transfer to America; and by looking at his size, no one would ever have guessed he was that young.

Furious at this latest assault, Leroy decided to try to join the Bad Boys. After school, the members gathered to determine his initiation. The ghouls were eager to get Leroy into this group and alienate him from his parents and Christian upbringing.

Pete Jennings, a rebel just like his dad had been, was the leader of the Bad Boys, a group of motorcycle riders, and he was the devious decider of all the initiation schemes. The demons owned him outright, and this time they easily gave him the ploy for Leroy to accomplish if he was to become a member.

"Your parents are Christians, aren't they?" he snarled.

Leroy winced. "Oh, no, here it comes," he thought.

The wheels were turning in Pete's head. Then one of the commandments that he knew leaped into his mind. 'Thou shalt not steal' (7th commandment Ex25:15) "He won't want to steal," Pete thought.

"Okay, Leroy. First, go to Cooper's toy store and steal a bike; and when you're done, go plant it at David Beam's house and come straight back here afterwards with your mother's Bible."

Leroy began to question his orders, but was chided by a thought penetrating his mind. "This will get them all off your back once and for all."

"Okay, I'll do it," he responded. The demons applauded, knowing the potential this little charade could hold for them.

That afternoon, with his heart pounding louder than a drum, Leroy sneaked into the warehouse of Cooper's. The Holy Spirit was speaking and moving strongly on him in conviction, but Leroy's ego was at stake now. If he didn't return with the mission accomplished, he'd be a whole year with these sixth graders bugging him.

"I've just gotta do this without getting caught," he rationalized.

He looked for Mr. Cooper and saw him by the cash register. Spying out a boy's black and gold ten speed, Leroy sneaked over, grabbed it and then shot through the back door, pedaling as fast as he could. The fear was intense, but as he got further away, a smirk came on his face.

"One down, two to go."

When he reached Sheriff Beam's house, Leroy walked guardedly. There on the porch was the grandfather, Willy, and recently retired Sheriff Beam. He was now very old and stocky; and Leroy figured that even if he did see him, he'd never be able to catch him. Like a snake, Leroy slithered into the shed, leaving the bike there and once again was gone in a flash. As he got closer to home, he began pondering how he could take his mom's Bible without her noticing.

"Why did Pete want the Bible?" he wondered.

"Because it will hurt her," came to his mind.

"But I don't want to hurt mom."

Another voice sneered, 'She can get another one.'

Leroy strolled past his mom with his thoughts on one thing, going straight to her room, stealing the book and then heading straight back to the group before his time limit was over. "Honey, would you please rake the leaves before dinner," his mom called to him. "I can't, mom."

"Leroy, I'm asking you to rake the leaves, please; and I expect you to do it."

"I have to go back to the café where I forgot something.

Thinking for a second, he then responded, "It won't take me long

"Okay, but I want it done as soon as you get back."

As Leroy climbed the stairs, a heaviness came over him. He'd never lied to his mother before. Darkness was asphyxiating the light in his heart and God's Spirit was grieved. On his mom's bedside table was her Bible. Leroy opened it. To Tanya,' it read. 'May you cherish this book and keep God's Word close to your heart. Love, Mother.' It was dated 1965.

"Come on! You've gotta hurry" The words interrupted his thoughts.

Throwing the Bible into his backpack, Leroy ran down the stairs and out the door towards school. An ugly, vicious demon followed behind to make sure he got there. The boys were all in a huddle. Pete sported a big grin when he saw Leroy coming around the corner.

"Did you do it?" they all called.

Certain he was now one of them, he let out a chuckle as he waved the Bible and nodded his head. "You're almost in now," one of the members called. "There's just one more thing." Handing him a book of matches with a vicious look in his eyes, Pete commanded him,

"Burn it."

The words stung. Everything in Leroy screamed, "No! Don't do it!"

He stared at Pete and Pete stared back, unblinking. "Come on, chicken! It's only a book!"

The creatures in the spirit realm were flitting all around. Little darts of arsenic shot into Leroy's heart. "Do it! Do it!" they pounded.

Placing the book on the ground, the boys huddled around as he struck a match. Putting it to the pages it wouldn't catch a light until the match went out. Relieved, Leroy said, "It won't bum, it must be damp."

"Try it again, you shrimp," they taunted.

Hurt by their cruelty, he lit another one, but again the book wouldn't light. In the spirit realm, two angels stood guarding God's Word and then like a huge vulture, a scaly bird-like creature swooped above them.

"You can't do that!" it demanded. "Leroy made his choice."

The two angels looked to heaven and God searched Leroy's heart. The Lord understood the pressure to be one of the boys, but Leroy had a mark on him. God's seal was already on him. His mother had prayed a salvation prayer with him at six years of age. The Lord silently gave a nod and the angels stepped back. As soon as they did, the Holy Bible burst into flames, shooting several feet into the air and singeing Leroy's hair. All the other boys stared at each other in horror and then scampered off in all directions, leaving Leroy standing there wondering if he was now a member or not.

"He might be in with the boys," the angel said, "but he's just broken fellowship with God." As the guilt flooded him, he hardened his heart and then rushed home, blocking this out of his mind. "It will be worth it," he told himself.

Over dinner, he couldn't face his mother, but both she and Walt noticed his burned hair. "What happened to your hair?" she questioned.

Leroy couldn't think of an answer.

"Leroy, answer your mother! What happened to you?" Walt demanded.

Tanya reached over and gently stroked her husband's hand. She knew he had a temper problem and to yell at Leroy wouldn't enhance his example of a Christian parent.

"Honey," Tanya said gently, "have you been playing with matches?"

"No, mom. Some kids were smoking, and I tried to tell them that it was wrong. One of them threw their cigarette at me."

The Holy Spirit touched Tanya. "Leroy, that doesn't sound right. Are you lying?"

"No, it's the truth."

"Okay, if you say so. As far as I know, you've never lied to me, so I'm going to trust you're telling the truth."

Leroy finished his dinner in dead quiet; and although he had been served his favorite dish, he couldn't enjoy it.

The conviction of God was on him, but as he ignored the weight, his heart engulfed more darkness and the lying spirit hovered nearby. Glancing at his partner, Deception, he spouted, "We know who the father of lies is, don't we?"(John 8:44) and off they flew to go and pervert some other child.

Chapter Thirty-Six
Spirit of Bondage

The week in school, all three offspring were at the center of an attack. The ghouls were determined to ruin the parents' walk through their children with whatever legal grounds that they had. The enemy would cultivate it in the teenagers.

Lilly's substitute teacher lectured on birth signs and astrology. The children were captivated as so much of what he said made sense. The teacher implied that even stronger powers could be attained by wearing their personal zodiac sign somewhere on their bodies. He would be selling them after school if anyone was interested.

Once back at home, Lilly contemplated how she could get ten dollars to buy one of these fascinating symbols. Being born in August, her sign was Leo and she rationalized that maybe wearing a lion would prove to somebody somewhere she wasn't a loser after all.

Walking over to her jewelry box, she retrieved a long-forgotten item. It was a gold cross necklace which Josh had given her the day she moved in. She stared at the golden piece, glittering in the sunlight, pretty but just a trinket. It seemed so useless, almost empty. What did it really stand for? What could it achieve for her? What power did it hold?

Witchcraft stood by her side. This demon resembled a big lizard and, as its long tongue darted in and out, thoughts flashed into Lilly's mind. "It's baby stuff, that cross. There's a greater power inside. Tap into that and you'll be somebody."

As she stared at the cross, the demon reached over and cruelly squeezed the sides, bending the emblem. "Incredible!" she said, aghast. "I bent it with my mind! I've got it! I've got the power!"

A knock on the door interrupted her excitement. "Yes, what is it?"

"Honey, it's me," Sharon replied. "We have a surprise for you. Can you come downstairs?"

Apprehensively, Lilly opened the door and cupped the cross in her sweaty hand. There was no way she could tell her parents what she'd done.

"Come downstairs quickly. There's someone we want you to meet."

Glancing in the mirror before leaving the room, she sighed deeply. "I'm so fat and ugly. But now I've got a special power."

Lilly was taken aback when she reached the landing. A handsome young man around nineteen years old stood at the bottom of the staircase. Josh and her stepmother had big grins on their faces.

"Honey," her dad said, hugging her closely to him, "this is Mark Barta from New York."

"Hi," Lilly said cautiously, trying to keep her heart from being drawn into this good-looking guy's soft blue eyes.

"Hi. I'm your new piano teacher."

"Dad? Is it true?" she exclaimed, squeezing his waist and kissing him excitedly on the cheek. "But we don't have a piano."

"We do now," Josh replied, gesturing towards a large upright standing predominantly in the living room.

"Oh, daddy, thank so much!"

"Lilly, Sharon helped pay for it too, so I think you should thank her as well, don't you?" Glancing over at her step-mother, Lilly smiled cautiously. Deep inside, she feared rejection from Sharon and didn't want to let her emotions get involved. "Thanks, Sharon," she said, then quickly walked over to the instrument and began tinkering on the keys.

"Well, you two have the next hour for lesson number one, so we'll leave you to it."

Lilly was nervous. She was immediately attracted to Mark. His dark brown hair worn over his collar, sparkling eyes which peered from under his neat bangs, and his beautiful smile were more than enough to stir her. Much to her surprise, hanging around his neck was a little lion and a sparkling crystal.

"Wow! Are you a Leo?" she exclaimed in wonder. "So am I."

When the lesson was over, Mark had given his necklace to her, including the crystal which he claimed had divine power. Lilly was on her way to tapping into her "inner power," and to add to her deception, she thanked God for answering her prayers.

The Holy Spirit pricked her conscience that this was not of Him, but Lilly's heart was dark and the sin that was there drew her into coveting this mysterious force. On the off chance it really was wrong, she decided to hide the necklace from her parents, and so her deception was solidified. The ghouls had set this up, not only to pull Lilly into dangerous territory but in the end to add to her self-rejection.

Lilly couldn't wait to get to school the next day. She bubbled over at the fact that she had made contact with something supernatural and couldn't wait to tell the others. As the last of the students sidled into their desks, Lilly sat ecstatic, waiting for the teacher to ask who had been successful in finding their inner guide. "Class," Mr. Rankin began, "how many of you spoke to your 'guide'?"

Pride eclipsed her heart and Lilly's arm shot straight up. "I did! I did!" she exclaimed gleefully.

Mr. Rankin looked around the room. "Lilly, it looks like you were the only one who did. Tell us what happened."

Proudly, Lilly stood and told the class all that had transpired the night before. "Today, I'll find out his name!" she added.

"Class, I think she deserves a hand." The applause was music to her ears, but then the day dragged on as she tuned out the other classes, contemplating her venture for that afternoon.

When Lilly opted to skip her usual cookies and milk, Sharon's antenna went up, wondering what the motivation was that caused her stepdaughter to forego this special treat. The Holy Spirit moved on her. "Something is wrong." Sharon decided to finish icing the cake she had just baked and then she would follow Lilly upstairs to see what it was that was enticing her from this afternoon snack. Unfortunately, the phone rang just as she was ascending the stairs and Sharon was detoured from her mission.

Lilly, assuming all was clear, pulled the drapes, locked the door and lit some candles. Then, crouching into the Lotus position again, she began to chant. "Come, guide, come." She softly repeated these words and then suddenly, just the way it had happened last time and as if a window had opened, a gust of wind blew the candles out. Chills ran up her spine, but she embraced it. In fact, she relished the feeling of being scared. The hereditary spirit of fear from her mother, Debbie, hovered nearby; and the ghoul was ready to enslave Lilly the same way it still did Debbie.

Running its long talons up her back, shivers ran through her body and Lilly knew she wasn't alone. "Guide, is that you? You're scaring me."

The spirit of fear signaled Witchcraft and the two, like little puffs of smoke, entered Lilly's mouth. "Lilly!" Fear tightened its grip as Witchcraft spoke. "My name is Lance. I am your guide, and I will protect you."

A sense of security came over her and a counterfeit peace invaded her mind. She had found her guide; and over the years, those forces would lead her down a destructive path. How could this happen in a family where the father was a Christian?

The child had chosen to follow into a realm forbidden by the revealed Word of God. It should have been explained to Lilly by Joshua before the initiation of the unseen raided his daughter.

The following Sunday, Josh felt strongly to keep Lilly in church rather than let her go off to Sunday school. The Holy Spirit was doing His best to warn Lilly she was on dangerous ground. Unfortunately, she was content with a small book she'd kept in her purse; and satisfied that her eight-year-old sister was actually quiet, Lilly listened intently to the message.

Pastor Burrows preached from Deuteronomy 8. Let none of you practice divination, foretelling the future supernaturally, or sorcery, which is the use of supernatural powers to produce supernatural effects, or magic, contacting spirits or calling up the dead.' (Lev 0:6) "Brothers and sisters, let me warn you. In these last days, much of this occult activity will be practiced in the home of church-going families. We must be on our guard for these evils carried out by family members who give demonic spirits legal grounds in our homes."

As the congregation sat transfixed, Lilly began getting restless and opted for a trip to the bathroom. Witchcraft was determined she wouldn't hear any more, even if only in her subconscious. The Pastor continued, "Some paraphrased Bibles state that if we call on astrology or stargazing for our future, we're calling up the demons to go and make these predictions come true. Only God has the right to tell us our future if He so desires. (Is 47:13) Some of you may have noticed that the Lawson's newspaper has taken out the astrology section. It has been replaced with a Prayer Request column and stories of answered prayers. Let's pray for God to use that in our community.

Now I know all the magazines and television guides have the star signs stating your future. If you must buy the magazines, please rip out those pages. Don't condone their message by having them in your home."

Lilly crept back into the sanctuary just as Pastor Burrows began singing the final hymn. Carras was grieved and turned to Stirling. "The enemy is getting a foothold into our charges' homes. Soon, we'll have to confront them daily if something isn't instigated to stop them. Darkness is bringing in more influence from every area."

Smiling, Stirling glistened. "The Lord is almighty and powerful. He'll bring glory to His name, but Lilly needs to release her mother and realize her authority against the enemy and do battle."

"I know." Carras shrugged. "But she hardly reads her Bible anymore, and she watches too much television with Josh.

"I've got an idea," Stirling exclaimed. "I'll be right back."

Carras watched with delight as Stirling followed Amanda down the sidewalk. He escorted her between all the other parishioners leaving the church. With her bible she was also carrying a book entitled 'Jesus Gives Authority.' She often brought other books to church in case she arrived early.

As she searched for her keys, Amanda placed the books on the roof of the car, then when she went to open the door, Stirling softly tapped her shoulder. Turning to see who was there, Amanda reached for her books but only picked up the Bible. Not noticing the other book still sitting where she'd placed it, she drove off and it fell to the ground.

Lilly turned just as it fluttered into the gutter and rushed over to retrieve it. When she saw the title, the Holy Spirit energized the words to her spirit. She knew that that was a book she should read. She tucked it into her bag promising to call Amanda and tell her that she would return it later. The book was called "God Speaks to the Weary Heart".

Again, the Holy Spirit gently touched her spirit and suddenly, she remembered what Amanda had told her at Christmas time. "Yes," she thought. "That was the same thing the pastor talked about today from Deuteronomy 18, consulting the dead. Maybe I do have a curse on me."

Chapter Thirty-seven
Idle Hands or Burnout

Amanda arrived home from the newspaper and carelessly tossed her slim fitting, tailored jacket over the hallway table before placing a few logs in the smoldering living room fireplace. Then relaxing into an old leather easy chair, she let down her long silvery hair from its usual French twist, allowing it to softly tumble around her shoulders and giving it freedom to dry the snowflakes which had settled there.

The fire felt good, relaxing, yet in Amanda's heart a void was enlarging. Her Editorial and Pray Request columns had become a burden. At first, they'd been a challenge along with the other adventures from Operation Matthew 25; but now a few years later, she was unchallenged and unfulfilled. In fact, boredom was settling over her life.

As the letters poured in with neighbor's hurts, traumas and anguish, Amanda had nothing left to give. She was burned out.

Standing behind her, a spirit which had followed her home was smirking sinisterly at her. It was the demon of bondage and the same creature which had succeeded in bringing Esther down for three years only now it had its new prey.

Valla, her angel, waved its wing across her shoulders, impressing on her the need to fast and pray and press into God. Amanda had fallen into a usual snare of busyness and not spending enough time in the Word.

The fire snapped and crackled as she remembered her college days where sipping wine in front of the fireplace had been a relaxing endeavor.

Jesus had changed all that; and being a Christian, both she and her husband had stopped drinking alcohol a long time ago. Amanda hadn't thought of booze in years, but now with boredom such a constant companion, and the enticement Bondage was releasing, the thought of a cool glass of wine sounded very tempting.

"But there's none in the house," she thought. "I know! I can get some delivered."

The Holy Spirit immediately quickened something she'd read a long time ago. 'Avoid all appearances of evil.' (1 Thes5:22)

"That's right, everyone in town knows that I'm a Christian. What would they think if the liquor van pulled up out front?"

She kept toying with the idea and bondage kept inflicting its desire.

As God always promises a way out of every situation, He kept His word; and just then Joshua phoned.

"Hi, Amanda. You dropped a book at church the other day and Lilly picked it up."

"Oh, is that where it is? I wondered where it had gone."

"Would you mind if I borrow it?"

"Not at all, but call me in a week if you haven't finished it because I'll forget who has it. I lose so many books and tapes that way." Laughing, Josh agreed. "Sometimes I think I'll start asking for a deposit."

After hanging up the phone, Amanda decided to take a nap, her desire for a drink had waned during the phone call.

Valla and Bondage stared at each other, determination in each gaze. "I know you're only doing what you do," Valla remarked, "but why not go and infect someone else?"

"She's in the flesh too much," Bondage quipped. "She'll be easy to bring down." Then swiftly, it vanished to set a trap.

The next day at work, Amanda was again running on empty. The morning was hectic with petty problems and her husband's unexpected overseas trip added to her already full workload. Decisions she usually made prayerfully were decided by what seemed best at the time. A knock at the door interrupted her frenzy. "Not another problem!" she hissed through pursed lips.

Surprised by this unusual outburst, her secretary grimaced and murmured, "No, it's just a luncheon appointment with Mrs. Boyer from Los Angeles. She was supposed to meet with your husband or Ted from advertising. I thought I'd ask you first if you wished to talk with her." Realizing a little tact wouldn't go astray, she added, "The lunch is on her, by the way."

"All right. It sounds like it might be a good escape, and that's what I need right now."

As twelve-thirty neared, Amanda powdered her nose and anticipated a good, hearty meal, something she hadn't been able to pamper herself with for quite a few nights as her time just wasn't her own anymore. She was hungry and ready for a big, thick steak at someone else's expense.

"This must be a treat from the Lord," she mused, chuckling to herself. "Thanks, Father!" she exclaimed, glancing upwards.

Shaking his head sadly, Valla whispered, "No, Amanda, it isn't. You should never assume. Ask the Father before you enter into anything." Unfortunately, Amanda wasn't listening.

Mrs. Boyer appeared to be very conservative with a severe hairdo pulled back from her face and a very masculine business suit. Amanda noticed a cross dangling from her neck. "Good, I don't have to witness at lunch," she thought. "I can just relax. She must be saved to wear one of those at her age."

Shaking hands, the woman smiled. "Hello, I'm Sue. Cedars Restaurant was recommended to me.

How do you feel about going there?"

"It's awfully expensive. Are you sure you don't mind paying for this?"

"Oh, honey, I'm not paying out of my pocket. This is a business lunch. Let's just remember that while we're gorging ourselves."

"Okay, let's go. I'll drive."

Once seated at a corner table, the waitress came over with a wine list. "Would you ladies like anything from the bar?" She smiled sweetly.

After glancing at the list, Mrs. Boyer quickly replied, "Yes, we'll have the bottle of Chablis White."

Amanda sat there, alarm bells ringing in her conscience. "Don't drink any." But she sat there, seemingly unable to respond. Once the glass was poured, picking it up and sipping it seemed a most natural thing to do. To be honest, she enjoyed its bite and the coolness as it trickled down her throat.

As the waitress left with their order, Sue signaled her to come back. Can you give us 15 minutes before you put the order in? Amanda noticed her lunch date seemed more interested in the cocktail time than lunch. By her third glass, the business was finished and now the women were discussing Amanda's column and some of the prayers that had been answered. Amanda's gift of evangelism surfaced.

"Are you a Christian, Sue?"

"Yes, I grew up in the Bethesda Church. I've gone to church my whole life." Suddenly, an uneasy feeling came over Amanda. "That's why she drinks so easily. That church is very lenient and compromising."

"But what harm is it?" Bondage questioned her.

Amanda mulled over the thought and then after a couple more glasses of wine, finally ordered lunch. By the time it was set before her, she was feeling very lightheaded and giddy. The pressures of work seemed so far away ... and so did the Lord.

Over the ensuing days, whenever a problem arose or pressure was on Amanda, she related back to her relaxed time with the wine. Trying to justify this desire to drink, she rationalized, "A lot of Christians drink wine, so why can't I?"

Bondage was leaving his mark and, on the way, home one day, she purposefully drove the long way round and pulled into an obscure liquor shop to buy a flagon of wine.

"Now, I won't abuse this," she said to herself. "It's just for when I feel down."

"What about prayer?" the Lord spoke.

Amanda froze. Conviction raced through her spirit, but Bondage quickly draped itself over her shoulder.

"I won't have any now. I'll go and take a nap instead."

When she woke, the Holy Spirit was heavy on her with conviction. Consequently, she felt guilty and this pushed her further away from God because she knew if she had a prayer time, the Lord would convict her further; and so she chose not to. Her body craved the effects of alcohol. She had to relax and ease her tension.

She was walking on thin ice and if it broke, so would her fellowship with God. The Holy Spirit wouldn't give up, but would Amanda?

God's convicting power was heavy on Walter too. It seemed he was foregoing church too often in lieu of racing. As weeks went by, the only thought he had of Jesus was when washing the car, and he saw the name that was emblazoned on the back, or when he did well in a race he gave a quick prayer of thanks towards the Heavens.

A sleeping enemy was awakening in Walt. Now that he was popular and had become an idol, Walter made a point of being rude to those who he'd grown up with who had abused him. The old hostility was there from all the jeers and prejudices and remarks that he had endured. Instead of forgiving and forgetting, Walter, in his pride, maintained his hatred towards those who had hurt him.

Regal, his angel, did his best to steer him into a good quiet time so the Lord could speak to him. Unfortunately, to get him to stay still was difficult. One afternoon, Edward approached him cautiously. Knowing Walt's temper, he was reluctant to tell him the bad news.

Unable to meet his eyes, Ed began, "Walter, I hate to be the one to have to inform you, but . . . the sponsors have decided to drop you." His voice ended in a whisper.

Anger transformed his face. "How dare they? Why? What happened? Don't they know I'm a winner?"

In a soothing tone, Ed continued, "Walt, from what I understand, they don't want to be identified with Jesus' name painted on your car anymore. They say it offends some of the other drivers."

Without a thought, Walt replied, "Then we'll take it off." Regal winced and spoke gently to Edward. "Idolatry."

"Walter, no. I'm sorry, but I just can't favor that. Your racing was to bring glory to God; and when it ceases to do that, I'm not sure I want part of it."

Anger tightened its hold on Walt's heart, and he responded by throwing a wrench against the wall. "Why does this always happen to me? Can't anything ever go right?" With that, he stormed out the door, his face set in a determined way and sin crouching at the door. (Genesis 4:7) At his home a few minutes later, the spirit of violence, which was tainting Leroy, decided to take Walter on. Smirking to Anger, he gave the signal and the two demons circled the room sinisterly, letting off gusts of darkness. The secretion was invisible to humans but was very effective on emotions.

Leroy was watching a Kung Fu movie; and as the fighting had stirred him up, he was already wired when his dad came through the door. Giving vent to his aggression, Walt slammed the door shut and stormed into the living room. "Turn that thing off."

Rebellion manifested. "No!" Leroy snapped.

"Don't you say 'no' to me, young man?"

"I will if I want to. No!" he repeated, growling at his father.

"I'm warning you, Leroy. Don't you say 'no' when I tell you to do something!"

Aroused by the violence he had just been watching, Leroy stood to his feet and immediately positioned himself into a karate stance. The spirit that had driven him into this form of entertainment expelled its desire and Leroy was unwittingly trying to draw his dad into a fight.

Moving like a cat and circling his father, Leroy's adrenaline surged. Then swinging around in a martial art turn, Leroy's heart turned black as the defiance towards his father multiplied. Rebellion and Violence had waited a long time for this moment, and both screeched with delight as Leroy spun around, kicking Walter straight in the stomach, sending him reeling backwards into the breakfront. The glass broke which sent dishes tumbling off the shelves, adding to Walt's anger.

Tanya walked through the door just at the moment, shocked by what she saw. There was blood on Walt's back from where the glass had hit him and little slivers of glass were impaled in his flesh.

"What on earth are you two doing?" she shouted.

Anger expanded and consumed Walter momentarily. He responded by slapping her across the face. "Stay out of this!"

Tears welled up in her eyes as Anger wrapped its cords of disease around her. She responded by throwing a china bowl at Walt. All three stared defiantly at each other and then fled to different rooms.

The demons jumped up and down in ecstasy. "We'll destroy this family too!' they shrieked gleefully at each other.

Regal determinedly looked to heaven. "Lord, touch someone to pray for this family before it's too late."

Walter jumped in the car and sped off. He had no idea where he was going; he just wanted to get away. He knew once he was behind the wheel, it would settle him down. Guilt flooded him as he recalled the look on his Tanya's face when he hit her.

"What makes me so angry?" he thought. "I can't believe I slapped Tanya. I love her, I don't want to hurt her." She is my best friend and my wife.

Bondage, which had been working on Amanda, landed on the front seat with Walt. The spirit shot thoughts into his mind to go into a bar and calm down. "You're popular. Go where they know and respect you. Go and relax with a couple of drinks."

Walt entertained the thoughts and without much opposition, decided to do just that. A few drinks probably would settle him down.

Later that night when Walter came home, Tanya was already asleep. Trying to be quiet, he slipped into bed, not wanting to talk to her. After a restless night's sleep, he went to the breakfast table where Tanya had laid his eggs and toast out ready for him. Waiting for him to make the first move, she quietly went about the rest of the morning chores, but pride and guilt kept Walter from apologizing. Instead, he acted as if nothing had happened and gave her a cordial, "Morning."

Tanya, figuring that he was under a lot of pressure, didn't bring the subject up either. So, the two ate in silence. Leroy hid until his dad had gone to work and then mumbled a quick "See ya, mom," before rushing out the door.

Tanya glanced through her daily devotional. Her times with God hadn't seemed the same without her own Bible. God's Word was always so rich to her, and no commentary could compensate for it. "Maybe Josh can run me by a bookshop during our lunch break so I can get a new one," she thought. "I still can't understand what happened to mine." A slight feeling of loss was with her as if something very personal had been stolen. Getting a new one would bring disaster.

Then slowly shaking her head, she sighed. "I always thought I'd take that Bible to my grave. Oh, well, I'll just have to take another one instead."

A horn honked, breaking her thoughts. It was Josh.

"How's it going, Josh?" Tanya smiled as she got in the passenger side.

"Teenagers," he quipped, "Who can understand them?"

Nodding her head in agreement, Tanya asked, "Do you think we were that bad?"

"I wasn't. Were you?"

"Some kids have fear of God when they grow up; others have fear of their parents. I had both!" She laughed. "Josh, would you be able to drive me to the Christian Bookshop during lunch today?"

"Yeah, sure. We could even dart over there now if you want," he stated, whipping the car around in a U-turn.

Just then another car, driving very fast shot through the yellow light and slammed straight into Josh's passenger side. Tanya was brutally thrown into the windshield. Josh, badly shaken, jumped out of the car to flag down help.

Spotting a woman on the other side of the street, he screamed at her, "Go and get an ambulance! Quick! There's a lady stuck in here."

Racing back to the car, Josh tried talking to Tanya, but there was no response. The other driver, panicking at Josh's reaction, hurriedly reversed and sped away. Josh couldn't read the license plate and was more concerned with Tanya than chasing after the culprit.

Once the paramedics and police were on the scene, he explained what had happened. "Wait a minute!" he yelled. "What are they doing?"

He watched a paramedic pull a white sheet over Tanya and then slide it gently over her head. "She can't be dead! We weren't hit that hard!" he screamed at the man bending over her. Racing over, Josh tried pulling the sheet away. "Leave her alone! She can't be dead."

"Come on, sir," the other medic tried taking his arm and escorting him to the police car. "We need to take you to the hospital to run some tests."

Fear gripped Josh's nerves. Helplessness strangled his spirit. "Oh God. Please don't let her die!" he pleaded. "Not her. She's too good to die yet. Please God, don't let her die!"

They admitted him for observation and before long, Esther, Sharon and Lilly were at the hospital by his bedside, thanking God that Josh was safe.

All of **a** sudden, a crash resounded around the room as the door was nearly knocked off its hinges. Walt stormed in. Esther recognized that look in his eyes. She'd seen it in Sam's. "I hate you! I hate you!" Walter lunged at Joshua, sending his dinner in all directions as he hit the counter top." You killed her and I'll never forgive you. Never!" Then like a wounded animal, he retreated out the door and down the hall.

CHAPTER THIRTY-EIGHT
HE WHO STARTED A GOOD WORK

Cambridge High had attempted to keep up with the times. The last week the teachers went all out in deception. They had brought in a specialist in the area of ESP and telekinetic so machines were brought in to test the students in these areas. They were interested to see who might want to earn some money by being a part time 'guinea pig' for their experiments after school.

At first, they used cards, laying them on one side of the table with a small divider in between and then letting the student use 'mind power' to identify what was hidden on the other side of the divider. For each child, a spirit of witchcraft spoke into their mind what each card displayed.

Lilly had answered correctly every time. Mr. Warier, who was conducting the experiments, commented on her accuracy. "Few of the others did as well as you today. What do you attribute your success to?"

Trying to sound blasé, she replied, "I've been in tune with the spirit world for years. I used to have some living in my bedroom."

"Really?" He smirked at her attitude.

"Yeah, and I've developed mind power by using this crystal as well," Lilly said proudly, displaying the glistening article for him to see, "I can tell my spirit friend to do what I wish or concentrate with my mind and make my wish come true using the crystal."

"Does your family know about your gift?" he asked inquisitively.

"Oh no! They don't believe in this sort of thing," she scoffed.

"Lilly, you tell them that psychic experiences and clairvoyance is becoming an accepted science, practiced by major oil companies to find gas and oil." Lilly's eyes widened, thinking of the prospects of future payment for her services.

Mr. Warier began clearing away the small objects, then paused thoughtfully before speaking again. "You know, young lady, it wasn't too long ago that medical science was thought to be black magic." His eyes narrowed sinisterly. "No such thing as magic. It's all a matter of releasing the power within."

"My dad's a Christian. What do you think God thinks about all this?"

"I'm sure God is the one giving you this power."

Deception grinned at Witchcraft and shot an arrow of darkness into Lilly's heart.

"You just keep tapping into that power." Mr. Warier winked. "Some of the big companies might hire you some day to find them oil, and then you'll be rich!"

"Okay, sir. I won't let anyone take this talent away!" Lilly's face lit up at the thought that finally she could prove she is a somebody.

"Good girl," he uttered as he affectionately patted her head before leaving.

In the spirit world, another creature landed in the room. Its name was Rebellion and this demonic instigator looked like a little spider monkey which then jumped on Lilly's hip, determined to start harassing Joshua and Sharon using her as the bait.

It didn't take too long for the opportunity to arise. Once at home, during dinner, Josh brought up the question of why Lilly was staying after school each day.

"I'm working on an assignment," she stated matter-of-factly.

Sharon looked at Josh, then turned to Lilly. "What is it, dear?"

Caught off guard, Lilly stared at her plate for a few seconds, desperately trying to think of something. "Um Um . . . a science project," she eventually blurted.

"What about?" Josh asked, reaching for the pitcher of milk. "Um . . . the heart."

"That's interesting. Are you going to describe how Jesus lives in your heart?"

Lilly sat, pondering this. She flashed back to the days when she called upon Satan as her father. It seemed so vivid in her memory. She thought of how Christianity would not allow for her new ESP adventures and the riches she would miss out on if she did as God commanded. Rebellion moved slowly nearer, and Witchcraft expanded inside. Determination etched on her face.

"No, I'm not because Jesus isn't in my heart." Rebellion saw the black appear around her heart and rushed in, staking its claim.

Josh put his fork down and glanced at Sharon before speaking. "What do you mean, Lilly? We've taught you all about Jesus."

"I know you have, but that doesn't mean I want Him!" Rebellion relaxed. He had his mark.

Stunned, her father stated, "That's it, young lady. You go to your room until you can show proper respect for our Lord."

Lilly's temper flared and defiantly she stood and slammed her hand into the pitcher sending its contents splashing all over the tablecloth.

Josh jumped up to challenge her, but Sharon cried out, "No, let her go, honey."

Little Rhonda sat there aware something was going on but unsure of what it was. Desiring to get some attention herself, she picked up her plate and tossed it on the floor.

"Oh, that's just great!" Josh snapped, forcefully setting his chair under the table. "We really need to do some praying after dinner."

"That sounds good. I'll meet you in the den in a few minutes."

While Sharon put Rhonda to bed, then percolated some coffee, Josh silently waited on God to get a word.

'Be ye not deceived . . . A man reaps what he's sown.' (Galatians 6:7-8)

"Josh, you've been too busy," the Lord whispered. "You don't realize what she's been getting into."

"What, Lord!" he asked, puzzled. "Witchcraft!"

Suddenly, Josh felt embarrassed. Guilt flooded him as he realized he had assumed all this time that his one prayer over Lilly years ago had been enough. Now he was certain it hadn't been, and the devil had his claws deep into her being and wasn't going to let go easily.

Joshua sat there helpless. He knew it was true. With all the activities he was doing for God, they were all being done by him and not with the anointing of the Holy Spirit.

"Those in the flesh cannot please God,"(Gal 6:7) permeated his mind. Ready to defend himself, Josh sighed deeply; but before he could even get out his defense, another verse buoyed in his spirit.

'Jeremiah 3:10 . . . and yet in spite of all this . . . did not return to me with all his heart, but rather in deception."

That word 'deception' was like a sword slicing and dividing his soul from his spirit, his joints from his marrow, judging his thoughts and attitudes. Nothing was hidden.

"Josh," the Holy Spirit spoke, "you have served me in deception. You have found it entertaining and profitable to do the works of God, but I don't have your heart. It is far away. And you honor Me with only your lips. Repent, therefore, that times of refreshing may come on you by the presence of the Lord." (Acts 3:20)

"But, God, I try to do well."

"There's not a man who continually does good. Many shall call Me Lord, but he who does My will shall enter. Stop making decisions without My guidance."

"What do you want me to do?" Josh asked sincerely. "How will they know if no one tells them?" (Rom 10:14)

"What?" Josh gasped.

"I want you to preach My word."

"God, years ago I swore I'd never speak in front of people again."

"Yes, but that was before you became a new creature in Christ. You can do all things through Me in My will."(Phil 4:13)

"Where do You want me to preach?"

"Wherever I open the way. I want you to start with the schools."

His reply was sarcastic. "They won't let me in!"

"You go in talking about saying no to sex, drugs and rock and roll, and the teachers will let you in. I'll open the way."

With his eyes fixed towards heaven, Josh inquired, "What good will that do? What does that have to do with Jesus?"

"It is those things which detour the young people away from Me."

While Josh was deep in thought, Sharon walked in with a steaming cup of coffee. Handing it to him, she remarked, "Looks like you've had an encounter of the 'first' kind!"

Josh smiled sheepishly. "You're right. The Lord let me have it too. Right between the eyes!"

"Feel better?" she asked, snuggling next to him on the comfortable sofa.

With his arm encircling her and his head resting on hers, he replied, "Yes. He busted me like a true gentleman and then showed me His love by giving me a job to do."

Sharon reached up and kissed him lightly on the cheek. "God sure blessed me by giving me a man after His own heart like you, honey."

"I'll remember that the next time I get too slack." He smiled and returned her kiss.

The n picking up the television guide, Sharon casually asked, "What are we going to do about Lilly?"

Josh shook his head despondently. "I dunno, sweetheart. I really don't know."

"Look, there's a good movie coming on. Let's relax for a while and we can deal with Lilly later."

Turning off the light and hitting the remote control, Joshua and Sharon reacted with the most usual response to a trying situation ... they escaped.

A demon mockingly commented over in the corner to one of his comrades, "When you don't know what to do and you don't feel like praying ... block it out for a while with the television. It works every time. Meanwhile, the Holy Spirit's opportunity disperses.

Days after Tanya had been buried, Leroy and his father, Walt, got in a terrible argument over his choice of a video he'd brought home from the store. "After all these years, you think you can tell me what to do" Leroy snapped. "Just because you're feeling guilty, don't take it out on me!"

Walt's blood pressure rose. "What do you mean by that, young man?"

Defiantly, Leroy retorted, "Mom's dead because of you!"

Anger squeezed its lethal tentacles, but Walter didn't respond. Those words cut deeply into him and the hurt was too raw which created an atmosphere for Anger to keep pestering. He sensed, though, that Leroy's nastiness was only because of his grief; and so, after taking a deep breath, he asked, "Why are you blaming me? Josh is the one who drove the car, son."

Unwilling to let it go, Leroy responded, "You didn't kill her, no, but on her last day alive, because of your horrible temper, you slapped her and that's why you're feeling guilty. So don't take it out on me!"

Walt stood there, unable to respond.

"You call yourself a Christian!" Leroy kept on with his poisonous tirade. "What a joke! You never do anything with or for God."

Sensing he might have gone too far and seeing the anguish on his father's face, Leroy decided to drop the subject. He'd cut his dad enough, and both of them backed down.

Anguished, Walter went to his room and closed the door. Turning to see the bed unmade and his clothes in a pile on the floor, the absolute reality of how different things were going to be now that Tanya was no longer with them hit him. She'd always loved tidiness, but now she wasn't there to clean up after him. He was left to fend for himself.

He stretched out across the bed and then, curling the pillow up into a ball next to him, he clutched it to his cheek, blinking back the tears and encompassing his heartache. A feeling of abandonment and condemnation from God overshadowed him. "God, how did you get so far away? What did I do to have You treat me this way? I did my missionary bit in Japan for you, didn't I?"

Jeremiah 2:17 came to his mind. Reaching under the bed, he pulled out his Bible. Dust and traces of mold snaked across its leather cover. Reading amidst his tears, God spoke these words into his mind." Have you not done this to yourself by forsaking the Lord your God when He led you in the way?' (Jer 2:17)

Walt lay there, convicted. The word had pierced his spirit as sharply as a fine dagger, yet it was so true, and Walter felt God's hurt in his wayward son's complacency. Then Jeremiah 2:5. "Walter, what injustice did you find in Me?"

Randomly, he turned the page until his eyes fell on Jeremiah 3 and the words from the thirteenth line stood out on the page 'acknowledge your iniquity.'

"What is it I've done that's so awful, God?"

"You're neither hot nor cold," was the stem reply. "My people have committed two evils. They have forsaken Me and hewn for themselves cisterns, cisterns that can hold no water." (Jer 2:13) He was bewildered. "What does that mean?"

"Walter, you've gone after the pride of life. You've tried building a life that won't hold."

"Why did You take Tanya away?" Silence enfolded his spirit. "Why?"

No word was forthcoming. Silence mocked him.

Then the phone rang, startling Walt from his questioning. It was Edward. "Hi, Walt, I was wondering what you're going to do about the race next week. Timothy from General Feed will sponsor you if you take the, as he called it, "religious jargon" off your car."

Regal moved closer to Walter and praised the Lord, waiting to see what God would do. The Holy Spirit blew across him and whispered, "Don't do it, Walter."

Sitting there, aware of the emptiness of the house and his life without a wife, he opted for the things of the world.

"Tell him Okay," he declared.

Edward spoke with slight conviction. "Walter, I'm not with you if you don't want to do this for the Lord."

Exasperation was evident in Walt's reply. "Ed, give me a break! People do things all the time in business that don't give glory to God. What difference does it make? I'm not a missionary anymore. I'm now a businessman, and I have to think like one." Before Edward could reply, he added, "And I give my tithe with what I make, so I'm honoring God by doing that."

There was a long, drawn-out pause. Both men it seemed were now taking their eyes from being Christ's ambassadors and instead focusing them onto the things of the world.

With a reluctant sigh, Ed replied, "Okay, let's do it."

And for Walter, the parcel that God had placed so many years before in his heart was still far from being used. Regal gave a sigh while quoting from Jeremiah ... 'They did not listen or incline their ears, but stiffened their necks ...' (Jer 17:23)

Although Amanda was less stressed out with her newly acquired habit of wine-tipping, it seemed that repercussions were going on in the heavenlies. Sitting in her breakfast nook with a cup of coffee early one morning, she began her daily quiet time. It was always a wrestling affair now, as the day's activities and phone calls she needed to make would drift in and out of her mind during her prayer time. Even though she stopped to jot them down, she still got flustered, concerned she wouldn't remember everything which needed doing. As a result, her prayers were very erratic. She pondered over the dream she'd had the night before, hiding in a house and making sure the front door was locked. In the dream she was caught off guard as these ugly men with bottles of wine sneaked in behind her through the back door.

"God, I don't know what to say to You. I don't even feel like praying anymore, and I don't know what the matter is. I've tried to serve you faithfully all these years, but now I'm too tired to bother. Lately, my relaxation comes from alcohol instead of You; and then because of the booze, I end up sleeping too much. And Lord, I'm not the same person anymore. I feel guilty and my relationship with You is empty."

Bewildered, she gulped her coffee down, almost as if she expected God to walk in through the door and tell her everything would be all right. Once she'd drained her cup, Amanda leaned back and stared up the hallway while Bondage hovered nearby, hissing, "Fix a drink."

The impulse came with the words, but she didn't move. The instruction came again, this time more insistent. "Go on. Fix a drink."

Amanda looked at the clock. It was seven forty-five. Shaking her head, she murmured, "I can't believe I'm wanting a drink at eight in the morning! Am I addicted to alcohol? I feel like the enemy is all over me and winning."

"Amanda," the Lord said. You're very precious in my sight, but unless you remove these things from your midst, you will not be able to withstand the enemy. Read Timothy 1:18. I give you this instruction in keeping with the prophecies once made about you so that by following them you may fight the good fight, holding onto faith and a good conscience. Some have rejected these and so have shipwrecked their faith.'

"What instructions, Lord?" she inquired.

"The Lord is a shield to those whose walk is blameless." (PS. 84:11) "What are You saying to me?"

"Those who are in the flesh cannot please God. (Rom8:8) You're trying to do My work in your strength and counting on booze to ease the burden. You know it's wrong, so you feel guilty. Where there's no blameless walk, there's no clear conscience, so consequently, no shield. The dream you had showed the spirit of bondage has come in the back door."

Concerned, she asked, "How did that happen? What can I do?"

The Lord brought to her mind the scripture James 5:16; and as she turned to it, Amanda felt almost relieved that her secret was out and God was going to break this yoke which had subtly crept into her life.

"Therefore, confess your sins to one another and pray for one another that you may be healed."

"Do you want me to tell someone, Lord? Isn't it enough that You know?"

"I want you to call Esther."

"What?" she exclaimed.

The Lord was silent as He waited for her to prove her obedience to Him and Amanda's angel stood by her singing praises to God.

"Yes, Lord." She smiled in agreement at her maker. "Esther is the perfect one for me to call. All Your ways are just and perfect, merciful art thou, oh God."

The handle on the big steel door turned, making a loud squeak. The huge gate swung open and in walked Sam. Esther sat nervously in the prison visitors' section, eyeing him as he approached, her hands fumbling with the clasp of her handbag.

Surprisingly, he looked good considering he'd just spent years locked up in jail. A flame was rekindled in Esther as he grinned at her and sat down.

Surprised at her own nervousness, she gave a coy smile in return. "Hi, Sam. You're looking good." She reached into her purse. "Here, I brought you a few things."

Esther placed on the table between them some writing paper and pens, a packet of gum and a carton of cigarettes.

"Thanks for the thought, but I don't need these now. I don't smoke anymore," he stated proudly and pushed the carton away.

Stunned, she silently replaced them in her purse.

Sam realized her bewilderment and smiled confidently at her. "Esther, the Lord delivered me.

Thrilled by his words, she replied excitedly, "Sam, it's so wonderful to know you're a Christian!" Then, sobered by the reality of her surroundings and the depravity of the people who were his daily contacts, she inquired with concern, "But how do you manage to keep in your walk with the Lord? It must be hard to be different."

"Esther, it gets better each day. I prayed for a guy last week who suffered from severe arthritis and guess what, God healed him! Isn't that wonderful? God is so faithful when you ask believing He'll do it and you know it's His will." Sam beamed with the joy of the Lord as he spoke.

Esther sat silently, unable to say anything. She was so overwhelmed at the change in him. "Anyway, tell me, how are Josh and our granddaughter?" he asked.

"Not very good. Lilly's not doing too well. Josh says she's getting more and more defiant and is totally turned off to God. She also puts up quite a fight about going to church now too."

"Let's pray about it." was Sam's response.

Sam reached over and gently took Esther's hand. Then bowing his head, he hesitated, waiting for the Spirit to prompt his prayer. Esther watched him cautiously. She felt her heart melting but was determined to remain aloof. After all, what good would it do to fall back into love with a man doing life in prison? She searched his face, remembering how much she'd once cherished him and pondered what would have happened to their marriage if Larry hadn't come along.

Watching him, her eyes became moist with tears. Then unable to contain her emotions, she rose from the table and came around to his side, where she knelt and hugged him. "Sam, please forgive me. I'm so sorry I've ruined your life."

Sam returned the hug and he meant it. An old love for her was rekindled in his heart too and then, holding her at arm's length, he stared deeply into her eyes. "I forgive you, sweetheart. I want you to know that I really do forgive you. Even though I will spend the rest of my life in here, I don't hold it against you. Gods in control of my life now, and He'll make good out of this tragedy."

This made Esther feel even guiltier and as the tears surfaced again, she held on tightly to Sam.

"Esther, I wouldn't have found God if this hadn't happened. In here, I don't have worldly temptations and for once, I can be different and special and know it's for the right reason. Men look up to me in here and come to me for counseling all the time. God has been giving me gifts of discernment and words of knowledge and wisdom. It's great! Just like in the book of Acts, I feel like one of the early disciples."

Wiping her eyes and blowing her nose, Esther interrupted. "But, Sam, we could've been sharing all this together and serving God as a couple and growing in His love and power instead of separately."

"Honey, obviously God didn't destine for that to happen, but He has used this to break me and bring me to a place where I'd listen to His voice."

Suddenly, Esther remembered a prayer she'd uttered innocently many years before. "Do whatever it takes to bring him to You."

"Sam, what can I do to make your life more bearable?"

"You just keep praying for God to use me in here and you can also bring some good Christian books to read. I need to learn as much as I can to help others."

"Sam." Esther reached over and took his hand. "I love you."

Squeezing the soft palm delicately resting in his, he replied with tenderness, "I love you too. Will you come back and see me in a few days?"

"Of course, I will. I'm here for you from now and forever and it's true that even death won't separate us."

Esther drove home very subdued. On one of these trips, she would have to tell him about Sam Jr. becoming gay. "I wonder what that will do to his faith?" she asked aloud.

As she came in the front door, the phone rang. "God," she said, "How do they always know when I get home?"

She recognized the voice on the other end of the phone.

"Esther, its Amanda. I really need to talk to you. I've got a problem, and I think you're the only one who will understand."

"Hi, Amanda. What's the matter? You haven't been hitting the booze, I hope." she uttered with concern.

There was silence. Then Amanda replied in a somber tone, "How did you know?"

"I didn't," Esther stated sadly. "I guess you could say I had a word of knowledge. The only thing that matters now is, are you ready to repent?"

"Yes, I am."

"Okay, well how about you come over and we'll break the power of Satan in this area and cut him off."

After Amanda had hung up, she stared out the window. "After the way I treated her she's still willing to reach out and help me," she remarked to herself. "She's so like You, Jesus. Why can't I be like that?"

"He who started a good work in you will complete it," surfaced in her spirit. (Phil 1:6)

As often is the case, the spirit of bondage was a persistent invader into Amanda's thoughts; but by a choice of her will and a growing love for God, she didn't give in after that. Consequently, the foothold was completely broken. The spirit left to go and corrode someone else, and Amanda had the victory in Jesus' name.

Down the street Eva reached for her mug of herbal tea and closed Amanda's book which she'd been reading over the last couple of weeks.

She'd taken her time, trying to digest every bit of it and now there was a sense of strength in her spirit. A knowledge that she wanted to do battle. Glancing over at Johnny lying asleep next to her, she sighed to herself, imagining that this must be what Esther had endured with Sam for so many years — a husband to which she was unevenly yoked.

"How could I have been so stubborn?" she asked out loud. "God, you gave me plenty of warning. I can't blame You."

She looked at the title of the book and tried recalling some of what she'd learned. "God, in Genesis You gave man dominion over the beasts of the earth, fish of the sea and the fowl of the air and in the spiritual realm I am to have dominion over my beasts, which are carnal desires and fleshly lusts and my fish, which can be the subconscious sphere, including early childhood traumas and bad dreams and lately, the fowls of the air, which is my thought life and the enemy that tries to persuade me and manipulate me there. Jesus also said, 'All authority has been given me over the enemy' (Mat 28:18) so I can bind these forces of darkness, using that authority given to me as a child of God."

"But, Father, I'm afraid I won't be able to do it right."

"You're always afraid," the Lord spoke.

Eva was jolted by the words.

"I didn't give you a spirit of fear." (2Tim1:7)

"Okay, Lord, I'll try it."

Reaching over and placing her hand above Johnny's head, Eva did battle. She had no idea of the effect, but she wanted to at least make an attempt in setting her husband free.

"I bind you spirit of pride that stops him from seeing his need for Jesus."

The entity in him squirmed, waiting reluctantly for the inevitable light shaft to blaze upon him and mark him.

As Eva stated her command again, light was released from her, catapulting towards heaven and then plummeting down precisely on top of the demon. This was the cue that it had to stop influencing John as long as she was interceding.

Eva continued down the list of areas she had to bind. She well knew which strongholds were in her husband, areas of his life which were preventing him from coming to the Lord. Rebellion, independence, mocking, anti-Christ... these were the forces which were holding him blind to the gospel.

"Father, I claim John as one that You've died for, and I ask that You to release an angel to minister to him as one who will receive salvation."

Just then, as Vester arrived to take his place by John, a huge snake-like beast slithered across the roof. It was Unbelief, and with a loud crackle, it summoned all the demons in the house to come at once. His buddies, Witchcraft and Deception, were already aware of the new battle which was about to begin in this home and quickly responded.

"Comrades, Jesus said the enemies of a man would be members of his own household. (Matt 10:26) Right now, instead of inflicting your usual characteristic, you are to instigate arguments between these three humans. I'll work on the mother so that she becomes frustrated and gives up on the spiritual warfare."

"How will you do that?" mocked Deception.

"I'll let her believe it doesn't work. I'll talk her out of it."

Vester and Carras called for Bega. These three mighty beings left at once to go before the Lord. "Your Majesty?" Vester asked, "Are there many prayers stored up from Johnny calling upon Your name?"

"No, there aren't. He's heard the gospel many times, but his heart was too hard and the Word was never absorbed."

"Then, what should we do on your behalf to soften his heart, for only You alone can draw man unto Your Son?"

"Yes, but he has his own stubborn will, and I won't cross that," God stated. Is it not from the mouth of the Most High that both good and I'll go forth? (Lam3:38) He must be brought down like many men before him. His foundation of believing in himself must be demolished."

"You're going to turn him into a cow like you did King Nebuchadnezzar?" a little angel asked. (Dan 4:30)

"You'll see. Meanwhile, minister extra protection to Eva so that she doesn't grow weary and give up."

Almost as though a jinx had been let loose on Johnny, his self-made world crumbled. The head injuries, sustained many years before in a car wreck, surfaced with assorted problems. Constantly, he'd have a headache and his eyes became hazy at the most crucial times. Within a month, they had pulled his driver's license, saying that it was too dangerous for him to drive; and consequently, he was found to be unsuitable for his present job at the railroad. This brought about him being immediately downgraded into handling the luggage. Besides a cut in pay, this totally deflated his ego.

During the same week, his beloved boat blew the engine, and it was obviously impossible for him to find the money to have it fixed. On top of all this, his other hobby, golf, was severely interrupted by the golf cart blowing its engine. Now, it too collected dust in the garage. Meanwhile, John was forced to spend more time at home and usually that time was spent downing beers in front of the television.

In desperation, Eva cried out to God for an answer. "Why are you doing this? My life is unbearable."

"Do you want him saved?" the Lord asked.

"Yes. But in breaking him, you're breaking me."

"Are God's consolations not good enough for you?"(Job15:11)

"I'm afraid this simply won't work, Father."

"You're always afraid." "Just like Rose your mother"

Eva froze. All she heard was the pounding of her heart. "Lord, you told me that before."

"I didn't give you a spirit of fear. (2Tim1:7) You must repent. You have been delivered from that domain of darkness. If you walk in the light as He is in the Light, the blood of Jesus purifies you from all sin." (John 1:7)

"What are you saying?"

The Lord spoke gently and with compassion. He was about to unfold to his beloved daughter the truth behind the bondage in her life, the reason why she never ventured out to do things for God. "Turn to Psalm 18:28."

While Eva hunted through the pages, a confrontation was taking place in the heavenlies around her. As her heart was in direct communion with God, it illuminated a dazzling light which consumed the darkness around her heart. Bega and Carras glimmered and stood ready for battle as the irritant ghouls which had kept her in bondage stood ready to guard their domain. They knew the Holy Spirit was about to release Eva and transfer more of her inner man out of darkness and into God's marvelous light.

Coiled around her spine lurked Fear, which had made its entrance when she was six. For years it had come and gone, maintaining its hold as she would give in to its persuasion.

Off to one side stood Hate, the powerful perversion which had been given legal ground as Eva had kept darkness permeating towards her mother for years. Seeing her mom and forgiving her was the beginning of its end of reign in her life. Last but not least, was the spirit of Witchcraft, which had been in her family for generations and she had unwittingly allowed a place the day at the carnival years before?

As Eva read the verse, her heart leaped. 'The Lord God illumines my darkness.' The words she had read in the book registered in her mind. The words God had just spoken echoed in her heart. Suppressed tears hid behind her searching eyes. A lump formed in her throat as she tried swallowing. Fear expanded its presence, but Eva couldn't feel it.

Lifting her head towards heaven, she released the tears and anguish. "Father, forgive me for my fear and my mistrust of You and your sovereignty."

She remembered the fowls of the air and realized a spirit had invaded her thought life and emotions. She remembered the fish of the sea and her early childhood dreams and traumas.

"In the name of Jesus, I come against these spirits right now. I break your power over my life, and I command you to go in Jesus' name."

Fear squeezed harder but the light consumed the darkness and the spirit disintegrated with a howl. Carras inhaled the descending light shafts and exhaled them in a battery of bullets, directing them towards Witchcraft and Hate.

With unchecked tears streaming down her face, Eva released years of pent-up emotions and hurt. She thought of all the nights she went to sleep hating her mother.

"God, forgive me for my sin towards mom. Please forgive me for my hate of her and not honoring her."

As soon as she uttered the word hate, the flames of light plummeted the demon into oblivion.

Two were down, there was one to go.

To her mind, Eva remembered her palm reading. "Father, forgive me for the sin against You of going to another source for my future. In the name of Jesus, I rebuke the spirit of witchcraft over my life and command it to go in Jesus' name."

Carras stood there, stretching his immense wings up into the heavens and looked directly into the face of God, stating, "Holy, holy is the Lord God Almighty." With those words, myriads of light beams shot from his wings directly into Witchcraft and sent him sprawling into the expanse of space.

Broken now were these inroads into her life. Broken now were these powers of darkness into Eva's heart.

Now the captive had been set free to worship God respectfully and Eva dropped to her knees and raised her hands and spoke to the Lord with a deep sense of His majesty.

"Father, I love You and I thank You for what the Lord Jesus Christ did that I may know You. God, I relinquish my family to You, and I ask for Your blessing where the curse has been on my life that You would reinstate now favor towards me and You would take me in the direction of the destiny that You have for me. I willingly yield myself to Your sovereignty and surrender my will with Yours. In Jesus' name, I pray. Amen."

The New Year was heralded in with one of the worst blizzards the Midwest had seen in years. Snowdrifts looming as high as ten feet lined the icy roads and beckoned only the daring to attempt any kind of travel.

Amid the constant onslaught of intricately designed snowflakes, another light was plummeting down from the heavenlies. Angels, like flames of fire, appeared instantly in answer to the saints' prayers. As God's faithful cried out in intercession, myriads of tiny, bright beacons skyrocketed towards the throne room of God which claimed His instant attention.

Much had happened in the world over the past five years. 1986 took us to the skies again, only this time in tragedy and horror as the spacecraft Challenger, 73 seconds after liftoff, exploded in front of millions of viewers.

Russia had the world's worst nuclear accident which helped to fuel the helplessness of millions of teenagers who reluctantly accepted the fact the world around them hastened the possibility of a nuclear annihilation.

The music was ready to comply and ease the tension by offering a way out — peace through suicide — a means to an end. "You do it to yourself before they do it to you."

To add to the doom and gloom, in England in October 1987, approximately four thousand trees fell one day, blocking the streets to London from its usual barrage of commerce. This set of a chain reaction around the world caused the stock market to crash, instigating the loss of millions of dollars in a few hours. It was suitably named "Black Monday." The world was shocked into a bleak Christmas as we realized once again the skies were not immune to murder. Appropriately named the Lockerbie Disaster, a 747 was blown out of the clouds by radical terrorists trying to prove their point.

A protest march in Beijing showed the world how insignificant human life appears to be. Tens of thousands of soldiers moved aggressively on a youth-oriented group who demanded more freedom. Blasting into the crowd with machine guns, over five thousand were killed and ten thousand wounded. This was one answer to keeping tradition.

In Washington, DC, many thousands watched George H W Bush become President of the United States, unaware of the unforeseen tyrant about to emerge and challenge America to prove herself once again as a leader in the world.

Just before her seventeenth birthday in 1989, Lilly had a crucial experience. Graduation was fast approaching which meant the senior prom was only weeks away.

Sitting in her room after dinner one evening, she reached out to God for the first time. Her day had contained the usual jeers and cruel remarks about her weight and acne problems. The nasty words echoed in her mind as she crawled into bed and extinguished the lamplight. The room was lit only by the silvery shine of the moon filtering through the flowered curtains. As she lay there the powers of darkness hovered nearby. The blackest one, Suicide, which had unsuccessfully worked on her grandfather, Sam, for years, expelled his horrendous desires into the air around her head.

Painstakingly, she formed the words as unspent tears held themselves in reserve. "Jesus, I hurt so much inside. I don't know if I can take the ridicule anymore. If one more person calls me a fat nerd, I think I'll kill them or myself. I don't want to live this way anymore, and I want You to know I give up."

The tears trickled down her cheeks; and as she reached to wipe them away, in a moment, the years of anguish burst forth and she cried from the depths of her soul.

"God saves those who are crushed in spirit,"(Psalm 34:18) darted into her mind. Stirling stood guard, shining in ultimate brightness. The light hindered the demons from any activity. Meanwhile, the Holy Spirit beckoned her heart to know the Son.

Picturing in her mind ways she might take her own life, darkness enveloped her heart, but the ghouls didn't respond. Joshua's prayers had finally paid off, and for now his intercession those past months had put a hedge of protection around his daughter. Stirling stood fast to claim it.

When she awoke, Lilly threw on her faded jeans and a loose checked blouse to disguise her figure. Walking down the street on her way to school, she was somber and emotionally void. Psychology that day would prove to be an obviously destructive subject. The teacher was discussing the risk of suicide and each student was to compose their own "farewell letter" and state why and how they would snuff out their own life.

Even the term 'snuff helped to desensitize the students to the real power behind the word 'death'. As a finale, the concluding sentences were to be written in the form of an obituary.

The powers of the air were ecstatic. A dense black mist hung over the room like a cloud, surrounding each student in the spirit world. The coldness added to the prick each was feeling in their emotions.

Lilly chewed the end of her pencil. Then in a burst of automatic writing, she penned the following, much to her own surprise and with the help of an ogre whispering the words. "Loneliness is a word I've grown to know. Not only in word, but deed. To be alone in life and have no purpose is God's greatest joke on mankind. To create us for His entertainment and like pawns on a chessboard, He moves us with the least amount of thought. If He doesn't care, why should I? Today I will take my life, so He doesn't get the satisfaction of doing it to me Himself. How? As you have found this note, you will find me in the lake where once my mother almost died. This time though, I'll succeed. I go now to take her place. My obituary? 'Deceased — Lilly Evans. Born out of wedlock, rejected by mother, nanny to half-sister, hounded by father, teased by peers. Fat, ugly, lacked esteem. Power within sought vengeance. Now at peace'."

As Lilly slowly replaced her pencil, the teacher noticed she was the only one finished. To use her as an example, she was called up front to stand while her work was read aloud.

While she listened to the oration of her own composition, Lilly stood motionless. Stirling waited nearby, poised to challenge Suicide who was ready to pervade her emotions.

Suddenly, a rod of light broke through the atmosphere and smashed into the demon. The other spirits already binding her were silenced immediately. The presence of God descended on her and in exuberance, manifested in her spirit. Lilly's cold heart thawed for a brief moment and she felt Life for the first time, flooding her very being. This wasn't a normal sense of awareness. This was the kind of life that can only come from the Creator of everything.

When Lilly returned to her seat, she felt an insatiable desire to live, to lose weight, to care about herself and to find God. Her whole motivation was changed because of the battle that had raged in the invisible realm around her.

That afternoon, Witchcraft was ready to instigate its evil. While sitting at the bus stop, Lilly glanced at the local newspaper, in the corner was an ad. "Are you tired of being fat? Hypnosis is the answer. We will hypnotize your appetite away with only one lesson. Satisfaction guaranteed."

All the way home on the bus, Lilly reflected on those words and then back in her room she contemplated how she could get the twenty-five dollars to pay for the appointment. There was no way her parents would give it to her.

"God, please show me a way to get it," she prayed.

Days went by and she continued faithfully in this prayer, but nothing happened. With every step she took, her eyes surveyed the ground in front of her, desperately searching for any stray coins that may happen to be in her path.

A few Saturdays later she was waiting at the bus stop with Leroy. Ironically, both had something in common and that was the spirit of rejection. They had each received it in different ways, but it manifested itself in the fact that neither like themselves very much.

"Leroy?" Lilly asked. "You've got friends on the street. What can I do for a quick twenty-five dollars?"

Curious, he replied, "Well, it depends what you want it for."

"I want to be hypnotized," she stated matter-of-factly. "I read an article that said they can go into your subconscious and alter your appetite and impulses to eat while you're under their power."

"For what it's worth," Leroy warned, "I read a leaflet my mom had years ago, and it said that under hypnotism demons can enter you and that many people who compulsively eat, have a demonic problem which can be severed through the name of Jesus Christ."

Lilly felt chills run up and down her neck. "Are you telling me I have a demon?"

Leroy raised his eyebrows and shrugged his shoulders. "I'm not really into this God stuff too much, but I saw enough through mom that God does take care of things like this through prayers from His people."

He paused for a moment, then said wistfully, "But why God took mom instead of dad will always baffle me."

Concisely, Lilly cracked, "Since she was a Christian, maybe He needed her to come and help Him in heaven."

"What? Say that again." Leroy was brought quickly to attention. Without batting an eyelash, Lilly repeated her statement.

Just then the bus arrived. Both separated and sat by themselves, deeply pondering the situation in their isolation. The Holy Spirit kept echoing those words to Leroy and it melted away some of the bitterness and questions he'd harbored. A plaque Tanya had hung in the library surfaced in his mind. "God is just and kind in all His ways." (Psalm 145:17)

For the rest of the year, our friends in Cambridge continued contending with the forces of darkness, and while some struggled more than others, many grew in their love and trust for God's gracious presence in their lives. After his chat with Lilly, Leroy decided to get more involved at Real Life church. Soon he found a place in the choir and one evening had a real encounter with God. Marcia Miller had returned for a youth rally and called for those who were ready to follow the Lord to stand at the end of the service. "Even if you've said a prayer before, today will add to your commitment."

Hesitant, Leroy stayed seated, assuming he was already a Christian. Then a warmth overshadowed him like melting wax being poured over his head. Jesus spoke to his heart,

Chapter Thirty-nine
He is the Author and Finisher

"I have come as a light to the world, that everyone who believes in Me may not remain in darkness."(John 12:46)

Immediately, he realized that his thoughts only had included God the Father, he didn't know Jesus.

From the pulpit the words pieced his cold heart. "No one goes to the Father, except through the Son." (John 14:6)

Boldly, Leroy stood to his feet and tears blinded his eyes, spilling down his cheeks as he received the Holy Spirit.

An encompassing joy arose within him as he raised his arms and prayed in tongues. People turned to watch, but Leroy was oblivious to the peering eyes. The hurt, bitterness and anger that had ravaged his heart because of his mom Tanya's death, dispersed, taking the darkness with it. In the spirit realm, descending upon and then from within, God's Shekinah Glory encircled him, swallowing up the remaining darkness and leaving a new soft heart, with God's Spirit dwelling within. His Christian heritage was birthed.

Joshua was well received in the schools, just as God promised he would be, and soon his next assignment came into view. Pastor Burrows, who had died suddenly, and had left the leadership of his church to Jack, his thirty-year-old son. With all the gifts and discernment that Pastor Burrows had walked in, it was unbelievable that he didn't realize Jack had never been born again. Sometimes, those growing up in church could play at being a Christian so well that even they themselves didn't realize. But the forces of evil knew, and what they would do was anyone's guess.

But God had a plan, and as Jack and Joshua preached here and there together, Josh soon stepped into his mantle as the Real-Life resident evangelist to stir up and equip the Body of Christ. Josh knew that the leader wasn't saved, but God encouraged him to wait as a better plan would soon emerge. In a dream God spoke to Josh, and soon a door-knocking venture called "For Sure" was born. All registered members of Real Life, which now consisted of four hundred or so, would have a formal visit to determine when they were exactly born again. That way not only could the elders determine who really knew Jesus, but maybe the pastor could get saved in the process? It was worth a try.

Most of the congregation loved it, sharing their conversion stories over cups of coffee on a one-to-one basis. Of course, the proud and arrogant got ruffled; but as the Holy Spirit moved, one hundred and eight souls were born again from above. Jack's day would come, but the year ended with God doing a deeper work in the lives of the church members. It was time to pass from the elementary things and grow up into all aspects of Him. (Eph 4:15)

Esther and Sam's relationship blossomed with their many visits together. The love was being fueled from above. The success of Edward's prison ministry had prompted Esther to do the same in the next state at the girls' correctional institute. The drive itself was quite long, and often Esther spent days across the border.

Sam Jr. had free rein of the house which allowed unwanted oppression to harass Esther whenever she slept. Consequently, the day came when she knew she had to make a stand. The cause of demon oppression would have to find his own apartment and take his lasciviousness with him.

Lovingly, yet firmly, Esther gave her son the news that he had to move out, knowing that wherever he went, in the end it was God who would have to save him. Tossing him out was the best she could do in the long run. It would force him to rely on God. He was old enough to get a bank loan if he went to apply minus the dress.

Lilly never did get hypnotized. She had heard on television, with Sharon and Josh, that while hypnotized, demons could enter you. Unfortunately, she went in and out with her desire to get close to God. She didn't want the Christian way because she couldn't use 'the power.' On the other hand, she longed for the peace and joy she saw in Josh and Sharon.

The greatest miracle happened near Thanksgiving at the corner of Swanson and River Streets, in the First National Bank. One bitterly cold afternoon, Walter found himself in line behind Joshua. It had been years since they'd spoken, but he recognized the voice immediately and it awakened the hurts and anger which ravaged Walt's emotions. Memories of the car crash raced through his mind.

Gritting his teeth, Walt speculated on whether to say anything to his old enemy. Suddenly, the door crashed open and two hooded men appeared with sawed off shotguns protruding from their overcoats. "Up against the counter and be quick about it!" one snarled.

Josh, Walt and two elderly ladies shuffl ed into position, facing the intruders. Th e tall robber went over to the window and made his demands. His partner stepped forward, shoving the barrel of his gun deeply into Walter's throat. "Okay, nigger, give me your money!"

Walt stood still as beads of perspiration dotted his forehead.

"Give it to me now!" he demanded, jabbing the gun quickly.

"Leave him alone," Josh snapped.

"Oh," the attacked sneered, "are you a nigger lover?"

"He's, my friend! Leave him alone!" The words flowed freely as he remembered their childhood together. "Take my money instead," he added, handing him the receipt curled around a wad of cash.

The man grabbed it, then pulled a switchblade from his pocket, ejecting the blade from its closed position. Without warning, he thrust it into Walt's side then hurled him backwards. In an immediate reaction, Josh kicked the man heavily in the side, sending him sprawling to the floor. The tall one grabbed Josh from behind, a thatch of hair bunched in his fist. "Come on bro," he sneered to his friend. "He's all yours!"

The man jumped to his feet and lunged towards Josh to stab him. Hastily, Stirling stood between the two opponents and the knife couldn't penetrate. Without materializing, Stirling expelled his breath and blew the man clear across the bank floor, smashing him up against the brick wall. The tall one released Josh and headed for the door, with his startled partner running right behind him. Josh lost a hundred dollars and the bank lost a few thousand dollars, but it was worth the gain of two dear friends making a reconciliation.

While Walt recovered, Josh hardly left his side, and the day came when Walt's unforgiveness was melted while he cried away his hurt, realizing and accepting that Josh didn't take Tanya away, but it was God who had. It took some time to heal the wound, not only in his side but also in his heart. Josh prayed in the spirit with words that God would heal his friend's broken heart and restore him to the joy of walking with Jesus Christ.

EASTER 1991

Walt sat nervously at the outdoor sunrise service, almost as if he were a fish out of water. He had attended mostly from a sense of duty and example to his son Leroy. It had been years since he'd been to church and his spirit longed for reconciliation with the Heavenly Father. Now that he and Josh had made up, gone was some of the anger and hate, but still in the recesses of his heart was an unopened package surrounded by a sleeping enemy that was yet to accomplish its mission. Walt still had the chance to unleash the gift to freedom, but would the darkness strangle it?

He wiggled around during the preliminary announcements and children's talk, anxious to get home and catch some sport on television.

Rev Jack Burrows came to the platform to begin his sermon and in an instant, Walt felt his eyes get very heavy. Tiredness overpowered him and, in a response, he yawned, shifting his weight in the seat. "Wake up, oh sleeper," Jack bellowed. "And Christ shall shine on you."(Eph5:14) The words, like electricity, shocked Walt and he sat up a bit embarrassed, sensing the words had been directed to him. "God, help me to stay awake."

Regal illuminated, stretching out his enormous wings to block the spirits from distracting him. Walt thought "Why is it Jesus is the only way? And why did he tell his followers to forsake all to go disciple nations?" (Matt 28:19)

Signaling the musicians to sit down, Jack opened his Bible. "Turn to Psalm 73, verse 20."

Throughout the assembly, you could hear the rustling of pages, and then all went quiet. Not a sound from the children, only a few birds in the whispering trees calling to their mates that spring was in the air. "For the dark places of the land are full of the habitations of cruelty." (Psalm 74:20)

"How many of you have been overseas?" A few raised their hands. "How did you find the people there?" No one responded, unsure as to what he was getting at.

Walt pondered his time in Japan. How reserved the people were, how different from the assertive Americans, how suppressed.

"Many heathen nations," Jack continued, "are governed by fear. The people's hearts are gripped by the darkness. They live in accepted dread of evil spirits and what they will do if not appeased. These demonic entities manifest themselves in order to keep the cycle of terror in the lives of the souls they own. Blessings are embraced or sufferings inflicted, and the end results are chocked up to fate or Karma."

"In one country the death of an infant summons the local witch doctor, who is then to determine the cause and appease the rulers of the air. The doctor turns slowly and points to a haggard looking woman who may or may not have a family and is commanded to prove her innocence by climbing to the top of a cliff and jumping. If the angels don't catch her, then her life is given in exchange for the child who was taken. No one's been caught yet."

"Where did this barbaric custom come from? Religion? This religion demands this practice, and yet we say 'Leave them alone. They have their own way to God'."

"So, we don't take them the truth. In another land not too far away at the simultaneous event of a birth and a death, human sacrifice is instituted. The infant is sent back to be reborn, with a death by having sand poured down its throat. This appeases the spirits but seals damnation for the accomplices. Should we leave them to their own religion and not bother them with the white man's way?"

"In some places, at the death of a husband, his wife is tied alive and kicking to a float which is set ablaze and pushed down the river to meet up with her mate in the next world. Why? Because their religion calls for it."
"My people are destroyed by lack of knowledge." (Hosea 4:6)

"The dark places of the earth are full of the habitations of cruelty, and that's why we're commanded to go there. What some say is a disturbance of culture is the calling of repentance from the traditions of men who conjured up ways to make peace with the other side. If you won't go, then help finance someone who will. But don't do nothing, for their blood is on your shoulders."

The organ began playing and Walt heard a beckoning in his heart. "I want you to return to Japan. "Letting down his defenses and the grief of going back without Tanya, Walt surrendered, allowing the power of God to snip the ribbons around his parcel and liberate the Life that was within.

Walt stood to his feet and shuffling past the many who stood in line for prayer made his way to the alter. Jack came over cautiously. "Walt, what do you want to say to God before I pray for you?"

Walt closed his eyes and raised his hands, boldly declaring, "Here am I, Lord. Send me!"

The two men embraced and cried tears of joy as the Watchers in the heavenlies sang, "Hosanna in the highest glory to the Almighty King."

And the Lord passed by, proclaiming, "The Lord, the Lord God, compassionate and gracious, slow to anger and abounding in loving-kindness and truth who keeps loving-kindness for thousands, who forgives iniquity and sin yet He will by no means leave the guilty unpunished, visiting the iniquity of father on the children and on the grandchildren…" (Ex34:7)

Heavenly hosts bowed low and then spoke in unison. "We exalt Thee, O Lord, and give thanks, for Thou hast worked wonders, plan formed long ago. Therefore, a strong people will glorify Thee. Cities of ruthless nations will revere Thee. For as we observed, all the sadness and oppression being done under the sun saw the tears of the oppressed knowing that there was power on the side of their oppressors. We also know that you, O God, loved them so much that You sent Your only Son that whosoever would believe on Him would not perish, but have everlasting life." (Jn 3:16)

"There are thousands of little towns whose residents have the same type of conflicts. Most of the residents have no idea what makes them tick. Cambridge was a made-up town for the sake of this book to show the characters are no different than what you would find anywhere. When those of us who have everlasting life reach Heaven, God will say, "turn around" and amongst the sea of faces you will see those who are there because you prayed for them. Maybe you planted and someone else watered and someone else harvested them. But what a glorious day it will be when we all celebrate those in Heaven because we took some time to bind demons and called for ministering angels to be involved.

It's our own evil heart that the entities feed on. To understand generational sin and scripture being fulfilled is one verse that stands out. "Our fathers sinned, and we have borne their iniquity" (Lamentations 5:7)

THERE'S ONLY ONE WAY TO OVERCOME...